Horses of War

Horses of War

BY

DUFF HART-DAVIS

St. Martin's Press
New York

HART

Library of Congress Cataloging-in-Publication Data

Hart-Davis, Duff.
    Horses of war / Duff Hart-Davis.
      p.   cm.
    ISBN 0-312-07787-4
    1. Soviet Union—History—Revolution, 1917-1921—Fiction.
I. Title.
PR6058.A6949H67   1992
823'.914—dc20   92-4039
                                              CIP

First published in Great Britain by Sinclair-Stevenson Limited.

First U.S. Edition: May 1992
  10 9 8 7 6 5 4 3 2 1

FOR
Phylla

Contents

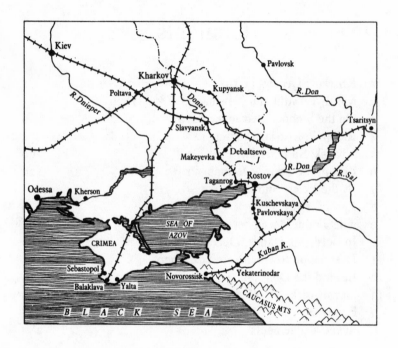

ONE

Kharkov: December 1919

THE TELEPHONE gave a faint tingle. Joseph Clements reached out for it, lifting the earpiece from its brass rest with his right hand and holding the tall stalk of the instrument with his left.

'*Da?*'

Through a storm of interference he just made out the voice of young Grigor, his man on the main gate. 'Bandits!' he was shouting. 'Armed men, demanding to be let in.'

'How many?'

'Five.'

'Keep them out. I'm coming down.'

He started for the door of his office, hesitated, strode back and took his 9mm Luger pistol from the top drawer of the desk. He strapped the belt and holster round his waist, then concealed both by donning his wolfskin waistcoat. He glanced round the bare office. Even if the worst happened, and the place were attacked, there was little of value for anyone to take. Already he had removed the stud's breeding records and buried them in the steppe. The Imperial roubles in the safe had been rendered worthless by inflation. There were no Kerensky roubles to speak of. The primitive typewriter was broken and missing a part. The copper samovar was like any other in a million Russian homes, the desk and chairs home-made. Even the telephone was makeshift – part of a field communications system abandoned by the German army when they pulled out of the Ukraine the year before, and reconstructed by Joseph himself to link the outlying buildings of the farm. No – there was nothing worth stealing here. He closed the door and did not bother to turn the key.

Outside, he called across the inner yard to one of the stable lads to bring out his hack. Donetz, a sturdy chestnut gelding from the Kuban steppe, was already saddled, for Joseph had been about to

I

ride out on his morning round. A boy led the horse across and drew off the thin blue rug which he had thrown over its saddle.

'Trouble at the main gate,' Joseph said tersely. 'Tell Makar and Petro to follow me down as soon as they can.' He checked the bridle, felt the girth, pulled it in one more hole and swung up into the saddle. The boy nodded and watched him trot away.

For the rest of his life Joseph had cause to remember that morning, 8 December 1919. The weather was cold and raw. Snow had fallen in the night, and the wind had blown it into shallow drifts, so that the paddocks were mottled with white, and on the bare patches frost had turned the grass pale grey-brown. Winter had not yet sunk its claws deep into that huge, gently rolling landscape: the great cold had scarcely begun. Yet the menace of its approach was already tangible in the scattered snow, the dank air and the leaden, lowering sky.

But a more dangerous and far less predictable menace was looming: the new Bolshevik advance in the civil war. For two years the hideous violence let loose by the November Revolution had surged and counter-surged across the south of Russia. Not only Joseph Clements, but most of the men who worked with him at the former Imperial Stud outside Kharkov, had been bewildered and dismayed by the changes that rolled over them.

Early in 1918, with the war against Germany still in deadlock, Ukrainian leaders had proclaimed themselves independent of Moscow and invited the Kaiser's army to move in. From the central *Rada*, or council, in Kiev they began to issue directives of their own, and at a lower level local leaders styled *hetman* or *ataman* seemed to declare themselves almost every week. Ostensibly, the Ukrainians wanted the Germans to restore order; in private, they were hoping, by inviting them in, finally to engineer the escape from Moscow's domination of which they had dreamed for centuries. The Germans had come, and for a few months they had done their Teutonic best to keep the peace; but the defeat of their fatherland in the world war had undermined them, and the head of revolutionary steam building up in the north had proved too strong for the Ukrainian separatists to resist. At the end of the year the Germans had been forced to retreat, leaving behind immense quantities of weapons and equipment, among them Joseph's Luger and his beloved telephone. Within weeks the revolutionary forces had swept southwards to occupy Kharkov, Kiev and the other cities of the Ukraine. Then, in the summer of 1919, the tide had turned so strongly that by July the

Whites, under Admiral Anton Denikin, were surging back towards the north. On the 24th they recaptured Kharkov, a week later the ancient town of Poltava, away to the west. So powerful was their momentum that by early October they were as far north as Orel, barely 200 miles short of their ultimate objective, Moscow. That, however, proved the zenith of their success, and now, scarcely six weeks later, they were again on the retreat, being rolled back southwards once more. With every day that passed the Red tide was creeping closer to Kharkov.

Often, in those months of ever-increasing confusion and anarchy, Joseph had felt like a football, kicked back and forth and trampled underfoot by the opposing teams in a global match played (or fought) without rules or referee. Germans, Reds and Whites had crashed over him, and now, judging by the rumours, the Reds were about to come again. The prospect appalled him: even though he was a foreigner, and had never had the slightest desire to take part in Russian politics, he was by nature conservative, and so on the White side of the struggle. His career, both here and in England, had made him a monarchist, and as he was a man of orderly habits, devoted to his horses and their routines, he detested the Soviet revolutionaries, whose destructive violence struck him as not merely criminal but senseless too.

Every day rumours of fresh atrocities came seeping through. The latest told of an effective new method invented by the Red terrorists of extracting money and goods from well-to-do citizens: in Tula they had packed over two hundred people into a single room, forcing more and more in until bodies were jammed upright, tight against one another, and there they left them for three days, without food, water, air or sanitation. When at last they let the victims out, twenty were found to be dead, still standing, and those who survived were in no state to resist the demands of their torturers.

So far Joseph had survived the revolutionary warfare by a combination of guile and good luck. In the absence of Semenov, his manager, who had disappeared in drunken pursuit of a Cossack girl six months before, never to return, he had taken charge of the stud. With the poor peasants – the *muzhiks* – deliberately set against the *kulaks*, or more prosperous ones, by revolutionary activists, with Government food-collectors harassing every household, with spies of all political colours rampant, he had in effect become a local guerrilla leader, arming his own little band with the German rifles and fortifying their camp to repel attacks from neighbours or casual raiders. Nobody

3

had given him authority to do this: in that fragmented world, no clear-cut authority survived. But equally, nobody had found the time or the means to suppress him.

The farm was far too large for the staff to defend its entire perimeter. Extending over more that 2,000 acres, it covered a block of land roughly rectangular, some three miles by one (even after spending more than half his life in Russia, Joseph still thought first in English measures – acres rather than *desyatins*, miles rather than *versts*, the height of a horse in hands rather than in *arshins* and *vershoks*). Most of the stud buildings were sturdily constructed of mud-brick and plaster, painted over on the outside with an attractive, pale-yellow wash; there was a formal entrance block in the English manner (except that the archway was surmounted by an onion-domed clock-tower), and the yards extended from the back of it, some boxes made of mud-brick, some of wood. Around them, the paddocks in which the horses grazed were bounded by neat wooden post-and-rail fences; but beyond this inner sanctum the huge fields of black earth in which they grew wheat, oats, beans and potatoes swept away undivided to the horizon.

When the emergency began, Joseph had asked for a military unit to protect the valuable livestock, only to be told that no troops could be spared from the front. (This was all too true, for by then soldiers were deserting in thousands and straggling home by any means of travel they could find.) All he had managed, in the way of defences, was to build a heavy wooden gate across the approach road, to fortify the hut beside it as a block-house, and to make the rail fences either side of it more formidable by digging a ditch in front of them, like the ha-ha round an English park.

Now, as Donetz trotted swiftly down the hill towards the boundary, he drew whinnies of greeting from right and left. Unless the weather became really bitter, it was Joseph's policy to turn all the horses out during the day. For most of his career he had struggled to make the Russians realise that excessive heat was more damaging to a horse than cold fresh air: when it came to getting a mare in foal, he kept telling them, a half-baked stallion was about as much use as a pickled cucumber. Just as he campaigned for better ventilation in the stables, so he always insisted on the horses going out for a period every day, so that they could move around freely and get their circulations going. Now, thanks to him, every field had a curved wooden shelter with its back to the prevailing east wind. In the first paddock, on his right, the stallion Saltpetre, son of the great St Simon, was rolling ecstatically, and rose to his feet with a snort as Donetz went by. 'That's my boy,' Joseph called. 'Give 'em air. Shake 'em about.'

Soon he was in sight of the gate. Sure enough, the barrier was closed, and a posse of riders had gathered beyond it. They looked like a gang of freelance raiders, of the kind which had been infesting the country for months, and they were hardly strong enough to storm the stud; equally, they might be the advance guard of some larger formation. He had better be careful. To avoid giving any sign of panic, he reined Donetz back to a walk and came to a gentle halt. The strangers looked a rough crew. Although they wore uniform of a kind, the different parts of it did not match: there were khaki and grey overcoats, blue breeches, green jackets. Two of the peaked caps bore no badges. Yet there was no doubt of the party's political and military allegiance, for their bridles sported little red pennants; besides, they carried rifles slung on their backs, and their torsos were criss-crossed by bandoliers of ammunition.

'*Dobry den*, comrades.' Joseph raised his fur hat. 'What can I do for you?'

'Open the gates,' snapped a foxy-looking, ginger-bearded man on a black horse. 'We have orders to search the farm.'

'Orders from whom?'

'Headquarters of the Eighth Revolutionary Army.'

'Where's your warrant?'

'We don't need a warrant. Open up!'

'This is Government property. No one comes in without proper orders.'

'Government property!' The leader gave an abrupt, sarcastic laugh. 'You're out of date, my friend. *We*'re the government now. Who are you, anyway?'

'My name is Klementz.' He pronounced the word in Russian fashion, with the stress on the second syllable. 'I am the manager here.'

'A foreigner!' The leader sounded incredulous, mocking. 'A German?'

'No. English.'

'*Anglichanin!*' Why are you here? This is no place for you.'

Joseph felt his temper rising at the man's insolence, his xenophobia, his immediate assumption of superiority. But he said coolly, 'Well, I've been in Russia for more than twenty years.'

'I knew it!' cried the bandit. 'An imperialist lackey.'

'Rubbish. I just look after horses.'

'Exactly. You look after imperialist horses. Well, that's all over. The horses belong to us now.'

'Don't be an idiot.' Clements let his voice rise more than he meant to. 'How can a horse be imperialist or anything else? Look at you. You're all riding horses. Russia needs horses by the thousand. That's all we're doing – producing good horses. Go and fight your bloody war somewhere that people aren't doing anything useful.'

A big, heavy man, all bun face and bushy black beard, moved up beside his leader. 'I smell *kulaks* here,' he growled, in an unpleasant deep voice. 'I smell hoarded grain. It is people like this who think they can starve the cities into submission. They are the advance-guard of the counter-revolution. It is our duty to weed them out.'

He began to unlimber his rifle, but his horse providentially swung round and bumped him hard against his neighbour, who was knocked sideways half out of his saddle. Suddenly all five horses were jigging and prancing, while the riders swore and hauled on their reins. The commotion gave Joseph a few seconds' grace, and to his intense relief he heard hoofbeats descending the track behind him. Glancing round, he saw three of his men galloping down, with rifles in their hands: five against five.

The arrival of reinforcements seemed to disconcert the raiders. They moved off a few paces, and held a brief muttered conference. '*Katsapy!*' exclaimed one of the defenders, spitting the word out. Literally 'billygoats', it was the Ukrainians' contemptuous name for northerners. Whether or not he heard the insult, the leader shouted, 'You will regret this. Today we are five. Tomorrow we will be five hundred.'

He gave a command and cantered away. After a few yards all five men turned left and began to ride parallel with the perimeter fence. As Joseph watched, they fell into line-ahead formation and unlimbered their rifles. Damn it, he thought: they were riding beautifully, right down in their saddles, part of the horses.

His involuntary admiration was cut short by a dry rattle of shots. Instinctively he ducked, only to realise that he and his men were not the target. First, way out along the perimeter fence, a piece of wood flew off one of the rails as a bullet smashed through it: then, in a paddock on the side of the hill, a group of mares and foals plunged forward and began to run. Joseph stared, frozen with horror, as one animal gave a violent jump, galloped a short distance, fell behind the rest and was left on its own. Then it tottered a few steps to either side, spun round, reared over backwards and crashed to the ground, where it lay prone in a patch of snow.

'The devils!' shouted Petro, the hot-headed young Cossack groom. 'They've killed Nadine.'

'No,' cried someone else. 'It's Milanaise. Look: there they go.'

Joseph gasped for breath, unable to believe what he was seeing. Already it was too late for retaliation; the marauders had turned away from the edge of the farm and were riding hard for the north across the open steppe, half a mile away. At that range his pistol was useless, and so were his companions' rifles.

'Swine!' bellowed Grigor, the gate-man, who had been cowering in the guard-house. The rest broke into a volley of oaths. '*Skoro!* Quick!' Joseph turned Donetz and set him galloping back up the road to the point where an access track led off between the paddocks. Arriving at the gate, he vaulted out of the saddle, tied his horse to the rails and ran across the field.

The mare lay dead in a patch of snow, belly towards him, so that he could not be sure of her identity until he came within a few yards. Then grief welled up to compound his shock and anger, for he saw that the casualty was neither Nadine nor Milanaise, but Sestritsa. Sestritsa – Little Sister! That was the name by which Katya was known in the hospital. Almost every patient called her that – so naturally he associated the mare with her, and loved her above all. Of course it was her: that was her foal Petrushka, hovering uncertainly just out of reach.

A single bullet had hit her high in the ribs, just behind the shoulder. Blood oozed from the hole; more had frothed out of her nostrils, and more still spread from underneath her chest, melting scarlet channels in the snow. Nerves in her eyelids and flanks still twitched. But she was dead. With one awful glimpse he saw how much worse it would have been if the bullet had broken her back, and she had been lying there paralysed but alive, beseeching him with her eyes to finish her off.

To anyone who loved horses, the sight would have been sickening; to Joseph, it was like a blow over the heart. He realised that he was suffering from shock: he was moving and speaking like an automaton. Miraculously, no other animal seemed to have been so much as scratched. Perhaps it was that lout with a black beard, he thought darkly: maybe it was only he who had aimed at the mares, and the rest had fired into the air.

'Catch the foal,' he said gruffly to young Petro, who had come up beside him. 'Then we'll check the rest and make sure they're all right.'

Trapping the little colt proved no easy task, so agitated had he become. Instinct kept pulling him back to his dead mother, but he would not let any human approach him. In the end they had to drive the whole group of horses back to the yards and pen him in a foaling box. For him, the disaster was traumatic, but it could have been worse, for he was already four months old, and would soon have been weaned anyway. Seen in the most practical terms, the attack had only accelerated a natural process.

In less desperate times, Joseph would have made sure that the mare got a decent burial somewhere out in the steppe; but now, with famine threatening, it would have been a crime to waste so much fresh meat. Although he himself never ate horseflesh, almost everybody in Kharkov did, and he knew that if he could get the carcase to Mischa the butcher, people would flock to buy cuts of it. Before that could happen, though, someone would have to disembowel the body, so that the meat could cool down quickly; otherwise it would go bad. As always with some unpleasant task which lay outside the normal run of duty, he felt that he could not easily order any of the men into action. Rather than wheedle with them or become bogged down in argument, he found it easier to do the job himself.

'Bring a *telega*,' he told Petro as he sharpened his sheath-knife on the grindstone in the tack-room, 'and something to cover her. Also some planks to drag her up on.' Then he walked down to the field, dreading the grisly task.

In the event he found it easier than he had expected, for in death the personality of Sestritsa had departed, and what he saw on the ground was not so much a mare as a heap of meat. There was no need to bleed the body, for the bullet had ruptured the lungs and drained off the blood into the chest cavity. By the time Joseph returned to the corpse, gas had inflated it into a taut mound, and when he slit the skin of the belly, he accidentally punctured the stomach, so that a blast of foul air and partially-digested food rushed out into his face. Recoiling sharply, he scraped up some snow to wash his face and hands, then quickly pulled the collapsing stomach and the fat, grey, moist coils of intestine out on to the ground. Once he had punctured the diaphragm to let out the accumulated blood, the job was done, but it left him shuddering with revulsion, and he was glad to pitch into the hard physical work of dragging the body up into the wooden cart.

Kharkov lay only five versts, or three miles, off; but Petro had grown nervous about venturing beyond the relative safety of the farm. 'What if that gang comes back?' he demanded.

'They won't,' said Joseph, with more conviction than he felt. 'They've gone back to their army, wherever that is. But it can't be very close to the town yet, or we would have heard. And if anyone tries to take the body off you, tell them the mare died of disease.'

The incident forced Joseph to a decision. For weeks he had been wrestling with the problem of what he should do. It was tempting to sit tight and trust that his luck would hold out, that life would eventually settle down – and the White successes during the summer had fostered hopes of a return to some sort of normality. Yet during the past few days the news had become increasingly ominous: it was clear that Denikin had over-reached himself, and that his forces were now pulling back in disorder. The whole White cause seemed to be crumbling. Joseph felt instinctively that it was doomed – and now this raid, by a small body of Red agitators moving freely through the land, had reinforced his conviction.

If the Bolsheviks gained full control, the stud farm would be a natural target. It had already been declared state property by revolutionary decree, and the horses had in theory been nationalised; but the place inevitably retained associations with the Tsarist regime and represented everything the Reds hated most: the old aristocracy, money, the idle rich. Besides, there was more than a grain of truth in what the black-bearded man had said about *kulaks* and hoarded grain. The farm had already twice been searched by odious officials of Narkomprod, the provision-gathering commissariat set up by the Bolsheviks. They had found nothing; yet under Joseph's direction five tons of oats and wheat had been buried in barrels beneath the fields, against emergencies or confiscations. There were also great quantities of carrots, buried in sand, which he relied on to keep the horses healthy in winter. If these secret stores were discovered, recriminations would be savage. A Bolshevik decree had laid down that no horse was to get more than three and a half pounds of grain a day – a fatuous pronouncement, but one on which bureaucratic enforcement officers could base the most damaging calculations.

Already, in the first phase of the civil war, Red Guards had stolen some of the brood mares. Now, if they returned in force, God knows what they might do. There was only one sensible course of action, Joseph decided: to leave. A story had filtered through from Odessa, on the Black Sea, of how an entire racing stable had escaped from under the noses of the Bolsheviks: at 6 a.m., on the day in April when the Reds first entered the town, owners, trainers, jockeys and stable-boys had joined forces to saddle up all eighty-five horses and set out on foot for the Rumanian border, to the west. How far they had managed to go, Joseph did not know; but now he was determined to emulate them and evacuate the Kharkov stud to comparative safety in the south. The snag was that with over sixty horses and only a dozen men, it was physically impossible to walk the animals away. Besides, there was no friendly border within reach, as there had been for the people at Odessa. What he needed was a train.

At lunch, which everyone ate together in the canteen, he said nothing about his plans, not wanting to raise hopes prematurely. As always, the food was simple but good: a big tureen of *shchi*, or thick cabbage soup, brewed from meat stock, with other vegetables in it, hunks of freshly-baked black bread, and *vareniki*, or pancakes sweetened with honey. The atmosphere was subdued and apprehensive; after one attack, everyone expected more. Although some of the men were older than Joseph, they all looked to him as a father figure for advice and instructions: he sat, symbolically, at the head of the bare wooden table, and tried to reassure them.

After the meal he rode into town. Until the revolution, Kharkov had been a flourishing industrial and commercial centre. Although it had nearly 250,000 inhabitants, it felt smaller – a civilised and attractive place, trisected by two little rivers which ran together, broken up by parks and gardens, boasting a university, a new opera house, a theatre and several museums, as well as plenty of restaurants and *traktirs*, or cheap eating-houses. During the seasonal fairs – five of them, with the largest in October – the streets were flooded with country people, who poured in to buy and sell cloth, wool, cattle and horses, and the horse-market – in Konnaya Square, in the south-eastern suburbs – became a particular whirlpool of activity, not least when wild horses rounded up on the steppe were being sold by the drove.

Now, on this dank December afternoon, the town seemed unnaturally quiet. In the outskirts, where the primitive shacks were made of mud, things felt normal; but further in, where the stone buildings began, there was hardly anyone about, and the noisy street vendors, with their carts of merchandise, had disappeared. As he rode in,

Joseph soon sensed something amiss, but it was not until he reached the railway station that he realised what was happening. The station had been engulfed by hordes of people. It was as if they had arisen from the suburbs like a swarm of bees and settled on the railway, leaving the streets empty. Such was the press that he could scarcely force his way into the main building's forecourt:

'What's happening?' he asked the *izvozchik* in whose care he left Donetz.

'Panic,' answered the cab-driver succinctly. 'Everyone's trying to get out.'

Joseph had to use physical force even to reach the entrance of the building. The booking-grille was under siege, the platforms packed solid to the very edge with bodies. Most of the people were civilians, but among them were soldiers who had deserted from their units – not wounded, but sound in wind and limb – still shamelessly wearing their uniforms. He elbowed a way through the crowd, heading for the office of the station manager, Naryshkin, an old friend with whom he had done much business in the past, moving horses to and from the stud.

Naryshkin also was besieged. A stocky, red-faced man, inclined to be choleric but essentially good-natured, with curling, gingery beard and grizzled hair, he worked in an office dominated, and heated to a fearsome degree, by a tiled stove which took up the whole of one corner. Joseph found him hemmed in – almost pinned to his desk, at which he stood upright – by five White Army officers. The spectacles which he wore for reading were pushed to the very end of his nose. His dark-blue uniform looked as if he had slept in it for a fortnight. '*Nyet!*' he was bellowing into a telephone. 'I repeat. We have no further capacity whatever. No more rolling-stock and no serviceable engines. This week alone I have had four locomotives destroyed by military action. What? Yes. No!'

The moment he replaced the receiver and turned round, the officers opened verbal fire on him, bombarding him with demands for transport.

'Gentlemen!' He glared at them over his spectacles, with his head tilted forward, and held up both hands, palms facing them. 'Please! You heard what I said. There is nothing I can do – today, anyway. And tomorrow – God knows.'

'This is not a request, but an order,' said one, with the insignia of a colonel on the epaulettes of his overcoat. His voice was loud and agitated. 'I *order* you to produce a train.'

'I am sorry, sir. It makes no difference.' Naryshkin gave a weary gesture. 'You can issue orders until you are black in the face. Arrest me if you like. Shoot me. It will get you nowhere.'

The message sank in. The officers turned, arguing angrily with each other, and trooped out. Seeing Joseph, Naryshkin suddenly looked more jovial. 'Joseph Petrovitch!' he exclaimed. 'What brings you here at such a time?'

'The usual. I need transport.'

'For horses? Not now! It is impossible.'

'Are you sure?'

'Even for a friend. Look – you will see what I mean.'

A whistle had sounded, and through the window they watched a train roll slowly into the station from the north, smoke puffing from the engine's funnel, steam hissing from its pistons. The waiting crowd, suddenly full of hope, surged forward, knocking several people off the edge of the platform on to the track. What happened to them – whether they were cut in pieces or survived – Joseph could not see. What he could see all too well was that the train was not only packed to the windows inside but festooned with human beings outside. Like barnacles, they clung to every possible point of attachment: the roofs of the carriages were encrusted with them, and more balanced in suicidal positions on the couplings between wagons. Their faces were white, almost blue, with cold, their eyes glazed, their expressions dead. Quite clearly, it was physically impossible for anyone else to board that train.

This self-evident truth did not prevent a general rush forward. Yells of anger rose from both sides as the would-be travellers tore open the doors and battled to gain access, while those already on board fought with equal ferocity to repel them. A huge wave of pressure, originating at the back of the platform, drove those at the front bodily against the side of the train and pinned them there. Straight opposite Joseph, a man jammed inside one of the doorways, with his head swathed in bloody bandages, swung some heavy object downwards and hit a peasant woman over the head so fiercely that she crumpled and collapsed out of sight.

'*I gave orders that he was not to stop!*' groaned Naryshkin, appalled by the violence erupting in his own station, but powerless to control it. 'He should have gone straight through. Nobody wants to get off at Kharkov now – and he can get water further down the line.'

As if the engine-driver had heard him, he gave a long blast on his hooter and set the train creeping forward. The few extra passengers who had managed to lay hold of it were dragged bodily sideways. Most were brushed off like flies by contact with the rest of the crowd and fell off among them. One or two had the strength to cling on, at any rate until the train had cleared the platform.

'Now you see, Joseph Petrovitch.' Naryshkin wiped the sweat from his forehead with the cuff of his uniform and sat down heavily on a stool.

'Shouldn't we do something . . . ?' Joseph began. 'People must have been hurt.'

'Killed, probably. We had ten fatalities yesterday, at least.' Naryshkin seemed quite unconcerned. '*Nichevo.* Don't worry. There are plenty of responsible army officers out there to organise things. In theory the great White Army has taken over the station. Let them get on with it.'

He lifted the flap of his desk and produced a half-bottle of home-made vodka. 'Glasses behind you, if you don't mind.'

At Joseph's shoulder, among the reports and timetables that filled the shelves, sat a tray of small green glasses. He reached two down and handed them over. The station-master filled both and passed one back.

'To hell with all Bolsheviks!'

'To hell with them!'

They touched glasses and threw back the fiery spirit.

'Yes.' Naryshkin licked his lips. 'God rot them all. He will in the end, for sure, but not soon enough for me.'

He got up, crossed the little room, locked the door on the hubbub outside and refilled the glasses.

'What did you want, my friend?'

'I want to take my horses away to the south.'

'How many?'

'Nearly seventy.'

'Good God! You've left it too late.'

'So it seems. Where is the front now?'

'The front! The front!' Naryshkin suddenly became sarcastic, not against Joseph, but against the futility of the civil war in general. 'The wretched front – it jumps back and forth like a grasshopper. One minute it is here, the next twenty versts away. But now it is coming this way all the time. They're saying that the Reds are at Kursk. If that's correct, they'll be here in two days, or even tomorrow.' He looked keenly at Joseph over the rims of his glasses. 'Where had you thought of going?'

'I don't know. Anywhere south. The Crimea, perhaps.'

'No!' Naryshkin was emphatic. 'Not the Crimea. That will fall first. Go further east, to the Caucasus. But first go to Taganrog, on the Sea of Azov.'

'Taganrog? Where's that?'

'There, on the map, to the west of Rostov. On the sea, and on the railway.'

'How far is it?'

'Five hundred versts, by train.'

Five hundred versts! Three hundred miles – more by road. Evidently Naryshkin noticed Joseph's look of abstraction, for he said testily, 'You know – the British have been fighting for Denikin and the White Army. You must have heard.'

'Yes, yes,' Joseph answered, but Naryshkin charged on. 'Yesterday a whole trainload came through on their way south. English aviators, with their machines dismantled and stowed on flat-cars. Poor fellows – only a few days ago they thought they were going to bomb Moscow. Imagine that! That would have woken up our friend Ulyanov, or Lenin, or whatever he calls himself. If only they had landed one on him!'

'*They* had a train, then,' said Joseph wistfully. The idea of a British-manned train going through the station, on its way to safety, wrenched at him.

'Yes, but they didn't get it here. They'd come up from the south on it. It was their base. They were living on it. They'd been on it for six weeks. That was the difference. What's more, they were the last of the British to go. They told me.'

'Maybe we'll have to go on foot, then.'

'Well – I can only wish you luck.'

'Thanks. And thanks for the drink – and for all your help over the years.' He stood up and held out a hand. The burly station-master gripped it hard, and Joseph thought there were tears in his eyes as he said, '*Do svidaniya*! Till we meet again.'

The crowd in the station was, if anything, still more dense. He slipped the cab-driver who had looked after Donetz a hundred Kerensky roubles. A year ago, such a tip would have seemed fantastic, the gift of a lunatic millionaire. Now it was almost an insult, and would scarcely buy a glass of tea.

Full of foreboding, but gripped by a desperate resolution, he rode eastwards along the Yekaterinoslavskaya, the main thoroughfare into the city centre. The short winter day was already dying. A few flakes of snow floated down. Straight ahead of him, the high, onion-topped spire of the Uspenski Cathedral shone with only the dullest gleam of gold. He saw that many shops had been boarded up, and in the city centre he found a horde of people on the move, all heading out for the bridges which led over the Kharkov river towards the south. Most were travelling in horse-drawn carts piled high with their belongings, but many were on foot, carrying what they could.

He turned left, against the flow, towards the University Park and the general hospital. The image of Katya grew bright in his mind as he drew closer to her. He saw her high cheekbones, her slanting grey-green eyes, her fine fair hair; he felt the softness of her body so clearly that he began to grow excited. Then he pulled himself together with a jolt, facing the certainty that nothing but misery and danger lay ahead.

Outside the hospital there was no one to take his horse, so he rode into the courtyard at the back and tethered Donetz to a rail. Inside the front entrance he was stopped by a stout, bad-tempered woman who crouched like a dark-green frog behind the reception desk.

'No visitors!' she grunted, pointing to a notice on the wall.

'I'm not visiting a patient. I have to see Sestra Mironov on business.'

'She is on duty now.'

'I know – but this is important.'

'We are very busy with wounded.'

'Even so . . .'

'Write your name.' With a heave of disapproval the woman shoved a piece of paper across the desk, and, when he had scribbled on it, gave it to a small boy who emerged from a cubby-hole behind her.

'Ward D,' she told him. 'Second floor' – and then, as he scuttled out, to Joseph, 'Wait.'

He sat on a wooden bench against the wall. There was nothing in that bare, dingy room to entertain him. His heart beat fast with apprehension, his natural anxiety reinforced by the smells of the hospital: disinfectant, ether, floor-polish. For Katya, he knew, they were normal, part of the fabric of her working life; but for him they evoked memories of broken limbs and operations, of visits to sick people, of death.

Presently the boy reappeared and handed him back the piece of paper. On it she had written in English, '2nd floor landing, in five minutes'. Finding that the lifts were out of action, he went straight up the stairs, but then regretted not staying where he was. On the landing of the second floor there was nowhere to sit or wait. A constant stream of nurses and orderlies flowed in and out of the double doors leading to the ward. All stared at him, and one or two asked what he wanted. After a minute he went back to the stairs and hovered there, returning only when he thought the time was ripe.

At last the swing doors opened yet again – and there she was, looking pale and drawn, with dark smudges of exhaustion beneath her eyes, but wonderfully tall and slim in her white uniform and head-veil, wonderfully alive, wonderfully beautiful. Her face lit up when she saw him, but she kept at a distance and gestured that he should follow her through a door to the left. After a few steps down a corridor, she opened another door and turned in.

The room was tiny – a consulting or interview cubicle, not much larger than a cupboard, with one small window high up the wall, a narrow table, two chairs, and no form of decoration on the dingy, cream-coloured walls. Once he was inside, Katya closed the door and slid a red card across the central aperture to indicate that the room was occupied; then without a word she came to him, placing the whole length of her body pliantly against his and clasping her arms behind his neck. For fully a minute they stood there, drawing strength from each other.

It was he who pulled away, still holding her, but at arms' length. 'Rusalka, I have bad news.'

She looked at him steadily, with a hint of amusement in her grey eyes. 'All the news is bad now.'

'I know, but this is really bad.' He swallowed and said, 'I'm going away.'

'Oh God! Where?' The question came out in a little gasp. She drew the fingers of her right hand down over his lips, as if to stop him saying something dreadful.

'To the south. To Taganrog.' He explained about the attack on the stud, without saying which mare had been killed, and about the lack of trains.

'Well?' she prompted.

'I've decided I must save as many horses as I can,' he said rapidly. 'I can't take them all. So I'm going to take just two. I'll walk and ride them.'

'To Taganrog?'

'Yes. It's only five hundred versts. The British army has a base there. If I can get them that far, they'll be safe.'

'Which horses, though?'

'Oh!' He realised that he had run ahead of himself. Knowing his own decision, he somehow thought she must know it too. 'Min and Boy,' he said.

'The English stallions.'

'Yes.'

She closed her eyes and laid her head on his shoulder. 'Oh, Martyshka!' Her sigh was full of fear and loneliness, like the wind on the steppe.

'Do you blame me?' he asked.

'No! Why should I?' She looked up fiercely. 'You know what you must do. Do it.'

'I know I should stay and try to look after them all. But it wouldn't achieve anything. If the Reds come, we'll be overwhelmed, shot to pieces. I feel I'd do better to save two, if I can.'

'Good!' She forced a little smile, wrinkling her mouth slightly to the right, in the way that he loved. 'And which way will you go?'

'I don't know. I'll head for Slavyansk first, I suppose. It depends what the roads are like.'

'Will you get someone to go with you?'

He looked her straight in the eyes and said, 'You!'

'Me?' Her face lit up, then clouded. 'Oh, God! It would be wonderful – the best thing in the world. But how can I? We're at our wits' end here, with the casualties. We need every nurse we can get.'

'I know, I know. But I wondered . . .'

'Anyway, I'd hold you back. You know what a terrible rider I am.'

'Don't joke. I can't bear it.'

There was a long pause. Then she asked, 'When will you go?'

'Tonight.'

'Tonight! God!'

'The Reds are at Kursk already. They'll be here in a couple of days.'

She said nothing, and he went on: 'I'm worried sick about what will happen to *you*, if you stay. I hear terrible stories about what they do to women.'

'Oh!' she passed a hand wearily over her forehead. 'I'll be all right. They don't molest nurses. They need us for their own wounded. I suppose I'll just change sides for as long as I have to.'

'Yes – but your name will be against you. They'll sniff out your background.'

As if to underline what he had said, out in the corridor a man came calling: 'Sestra Mironov, Sestra Mironov.' She glared at the door, willing it not to open, until the voice had gone. Then again she clung to him so tightly that he could feel her breasts flattening on his chest. At last she drew away and whispered quickly, 'Wait here for five minutes, and I'll fetch some things for you to take with you. Medicines and so on.'

With a rustle from her starched uniform, she was gone. He sat at the narrow table with his head in his hands, fighting despair. He had never really believed that she would come: her sense of duty was too strong. Yet he had not been able to stop himself hoping. He knew in his bones that he would never return. If she did not travel with him, he might never see her again. As he waited, the feeble electric bulb overhead flickered and went out, and he sat there perfectly still in the gathering dusk.

In a few minutes she was back with a bundle neatly done up in blue cloth. 'There. You've got iodine, for wounds, quinine tablets for fevers, bandages, morphia. All labelled. I hope you won't need any of them!'

Joseph found it difficult to speak. 'Have this,' he said. 'Perhaps it will keep you safe.' He handed her a medallion on a chain.

'What is it? I can't see.'

'Minoru's medal. The one the King gave me at Newmarket.'

'Oh – but that's yours.'

'I want you to have it now.'

She looked down at the medal, up at him, down again, her eyes glistening. Then with quick movements of her hands she unbuttoned the neck of her blouse and brought up a small cross which hung on a chain round her neck. 'Have this. It's my little icon of St Nicholas. Wear it, and think of me.'

He fastened the chain round his neck and shook it down inside his collar. Then he took her in his arms and kissed her passionately. There was nothing more he could say. Out on the landing, in a mist of tears, he heard her whisper, 'God be with you.' Then with a swish the double doors from the ward burst open, and some desperately injured man, all blood and bandages, was bundled past on a trolley, attended by a doctor and a scurry of nurses. One of them caught Katya by the arm and physically drew her away: suddenly she was gone, caught up again in the dreadful carnage of the war.

The stud had no electricity, but he examined the icon by the light of an oil lamp, wondering how it was that he had not seen it before. It was a beautiful thing – a small gold cross, with a miniature image of St Nicholas fashioned in porcelain and encircled by a golden frame. He hung it round his neck, feeling her presence very strong. The icon was much finer than the badge which he had given her, and the difference between the two tokens pointed up the disparity between their characters: the badge was a worldly prize, given in recognition of sporting success; the icon was a religious object, reflecting the faith of its donor.

His packing was quickly done: he had been subsconsciously planning the journey for weeks, and knew exactly what he could carry. For each of the stallions he had devised a pair of leather panniers which could be slung behind the saddle, and these he filled with the barest essentials: grooming kit, spare shoes, leather straps for repairing harness, farrier's tools and lightweight rugs, leg-bandages, as well as all the crushed oats that the bags could hold. The horses' thick rugs – one each – could travel rolled up across their backs, behind the saddles.

His own effects were more elaborate, but took up still less space. The most important was a money-belt containing fifty-five gold roubles and ten English sovereigns, each wrapped in a small piece of silk so that it would not clink against its neighbour. With his life savings of 300,000 roubles, or £30,000, gone up in the smoke of rioting inflation, the bullion represented his entire worldly wealth. Next most vital was the Luger pistol, in its holster, and fifty rounds of ammunition in a bandolier. Into a German army knapsack went two clean shirts, socks, underclothes, a towel, washing and shaving kit, a jersey, a spare pair of breeches, Katya's bundle of medicines, some salt, tobacco, matches, a favourite pipe, a folding saw and knife combined, and another bundle of food which Mariusha, his housekeeper, had packed for him. On to his right wrist he strapped a compass, like a watch. The idea of leaving behind the rest of his possessions did not worry him: they were few enough, and he had never been much of a collector. The only objects he would miss were his racing mementoes – the cups and horseshoes and certificates; but these were already sealed inside a large earthenware jar and buried in one of the paddocks. If the country ever settled down, he could come back and reclaim them.

Last to go in was a packet of documents: a rudimentary map of south Russia, papers authenticating the pedigree of the horses, and his own passport. Staring at the photograph in the front, he could not help smiling: no wonder she called him Martyshka. The word meant 'marmoset', the term of endearment 'monkey face.' Without knowing that in Newmarket he had always been known as 'Monkey Clements', she had put her finger unerringly on his most obvious characteristic: the slightly simian expression produced by a deep upper gum, wide teeth, and slightly upturned corners to the mouth. He fastened the haversack, ready to go outside.

He did not worry about feeding himself. He would always find something to eat. But he was concerned about how to feed the horses, especially now, as winter went into its harshest phase and there was no casual grazing to be had. How would he come by enough oats or beans? How would he find hay? He tried to reassure himself by reflecting that Russia had more horses per human head of population than any other country in the world, and that food for them must exist somewhere.

About the horses themselves, he felt quietly confident. Most stallion men, he knew, would think it madness even to consider the journey which he proposed. Conventional wisdom had it that stallions were vicious creatures which fought one another with teeth and hooves if they could only come within biting or striking distance. The idea of one man taking two on a 300-mile walk would strike most experts as suicidal. Probably it would have been, with most horses; but his own two defied normal classification. Just as stallions usually fight, so, occasionally, two seem to enjoy each other's company and get on well. Minoru and Aboyeur were such a pair – and because their characters were very different, Joseph saw them as complementary, a case of opposite natures fitting together to make one whole.

The only thing they had in common was that they had both won the Epsom Derby - Minoru, carrying the colours of King Edward VII, in 1909, and Aboyeur in 1913. Minoru was outstandingly calm and easygoing, a real gentleman; it was said that he would even let a stranger into his box to feed him, though Joseph had never allowed it. Aboyeur was the exact opposite: a rogue and a bully, with a particular reputation for biting. Joseph had always been amused by the prescience of his owners in giving him his name, which was the French for 'bastard', in the pejorative sense of the word. 'How did they know what a bugger he was going to be?' he would ask incredulously. 'How could they tell?' And yet, in spite of Aboyeur's lack of social grace, he had grown fond of him. Also, he admired the horse enormously. Had he himself not been present at Epsom, after all, when Boy had won his greatest race?

At first glance the pair looked much alike. Both bays, both a shade under sixteen hands, they had similar profiles and conformation; but in fact Min was slightly the darker, with very dark points – his lower legs and mane were almost black – as well having more powerful quarters. He also had a secret weapon which might prove invaluable during the journey. One winter – to the unconcealed disapproval of his men, who considered it demeaning – Joseph had broken the stallion to harness and taught him to pull a cart. At the time, his main purpose had been to stop the horse becoming bored; but now it looked as though his investment of time and patience might pay off.

As Joseph prepared to leave, he eased his feelings of guilt by telling himself that even if these two were his favourites, they were also the only two which he could manage on the road. The idea of leaving the rest depressed him heavily. He loved the other stallions – Saltpetre, Blackadder, Louviers – scarcely less, and he mourned the quality he was about to leave behind. Equally, he was much attached to the mares. The best he could hope for was that when the Bolsheviks came, some reasonable and horse-minded officer would be in charge of the unit which reached the place first. If that happened, it was possible that the stud could carry on much as before, producing fine horses for the cavalry, rather than for racing, which the new government had condemned as a bourgeois, reactionary and aristocratic pastime. If the worst occurred ... Already repulsive stories had come back of the atrocities committed at the Antoniny and Slavuta studs in Russian Poland, where Bolshevik sadists had put out the eyes of the mares and foals with red-hot pokers before burning them alive, and then hanged the mutilated stallions on a scaffold built for the purpose in the market-place.

Stunned silence greeted him when, at 9 p.m., he summoned a meeting of the stallion men and told them what he proposed to do. Makar, who looked after Minoru, and Vladimir, Aboyeur's man, seemed unable to grasp what he was saying. Both local lads, they had never been more than twenty versts from Kharkov in their lives: the notion of walking two horses five hundred versts, to places they had never heard of, was beyond their comprehension. It was precisely their parochial nature and lack of experience that had made Joseph decide to leave them behind. He could have ordered them to go with him; but that would have been unfair on them and a risk to him. If they stayed where they were, they could probably go through the motions of becoming Communists and carry on working as harmless country lads; if he took them with him, he would lead them out of their depth and, quite possibly, to disaster.

He did not tell them where he meant to go. In fact, he misled them deliberately by suggesting that he would head south-west, towards Kiev, hoping that thus he would divert any attempt at pursuit. It was not that he thought any of *them* might come after him: their loyalty touched him to the heart. Rather, he feared reprisals from incoming Bolsheviks who might try to extort information. It would be better if his lads guilelessly sent unpleasant people in the wrong direction.

He spoke to them mostly in proper Russian, with a sprinkle of Ukrainian words thrown in. 'Remember,' he told the circle of young, baffled faces, blinking in the lamplight, 'none of you knew I was going. I just disappeared in the middle of the night. If you say that, they can't do anything to you.'

He sought to soften the blow of his defection by pretending that he would return. As soon as the horses were in British hands, he said, he would be back. When he had finished, he simply stood up and said, '*Do svidaniya*', and they muttered various replies.

Outside, the clouds had cleared. The sky was hung with brilliant stars, and frost had come cracking down. In the boxes, the stallions were asleep, Boy on his feet, Min lying in his deep bed of straw. They blinked like owls when the lamplight fell on them, and Min struggled to his feet, giving a shake and a snort – a greeting which Joseph answered by blowing out through his lips until they fluttered and made the same sort of noise. The boys carried in the saddles and loaded panniers. 'You do Boy', said Joseph to Vladimir. 'I'll see to Min.'

Like most stallion men, he had a habit of talking to a horse more or less continually while he was working on him. Sometimes he spoke in Russian, sometimes in English, reverting to the cheerfully obscene and blasphemous vernacular favoured by stable lads at Newmarket; whatever language he used, the horse would listen intently, flicking his ears forward and back as the monologue rose and fell. Even if the animal did not understand the words, he certainly derived confidence and pleasure from the soothing flow of communication, and became that much easier to handle. Now, as Joseph entered Min's box, he addressed him like the old friend he was.

'Well, old man. Bit of a surprise. We're going for a walk.' He produced a palmful of crushed oats from his pocket, and while the horse nuzzled it he ran his other hand down the side of his neck. 'Middle of the night, I know, but that's the only way to beat the sodding Bolshies. Won't half annoy them, finding you've gone. That bugger with the black beard – I hope he ruptures himself. I should have given the bastard one with the Luger while he was so close. Sorry, old boy: no more jig-jig for a bit. Have to tuck it up for the winter, won't you . . . ?'

Still talking, he slipped a bridle on to the stallion's head, put the reins over his head and fastened the neck strap under his chin. With the same easy, slow movements he slid the thick rug off over his tail and settled a sheepskin numnah on his back. Then he took the saddle and panniers from Makar and lowered them into position. Minoru flinched as the cold leather touched his flanks, but otherwise he stood still.

'Roll up the rug,' Joseph told Makar. 'Double it longways, and then roll it tight. Get on with it, now.'

From the next box came a thud and a curse. '*Vsio v-poryadke?*' he called. 'You all right?' And back came the answer, 'Fine. He's just messing about, as usual. I'm ready.'

'Stay with him for a minute. I'll just get my coat. Oh – and before I forget: take down the boards in the morning.' He indicated the black and white boards mounted on the wall beside the door of each box, giving the name and pedigree of the occupant. 'Burn them,' he said. 'Destroy all traces.'

For the last time he walked across to the little house which he had come to think of as home. His housekeeper had made a great fuss, but he himself did not feel in the least sentimental about leaving it, for his heart was elsewhere; all the same, it was odd to shut the cupboard door on his spare clothes, to leave his row of books on the shelf in the living-room, to close the front door on that chapter in his life.

Already he was clad in his wolfskin waistcoat, a garment of his own design, with the fur on the inside and the skin outermost. Known locally as a *dushegreyka*, or soul-warmer, it had a collar high enough to turn up over his ears and a tail long enough to cover his behind, with twin vents at the sides so that it rode up easily when he was in the saddle. On top of it he pulled his *shuba*, a splendid three-quarter-length coat of sheepskin, flared and vented for riding, and between them the two layers of fur and wool made him entirely frost-proof. Wolfskin gloves and a fore-and-aft fur hat completed his defences.

'*Horosho!*' he said heartily as he came back to the boxes. 'Good!

We're off.' He did not feel at all sound inside. Nervousness about the welfare of the horses, anxiety about his own stamina, fear of the unknown – all combined to set adrenalin racing round his blood-stream. But there was no stopping now. As the boys led the stallions out, he took Min's reins in his left hand, Boy's in his right, and moved off at once, calling quiet farewells over his shoulder. At the sound of the hooves on the gravel road, some other horse gave a whinny from inside the yard, and Boy screamed out an answer, throwing up his head.

'Cut it out, you bugger,' growled Joseph fiercely, giving neither stallion any chance to stop.

Even without a moon, there was plenty of light in that crystalline darkness. Frost sparkled on the surface of the track, and the horses' breath smoked white in the air. Glancing upwards, he saw a shooting star fall down the tremendous sky straight above him. Was that an omen? For good or bad, he was on his way into the unknown.

TWO

Merthyr Tydfil and Newmarket: 1878–1896

IF ANYONE asked Joseph when he was born, he would answer confidently 'third of June, 1878', and if they asked where, he would reply, 'Merthyr Tydfil, South Wales'; but his responses masked a basic uncertainty, for he possessed no birth certificate, and he had never been sure of his origins. Just as he might have been born in Merthyr, or in one of the valleys round about, so he might have been the son of Peter Clements, miner, of Abergele; but he had nothing to prove it. When he grew up, he consoled himself by asking rhetorically, 'What difference does it make?' But when he was a boy his lack of a solid background induced such deep insecurities that it shaped his whole character and life.

All he could say for certain was that he *lived* in Merthyr: to be precise, in Dowlais, once a village, but by then a suburb of the sprawling industrial town into which Merthyr had grown. Coal and iron were the mainstays of its economy. Most of the men worked in mining or smelting, the women in brickworks; and everywhere tall chimneys belched smoke skywards, so that the air was laden with sulphurous fumes and rent by the groans of pithead winding-gear. Coal dust invaded every corner and crevice of the town: window-sills were dark with it minutes after they had been wiped clean, children came in from play looking like Christy minstrels, and whenever it rained – as it seemed to for days on end – the streets ran with liquid black as ink.

Underground accidents were common: tunnels collapsed, shafts were flooded, men were crushed, buried and drowned. After every fatal disaster, work stopped throughout the town: factory hooters sounded and the men processed home through the narrow, sloping streets, singing dirges for the dead.

Joseph's father – he was always told – had been killed in a pit disaster when he was a baby. About his mother he knew nothing at all. He lived with a family called Evans: Dan – another miner – his wife Florence, and their two boys Evan and Morgan, one older and one younger than he. To Joseph, Mr and Mrs Evans were Uncle Dan and Auntie Florence, and she treated him like a third son; yet as he grew older, cautious inquiries revealed that she could not be his father's or his mother's sister, and was not his real aunt at all. Who was she, then, with her strong good looks, and her thick, raven hair swept back round her head from a central parting to a neat bun at the back? And how had it come about that he was living with the Evanses, at 96 Cregrina Terrace?

His life was by no means unpleasant, for his foster-parents were kind and looked after him well. The house was small and primitive, wedged in between its neighbours on a hillside steep as a roof, and one of Joseph's earliest memories was of watching Dan take his bath in a steaming tin tub set before the fire in the living-room. But its discomforts were not of the kind to worry a boy. Florence fed the family substantially, kept them reasonably clean and saw that their clothes were presentable. Every Sunday they went to the chapel in the valley, where the preacher thundered out denunciations of sins that the boys could scarcely imagine.

Joseph was not the sort of lad to complain. From somewhere in his ancestry he had inherited an overriding desire to work: to get on with whatever he was set to do, to forge ahead, not to waste time. In school he applied himself diligently to his lessons, and, although not greatly gifted, won several prizes, for endeavour rather than for achievement. At home, he helped cheerfully with household chores like bringing in the coal, and even before he had the strength to be much use, he joined Dan in digging the vegetable plot which climbed away behind the house.

For recreation, he took to the wild hills which surrounded Merthyr on every side. Green in summer, brown with bracken in autumn, sometimes white with snow in winter, they rose open and inviting beyond the grimy limits of the town, and the transition from industrial wasteland to virgin mountain was extraordinarily abrupt. Walking out of Dowlais Top, young Joseph could pass in a few moments from a landscape ravaged and ruined by man to one still untouched, in which rabbits gambolled, peregrine falcons hunted, and clear streams came flashing down: up there, he had trees and rocks to climb, caves in which to make camp, pools beneath waterfalls to swim in, and endless smooth turf over which to run.

Best of all, he had horses. Where it came from, he could never tell, but from his earliest remembered days he had harboured an obsession about horses; and one day out in the hill country above the town he came on a farm alive with the creatures. Later he realised that it was a place of rest and recuperation for the pit-ponies used in the mines; but when he found it, he just took it for some kind of miracle, put there for his special delectation. He did not see that the inmates of the farm were small and work-worn, with thick legs and shaggy fetlocks: to him, they might have been priceless bloodstock, Derby winners all.

The first time he glimpsed them, he came up out of an oak wood bounded along its top edge by a high stone wall. The horse flies were fierce that day, he remembered afterwards: the long, grey insects kept dropping onto his bare arms and legs, and unless promptly smacked flat, gave a penetrating bite. When he climbed on the wall and peeped over, there they were – ten or a dozen ponies, grazing peacefully. As he watched, he fell prey to an irresistible temptation. Even though he knew he was on someone else's land, that technically he was trespassing, that he had no right to enter the horses' field, still less to touch them – even so, he felt an absolute compulsion to ride one of them. So he had waited, crouching breathless with excitement behind the rough stones, until a black pony with white blaze had come grazing right alongside the wall. Then suddenly he had scrambled over and jumped down on its back. Almost certainly the animal had never been ridden in its life; without any doubt at all it got a severe fright. The outcome was inevitable. The pony took off up the sloping field like a racehorse, and after a few highly uncomfortable seconds Joseph was bounced off onto the ground, where he lay winded, feeling both sick and guilty.

Yet the fall did not put him off. Far from it: he found out that the farm was called Pentwyn, and he continued to visit it so often that Dai Thomas, the owner, eventually accepted him as a kind of unpaid junior groom and stable-boy. Thus Joseph acquired some rudiments of horse management, and also learnt to ride: on a stocky Welsh mountain pony, he would go out with Dai to round up the sheep, cantering along the smooth, sheep-mown turf of the ancient drove-roads over the hills. At first Florence was worried by his protracted absences from home, but when she discovered what he was doing, she encouraged him.

The long hours he spent outdoors fostered his natural interest in the country. He learnt where foxes had their earths and badgers their setts. In spring he sought out birds' nests and started a collection of eggs, taking one from each nest, piercing either end with a needle and blowing out the contents, to leave the shell dry and empty. Hearing that black-backed gulls were regarded as vermin, he waded out to their nests in the tufts of reed that grew in boggy tarns, and brought back the mottled eggs to Auntie Flo, who considered them a great delicacy and boiled them for tea. In summer he would take off his shoes and go barefoot over the coarse mountain grass, feeling far more comfortable than if he were shod with leather. Subconsciously, his inborn inclination to work matured into a feeling that the best thing of all was to work *with nature*, in some occupation like farming.

And so, until he was ten or eleven, his existence was happy enough, even if he remained solitary, keeping himself to himself. Then things began to change. The first unwelcome development was that Uncle Dan became increasingly erratic. He started coming home in the early hours of the morning, or not at all, and when he was about the place his temper grew unpredictable. He began to shout at the boys, even occasionally to hit them – something he had never done before. Neither Joseph nor his foster-brothers discerned that the trouble was drink, but they could not help feeling the tension which Dan's behaviour set up in the house. Auntie Flo became nervous and irritable, less confident in her dealings with the boys.

That was one factor which unsettled Joseph. The other was deeper, darker, more personal. He had developed a dread of the mines. The idea of descending into the bowels of the earth, of spending his life in low, airless tunnels which might collapse, of being trapped in some pitch-dark, confined space – all this scared him speechless. The trouble was, no other future faced him. In Merthyr it was taken for granted that all boys would follow their fathers into the mines. Evan and Morgan had both put their names down to join the Dowlais Iron Company, for which Dan worked. Joseph was expected to do the same. Besides, in those days boys left school at thirteen, and started work on or soon after their fourteenth birthday.

By the time Joseph was twelve, a terrible fate seemed inescapable. Again and again he woke sweating in the night, unable to breathe, pursued by claustrophobic nightmares. Sometimes his shouts of fear roused the other boys, whose room he shared, and they would shake him into consciousness, crying, 'What's wrong, Boyo Jo?' But that was his problem: he could not admit that anything was wrong. To tell them that he was scared of the mines would be an intolerable confession of weakness; they would despise him as a weakling, who would never make a man.

The older he grew, the closer the time of going to work approached, the worse his phobia became. He was even taken to see the colliery manager – a kindly man, who nevertheless filled him with still deeper dread. In the end he took the only escape route he could see – by running away. He realised that his defection would alarm and sadden Auntie Florence, so he scribbled a note on a piece of paper and left it in his bed, where he knew she would find it eventually, but not at once. 'Dearest Auntie Flo,' he wrote. 'I am sorry to leave you but I want to go to sea, don't worry, will be alright. Your loving Jo.' Then, taking nothing with him but some sandwiches for his tea, he set off, one afternoon in May 1890, ostensibly for the farm.

He was a month short of thirteen, and still small for his age, but with greater wiriness and stamina than his slight frame suggested. Apart from this, he had nothing in the world but his wits and a prematurely powerful resolve. His mention of going to sea was a red herring: he hoped it would decoy the hunt for him away to the south, to Cardiff and Swansea and the other south coast ports – as indeed it did. In fact he had made two fundamental decisions: one was that he would not work in the mines, and the other that he would work with horses. He had no idea where to go, except to head north, away from the direction in which people might be looking for him; so as soon as he had cleared the outskirts of Dowlais he carried straight on until he came to the valley of the Taf Fechan, and followed it upstream into the hills. His lessons had given him some slight idea of local topography, and he knew that the infant Taf would lead him to the north-east.

He walked all that day and much of the night, eating his sandwiches when he was hungry and drinking from the stream. Then the stream gave out and he kept on along a rough road that led over the mountain. Having no watch, he could not tell what time it was when at last exhaustion overcame him, but the night was warm and he fell asleep in the open, lying against the foot of a wall. When dawn woke him, he went on, heading north-east (as he could see by the sunrise), and in mid-morning he came down, ravenous, to the hamlet of Talybont. A signpost showed that Brecon lay ten miles off to the left, so he set off that way, footsore and apprehensive.

Luck rescued him from further punishment. As he passed a side road, there emerged a horse-drawn cart loaded with chickens in wooden crates, evidently on their way to market. The farmer leaned over from the driving seat and offered him a lift. A whiskery old fellow, with a felt hat pulled down over his ears, and leather gaiters, he hardly spoke a word, except to say that he was going all the way to Brecon. When Joseph asked him the name of his mare, he replied, 'May', and left it at that; but later, when he pulled a packet of bread and cheese from a knapsack under the seat, he gave the boy some without being asked. Joseph was glad of his taciturnity; for one thing, he did not have to make up stories, and for another, the warmth of the sun combined with his own exhaustion to overpower him with drowsiness. Dozing, reeling in his seat, scarcely seeing the strangely-shaped fields and hills all round, he was carried towards the town.

Just as they reached its outskirts, the farmer stopped to address a friend coming the other way, and in a field beside the road Joseph saw something that fascinated him. A handsome pony, with red ribbons on its bridle, was going round in circles. That was what he noticed first. Then, as he concentrated, he realised that the horse was being lunged by a slim, fair-haired girl wearing a dress of apple green. Looking harder, he saw that a small circus had set itself up in the meadow: there were several living caravans, with hooped roofs, and one much larger, bulkier wagon, elaborately painted and embossed, with the legend THE MAGUIRE WILD BEAST SHOW emblazoned in ornate gothic letters, gold against a red background. More horses were tethered to a rail, and in front of one of the caravans a woman was cooking over an open fire.

Bacon! That was what she had in the pan. The smell wafted across irresistibly. Whether it was that, or the sight of the circus horses, or the wild beast legend, Joseph never decided; but the combination of smell and spectacle drew him as surely as the sight of the pit ponies had drawn him on his first visit to Pentwyn. He found himself thanking the whiskery farmer and climbing down from the cart. The next thing he knew, he was standing in front of the big wagon, gazing at the exotic designs of palm trees, lions and tigers that covered its front.

'Hullo, son. What do you want?' The voice, coming from inside a living wagon to his left, made him jump. A tall man appeared in the doorway, dressed like a cowboy: light blue stetson, leather chaps, high-heeled boots, a belt full of metal studs and a dashing scarlet scarf tied lightly in the neck of his clean white shirt.

'I – I'm looking for a job.' The words came out unrehearsed.

'You don't look hardly old enough.' The man stepped down to the ground with loose, easy movements and from his own considerable elevation sized up the newcomer. 'How old are you?'

'Thirteen.'

'Been to school?'

'Yes, sir.'

'Read and write?'

'Yes, sir.'

'What else can you do?'

'Well – I can ride.'

'Can you now?' The man turned and called into the living wagon. 'Here, Bess, will you look at this?'

Out came a woman, also slim and tall, but with long blonde hair, wearing a dark, flowered red waistcoat over a pale lilac dress: even to a twelve-year-old, a glamorous figure. 'By the powers!' she exclaimed, and for a few seconds she stared at the boy; then her face softened into a maternal smile and she asked him his name.

'Joseph Clements, ma'am.'

'And where do you come from?'

'Mer . . . from Newport.' He knew at once that his hesitation had given him away. The woman looked at him keenly, then laughed.

'God, but you've run away from home! That's what you've done.'

In his state of exhaustion, the shock of being discovered was too much for him. Not sensing the kindness behind the words, he burst into tears.

'Come on.' The woman put her arm round his shoulder. 'I expect you're half-starved, too.' She took him across the grass and up the steps into her wagon, sat him down on a padded bench, and pulled up a flap from the wall opposite to make a small table. With eggs and bacon, bread and jam and a mug of tea inside him, he recovered and made a full confession, not least about his fear of the mines. Within an hour, to his astonishment and infinite relief, he found himself taken on as assistant to Captain Harry Maguire and his wife Elizabeth.

That summer proved the happiest of his life. The circus was a compact family unit, in which most of the performers were Maguires of one kind or another, originally from County Sligo. Having been in the business for generations, they had the tradition in their blood, and every one of them excelled at some act. Their shows were extremely modest: they did not even have a tent, but set out a makeshift ring in the open air, with the big wagon drawn up at one side as a backdrop against which acts could be staged. Although in wet weather a long awning could be pitched round half the ring, opposite the front, giving the first few rows of the audience some shelter, most spectators had to remain in the open. Yet the high spirits and good nature of the performances were so infectious that they drew appreciative crowds wherever they stopped.

Harry – no more a captain than Joseph – acted as ringmaster, wielding a trombone like a conductor's baton and blowing raucous blasts on it as he introduced the acts in a loud, theatrical voice. His younger brother Michael played the clown and wrestled with Bruni the bear. Rosaleen, billed as 'The Child of Promise, Now about 10 years of Age,' was in fact fourteen, and walked the tightrope, besides presenting Percy the Perspicacious Pig, who could count and tell fortunes. She also showed Black Beauty, the Talking Horse, and the family's dogs – mainly collies – which would fetch and carry things with apparently perfect understanding of English.

Behind these and similar acts was a strong element of bluff and a great deal of skilful training. Percy, for instance, responded to the clicking of his handler's finger-nails: the signals were so faint that the audience could not detect them, but they were enough to stop or start the pig as he paraded round the ring, and so enabled him to tell fortunes by halting at one or other of the giant playing cards laid out in a circle. Black Beauty reacted to similarly cryptic commands, counting up to ten by striking out with one forefoot, telling the time, and prophesying who in the audience was or was not going to get married by stopping opposite them. The only non-family turn, that of Jack and Jill, the giant and the midget, also made use of gentle deception. When Jack first came on, he walked with absolutely rigid legs, and a planted member of the audience would shout out that he was cheating, using stilts to increase his height – whereupon, looking greatly aggrieved, he would strip off, down to his underwear, revealing that every inch of his seven foot eight was his own.

The climax of every show was the act known as The Untameable Lion, which brought the audience to its feet and left many of them in a dead faint, unconscious with fright. The first time Joseph saw it, he too nearly passed out, for, like everyone else, he thought that Michael Maguire was about to be killed, or perhaps even had been.

With much ceremony, and many fanfares on the trombone, the family's lioness Cleopatra was wheeled up in her travelling cage, which had iron bars along the front. Captain Harry then told an elaborate tale of how it had proved impossible to tame her, how she was too savage to be used in any ring, but how, for the especial benefit of tonight's audience, and to avert disappointment, Mr Michael Maguire would enter her cage. That was all he could promise, all he could do. He would go in and come out. To try more would be as much as his life was worth. Was everybody ready?'

Although the warm-up took several minutes, the act itself was over in seconds. An assistant worked the door, at the right-hand end of the truck. Captain Harry himself stood by with a long pole, to ward off the lioness if anything went wrong. Then came the action. The door opened. Michael stepped into the cage. From the far end of the wagon the lioness launched herself towards him with a roar. As one, the audience screamed, for all they could see was a terrifying blur of lion, man, lion, one passing the other, apparently in contact. Then with a clang of metal the door slammed shut – and there was Michael on the grass outside, unharmed.

It took Joseph weeks to learn the secret of this spectacle – that Cleopatra, far from being untameable, was an old circus hand, and a bit of a pet, who had more or less invented this trick herself, and regarded it as an agreeable form of ballet. What happened was that when Michael entered the cage, with his back to the audience, her spring carried her along the back wall, in front of him. Then, as she passed and went hurtling round the end, he stepped forward, so that as she came back along the front of the cage, she passed behind him, never touching him, or trying to.

For Joseph, the Untameable Lion came to epitomise the spirit of that little circus. With its risks, its hidden skills, its showmanship, its exotic nature and its element of bluff, the act summed up what all the performers were trying to achieve. Captain Harry was a master at what they called 'telling the tale' – spinning a yarn to build up his next performer – and Joseph became intoxicated with the mild form of deception practised nightly on willing audiences. He knew full well (for instance) that The World's Only Mummified Mermaid – exhibited nightly in a huge glass jar of 'embalming fluid' – was in fact made of wood, cunningly painted, and that between stands she was taken out of her jar and travelled, dry, in a wooden box because the water in which she appeared was too heavy to transport. But never in the world would he have revealed her true nature to an outsider, so strongly had his loyalty been engaged.

Playing for one or two nights, then moving on, the circus progressed slowly eastwards on a time-honoured course which took it out of

Wales and through the heart of England. From Brecon they went to Hay-on-Wye, then to Hereford, and on through the rich farmlands and orchards of Worcestershire. Everywhere a site was ready for them: Captain Harry seemed to know all the farmers in the land, and always a gate stood open at the entrance to a level field on the outskirts of the next town. From the farmer's wife they would buy fresh milk and butter, eggs and chickens, as well as vegetables and fruit when they came into season. Sometimes, if their journey was a long one, they would spend a night on the road, parked on the grassy verge, shaded by chestnuts or limes, and undisturbed by other traffic.

In this nomadic life Joseph found nothing but delight. He suffered one severe pang of sadness and remorse when his birthday came and went uncelebrated. Having claimed to be thirteen already, he could not admit that he was still only twelve, and on the 3rd of June he spent a miserable evening, thinking of the cakes that Auntie Flo used to make him, and of the pain that his disappearance must have caused her. After that had passed, though, he took happily to his new world. He loved the sense of freedom which constant movement brought, the feeling that there was always a new place, a new audience ahead. For him, in a continuous ferment of discovery, everything seemed to grow larger with every stop – the weather finer, the colours brighter, the hills steeper, the sky higher. The journey was like a protracted lesson in geography; having never seen anything but Merthyr and its immediate surroundings, he began to realise what variety lay beyond. One source of wonder was the way in which people's accents changed, from the lilt of central Wales to the fruity rustic twang of Worcestershire yokels; another surprise was the brick-red earth of Herefordshire, another the taste of strawberries, which he ate for the first time near Evesham.

Soon he was making himself useful on many fronts, watering the horses, taking them out to graze, grooming them, harnessing them to the wagons, and leading or driving them when on the move. The horses were all-important, for they not only provided some of the stars of the show, but also pulled the wagons from one site to the next, and anyone who could help look after them made a valuable member of the team. Only one old stager – a heavy Irish draught mare – would pull the lion wagon: the rest were terrified of the big cat's scent, but all had their special tasks. Joseph also did routine chores like collecting wood, lighting and maintaining the cooking fires, and filling the mermaid's jar. In the evenings, he took the money when audiences began to roll up for the performance; and then – far better – he himself began to take part. Noticing that he rode well and had good balance, Captain Harry taught him to walk the Rolling Globe – an old-fashioned act in which the performer stood on a large globe and moved it about by shifting his feet, while the master of ceremonies spun tales about the dark and dangerous continents on which he was treading. Out there in front of the audience, dressed in a shiny blue sailor suit, Joseph felt like a king.

Soon he loved not only the life but his companions too – and none more than Rosaleen, whose slender body was already starting to blossom, and whose fair good looks were causing her parents both pleasure and apprehension. Joseph admired her extravagantly, especially when she rode her ponies bareback, with her long thighs fiercely caressing their smooth summer coats; and, whenever it was possible without attracting attention, he compared her physical attributes with those of the mermaid. She, for her part, noticed that he often hung about her, but raised no objection so long as his devotion took the form of slave-like obedience and an immediate willingness to carry out any menial task which she wanted done.

At first he earned only a shilling a week, but after a month his wages leapt to four times that. Four shillings a week! To him that was a princely sum, most of which he managed to save. Sleeping on the top bunk of a fine old mahogany wagon, eating his meals with the family, he normally spent nothing at all – and in some mysterious way Bess Maguire managed to find him a complete change of clothes at no cost, even down to a second-hand but comfortable pair of boots. Afterwards, he assumed that the garments must have come in part-exchange from one of the other travelling families whose paths they crossed, for they often stopped in company with itinerant funfairs or gypsies who shared the traditional sites, and much barter was done. Easily the greatest of these gatherings was the horse fair at Stow-on-the-Wold, high on the Cotswold hills, to which dealers came from all over the south of England. Never had Joseph seen such an assembly, such a variety, of animals: little, short-eared ponies from Dartmoor, bigger ponies from Exmoor, shire horses of many breeds, big, raw half-breds straight from Ireland, finished hunters gleaming with condition, Arabs with their elegant arched necks and dished faces, tiny Shetlands, the Welsh mountain ponies which he knew already, and even a zebra, brought along as a joke by some enterprising owner of a menagerie.

The circus's finest hour came when, for a couple of weeks, they

borrowed an elephant. This grand beast, called Mary, belonged to
another travelling family – the Hudsons, friends of the Maguires –
who had been smitten with bad luck: first one of them went down
with appendicitis, then another broke his arm, so that they had to
suspend performances, and had lent the elephant, together with her
handler, for the duration. Walking at a stately place from one location
to the next, looming enormous beneath the chestnut tree to which
she was tethered in the evening, she created a sensation wherever
she appeared, and enormously strengthened the Maguires' claim to
be a Wild Beast Show. In the ring she performed some modest tricks,
but easily her best turn was the tug-of-war. 'Twenty men to pull the
elephant!' Captain Harry would cry. 'I don't want any weaklings,
either. Twenty good 'uns, if you're out there.' With much muttering
and bashful grinning, twenty husky youths would be sorted out and
lined up in a tug-of-war team along a thick hemp rope, the other end
of which would be passed right round the elephant – along her flank,
round her backside and up to her head again. In the middle, dividing
the combatants, a white handkerchief would be tied on the rope as a
marker.

'Twenty to one!' cried Captain Harry, as if in agony. 'Ladies and
gentlemen, this can*not* be fair! I wonder the elephant stands for it.
Sure to God, boys, you can pull her from here to Buckingham' – or
whatever the next town was – 'Nevertheless, I shall call "Are you
ready . . . get set . . . PULL".'

Although Mary held the rope in her trunk, it was through her
behind that she exerted pressure: she knew perfectly well that she
could pull the men over whenever she wanted to, but she was trained
not to put out more than minimum force until she got a particular
command. The boys would heave and curse, slipping and stamping
their heels in, until they were breathless: then, at a signal from her
trainer's hand, Mary would simply sit backwards and pull them flat
on their faces.

As the summer wore on, Joseph advanced rapidly in confidence
and physique. It was not just that the outdoor life gave him a healthy
tan: in response to the continuous physical exercise, he grew taller
and stronger, and by autumn looked altogether more formidable. His
dread that the law would catch up with him gradually wore off.
Occasionally, if there had been a robbery or an accident, a dogged
country constable would come round the wagons to make inquiries;
but no one ever demanded to see any documents, and if questions
were asked, Harry Maguire passed the boy off as his son. By the time

they reached Bedford, at the beginning of September, Joseph felt far
enough from Wales to be safe.

Yet like all glorious summers, that one came to an end. Joseph had
been so absorbed in day-to-day activity that he had scarcely looked
ahead, hoping, or assuming, that his carefree existence could go on
indefinitely. Then one morning Captain Harry called him into the
Big Wagon and said, 'Well, me lad. You've done us proud. But this
is the end of the road, and the question is, what are you going to do
when we close down?'

'Close down?'

'For the winter. We always shut up shop at the end of this month.
This year we're going to winter near Bury St Edmunds. We put most
of the horses out to grass, and there isn't the work. You'll need to
find something else.' He paused, then added, 'Horses are your thing,
aren't they?'

'Yes, sir.'

'Well – I have an idea. Let's see what we can do.'

When the show played at Cambridge, he sent word ahead to a
friend called Richard Marsh who ran some racing stables outside
Newmarket. Harry wrote that he had a promising lad who might
make an apprentice jockey: would Marsh see him when the circus
reached Newmarket in a week's time? Back came a positive answer:
Mr Marsh could not guarantee a place at Lordship Stables and Stud,
but anyone recommended by Harry Maguire was worth a look, and
he would gladly interview young Clements the following Saturday.

Newmarket was another revelation: only a small town, with most of
its houses lining the straight, broad main street – but the racehorses!
Joseph was amazed at the numbers which came out for morning
exercise. The Maguire family camped on the edge of Severals, the
open space traditionally used by circuses just to the east of the town;
and over this fine stretch of turf every morning came strings of horses
such as Joseph had never seen: thoroughbreds of exquisite grace and
lightness, every one an aristocrat, with little men and even smaller
boys perched on their backs like monkeys.

Lordship Stables and Stud, where Richard Marsh trained, lay four
miles out of town in the opposite direction, beside the London Road;
and on Saturday morning Harry Maguire drove Joseph out there
in the dog-cart. As they bowled along between neat hedges and

avenues of trees just starting to turn, the boy grew taut with nerves, not least about his appearance. Harry looked just the ticket, in a bowler hat and high-collared grey pea-jacket, but Joseph had been at a loss over what to put on. The sailor suit which he wore to walk the rolling globe belonged to the circus, and in any case was not suitable for a formal occasion of this kind. He had no suit of his own, nor even a jacket, and was wearing only a clean shirt and trousers. Naive and inexperienced though he was, he nevertheless felt under-dressed for an important occasion.

His apprehension increased when they began to pass paddocks laid out with geometrical precision and bounded by post-and-rail fences painted white. They turned off the main road beside a lodge whose garden was perfect in every particular: zinnias and dahlias blazed in masses beyond an emerald lawn, and there was not a weed in sight. Clearly, this was an establishment run to high standards.

At the house – a mansion, in Joseph's eyes – a manservant greeted them and asked them to wait in the hall. Never in his life had Joseph seen such a grand room, full of highly-polished dark furniture, with a grandfather clock ticking loudly beside the fireplace. The ceiling seemed very high, the pictures on the walls immense, the acreage of floor-boards intimidating.

After a minute or two they were ushered into the study, where Marsh himself arose from his desk to greet them.

'Harry - my dear fellow!' He came forward smiling and shook hands vigorously.

'Dick! Top of the morning to you. What a place you have here now.'

'Improving all the time . . . and this is the boy?'

'Yes – this is Joseph.'

'How do you do, young man?'

'Very well, sir, thank you.' Joseph tried to look at the famous trainer, but found it difficult. He could feel the keen grey eyes sizing him up. Then, as it was five years since the friends had last seen each other, they fell to catching up on news, and he had time to consider his surroundings.

Marsh was a spare, fit-looking man of middle age – in fact, although Joseph thought him ancient, he was only forty – and the most striking feature of his bony face was his nose, which must at some time have been broken, since it was bent slightly to its owner's right. He was formally dressed, in a tweed suit and stiff white collar. The walls of the room were covered with pictures of horses, at rest and in action, and with banks of framed testimonials and certificates. Beyond his large, roll-topped desk French windows gave directly onto a stable yard, surrounded by boxes, in which horses and lads were continuously coming and going. Suddenly Marsh was addressing him:

'What can you do, then, young man?'

'I can ride, sir.'

'Good. And what have you ridden?'

'Captain Maguire's horses, mostly.'

'Ever fallen off?'

'Yes, sir.'

Marsh chuckled. 'That's an honest start. If you'd said no, I'd have had my suspicions.' After a pause he asked, 'How old are you?'

'Thirteen, sir.'

'And how tall is your mother?'

The question flummoxed Joseph. Then he blurted out, 'I don't know, sir. Me mum's dead.'

'I'm sorry. My apologies. How tall was she?'

'Don't know, sir. I don't remember her.'

'Joseph's an orphan,' Harry put in.

Marsh raised his eyebrows. 'Who taught you such good manners, then?'

'Me aunt and uncle.'

'In Wales, was it? Your accent's Welsh.'

'Yes, sir. Merthyr Tydfil.'

After a few more questions Marsh stood up, crossed to the French windows, called one of the lads over and told him to show the newcomer the yard. Left alone in the study, the two men reminisced agreeably for a few minutes before Harry said, 'He's a good lad, Dick. I'd back him to do well, any day.'

'I can see that,' Marsh answered. 'But what happened to him? Something went wrong, I know.'

'I don't think anything *went* wrong. It was what might happen that scared him. He had a thing about going down the mines, see? He didn't want to spend his life in the dark.'

'Well – I can't blame him for that.'

'Will you take him on, then?'

'Yes – I'll take him: as an apprentice, on six months' approval at first.'

'Dick – you're a real friend.'

'He'll have to work, mind. You know what people say about Newmarket? It's the place where horses live in state and humans exist for their convenience. That's true of Lordship, anyway. And I'll have to tell his foster-parents where he is. Otherwise I'll be breaking the law.'

'Of course . . .'

'But if he's any use, I won't let him go – so he needn't worry.' Marsh got up and walked to the window, where he stood and looked out with satisfaction over his bustling yard.

'He's come at the right moment, anyway. When I arrived at Lordship fifteen years ago, this place was nothing but a hundred and twenty acres of farmland. Look at it now. Three yards, four miles of private gallops, hedges, avenues . . . It don't do to brag, even to an old friend, but things have certainly changed.'

Marsh drifted into a descriptive reverie, telling Harry how, when he came to Newmarket in the Seventies, he had only been able to rent the land at Lordship. Then, in 1890, even though he had made countless improvements at his own expense, the owners had demanded a steep increase in rent. Marsh, incensed, had privately incited Percy Heaton, agent for Lord Ellesmere, to buy Egerton House, the farm next door. Marsh's idea was that there, under his own supervision and for his own use, Ellesmere would build the most modern and best equipped training establishment that man could devise – and this, in due course, was done, at enormous expense, most of the money coming from the earnings of the splendid stallion Hampton. But at the last moment the owners of Lordship relented and let Marsh renew his lease for fifteen years at the old rent, so that he stayed on there as well and found himself with two properties to run instead of one.

At Marsh's direction, three handsome yards of stabling had gone up at Egerton – one of brick and two of timber, all equipped with electricity and the latest ideas in drainage and ventilation; the land, which had been growing wheat, barley, turnips and seeds, had been put down to grass, and round its edges Marsh had created miles of gallops. He had also ordered the planting of many thousand trees, in belts and avenues. Yet his special pride was an idea which he copied from France: a moss-litter gallop, one and a quarter miles long, which remained soft throughout the year and could be used when other gallops in the area, such as those on Newmarket Heath, had become too hard through drought or frost.

'That's our particular winner at the moment,' he told Harry. 'No one else has anything to touch it. Your lad's going to work in the most modern racing stables in the world.'

Joseph said goodbye to the Maguires with keen regret. He hated the idea of losing their company, and could not find words to express his gratitude for all they had done. 'Ah, go on with you,' said Bess when he began to stumble out his thanks. 'And who did all the work, anyway?' But she did give him a kiss and a hug, and Harry gave him a golden sovereign. 'We'll be at Bury all the winter,' he said. 'So come and see us. Next year we'll go west again, but I expect we'll be back in '92.'

So Joseph went into his first proper job in the place which claimed, with some justification, to be the hub of the racing world, its metropolis. Home of the Jockey Club and of Tattersall's, the leading auctioneers, patronised by royal race-goers, owners and trainers for over two centuries, Newmarket boasted more equine establishments than any other town in England – and at the time Marsh's were among the busiest of all. Not only did the horses in training have to be looked after and exercised: the programme of improvements created hundreds of extra tasks, and if any lad ever had a moment free, he was grabbed to lend a hand with carting earth, digging holes for trees or clearing up after the fence-builders.

Joseph signed on for a five-year apprenticeship. 'He shall not commit fornication nor contract matrimony,' ran the formal text of his indenture. 'He shall not play at cards or dice-tables . . . he shall not haunt taverns nor playhouses.' In return for his labours, his employers promised to pay him nine guineas in his first year, eleven in his second, thirteen in his third, and fifteen in his fourth and fifth; they also undertook to 'find unto the said apprentice sufficient meat and drink and also hat, coat and waistcoat'.

They got their money's worth. In summer the boys were up at cock-crow, and in winter before it. Their days were filled by a ceaseless round of work: feeding the horses, grooming them, mucking out their stables, riding them out, feeding them again, cleaning the tack, sweeping the yards. Their food was adequate, but not much more, and they were always ravenous. Discipline – at any rate during the day – was strict: no boy was allowed to speak a sharp word to his horse, nor a foul one to a superior human being, and to strike any

41

animal with a stick was a criminal offence, punishable by immediate dismissal. All were required to wear their tan-coloured stable-suits while on duty.

At night, things were rather different. The ten youngest boys all slept in a single long room, on the first floor above a range of stables, and into this dormitory they were locked at 9 p.m. Whether or not Marsh knew what went on in there, none of them was sure; the shrewder ones suspected that he must know – for had he not been a jockey himself, and apprenticed to stables at Newmarket, just as they were? At any rate, he took care never to interfere.

What went on – in a word – was horseplay, much of it with overt sexual overtones. After the old-fashioned courtesies of the circus world, the coarseness of the lads gave Joseph an unpleasant shock. Their language, for a start, was atrociously obscene and blasphemous: it was as if the civility and good behaviour which they were obliged to maintain in public pent up within them a head of filth, which poured out like steam as soon as they were locked away. Forbidden fornication by their contracts, and anyway lacking experience or opportunity, they discussed the subject endlessly in lascivious detail, their imaginations fuelled, and their phraseology coloured, by the daily spectacle of stallions covering mares. Boys of fourteen swore like veterans – and if anyone had criticised them for it, they would have justified themselves by citing the example set by their great hero, Fred Archer, the champion jockey, whose language was known to have been of positively heroic extravagance.

Their frustration also found release in violence – in the ritual stripping and painting of newcomers, in pillow fights and obstacle races round the dormitory, some boys acting as horses, others as jockeys. There was also an element of bullying, usually fostered by only one or two of the inmates. When Joseph arrived, the leading agitator was a thuggish, red-headed Scot called Angus Macleod, who sought to take it out of the newcomer by mimicking his Welsh accent, hiding his boots, and secreting leeks under his pillow, so that his bed stank of onions. Joseph stood the taunting for a while, then one evening astonished everybody in the dormitory by suddenly landing such a cracking upper-cut on Angus's chin as to put him flat on the boards.

That one lucky punch gave him a respite; but all next day hints kept reaching him that he had better watch out, as Angus intended to settle the score that evening, and his apprehension mounted as lock-up approached. There was no escape. No sooner had the dormitory door been shut than a couple of Angus's cronies pushed four of the beds away against the walls to form a makeshift ring and goaded him into the arena with loutish threats. Had he held back, they would have dragged him out to fight, so he went forward, trembling with fear but clinging to the precepts which Harry Maguire had taught him during sessions of open-air sparring. 'You've got long arms,' the Captain had told him. 'Keep that left straight out, and you'll come to no harm. Chin down, right hand in front of your face, and *watch your opponent*. Never shut your eyes.'

There were no formalities, no seconds, no timekeeper. With a snarl of 'All right, you whippersnapper,' Angus came lumbering forward. Luckily for Joseph, he had no technique, but merely launched wild, round-arm swings as fast and hard as he could. Joseph ducked, led with his left and felt his knuckles crunch into Angus's nose. The impact jolted his opponent's head back, but it also sent a shock up Joseph's arm and rattled his own jaw. A heavy blow half caught him on the top of the head, and although it glanced off upwards, it made his eyes swim and woke cold rage in him. This time he did not wait for a charge, but led again with another long left. Once more his fist thudded home. Angus gave a grunt and stepped back. Already blood was running from his nose.

Shaken, he began to circle crabwise, then launched another assault. Joseph ducked and led staunchly, but this time his left missed and he suddenly found himself at close quarters. The combatants grappled briefly, wrestled, came apart. Yet again Angus charged, to be brought up short by that jarring, ramrod left. He grunted with pain and spat out blood from a split upper lip. Lacking the wit to vary his tactics, he lumbered forward yet once more, and this time got a fist in the eye.

As yet Joseph was unmarked, except that his ears were burning from round-arm swipes. He was out of breath, but not distressed, and buoyed up by the incredulous realisation that he could take control of the fight. Then he made a fatal mistake. Instead of sticking to his well-tried tactics, when Angus came back at him, he tried to plant a right-handed uppercut on his chin, as he had the night before. The punch missed, and the impact of Angus's charge spun him round. A second later he was felled by a murderous punch in his right kidney.

He lay on the bare boards, disabled by pain. For a moment he was barely conscious. Then he became aware of a mêlée. Feet stamped and legs heaved all round him. Somebody fell over him, swore, got up again. As he lay still, gasping for breath, he realised that a general fight had broken out. His friend Wilf Collyer, infuriated by the blatant foul, had sprung to his defence. So had Basher Brown, a heavy-set boy whom he scarcely knew. Two or three others had come in on Angus's side and were slugging it out, toe to toe. As they fought, Joseph crawled away, sat up and was sick on the floor. Then, as abruptly as it had started, the fight ceased, and everyone retired to lick their wounds. Nobody spoke when Joseph crept away to bed, but there was no doubt that the moral victory belonged to him.

The fight did much to stabilise his existence. For the first few weeks he had suffered miserably, missing the circus and the gentle Maguires, loathing most of the rough crew among whom he had landed. Then, by standing up to Angus, he became a local hero, and was accepted as a fully-fledged member of the team. Of greater import, in the long term, was the way the battle shaped his character: it left him determined to pursue his own road quietly so long as he was unmolested, but to defend himself ferociously if anyone attacked him. Jealousies raged, of course, among the lads about which horses they looked after and what rides they got, but from that moment Joseph found it easier to stand up for himself in any argument.

As he gradually learned about racing, present and past, its glamour and traditions entranced him and drew him firmly into their grasp. He grew to love the work and the daily round of the stables; he discovered the thrill of sitting on top of a highly-bred, highly-charged animal, packed with explosive power; above all, he loved riding out in the early mornings, when mist hung low over the broad sweeps of the Heath, when the air was crisp and cool, and the horses' feet left trails in the dew. His admiration for his employer increased tenfold when he discovered that Marsh himself had been no mean jockey, especially over fences and hurdles, and that he had several times ridden in the Grand National, once finishing third. His immediate heroes became the jockeys who rode the stable's best horses, principally Jack Watts, famous for never having smiled in his life, but an admirably cool performer, and a kind, quiet teacher, always willing to pass on useful advice.

Yet for Joseph, as for all the lads, the name revered above all was that of Fred Archer – the Newmarket man who had been champion jockey for no fewer than thirteen seasons. His example gave them all hope, for he had started off very much in the way Joseph had – a horse-mad boy who would creep into stables illicitly and climb on to the animals' backs. Archer had gone to work for Matt Dawson, at the Heath House stables on the edge of the town, when only eleven, and had risen to dizzy heights from modest beginnings. Endless stories were told about him: how once as a boy he was found in tears because he had been able to ride only one of the horses that finished level in a dead heat; how he had won the 1880 Derby on Ben d'Or even though his arm had been savaged by an ill-tempered brute called Muley Edris after a gallop on the Heath only a few days before; how he had said little but always listened; how high-born ladies had proposed marriage to him; how, by merely appearing in the street in Manchester, he had brought the place to a standstill . . . The one fact which the boys found infinitely puzzling was that in November 1889 Archer had shot himself. Joseph knew that his wife had died in childbirth – but even so, how could such an immensely successful man have been driven to commit suicide?

In the autumn of 1892 excitement swept through the stables when it was learnt that the Prince of Wales, no less, was to send his horses for training there. Marsh already had many distinguished clients, among them the Duke of Hamilton, the Duke of Devonshire and Lord Hindlip, but patronage from the heir to the throne was something different, and pushed life at Egerton into a higher gear. Scarcely had the last of the new boxes been completed in November that year than they were filled with an influx of royal horses, and never had any establishment been more thoroughly scrubbed and polished than Egerton was before the royal party arrived to inspect the premises in January 1893. Every box and horse was made immaculate, every item of leather dressed and buffed, every bright buckle polished, every straw (almost) set in order. From Sandringham, with the Prince, came his racing manager, Lord Marcus Beresford, and the entire staff of the stud was lined up in the main yard to give three cheers. The fact that the place was brand-new worked both for and against it, in making a good impression: the buildings and their paint-work looked immaculate – dark green doors with black hinges – but the turf in the centre of each yard was poorly established, and the trees in the new shelter-belts were bare of leaves, besides being only a couple of feet high. Fortunately the weather rose to the occasion, and washed everything over with a pale wintry sun.

Along with the other apprentices, Joseph watched enthralled as the royal party descended from the carriage which had brought them out from the train. The Prince wore a pale grey overcoat of very fine wool, with a collar of black Persian lamb; he was even more portly and pop-eyed than in pictures, and his neatly-trimmed beard did not conceal the fact that his neck bulged over his collar, or that his complexion was ruby red. Yet he moved with surprising agility, and by the energetic inquiries which he made of Marsh he communicated his enthusiasm to the entire staff.

Among the lads, some ribald opinions were expressed about the quality of the eight royal horses which were boxed to Newmarket in a special train and walked out to Egerton on New Year's Day 1893. 'A ribbier lot of rubbish I never saw,' exclaimed Wilf Collyer, who considered himself an expert at the ripe age of fifteen. 'That Downey – you could put her through the bloody mangle and she wouldn't come out looking no different.' (Events went some way towards vindicating this precocious verdict, for of the new arrivals only the bay colt Florizel II proved to have any real quality, winning five races as a three-year-old.) A few days after the royal influx, another twenty horses came to Egerton – the entire stable of Baron Hirsch – and suddenly the establishment was at full stretch, with more than eighty animals in training.

As Joseph gained experience, he was promoted from the most menial tasks and given charge of particular horses, generally two at a time. His riding ability kept pace with his general competence, and he began to acquire a very good eye for a horse. Although he grew steadily taller, he remained very light and wiry, so that by the time he reached sixteen, Marsh started to tell him that he might yet make a jockey. So far he had had no chance to ride in a race, but Marsh began to put him up now and then on a fast sprinter when he wanted a light lad to act as pacemaker in the trial of a major hope.

In those years of his apprenticeship, Joseph heard scarcely a murmur from the outside world, and saw still less of it. The longest trip he ever made was to Bury St Edmunds – some twenty miles – where he visited the Maguires in their winter quarters during February 1893 and found them little changed, except that Rosaleen had become disturbingly beautiful, very much in her mother's blonde-haired, blue-eyed mould. Otherwise, his excursions were limited to Newmarket, which he visited on his occasional days off. Sometimes he also made illegal expeditions in the evenings, when he and a couple of companions would shin down a drainpipe from the dormitory window and leg it the four miles into town, lured by the excitements of the cock fights held behind the Greyhound Inn, the drinks slipped them surreptitiously in the back bar of The Crown by Annie Bloss, and the tremendous fights that broke out among revellers on the evenings after race meetings, when the town was full of trippers and touts circling the dark streets after easy prey.

There were plenty of legitimate attractions, too, among them the saddlers Boyce & Rogers, next to the post office in the High Street, who made the most beautiful harness and other equipment, and whose aged craftsmen could be watched as they worked in the back of the shop. At one stage the manager stationed a full-sized stuffed horse in his front window, attracting much attention and not a few warnings from passers-by, who thought it was real and might walk out through the glass. Another favourite rendezvous for growing lads was Moss's pie shop, where a plate of sizzling Newmarket sausages and potatoes could be got for twopence.

For Joseph, the town and its environs established themselves firmly as home. He grew very fond of the broad High Street, with carriages waiting for business parked down the middle, its constant processions of horses on their way to or from exercise, and on the south side that holy of holies the Jockey Club – a low, white building to which, paradoxically, no jockeys were admitted, but which had housed the governing body of racing since the late eighteenth century.

Yet even if Joseph did not travel, his life at Egerton gave him clear insights into the rigid stratification of society, not just in the racing world but in late Victorian England as a whole. The Queen, of course, formed the apex of society, and immediately beneath her the Prince of Wales, who would eventually succeed to the throne, came a close second. Beneath him were the aristocracy, great landowners such as the Duke of Hamilton (a frequent visitor) and the Duke of Roxburghe. Below them came the minor nobility like Lord Marcus Beresford, and below them again the professional classes, among whom, the boys supposed, Richard Marsh must be numbered. Argument smouldered among them as to whether or not Marsh was a gentleman; some said that he could not be, as he worked with his hands for superior masters, but others maintained that, whatever his exact social position, he was certainly a *natural* gentleman – and Joseph, seeing how gracefully and easily Marsh dealt with his employers, supported this view. (Another such, he reckoned, was Harry Maguire, whose courtesy and charm enabled him to move easily in any circle, no matter how high or low.) Joseph also perceived that it was possible to be a gentleman and, at the same time, a bit of a cad. One such, he suspected, was the Honourable George Lambton, who was mustard on his horses (as the lads described him), and who often came to Egerton dressed with such extravagance as to set every tongue wagging. From his curly-brimmed hats, via his lemon-coloured suits, with the trousers pressed into seams at the sides, rather than fore-and-aft, down to his gleaming brogues, he presented a picture of such sartorial elegance as to make people wonder whether or not he was quite the ticket.

It was generally agreed that, whatever else Marsh might be, he was definitely a sport: a man who had ridden winners himself, who knew the score, who was scrupulously fair, and who above all had a sense of humour that put him on the boys' side in many an argument, even if he could not immediately reveal his allegiance. Even when one of them committed some misdemeanour, he would look on it indulgently if it had been done in a spirit of fun or enterprise. He could always take a joke, and often hinted that he himself had not been by any means blameless as a boy. All the lads looked up to 'Marshy', and Joseph in a way loved him.

But then, the great question: could a jockey ever become a gentleman? Some reckoned that Archer had managed it, and cited the well-known rumour that a duchess had once asked him to marry her. The standard answer to this was, 'Well, he bloody didn't, did he?', and cynics pointed out that although Archer had been on unprecedentedly close terms with the owners for whom he rode, they had continued to address him as 'Archer', rather than 'Fred', until the day he put the pistol to his head. As for raw stable lads – they were the lowest of the low, unless by their own efforts they proved themselves capable of becoming something better.

All this Joseph noticed and tried to analyse, quite without rancour. This, he observed, was how society worked, and he did not consider it his job to try to change things. Yet he did quietly determine that he would improve his own lot as much as possible. The son of a miner was nobody, especially if he could not produce a pedigree of any kind. But what might he not achieve if he became a successful jockey, or even a trainer? The weapons he chose for self-advancement were conscientious effort and courtesy; nature had blessed him with an even temper, and just as he liked to keep his own person neat and clean, so he tried to preserve the decencies in his dealings with other people. 'Clean as a whistle', used of a person, became a favourite phrase of approval.

Many of his own ideals and attitudes derived from the behaviour of Marsh himself, who became a kind of substitute father. When the dread moment came for him to tell Joseph's aunt and uncle where he was, he did so in a straightforward letter, which he allowed Joseph to read. There followed a tense wait of more than a month, but at last the envelope was returned by the Post Office, opened and resealed, with 'Gone Away' written across the Evans's address. That brought Joseph relief, but also anxiety: he feared that Uncle Dan's drunkenness must have broken up the family, and that they had been forced to move. He felt sad as he imagined the little house standing empty – for if it were inhabited, the new people would surely have sent the letter on – and the vegetable garden on which he had laboured going to waste. Guilt plagued him, too, for he knew in his heart that he should have stayed, and paid back some of his debt to Auntie Flo by trying to act as mediator in the family squabbles. He himself wrote a contrite note, apologising for his apparent ingratitude, but when that also was returned, he let Merthyr gradually fade from his mind.

In 1894 a fresh development helped blot out the past. That August there arrived at Egerton a bay yearling called Persimmon – soon known to the lads, inevitably, as Percy, or Perce. Bred in the royal stud at Sandringham, a brother of Florizel II, he came with the highest expectations, for he was exceptionally well made and seemed to have infinite promise. Great was Joseph's delight, therefore, when Marsh assigned the colt to him, with a warning that the Prince of Wales had a special interest in this animal, and that their care of him would have to be outstanding. In particular, Marsh warned Joseph against the touts, who constantly lurked outside the gates, on the Heath and around the pubs in the town, hoping to pick up tips about the form of the horses.

'This one's going to be a real top sawyer,' declared Marsh, leaning over the door of Persimmon's box. 'We'll keep him as dark as we can, but those fellows'll be after him, for sure. If any of them accosts you, don't speak to him - and whatever you do, don't talk about the horse in town.'

As Persimmon matured, his quality proclaimed itself more and more clearly. If there were faults in his appearance, they were trifling: a tendency to lop ears – which he got from his ancestor Melbourne – and patches of curious mousy colour round his eyes and muzzle. In the winter he grew such an extraordinary, long, woolly coat that everyone said he looked more like a sheep than a horse. But he had a fine neck and a bold look, and behind the saddle he was outstanding – exceptionally long from hip to hock, and between the hip and the round bone. In the stable his manners were perfect, and he was no trouble to break and train. By the spring of 1895 he had grown into a big horse; when Joseph rode him on the gallops, he was thrilled by the length and springiness of his action. For the first time in his life, he had the instinctive but sure feeling of being on top of a champion.

Word of Percy's progress soon reached Sandringham, and one morning in May 1895 Lord Marcus Beresford came down to witness a trial. Joseph yielded his horse to Jack Watts, the professional who would ride him in races, and was put up instead on a four-year-old mare called Rags, herself no mean performer. 'Let him stride along the whole way,' Marsh told Watts, as he rode out with the racehorses towards their starting point on the Heath. 'Don't touch him with your heels or interfere with him at all. Then we'll see what he can do.'

Away went Lord Marcus and Marsh on their hacks, towards the Rowley Mile finishing-post. For a minute or two Watts and Joseph walked their mounts round quietly, watched by Ted Myers, the head lad. Then, as a flag went up in the distance, they wheeled into position beside each other, and Ted called out, 'Ready, steady, GO!'

The horses, sensing a special occasion, went off like smoke. Joseph's loyalties were uncomfortably divided. Personal pride made him want to win the gallop, but he was almost equally keen that Persimmon should prove himself superior. He need not have worried: even though the colt was giving away nearly two stone, he won in a canter and showed that he was in a different class. Lord Marcus went away highly delighted, and Marsh decided to enter Persimmon for his first race, the Coventry Stakes at Ascot.

Alas for his attempts to keep news of the two-year-old quiet! Word leaked out that Egerton contained a potential Derby winner, and the touts saw to it that he went to the starting-post for the first time at odds of only 2–1. On the racecourse, excitement mounted when the crowd saw the Prince of Wales himself go down to the paddock to inspect his horse: he did not often do that, and his visit clearly signified that he had a special feeling for Persimmon. At any rate, he seemed delighted with the animal's appearance: Joseph, who was holding the bridle, heard him say, in his thick, well-oiled voice, 'He looks a cracker now, Marsh. You've done him proud.'

So it proved. Persimmon ran away with the race – and then a few weeks later he did the same in the Richmond Stakes at Goodwood, again watched by the Prince, and this time at 2–1 on. Then in August came a setback, when he failed badly in the Middle Park Plate, over the Bretby Stakes course at Newmarket; but Marsh insisted all along that he was off colour before the race, and that he entered the horse only at the insistence of Lord Marcus. In spite of this disappointment, everyone at Egerton saw 1895 as a year of continuous development for Persimmon, and looked forward with the keenest anticipation to his career as a three-year-old.

If the year 1896 made Persimmon famous, it also changed Joseph's life, for in May he was twice abducted.

Perhaps he relaxed his normal vigilance; perhaps he was a victim of the excessive work required to bring Percy to the highest pitch of training. Either way, he and Wilf were set upon one evening by a gang of ruffians as they emerged from having a pint of beer at The Bushel, in Drapery Row. The attack was so sudden that it caught them off guard, and when Joseph tried to run, he was tripped and came down heavily. The next thing he knew, he had been dragged round a corner and was pinned in a doorway by three men, one of whom had him by the collar and held a drawn knife to his throat.

'You're the one as does Persimmon,' he hissed in a hoarse whisper. Joseph, who was still gasping for breath, said nothing, but glanced desperately to right and left in search of Wilf, who had disappeared.

'Look at me, young feller – and see this.' The knife blade turned slowly back and forth, inches from Joseph's nose.

'What d'you want?'

'Persimmon. You do him, don'tcha?'

'Not any longer.'

'Liar!' One of the other men cuffed him sharply from his right, knocking his head sideways.

'It's the truth. I used to, but a different lad's got him now.'

'The one who was with you?'

'No – another. Tom Turner.'

'The devil take him!' The knife-man sounded both angry and perplexed. But he kept up his bluster. 'You can get to him, though – get into his box of an evening?'

'Well . . .'

'Course you can. Look.' He handed the knife to one of his accomplices, and from his pocket brought up an envelope, which he held right in front of Joseph's face. 'See this? This goes into his feed on Monday. Right?'

Feeling the grip on him relax, Joseph looked down and took the packet, which was thick and soft, full of some kind of powder. 'What is it?' he asked faintly.

'Never you mind. Just see he gets it. And if he don't get it – if he wins the Two Thousand – just remember: this will be waiting for you.'

Again the knife flashed in the lamplight. Then the tight circle of men opened, and Joseph was running for home, with the packet clutched in one hand. Back in the safety of Egerton, he found that Wilf had escaped unscathed; but for much of the night he lay awake, racked by indecision. Should he throw the packet away and do nothing? Or should he warn Marsh that villains were after his star horse? There was no doubt where his duty lay; the difficulty was that in drinking at The Bushel he had committed a serious crime, for which he might well be dismissed.

At last he went to sleep, without reaching a decision, but he awoke with his mind made up. As soon as he could arrange it, he went to see Marsh in his study. The trainer was outraged – not by Joseph's behaviour, which he forgave in return for his honesty in owning up, but by the audacity of the gang.

'I'll have the law on them!' he kept saying. 'What did they look like? Describe them.'

Joseph did his best, but his recollections were hazy. He remembered little except that the men all wore trilby hats, had heavy moustaches, and were what he called middle-aged – probably in their thirties. The accents of the two who had spoken were lower-class, perhaps Cockney. A typical race gang, Marsh called them. He put the police on their trail, sent the powder for analysis and stepped up his security precautions on the stables, appointing an extra night-watchman to supplement the two already on duty.

Joseph's own predicament was solved by a fluke. Within three days of the incident Persimmon was found to be suffering from an abscess under a tooth, and had to be withdrawn from the Two Thousand Guineas at the last minute. The touts, not knowing the real medical position, almost certainly believed that their threat had been effective, and that Joseph had administered their narcotic – which was what the powder turned out to be.

So he escaped from that first entanglement. The second snared him inextricably.

Again he was coming home in the evening, this time after legitimate business with the ploughman at Cadenham Farm, to whom Marsh had sent him with a message about the amount of hay he was going to need. The sun was setting after a hot day, and the air was heavy with the smell of hay almost ready to be carted. As he climbed over a stile through a hedge, suddenly there was Cherry Green, kneeling in the grass ahead of him.

Cherry Green! He caught his breath. Although he had scarcely spoken to her, and hardly knew her, he knew all *about* her, for she was the nearest equivalent which that sparsely-inhabited corner of Suffolk could claim to the village tart. Her proclivities were famous among the lads, several of whom had been, or claimed to have been, seduced by her, and many an idle hour had been whiled away in weaving lecherous fantasies about her.

Now here she was, right in front of him, undeniably attractive, with her dark hair cut in a fringe straight across her forehead, her bright black eyes, her even white teeth and her voluptuous young figure. She wore a blue-and-white cotton frock buttoned up to her throat, but her arms and feet were bare.

'Oh!' she flashed a smile up at him. 'It's you. I wondered who it was coming.'

'What's up? Lost something?'

'Me brooch. I dropped it in the grass somewhere.'

Guilelessly, not thinking for a second that she had set an ambush, he knelt on all fours beside her and started to search. Suddenly she put her arm round his waist and brought her hand up flat against his stomach.

'Cor!' she said. 'You aren't half skinny.'

'Let go!' He tried to pull away, but she held tight, and all his sideways movement achieved was to draw her into his arms, face to face. A second later he was on his back, with her on top of him.

He seemed to have no time to organise his defence. Her hands were all over him, her wide mouth close above his, *on* his, her soft black hair falling round his face. He ought to get up, he knew very well. He should throw her off, cast her down, leave her grovelling on the ground. But he did not do any of those things. Instead, he succumbed to the delicious pressure of her body, the softness of her lips, the astonishing sensation of her tongue flickering round his. When her right hand went deftly to work on the buttons of his breeches, he answered only with handiwork of his own, which immediately told him that under her cotton dress she was wearing nothing at all. His natural inhibitions melted like ice in the heat of her lust and youthful experience.

With a few sudden twitches she pulled her dress over her head, jerked his trousers down and his shirt up. Then, still kneeling, she straddled him, pale as ivory in the dusk, and lowered herself on to him until she was well impaled – whereupon she rode furiously, as if she, and not he, were the aspiring jockey. Overcome by delicious sensations – firm breasts bobbing round his face, satiny thighs on the sides of his chest, a raging fire down below – he gripped her with all his might until a cloudburst swept him away. She let out a loud cry, half a groan, half a caw, like a rook, and moments later subsided quietly on him. Night settled over them as they lay together in the sweet-scented, half-made hay. 'Oh God, Cherry,' he muttered. 'What have you done?'

'Nothing,' she said comfortably. 'That was beautiful.'

Next day he was overcome by guilt, but also elated. Shame, excitement, fear, delight – all raged through him simultaneously as he went about his work. Riding out, he was so powerfully distracted by the memory of what had happened that he let his horse wander out of the string and was sharply reprimanded by the head lad. He tried to analyse his feeling of fear: he felt afraid, yes – but of what? Not of disease, for he had scrubbed himself minutely the moment he had come in. Not of exposure, for he did not believe that even if Cherry bragged about it, any of the lads would give him away. No – it was worse than that. Somehow he felt he had polluted and defiled himself, that he had let himself down. Much as he lusted to repeat the experience, guilt and shame gradually gained supremacy in his mind, and when Cherry once again managed to waylay him out in the country, he firmly resisted her advances, sending her into an angry sulk.

Needless to say, word of the encounter leaked into stables. The other lads chanted, 'Cherry ripe, up her pipe,' and similar pleasantries as they passed him, but he cheerfully told them to clear off and got on with his job. In time the pressure of work helped him regain equilibrium. Persimmon, by then, was in the final stages of prep aration for the Derby, and at Egerton tension mounted with every day that went by. The spring and early summer had been anything but easy; after the horse had recovered from the abscess on his gum, he seemed to improve dramatically, and so well did he come on that Marsh sent a telegram to London inviting the Prince to come down and see his colt perform on the eve of the big race: the answer was that not merely Edward but half the royal family would be pleased to visit the stables on 26 May.

Frenzies of preparation engulfed Egerton. Because Marsh had decided to hold the trial on his own moss-litter gallop, away from prying eyes, he ordered the construction of a special stand from which the royal party would be able to watch the horses run. Malicious rumours fizzed round the yards when, with two days to go, Marsh dismissed his cook and was left with nobody to prepare the royal lunch. Only a dash to the Savoy Hotel in London secured the services of a temporary chef and some waiters, who came down by train the day before.

At last the great day arrived. With the Prince and Princess of Wales came the Duke and Duchess of York, Princess Victoria, Princess Maud, Prince Charles of Denmark and a handful of hangers-on. Carriages brought them from the station out to Egerton, and by the time they arrived the horses they were to watch were already walking about, as if in the paddock before a race. As usual Jack Watts was up on Persimmon, and Otto Madden rode a colt of outstanding promise called Balsamo, belonging to the Duke of Devonshire and brought in specially for the trial. To ensure a fast early gallop, Marsh had included two lightweights, Courtier and Safety Pin, and as a mark of favour for good work done, he put Joseph up on the first of these, so that the boy got the closest possible view of the royal party as they strolled about the grass. Under the pretence of steadying his excited horse, he was able to move gently from side to side and let his eyes rove under the peak of his cap. He marvelled at the fineness of Princess Alexandra's long grey dress . . . but the smoothness of her complexion sent his mind racing to the creamy satin of Cherry Green's thighs. He was brought to his senses by hearing the Prince murmur in an aside, 'Damned if he doesn't look a real clinker, Marsh,' and Marsh reply, 'Yes, sir, I think he's going to do us proud.'

The trial went just as everyone had hoped. The lightweights set a rare gallop, as they were supposed to, but after six furlongs they were finished, and the two class horses drew away on their own; yet Persimmon was always toying with Balsamo, and he won by three lengths in a canter. So the visitors went in to lunch in high good humour, and emerged at three o'clock to inspect the stables and Lordship Stud in still more jovial fettle.

The Derby was to be run on Joseph's birthday, Wednesday the 3rd of June. Marsh arranged for Persimmon to travel to Epsom by train, and on the Tuesday morning Joseph walked him through the lanes past Hill House farm to Dullingham station, a country halt some five miles on the London side of Newmarket. There, however, some devil got into him: he took against the box cars which came in alongside the platform and refused absolutely to enter them. Again and again Joseph led him in a circle and made a fresh approach, talking steadily to him all the while, but every time he would stop short of the train, brace himself backwards and threaten to rear.

Marsh, in a bowler hat and new tweed suit, became increasingly hot and agitated. Two horse-specials from Newmarket pulled into the station, were loaded and pulled away without Persimmon. The third and last of the morning came in. Still the horse refused.

'Try him once more,' Marsh ordered. Doffing his bowler, he enlisted the services of a burly porter and tried to link hands with him behind Persimmon's hindquarters, so that they could lift the horse towards the wagon, while Joseph pulled him from the front. All that happened was that Persimmon let fly backwards, narrowly missing the porter, who withdrew in alarm.

By then a large crowd of spectators had gathered, one or two of them openly contemptuous. 'Look here,' Marsh suddenly called out. 'This horse has got to go to Epsom. Any man who helps get him into the box will have a sovereign from me.' The offer immediately sorted the doers from the gawpers: about ten men came forward, and with five or six joining together on either side to heave on a couple of short lengths of rope, they more or less lifted the horse through the doorway. Typically enough, the moment he was inside, he relaxed and tucked in to the feed of oats with which his handlers had spent the last hour trying to lure him. So nervous had Marsh become that he travelled the whole way in the horse-box, rather than repair to the first-class seat reserved for him.

Joseph's first visit to Epsom, his first Derby, should have been memorable – and it almost was. He was exhilarated by the scale of the meeting – the size of the crowds, the colour, the noise and the sense of occasion – but he did not see the race itself. Having sent his horse off to the start, he returned briefly to the jockeys' dressing-room under the stand, and then found it physically impossible to force his way through the crowd to a position from which he could see. All he could do was listen as the cheering built to a sustained thunder and then subsided into a general hubbub of excitement – but he learnt what had happened soon enough: having come down round Tattenham Corner a length behind his most dangerous rival, St Frusquin, Persimmon had hauled him down on the run-in and won by a neck. When the Prince himself walked down onto the course and led his horse into the winner's enclosure, the crowd went wild, roaring like the sea in vast surges of patriotic fervour and enthusiasm.

That was the high spot of Joseph's summer. Persimmon ran in two more races that year – the St Leger and the Jockey Club Stakes –

and won them both, to complete a glorious season as a three-year-old; but for Joseph neither Doncaster nor Ascot approached Epsom for glamour and excitment.

Then, in August, his life took a turn as unexpected as it was unpleasant. One morning Marsh summoned him to appear in the office at 11 a.m. As he went about his chores, he wondered if he was about to be offered his first ride in a race. His competence in the saddle had improved continuously, and his weight had remained within useful limits. At the age of eighteen, weighing only eight stone, and with a record of excellence in his manner with horses, he had become a useful proposition.

It was a shock, then, to find that Marsh received him frostily, even with a peculiar gleam in his eye.

'What's this?' he began, holding up a piece of cheap, lined paper that looked as if it had been torn from a child's exercise book; and when Joseph merely looked at him in surprise, he went on. 'It's a letter of complaint. Directed against you. I expect you know who from.'

'Haven't a clue, sir.'

'No? Mrs Green. I quote: "My daughter Cherry is expecting, it was your Joe Clements what did it." What do you say to that?'

Joseph blushed crimson. 'I . . . well, I . . .'

'Did you have carnal relations with this girl?'

'Well . . .'

'You went to bed with her?'

'No, sir. It was in the hay.' Even in his confusion, Joseph thought he saw a flicker of amusement cross Marsh's face.

'When was it?'

Joseph thought and said, 'May, sir.'

'Can you remember the date?'

'About the tenth.'

'I see.' Marsh gave a sigh and leant forward over his desk, weight on his elbows. 'You realise this girl is a slut?'

'Yes, sir. The village tart.'

'Then why on earth . . . ?'

'I dunno.' At this stage it was no use blaming her.

Marsh waited, then said, 'Well – I don't want to hear about it. But you've blotted your copybook, Clements. It's a shame, because you've done very well. You've shown a lot of promise, and until now I've had nothing but praise for you. But now you've broken the rules. You realise that?'

'Yes, sir.'

'That's one thing. The other is that this Green woman's after you. She wants you to marry her daughter. I presume you don't want that.'

'Jesus!' He let the word slip out, and instantly apologised. 'Sorry, sir. I meant No.' Again he thought he saw a flicker cross the rugged face opposite, and he asked, 'How does she know it's mine, sir?'

'You mean she's slept with other lads?'

'Oh yes – I mean, no. Not lads, sir,' he added quickly. 'Boys from the farms, and from the town.'

'I see. But she seems to have her hooks into you. It looks to me as though you'll have to give her the slip.' He stood up and crossed to the side of the room, where he took another sheet of paper from a tray on top of the bookcase. 'As it happens, I've hit on something that may enable you to do just that.'

Marsh came back with the paper and laid it on the desk. 'Ever heard of Prince Soltykoff?'

'Yes, sir. He's the Russian owner.'

'That's right. I have this letter from him, asking if I know any promising lad who would go out to Russia to work in his cousin's stables.'

Russia! The idea was so strange that for a moment it made no impact. Then Joseph's neck began to crawl at the thought of a huge country, so far away.

'How would I get there?' he asked faintly.

'By train, I should imagine.'

'I meant, how would I pay for the journey.'

'Oh – no need to worry about that. All your expenses would be paid. The Prince guarantees that. If you want to find out more, you'd better go and see him at the Kremlin.'

Joseph went that afternoon, riding into town on one of Marsh's hacks. His Serene Highness Prince Dmitri Soltykoff was well-known and liked in Newmarket. Having come to England for a three-month holiday after the Crimean War, in 1856, he had stayed (so far) for forty years. In the 1870s he had built Kremlin House, a substantial dwelling and training establishment just off Fordham Road, on the eastern fringes of the town. Under his racing colours of pink and black he had achieved many successes, not least with the Duke of

Parma, who won the Cesarewitch in 1877, and because he firmly upheld the old English creed of sport for sport's sake, he had become immensely popular in racing circles – the first foreigner to be made a member of the Jockey Club.

Joseph found him in his parlour – a small, elderly man with drooping grey walrus moustaches and a neatly-trimmed beard jutting from the point of his chin. He spoke English precisely, with a curious liquid accent, and his manner was friendly and direct. He did not ask why Joseph wanted to go to Russia – perhaps he already had an idea – but with a minimum of fuss he explained that his cousin, Count Scherbatov, was expanding his training stable and stud at Yarskoye, in Tula province, and wanted to recruit young English jockeys, who were becoming fashionable in Russia. The first contract would be for a year, and the annual salary would be 250 roubles – the equivalent of £30, more than twice what Joseph had been earning. All travel expenses would be paid, and accommodation in Russia would be free. The jockey who went out could expect to start riding in races next season - in 1897.

Joseph did not argue. Half appalled, half attracted by the idea, he knew quite well that he had better remove himself from Newmarket as soon as possible. Russia, he thought. Ye Gods! Snow. Ice. Wolves. 'Yes, sir,' he heard himself saying. 'I would like to take up your offer. Thank you.'

'Excellent!' said the Prince, waggling his little beard. 'How soon can you leave?'

'As soon as you like.'

'Very good. Then we must arrange your tickets, and a passport.'

At Egerton the news of Joseph's impending departure caused a mixture of surprise and envy; but he managed to conceal the real reason for his sudden move, and Marsh lived up to his reputation as a sport by agreeing not to answer Mrs Green's letter until it was too late, and he had gone. 'Don't go and do the same thing out there,' Marsh warned him genially, 'or you'll finish up in Siberia.' Thus primed, he went out to equip himself for the Russian winter by buying a new jacket, and within ten days was on his way to seek a new life in the east.

THREE

On The Steppe: December 1919

ALL THAT seemed far away, and yet very close, as he tramped beneath the glittering stars south of Kharkov. The immensity of sky and steppe appeared to compress time, bringing past and present together.

The main thoroughfare to the south was full of travellers, many with horses and carts. Fires glowed along the verges, where people had set up makeshift camps, but the road itself was alive with dark shadows lurching on over the ruts and potholes. Now and then a horse whinnied or a man cursed, but mostly the refugees stumbled along in silence, bowed down by the weight of their loneliness and fear.

Joseph, going faster than most, kept overtaking other parties. 'Where are you heading?' one man called softly. 'South, of course,' he muttered, and he hastened on to avoid becoming embroiled in conversation. He did not like the main road. The surface was diabolical, for the mud had frozen into irregular ruts and ridges on which the horses kept tripping and skidding. He would rather be in open country – and in fact he already had his first objective in mind: a house out on its own in the steppe, belonging to a *kulak* whom he had often helped in the past. Vassiliy Petrovitch Lubin would give him shelter, he felt sure – provided he and his farm remained intact. Joseph knew that Lubin had survived the first Bolshevik occupation, for he had seen him since, but how the farmer had fared during the past few months, he did not know.

Joseph felt well and strong. He was going easily, and so were his horses, apparently unworried by the drastic change in their routine. At first they had been nervous, starting and jumping whenever they heard a noise or saw a shadow blacker than its neighbours; but now they had settled down and walked on at a good pace. For the first couple of hours he led or rode Min, with Boy attached by a leading rein and walking at his companion's shoulder; then he changed them round, and after a short rest carried on. Min was naturally the better walker of the two: he always strode out with zest, no matter where he was going, whereas Boy needed constant impulsion to keep him moving briskly – unless of course he was heading for home, in which case he was hard to stop. Now, though, they both seemed to be on top form. Thank God they don't question the necessity for doing something, thought Joseph – and he reflected that their nature was rather like his own: when faced with a task, they just got on and did it.

Now that he was on the move, life seemed much simplified. At last he was not plagued by the need to take major decisions. At last his objective was simple and clear: to deliver the horses into safe hands. It was a relief to be thus unencumbered, and to be taking positive action. At the fringe of his awareness hovered the realisation that in spiriting Min and Boy away from the Bolsheviks he was trying to salve his own conscience – that after years of relative passivity, he was finally putting himself at risk on the horses' behalf. He could, after all, have slipped off on his own and fought his way aboard one of the packed trains, or merely walked down the road to the south. Without the horses he could have travelled faster, less conspicuously. Yet nothing on earth would have made him leave them.

After two hours, at about midnight, he came to the little wayside shrine which marked his turn-off point. The half-dome sheltering its figure of the Madonna stood out in silhouette against the stars, and without thinking he crossed himself as he passed. At the junction he stopped for a moment, pretending to check the horses' girths, but in fact making sure that there was no one close behind who might see him turn off the road. Then he took the track that led into the dark hills. Once he had left the main road, the night became absolutely quiet: whenever he stopped, and the creak of saddlery ceased, he could hear no sound at all. The silence reassured him, for it meant that he was on his own and less likely to be challenged. Also, it set his mind free to think back over his own life.

His train of thought was suddenly broken. Ahead of him, at the corner of a little wood, the track divided. The fork was perfectly even, and there was nothing to indicate which branch he should take. Right in the V of the fork, in front of the trees, loomed a rock as tall as a man – a landmark of a kind; but it bore no sign-board, and beyond it the twin paths stretched impartially away, light streaks running off into the dark along the edges of the wood. Around him the steppe lay absolutely black: no spark of light broke the darkness, and near the horizon only the bright scatter of stars distinguished sky from land. Although Lubin had often come to the Kharkov stud, Joseph had visited his farm only once, and then he had ridden out in the company of the owner, so that he had not paid much attention to route-finding. He did not remember this wood and junction at all. Now, after heading generally south-east, his instinct was to take the right-hand track, which would lead more towards the south, his ultimate destination; yet something made him favour the other path. He resisted the temptation to strike one of his precious matches and look about for clues, feeling sure it would do no good.

As he hesitated, Boy straddled his hind legs backwards and staled. A cloud of urine fumes rose warm and pungent into the freezing air. 'Good idea,' said Joseph out loud. 'I'll copy you.' As he did so, Min also followed suit, and for a moment all three of them were caught up in sharing their agreeable moment of relief.

Then Joseph saw Min's ears flick forward. The stallion turned his head and stared intently down the path to the south. Joseph heard nothing, but Boy too began to stare. Perhaps a wolf was on the move. Joseph listened, straining his ears. At last he picked up a definite sound: the click of a horse's shoes on stone.

'Come on, boys. Quick.' He spoke in an urgent whisper, hustling the stallions a few steps forward, until they were in the mouth of the left-hand path and hidden from the other track by the trees. Then he turned them round so that, still holding their reins, he could look past the rock and face the oncoming rider. He drew the Luger from its holster, made sure by feel that there was a round in the breech, and eased back the hammer with his thumb.

The approaching noise grew louder. Listening intently, Joseph detected one horse only. More would have made a continuous stream of clinks and scuffles, whereas all he could hear were intermittent sounds. He prayed that neither of his own horses would give themselves away by whinnying.

Now the stranger was no more than thirty yards off. What was the safest way of greeting him, the least likely to provoke a violent reaction? Joseph waited till the horseman was almost at the rock, then said quietly, 'Vassiliy Petrovitch?'

The strange horse gave a snort and reared. Its rider cursed. Min let out a roar of a whinny. The outburst of noise seemed to tear the darkness apart.

'*Kto tam?* Who's there? Vassiliy Petrovitch?'

'*Nyet*. Mikhail Vassilovitch.'

'Ah, thank God. This is Joseph Clements, from the stud at Kharkov. I'm on my way to see your father.'

'Joseph Petrovitch!' The rider vaulted from his saddle and came across. 'Whatever are you doing here, in the middle of the night? And what are these horses?'

Joseph told him. He could hardly see the boy's face, but he knew him well: a handsome, dark, ruddy-cheeked youth of about seventeen, who helped his father on the farm.

'Holy Mother!' he exclaimed when he heard Joseph's account of the raid on the stud and the latest Red advance. 'Is it really so bad?'

'Every bit. There's no telling what the bastards will do when they come for the second time.' Joseph told him about his visit to the station in Kharkov, the packed trains, the panic to escape southwards.

'At least you've saved me a nasty trip,' said Mikhail. 'We'd heard no news for ten days, so I was going into town to find out what's happening. Now you've told me, I'll turn round right here.'

'How far is it to the farm?'

'Half an hour.'

'May I come with you?'

'Of course! My father will be delighted to see you.'

'Is there somewhere I can stable the horses?'

'Plenty of room.'

'Good! What time is it?'

'Two o'clock, I should think. What time did you start?'

'About nine.'

'Five hours!' Mikhail gave a little whistle. 'The horses must be tired.'

'Not too bad. Let's go, though. You'd better keep ahead, if you don't mind. One of my fellows can be difficult.'

With Mikhail to guide him, the last lap of the journey seemed very short. Soon they were descending into a wide bowl among the hills. No light showed, and the first indication of a dwelling came to them in the form of woodsmoke, drifting on the air currents. Presently Mikhail said quietly over his shoulder, 'Stay here a minute, while I go and deal with the dogs. Come on when I call.'

Joseph waited until the bloodcurdling eruption of barking and baying was doused by a volley of human roars. At length silence fell again, and he heard Mikhail call him forward. By the time he reached the farmyard, the dogs had been shut into kennels or sheds, and he was greeted by growls and whines of frustration from all sides. The rest of the family had woken up: from inside the house the glow of a lamp lit up a frosted window, and Mikhail went to the door to reassure them. Then he came back, showed Joseph where he could stable the stallions in a barn, and helped him get them settled, producing a bucket of water and a feed of crushed oats for each. The horses were too tired to argue about their unfamiliar surroundings, and went into the barn docilely enough.

'You'll sleep in the house with us,' said Mikhail, as a statement of fact rather than a question.

'Thanks – but I'd rather stay with the horses. I've got a blanket. I'll be comfortable as a dormouse up there in the hay.'

'Please yourself. Don't you want anything to eat? No tea, even?'

'No, thanks. I'll just turn in.'

'At least you'll have breakfast with us in the morning.'

'Gladly. Thanks again.'

Going out of the frost, into the relatively warm air of the barn, Joseph suddenly realised how tired he was. Knowing the hellish temperature at which Russian peasants kept their living-rooms, and having suffered a hundred times from the foetid atmosphere caused by their refusal to open windows, he preferred to stay in the fresh air of the farm buildings, in spite of the cold; and he had scarcely buried himself in the hay, wrapped in a blanket, with the horses scrunching at their oats beneath him, when he sank into a dreamless sleep.

For the first morning in many years he did not shave. In a land where beards were the general rule, a clean-shaven man was immediately conspicuous, and that was the last thing Joseph wanted to be. A beard also gave some protection from cold, and he forced himself to tolerate the disagreeable feeling of bristles on his face and neck. With the horses, he adopted the same policy of minimal grooming. Their gleaming coats stood out, and he reluctantly took a decision to let them become as unkempt as possible. 'Pity you don't grow a winter coat like old Percy,' he said as he checked Boy's feet. 'Hup, now! Like a blasted sheep, he was. Come on – hup! People thought there was something wrong with him, to be so woolly. Hup, again. Wouldn't half keep you warm, a jacket like that. And again. That's a fellow. Sometimes they used to think it *was* a sheep, coming along.'

Across in the farmhouse, his mental forecast of temperature and atmosphere proved correct. The heat produced by the tiled stove was stifling, the air all but unbreathable. But Lubin and his wife Anna received him jovially and gave him a hearty breakfast of bread dipped in hot, fresh milk laced with sugar and cinnamon. Lubin was about forty-five, stocky and red-faced, with a high, bald cranium fringed by brown curls the colour of his leather jerkin. His habit of constantly asking questions suggested that he lived in a state of perplexity; but the impression was misleading, and the truth was simply that, tucked away in such an isolated spot, he rarely got a chance to interrogate a stranger.

'Tell me everything!' he urged. 'Who were they, these people who shot the mare? Who sent them? Where did they come from?'

Joseph answered the questions as best he could. As a bringer of news, he felt rather an impostor, for his information was not really much more detailed than Lubin's, even though it was slightly fresher. Nor was he any stronger on the political situation in general.

'What's happened to this fellow Semyon Petlura?' asked Lubin querulously, referring to the man who had proclaimed himself *hetman* of the Ukraine. 'I haven't heard much about him lately.'

'No,' Joseph agreed. 'He's gone out like a glow worm.'

'And who's this Admiral Denikin? I'd never heard of him till last year. Where the hell is he, I'd like to know?'

'He's supposed to be in Yekaterinodar, in the Kuban,' said Joseph cautiously. 'That's his headquarters, and his supplies are coming in through Novorossisk. You know it's us, the British, who've been sending him arms?'

'Novorossisk! Yekaterinodar!' Lubin gave a snort, quite unimpressed by the Allied intervention on the White Russian side. 'A fat lot of use the commanders sitting there, down in the Caucasus. Why don't they get a bit nearer the front and find out what's going on?'

'People say Denikin can't get on with his second-in-command, Baron Wrangel.'

'Then he should sack him. But what about Petlura?' Lubin demanded. 'I thought he was supposed to have taken charge.'

'He did, but he didn't last long. Like all those others.' To Joseph they were only names: Grigorev, the wild and unprincipled ruffian who had raised a brief rebellion in May that year, embodying the *kulak*'s hatred of Bolshevism and promising country people an independent Ukraine; Skoropadsky, the Tsarist general appointed *hetman* of the Ukraine by the Germans, who restored estates and manors to their owners, and then prudently retired to Berlin when the German forces withdrew; Makhno, blond and blue-eyed, who claimed to

65

oppose both Grigorev and the Bolsheviks . . . All had promised relief from the chaos of that year, but all had disappeared without trace – or rather, their names had gradually ceased to be mentioned.

'What about *you*?' asked Joseph. 'Have you had much trouble?'

'The Revkomy came, and the Narkomprod.' Lubin concentrated extraordinary sarcasm into the names of the Bolshevik organisations charged with the task of unmasking peasants who hoarded grain. 'And of course they took away most of what I showed them. But I didn't show them very much.'

'You've got some good graves dug, then?'

'Oh yes!' Lubin gave a bitter laugh. 'I've a few poods of wheat safely underground. And now that the frost has come, nobody will find them.'

'So what will you do if the bastards come back?'

'I doubt they will, with winter setting in. They don't like getting too far from their offices or the railway. Besides, there's nothing to interest them here. They know I can't read or write, so they can't accuse me of counter-revolutionary activity, or any rubbish like that. No –' Lubin sighed and shrugged his wide shoulders. 'I'm going to stay put. There's nothing else I can do.'

'What about me?' Joseph asked. 'Which way should I go?'

The question led to prolonged explanations. Lubin, being illiterate, had no time for Joseph's map. 'Paper! Paper!' he said contemptuously. 'That won't tell you anything' – and his scepticism was to some extent vindicated, as the scale of the map was far too small for it to show details of the kind that he started to expound. Nevertheless, he was fascinated when Joseph began to write down the instructions which he gave him. 'What's that?' he demanded, pointing his stubby, black-nailed finger at a word.

'*Perekryostok*. What you just said. A crossroads.'

'Yes, well, naturally it's a crossroads, as I told you. Only of course it's just two tracks that cross each other, not roads. Take the right-hand track, and soon you'll come to the source of the river. There's a small valley, and you'll see how a spring rises to the surface in the middle of a few alders. It freezes later, but it'll still be running now. From there you can follow the river for about five versts, till you come to the Wolf's Cairn . . . How far can you go in one day?'

'Perhaps forty versts.'

'Then you will reach Manino, easily.'

'What's Manino?'

'A farm like this. The owner is Lvov, Pavel Alexeivitch. Tell him

66

I sent you. He will take you in. Of course, you can stay here if you like.'

'Thanks – but the more distance I can put between me and the Reds, the safer I'll feel.'

'I know. You'd better go on. Pay attention to my directions, though, because I feel snow coming. Look at the sky.'

They went outside into the bright morning. The sun was still below the horizon, but the sky, though clear and blue, had a watery look about it, and the air felt moist. 'Yes,' said Lubin with a sniff. 'It will snow.'

Joseph was preparing to leave when the fat farmer came across to the barn. 'Take all the oats you can carry,' he said. 'And here is something for you to eat during the day.' He handed over a package wrapped in white cloth, and brushed aside Joseph's thanks – but with a slightly uncomfortable air which suggested that he was hoping for something in return. A moment later he added, 'My mare over there . . . she just happens to be in season. I don't suppose one of your horses could oblige . . . ?'

Joseph had been half-expecting the request, for the stallions and the mare had been whinnying at each other across the yard. What did surprise him, though, was that the mare had come into season during the winter. He had been to have a look at her and found that she was a good-looking riding horse of nearly fifteen hands, quite powerfully built, perhaps with a touch of Orlov in her.

'I'm afraid it would be very expensive,' he said solemnly. 'it would cost you ten thousand roubles.'

'My God!' Lubin creased his forehead. 'And who gets the money?'

'Comrade Vladimir Ulyanov, or Lenin, or whatever he calls himself. At least, I suppose he does. He owns all the horses in Russia now.' Then he grinned and asked, 'Which one would you like?'

'Which do you suggest?'

'This one. Minoru. He won the English Derby carrying the colours of King Edward. You couldn't get anything more anti-Bolshevik than that.'

'Very good, then. Is he ready?'

'Ever ready. What about the mare, though? Has she had a foal yet?'

'One.'

'See to her, then. Put a sack over her neck, because he's liable to bite her. And ropes on her hind legs.'

'She never kicks.'

'Maybe, but I don't want to risk it. And we'll have them in the open, on that piece of grass over there, if you don't mind.'

The preparations were soon made. Joseph led Min out to where the mare was waiting, and after a few shrill squeals of greeting she swung round to present her hindquarters to him. With minimum fuss he mounted her and drove home his attack, seizing her with his teeth through the sack which Lubin had tied round her neck. In thirty seconds his work was done, and he was back on the ground, retracting.

Lubin whistled. 'He doesn't hang about, does he! Think how much he could earn, doing it that fast.'

'Don't worry – he's earned a good bit already. Thrown some grand foals, too.'

'How old is he, then?'

'Born in 1906. That makes him thirteen. I reckon he's got another six or seven years at stud in him. That's why I brought him away. And the other – Boy – is only nine. He's got a long way to go.' As he turned Minoru away, Joseph brought out an impromptu rhyme:

'No foal, no fee:
But God knows
Where we'll be.'

'What shall we call the foal?' Lubin asked.

'If it's a colt, Edouard, after the King.'

'And if it's a filly?'

'Lilia.'

'Why that?'

'Lily – the same word in English – was the name of one of the King's lady friends. Whatever it is, I hope it has its father's temperament – he's the best-natured fellow you could imagine.'

As he was about to leave, there occurred a small but sinister accident. He was making final adjustments to the girth when Boy took a sudden step sideways and by sheer bad luck drove one steel buckle against his wrist. Because he was leaning into the horse's side, he could not shift his weight back instantly, and the pressure smashed the fragile compass on his left wrist. The damage was done in a second, but it was comprehensive: the glass was broken, and the pointer knocked off.

'Useless,' he said, taking off the mangled remains. 'We'll have to do without.'

'Never mind,' Lubin reassured him. 'You can't miss the way.'

'Famous last words!' Joseph said goodbye and went off amid mutual protestations of gratitude. He felt in high spirits, buoyed up by the feeling that he was being passed down a chain of helpers, from one pair of friendly hands to the next. If this went on, he would have no trouble.

As an experiment he rode Boy, with Min on a short lead following at his right heel. For as long as the track was reasonably wide, the system worked well, and the horses did not jostle or harass one another. After half an hour he changed the stallions round and carried on. Again he was glad to be in the open, away from people and their frenzied political posturing, in a landscape that had not changed for hundreds of years. The horses seemed to share his euphoria, as if they were enjoying their adventure. They stepped along briskly, casting keen glances to either side, and Joseph fancied that every now and then Min gave him a specially meaningful look. 'Slipped her a nice length, didn't you, mate!' he said as they walked. 'Shafted her good and proper. Boy's turn next.'

Following Lubin's instructions, he found the first few landmarks easily enough, so that his mind was free to admire the grand proportions of the steppe, which rose and fell in dun billows ten versts wide, like gigantic swells of the ocean. Pale sunlight washed over them, and the temperature rose until it hovered just above freezing point. Most of the ground was uncultivated, and supported nothing but the withered stalks of grass, poppies and other wild flowers. Occasional patches of forest, where trees huddled out of the wind in shallow valleys, gave splashes of dark green, but the general tone of the land was a dead grey-brown, with blankets of hoar frost still lying white in the hollows. For much of the time Joseph's little party was the only thing moving in that immense and desolate expanse, but sometimes he saw crows labouring over the sweeps of hill, and once he had a scare when a herd of wild horses appeared in the distance on their left, travelling swiftly along the horizon. Far off though they were, the stallions spotted them, and Boy – by then following – began to rear and neigh. Joseph was seized by a sudden dread that he would break loose and go after the strangers: he had a vision of one stallion taking off like the wind, and himself galloping in pursuit on the other. Gradually, however, they both settled down, and went on more easily.

His euphoria lasted until they came to the source of the river. There, just as Lubin had described, a spring rose out of the stony ground, forming a pool of crystal-clear water only three or four feet across. Ice had crusted round its edges, but the middle was clear. Looking down into it, Joseph saw fine grains of sand on the bottom lifting and fluttering as water bubbled up from beneath them; but from that little pool came images from another river which made him suddenly sad.

His vision blurred; his exuberance died away. When he looked up, he realised that a grey haze of cloud had crept over the sky, obscuring the sun. The stallions had not sensed his change of mood, for they were snatching eagerly at a fringe of grass that still grew bright green around the spring. For five minutes or so he let them graze, but then he set them moving again, for he did not like the look of the weather coming to meet him from the south.

Half an hour later the snow predicted by Lubin began to fall: fine, gritty flakes at first, then bigger, damper ones which started to settle and form a layer. Joseph replaced his fore-and-aft fur hat and sheepskin coat, but he left the horses' rugs rolled up across their saddles, for they were warm enough with the effort of walking, and would have heated up uncomfortably with coverings over them. There was nothing for it but to keep going, along the faint path which followed the left bank of the stream. Then the wind rose, whirling flakes straight into the travellers' eyes. Alarm began to needle Joseph. In a few minutes the blizzard had shrunk his world from a land of limitless horizons to a claustrophobic cell no more than twenty yards across; if it continued for any length of time, it would make walking difficult, impossible even. Too late, he realised how poorly equipped he was to deal with true winter weather, and started to regret that he had not stayed on the main roads, which at least offered shelter.

Here there was none. For the moment all three of them were warm enough; but when they stopped, things would be different. It was essential that they reached the sanctuary of Manino as early in the day as possible. Navigation became Joseph's most pressing worry. Without the compass, he was in trouble. It was easy enough to follow the stream, but Lubin had told him to leave it after only five versts, or three miles, and turn away to his left when he saw the Wolf's Cairn, a pile of big rocks on the opposite bank. Now the blizzard was plastering snow on to the ground so thickly as to obliterate all details: already it was impossible to distinguish rock from earth, earth from ice; and hollows were filling rapidly so that the ground was being evened out. Joseph, on his own feet now, and stumbling often, cursed himself for not having asked detailed questions. How big was the Wolf's Cairn? How far back from the bank of the stream did it stand?

Was it possible that in this storm he might go past without seeing it?

Back at the farm, Lubin's breezy explanations had made everything sound simple. Perhaps in clear weather it would have been – but now his doubts increased with every step he took. Checking his watch, he found that they had been going along the river for fifty minutes. Surely they should have covered three miles in that time? Stopping for a moment, and turning his back on the snow, he checked his hand-written notes again. 'Opposite cairn, small dry valley. Six versts, wood on hill.' He remembered Lubin saying that he would see the wood from the river, before he started towards it, because it stood out in the distance above him. No hope of that now. He could scarcely see across the stream to the far bank. He considered turning back, but he rejected the idea. It was already two o'clock, and he had barely two hours of daylight left. He had been on the move for four hours: if he tried to return, he would be benighted. The only course open to him was to continue.

The horses' backs steamed as snow settled on them and melted. Both constantly blinked and shook their heads to clear the whirling flakes from their ears and eyes. Looking them over, Joseph saw that they were uncomfortable, rather than distressed, but he fervently wished that he could put them inside some building, however primitive. As for himself – he was warm and dry in the body, but water had seeped through the soles of his boots.

He went on, shading his eyes with one hand in the hope of spotting the cairn; yet after another twenty minutes he still had seen no sign of it, nor of any ravine leading away to his left. Perhaps Lubin had got his distances muddled: perhaps the cairn was more than five versts from the spring. Still he continued – and then at last, an hour and a half on from the start of the river, he came to the dry valley. At least, he came to *a* dry valley: a flat-bottomed ravine, with banks about twenty feet high, leading away in the direction he wanted. He could not see the cairn opposite, but he decided not to waste time looking for it. The light was beginning to fail, and he still had at least an hour to go.

He took the horses down to the water and encouraged them to drink, not knowing what other water he might find. Then he turned left and started up the ravine. There seemed to be a path. At any rate, the ground was level beneath its white blanket. But already the snow was six inches deep; walking had become a trial for him, and a positive danger for the horses, who might, if they put a foot into a

71

deep hole, do themselves serious damage. To reduce the risk, Joseph lengthened his leading rein and went further ahead, stamping out a path and making sure no treacherous hollows undermined it.

For half an hour he found himself climbing gently; but then he went over a crest, where the wind was at its fiercest, and started down again. His disquiet sharpened into fear that something had gone seriously wrong. Lubin had said that he would come to the wood on the hill and go right through it – the wood that lay in sight of the stream. But now he had gone over the hill without coming to any trees at all. Undoubtedly he was on a path of sorts – generations of travelling feet had dug a groove between waist-high banks – and there had been no side turnings that he could see; but even with the limited view that he had, he knew that the topography did not match his expectation.

Snow fell as thickly as ever. Leaden twilight was closing down on the steppe. Joseph's legs had begun to ache; for an hour at least he had been walking automatically, and a great weariness oppressed him. He felt ever more sorely tempted to lie down in that comfortable, soft white blanket and go to sleep. Even a few minutes among those downy pillows would refresh him . . .

Thump! He came out of his reverie suddenly, face-down in the snow, where he had fallen, with the horses standing almost on top of him. He was shocked to think that he gone to sleep on his feet. He got up, shook himself, brushed the snow off his coat and told himself to carry on. Anger gave him new energy. 'It's my own bloody fault,' he said to the stallions. 'Sorry, lads, but no excuse. I should have stayed and waited for the storm to blow itself out. We're in a right mess, the three of us.'

By then he felt certain that he had missed the track to Manino. He knew that the chances of coming blindly on another dwelling, out in that immense waste, were neglible. On the other hand, the path he was on must lead *somewhere*, and if he kept on long enough, he would surely reach shelter. So logic told him; his difficulty was that daylight had almost gone, and to stagger on in the dark would be not only foolish but dangerous as well. Visions of disaster came at him with the flying snow: he imagined being attacked by wolves, or frozen to death and not found until the spring.

By now the dregs of daylight had turned a sulphurous yellow: the lumps of snow hurtling at him were still white, but they came out of a dirty, dun-coloured murk. And then suddenly, through the bombardment, he saw something black and solid ahead of him. At first his overwrought imagination told him that the object must be a building, but quickly he saw that it was a tree, the first of many, all mantled with snow.

FOUR

Riding in Russia: 1897–1912

I T WAS the cold of the Russian winter that had made the most powerful impression on him when he first arrived, and the cold that he wanted to convey when he sat down to write to his friend Wilf Collyer after supper on the first day of 1898:

Dear Wilf, (he began)

Probably you thought I'd been sent to the salt mines in Siberia, not having heard from me for so long! Well, here I am, fit as a fiddle. *Horosho*! [he wrote the word in Cyrillic]. That means good. You see, I've even learnt a bit of Russki! Mind you, I was all at sea to start with.

I'm on this estate called Yarskoye, about 200 miles south-east of Moscow. Outside, the temperature's thirty below zero, enough to freeze the balls off a brass monkey, you'd think, but in fact the air is so dry you hardly feel it. The snow's lying two feet deep, so it's all skis and sledges now. Inside, the temperature's about 80, courtesy of a stove as big as the corn-bin in the back barn at Egerton, covered with blue and white tiles. Very cosy. The flat's above some loose boxes, so I can hear the horses moving below.

My journey out was tophole. The Prince gave me a first-class ticket, luxury all the way. I'll never forget coming to the border. You have to change trains because the Russian gauge is wider, so it was all out and into the Customs House, where the Great Smell of Russia hits you. It's enough to suffocate you – but it's the same in all public places: sweat, cigarette smoke, leather, and above all incense, with the incense just about winning. The place was full of army officers in greatcoats covered with medals on the breast and gold bars on the shoulders. Most of them had swords clanking at their sides, and shiny black boots, and spurs going *zing, zing* as they walked about.

A great big fellow with a white beard down to his waist searched my luggage from end to end. The only thing that worried him was my old pack of playing cards, which he confiscated! (You know them – the ones with the horse-heads on the back.) Old White-Beard couldn't speak English, so he had to call another man to explain that the State has a monopoly of playing cards. No more patience after that, anyway.

From the Customs we went into a great big hall, a kind of restaurant, with food and drink for an army laid out on long tables round the sides. As it was the middle of the night, I wasn't hungry, but I could have had anything under the sun – beef, pork, lamb etc. Oh yes – and there was this whale of a fish, ten feet long, brown and grey, with a huge square mouth, all packed in ice. After I'd stood looking at it for a bit, I realised it was a sturgeon – the thing that caviar comes from.

As I'd expected Russia to be a backward sort of place, I was surprised by how clean and lavish it all was. People very friendly, too. They actually seem to like foreigners. The train was the same – carriages much wider than at home, and that much more comfortable. First-class carriages are painted blue outside, others tan . . .

Joseph broke off and put down the pen to wriggle the ache out of his fingers. How could he ever convey to Wilf the sheer size of Russia? He remembered how, in the morning, the train had seemed to be crawling, crawling, crawling over an immense and endless plain. Sometimes the landscape reminded him of the Heath, though of course it was a hundred times bigger: there was something similar in the way the ground rose very gently and openly to the horizon. All the way to Moscow it went on and on for ever, with hardly a hedge or tree in sight. In summer – he now knew – it became a mass of wild flowers, but in the autumn it was brown and bare. Every hour or so he spotted a village of wooden houses out in the middle of nowhere – not even on the railway line. Most of the houses were log cabins, trunks of pine trees laid one atop the other, and bleached to a pale grey, with only dust and a few sunflowers outside. The churches were made of wood, too, but painted, usually red or green, with small domes like golden onions nearly at the top of the spire.

When eventually he reached Moscow, a friend of Prince Soltykoff met him and helped him find the train heading south. Late that afternoon he got off at a place called Tula and was met by a *tarantass*, a big wagon pulled by four horses all abreast. A two-hour drive brought him at last to Yarskoye – a sizeable house, made of wood, in a park, with the stud behind, and the village at the park entrance.

'Count Scherbatov is a very decent man,' he wrote.

What little we see of him, that is. He isn't here much – and he seems to have a special fancy for English lads. Nothing sinister, I don't mean. Something to do with the fact that the Countess has English relations. Anyway, one of my jobs is to teach English to the eldest son Nikolai. Me, a teacher! I said to the Count, I'm not qualified. I mean, I hardly went to school. Never mind, says he. You speak English. Just speak it to Nicky. So that's what we do. He's a nice enough lad – coming up for ten – and he has a French tutor who teaches him English grammar, but with a cracking Frog accent. So Nicky and I chat about this and that, generally when I'm working, and I get him to teach me Russian, so it works both ways.

A lot of things are pretty rum about this country, I can tell you. One is the date. They're still working on the old calendar, which means we're thirteen days behind you. As you see, this is New Year's Day, but with you I reckon it's the fourteenth. People keep saying they'll have to catch up with the rest of the world, but they can't nerve themselves to do it. Another thing is, almost all the men have full-length beards – like the fellow in the Customs. Anyone clean-shaven like you or me stands out a mile, or else they're in the army. Because they don't trim their beards, you see big fat peasants with whiskers nearly down to their knees. Think of Farmer Brown from Dullington, and double him, and you'll have an idea of what I mean.

The peasants are called *muzhiks*. It's said that ninety per cent of them can't read or write, and I can well believe it. Ivan Ivanovitch looks as thick as a two-inch plank. You know – his hair starts growing just above his eyebrows. Mostly he wears a long red shirt outside his trousers, belted in with a greasy old bit of rope. In summer he goes barefoot, and in winter he wears boots made of cloth tied together with birch bark. Can't get much more primitive than that!

They're wonderfully superstitious, too. Most of them have never seen a train or any kind of steam engine, but the idea of any vehicle going fast without horse-power terrifies them. During the harvest we had to go out to a village in the back of beyond, and I saw a man standing on a box in front of one of the houses, giving a speech. Quite a crowd had gathered round, and they looked dreadfully worried by the loud hissing noises he was making. Guess what he was doing? Imitating a train that he had seen! Then one of the peasants ups and says, 'Lies! Lies! Wagons can't move without horses. The Devil's behind it.' And he spat three times over his left shoulder, crossing himself to ward off the evil eye, and saying '*Chort! Chort!*' – 'Devil! Devil!'

That's how advanced their ideas are. And the pong! You've never smelt anything like it. I mentioned the smell that you get in public places. This peasant pong is something more primitive. I don't reckon some of them have ever had a bath in their lives. It's like a mixture of horse and cow and human, but mostly human, with a few dead rats thrown in.

Talking of baths – a lot of people do have baths, but they have them all together, in bath-houses, men and women separate, of course. There's a bath-house in almost every village, and dozens of them in the towns. *Bania*, it's called. It's an absolute institution. We have our own one here at the stud. It's quite a performance. First you strip off and sit steaming in a hot room – the stove heats bricks too hot to touch, and someone throws water over them, so that the air's thick with steam. There you sit on rough wooden benches in the altogether until sweat's fairly running off you, and then you go out into the next room for a scrub-down and plunge in cold water. At this time of year the real thing is to go out and roll in the snow. There's men doing it all the time, bollock-naked. They come out of the bath-house red as lobsters and dive into snow-drifts, roaring like bulls. Don't believe me, if you like. But it's true. Men think nothing of walking down the village street to the bath-house stark naked – it doesn't worry them. And in summer they bathe in the river, also starkers.

Anyway, the bath's a great way to lose the odd pound. How's your weight, by the way? Glad to say mine's the same – just over 8.6.

That brings me to food. You'd never believe the amount people eat. You'd think they'd all be the size of houses – well, a lot of them are. Any posh meal begins with what they call *zakuski* – any amount of bits laid out on a table: caviar, raw fish, smoked fish, little cubes of pork, lamb, beef, cheese, radishes, boiled eggs, pickled cucumbers – everything you can think of, enough for a meal on its own. Then, when you've already eaten as much as you can, and drunk a few tots of vodka, they give you soup, meat etc., as in England, until it's coming out of your ears.

Talk about storing things – the ice-houses here are amazing. Ice-rooms I should call them, or cellars, because that's what they are – under the house. By this time of year the river's frozen solid. I suppose the ice is about eighteen inches thick, and next week we'll start cutting blocks of it. It's tough work – you have to saw the ice with big cross-cuts, and horses drag the blocks out with ropes. Then we load them up into carts and bring them back and pack them round the walls of the ice-rooms. They do melt gradually, but the temperature down there stays just about freezing right through the year . . .

Again Joseph paused for a rest, only to realise that he had taken up pages without coming round to his main news. He got up, drew some boiling water from the samovar, and thought out his next few sentences as he made tea. Then he sat down again and went on:

A friend of the Count's called Reske was suddenly stuck for a jockey. Tommy Sharp, another English jockey, who rode for him regularly, broke his arm, and they needed someone in a hurry. Next thing I know, yours truly's in for the Warsaw Derby on a horse called Claude-Froll. It sounds pretty grand, I know, and by the standards over here, it is. The big race, like Epsom, is the All-Russia Derby in Moscow, but Warsaw's a good second. A mile-and-a-half, like Epsom, and all the best three-year-olds. Anyway, to cut short the story, we won! 'Keep him back a bit till you're only half a verst out,' Reske told me. (That's about two furlongs.) 'Then push him through.' So I did just that, and we beat the favourite a length! Immediately Reske thought the sun shone out my backside – and so he might, as I'd won him 30,000 roubles. And all the more so when I also won the Warsaw Emperor's Prize for him on an awkward brute of a horse called Vrogar. A devil to ride, he was, as I could hardly keep him balanced, but he had plenty of go, and we cruised in three lengths in front. So you see, a beginner's got plenty of chances here.

That's something else rum – the system of racing. What the Russkis really like is trotting – their damned Orlov trotters are all the rage. Nice horses, often spotted, bred specially for the sport, and all started by a cove called Count Orlov in the eighteenth century, but not what you or I would call racing. At your average meeting first there's a trotting race and then there's a riding race, sometimes on the same track, which I'm sorry to say is cinders – no grass. The trotting races are all timed – competitors start off separately, at intervals – a slow sport, I reckon. In the riding races, everything is much more like at home, except that in some places you find yourself up against two different types of opponents. There's the proper jockeys, like us, in their silks, as in England, but also there are army officers in their uniforms and service hats, riding their own horses, and carrying their swords! Don't they go, too! Beautiful horsemen, a lot of them – of course the cavalry tradition is very strong here. In fact the whole country is horse mad – something which would appeal to you, I'm sure. I read somewhere that in Russia there are twenty-five horses for every hundred humans – more than twice as many as in any other European country.

All local transport is by horse power, and every vehicle I've seen – carriage or sleigh or whatever – has this high, rounded arch called a *duga* going up from the front ends of the shafts and over the horse's neck. To me, it's the hall-mark of all Russian vehicles. Even a *troika* or three-horse team has it – although only the one arch, over the middle horse: And you should see the way they drive! The draught horses are mostly a tough little breed called the Bitiug, very strong and quick, a bit like an Arab about the head, but straight and plain in the leg. They've got a real hackney action – and do they smack their feet down! In Moscow the streets are all cobbled, so it's a wonder they aren't all lame. But now, in the snow, the most amazing thing is the silence: out here in the country you see a horse and sleigh flying along a road, but *without a sound of hooves*, as if it was a ghost. That's why everyone has a bell on top of the *duga* – to warn others that they're coming.

As I say, the Russkis seem to be getting more and more English lads over – and this brings me to the point (at last). The Count wants to take on a second Englishman, and he has authorised me to send word officially. I suppose I should write to old Marshy, really, but this is easier. Why not come out, Wilf? I'm sure you'd enjoy it, and the opportunities are growing. From my own point of view, I can't imagine anything better. I've made some good friends here, and some money, but to have a real mate would be ripping. If it's not for you, pass the word around, and tell Marshy, anyway. Give the old bugger my regards, too, please, and say I've ridden a couple of winners.

There's something else I might tempt you with. The peasant girls are quite something. On the hefty side, but some of them are clinkers. As you probably learnt in school, all serfs were officially set free more than thirty years ago, but honestly you wouldn't know it sometimes. The country girls here will do anything you ask, as if you are their lord and master and they can't resist!! Especially if their husbands go off into the army or get sent away to work for the summer, as seems to happen quite often. No more of that here, but you know what I mean.

Well, Wilf old fellow, it's got late and I'd better stop. I've just been on to the balcony for a sniff at the night. The outside boards of the house are cracking in the frost, and the wolves are howling on the edge of the forest, about half a mile away. That's what it's like here. Come and see for yourself.

Your affec. friend,
Joseph.

In due course this missive achieved its desired effect. Wilf never managed to answer it, but he did obtain Marsh's permission to work in Russia, and came out to Yarskoye the next autumn, September 1898. Not until then did Joseph learn that his former charge Persimmon had more than fulfilled his promise. 'Magnificent' was the word that Wilf repeatedly used of him. He had grown into a magnificent animal, he said, with marvellous strength and speed and presence, the perfection of what a thoroughbred should be. In his first race of 1897, the Gold Cup at Ascot, he had beaten the much-fancied Winkfield's Price by no less than eight lengths. By the time he came to the Eclipse Stakes at Sandown Park, he was a 100-12 on, a celebrity, and much mobbed by the public, so that he sweated up and became seriously over-excited. Yet at the last moment he calmed down to run another perfect race and win by two lengths.

Then suddenly his racing career was over. The summer had been very dry, and the ground rock hard, and what Marsh had feared for weeks at last occurred: Persimmon threw out two spavins, one in each hock; and although the damage was not yet serious, there would always be a risk that it might be aggravated by further training, and his owner decided that he should retire to stud. So to Sandringham he went.

The news about Cherry was surprising. When her baby turned out to be a boy with a mass of coppery curls, she decided that the father must be Ginger Harris, the son of a local farmer, who worked in another of the Newmarket stables, and whose hair was that very colour; so she had married him and settled down in a cottage outside Exning.

Joseph was mildly annoyed by this discovery; but in fact he never regretted having come to Russia. Far from it. He felt it was the best thing he had ever done – and as time went on, his convictions grew. Unlike Wilf, who could never shake off his homesickness, and went back to Newmarket after less than a year, Joseph felt at ease among the Russians. He saw that they had faults, like anybody else – that they were lazy and fatalistic, and prone to gargantuan drunkenness, especially during the winter. Young officers tended to be astonishingly idle and arrogant: Joseph was nauseated by their physical softness, for, unlike their contemporaries in England, they played no games and shirked any mundane physical task with the fastidious disdain of creatures too highly bred for their own good.

All the same, Joseph liked the Russians, made friends everywhere, and saw no reason to return. He was realistic enough to see that in England he would never have reached the top flight of jockeys. No Archer, no Watts even, he would probably have been condemned to second-rank horses and second-rank races had he stayed at home, for he lacked the hard competitive edge, the burning need to win, which drove the real aces to the heights. But in Russia, where competition was less intense, he was good enough to shine, especially at first. Besides, he happened to have arrived at a particularly opportune moment, when interest in racing was on the increase, and the amount of money to be earned was growing fast.

One key factor had been the introduction, during the late 1870s, of the *pari-mutuel* betting system on racecourses. At first the minimum stake was only one rouble – about two shillings – but after a series of riots on the track in Moscow this was increased to ten roubles, in an attempt to stop poor people risking their money, and the large sums thus earned for the state went towards the creation of new racecourses and the increase of prize money. By the turn of the century the sport had become well enough endowed to attract a stream of jockeys and trainers from England and America – a migration of which Joseph had been an involuntary pioneer. The arrival of more professionals led to a general increase in standards, and during the same period the Cavalry Remount Department brought in more and more thoroughbred stallions from abroad – since the breeding of racehorses and the production of high-class animals for the cavalry went hand-in-hand.

Joseph's career as a leading jockey was brilliant but brief. After his successes in 1897, he rode regularly for Reske during the next few seasons, and in 1898, although unplaced in the Warsaw Derby, once

more won the Emperor's Prize on Claude-Froll, as well as several
minor races. In 1899 he scored another major triumph, winning the
Warsaw Derby for the second time, that year on a bay colt called
Pickwick, at odds of 7–1.

After that, however, nature started to work against him, for his
body belatedly began to fill out. Luckily for him, perhaps, he was a
late-developer, both physically and mentally, and he did not achieve
his full size until he was well into his twenties. Continuous riding
had rendered him strong and wiry, but although he grew to be five
feet ten inches tall, he remained so slim that for years his weight
stayed below nine stone without any particular effort on his part to
keep it down. Then, inexorably, it began to rise, and no amount of
dieting or exercise would stop it. He did for a while resort to purgatives
to achieve particular rides, but on the whole he fought shy of them:
were they not what had undermined poor Fred Archer, and driven
Jack Watts to drink?

The result was that although he continued to ride for Reske when
the owner-trainer shifted his operations to Moscow in 1900, he never
again recaptured his earlier form. After an amicable parting, he
transferred to another stable run with skill and energy - that of I. A.
Arapov. Yet with him, also, Joseph failed to win the big prizes, and
by 1905 he knew that his days as a jockey were over.

He never resented a change which he saw was inevitable. As nature
took its course, he accepted his fate with equanimity, and was happy
to move on from riding to management, which he soon found suited
his temperament. Apart from anything else, his riding career enabled
him to travel widely and see a good deal of European Russia. After
his early days in Warsaw and then Moscow, he journeyed at last to
St Petersburg. Until then he had never paid much attention to
architecture, but the size and scale of the buildings in the capital
struck him full of wonder. The first time he set eyes on them, he
came off the train from Moscow early on a spring morning and found
the city washed by low-angled sunlight. So delighted was he by the
pastel colours – turquoise and butter-yellow especially – and by the
gleam of golden cupolas, that he paid an *izvozchik* an exorbitant sum
to drive him round for an hour before he went to his appointment.
In the grandeur of the Winter Palace, the vast sweep of the Kazan
Cathedral, the width and surge of the River Neva, he saw a reflection
of the immensity of Russia as a whole, and sensed the awe-inspiring
power of the Tsar. At Tsarskoe Selo, the royal village some twenty
miles to the south-east, he was again dumbfounded, here by the scale

of the country houses which the Emperor's ancestors had seen fit to commission for themselves: the colossal Catherine Palace, with its blue and white facade two hundred yards long, and the smaller but still enormous Alexander Palace, all honey yellow, in which Tsar Nicholas II and his family lived for certain seasons of the year.

Of all the racecourses on which Joseph rode in Russia, the one at Tsarskoe Selo remained his favourite, not least because the surrounding parkland, with its hills and artificial lakes and specimen trees, reminded him of England. Another fact in its favour was that race meetings were held there in early summer, when the country was looking its best and freshest. The facilities were modest – but that, too, appealed to Joseph. Unlike the grandiose Hippodrome in Moscow, Tsarskoe Selo had no side about it. The only buildings of any consequence were two elegant stands at the finish, made of wood and painted green and white, with pillared balconies and elaborate fretwork round the eaves. The larger of the two, known as the Imperial Pavilion, was reserved for the Tsar and his guests, and on days when he came to the races was prettily decked out with wreaths of flowers; but it held no more than fifty spectators, and its minuscule size contributed to the intimate atmosphere which made the course so attractive. Funny, Joseph always thought as he glanced up at the monarch and his entourage with their braided uniforms and crinolines and high, white hats filling the imperial box: there sits the Tsar of all the Russias in a little wooden hut.

Riding in the races at Tsarskoe Selo, and visiting St Petersburg, Joseph could not help but notice the deep and rigid stratification of society, like that of England, but more extreme. He did not enter society himself, of course, but only skated across its fringes. Owners made much of him whenever he won a race, and increasingly sought him out at training stables, to ask his advice or to watch their horses in action; but he was never invited to dine in a princely household or to go to a ball in a palace – and if any such invitation had come, it would have alarmed him greatly, for he would not have known how to deal with it. The deprivation did not worry him: he saw it as in the natural order of things that some people should be born high, others low, and that although money could go some way towards bridging the gap between the two worlds, it would never unite the one with the other.

All the same, he did notice with ever-increasing unease the vast disparity between the rich and the poor. At Yarskoye, where he continued to live and work between riding seasons, he grew used to being attached to an upper-class establishment, but later he realised that it was moderate in every way: the house was of moderate size, the Scherbatovs a family of moderate distinction, moderate means and moderate behaviour. In Petersburg the grandeur of houses and people was alike immense, the behaviour of the aristocracy outrageously affected and artificial, and at the same time the poverty of the lower orders – the washerwomen and hawkers and street-sweepers – even more oppressive than that of the average *muzhik* out in the country. As for the royal family – the style in which *they* existed beggared description. The Tsar was said to be a man of simple tastes who disliked ostentation; but that was not how he appeared to outsiders. Did not the royal family maintain over one hundred and thirty palaces? Certainly at Tsarskoe Selo station imperial carriages seemed always to be waiting for royal guests, with coachmen and footmen wearing scarlet cloaks edged with white fur, and cocked hats of red and gold. In the park itself hundreds of workmen spent the summer cutting, snipping, sweeping and clearing, so that the lawns looked like acres of finest carpet, and no fallen leaf was allowed to sully the perfect swards.

Such extravagance made Joseph wonder. For the first time in his life he became politically aware, and he was not surprised when he heard that, in October 1905, a small earthquake of social unrest had shaken St Petersburg, and banks, newspapers, post offices and tram services had closed down as crowds armed with red banners took to the streets. By then he had gone home to Yarskoye for the winter, and the news did not filter through for several weeks; but when it came, it merely confirmed an opinion he had been forming for some time – that Nicholas was a weak and ineffective ruler, who had been losing touch with the needs of the country for some time. In merely thinking this, Joseph worried that he was being unpatriotic, for the close blood ties between the English and Russian royal families made him feel loyal to the Tsar as well as to the King; yet he observed the weakness as a matter of fact, and could not pretend that it did not exist.

Just as his body belatedly filled out, so his mind gradually broadened and extended, and it went on expanding long after those of his contemporaries had settled into a mould. It occurred to him that if he could have stayed at school for another year or two, things might have been very different; new ideas might have been implanted when he was thirteen or fourteen, new interests started and followed. As it was, he had been forced to concentrate on the mundane business of keeping alive and well, of holding his own, of making his way, first in the circus and then in the stables, so relentlessly that he had never had a chance to develop intellectual pursuits. Only when he achieved modest affluence in Russia did he find time to think and look around more widely. It was partly his success in learning Russian that gave him confidence; if he could do that – he reckoned – he must have a reasonable brain. He began to read, and was swept away by *War and Peace*, of which he found a tattered, second-hand English edition, going for a few kopeks in a shop in St Petersburg. One summer evening he summoned up his courage and bought a ticket for a symphony concert in Petersburg. Nervous doubts assailed him as he sat waiting for proceedings to begin, since he did not know what to expect; but within half an hour he was on the edge of his seat with excitement, swept away by the deep surge of cellos and double-basses, and then by the electifying beat of a fast, doom-laden march. Only afterwards, as he was recovering, did he discover what it was that had been played: the Sixth Symphony by a composer of whom, until then, he had never heard: Tchaikovsky.

His transition from jockey to horse-breaker, adviser and stud manager took place slowly, over several years, and he was much helped by the generosity of his first employer, who frequently gave him time off to carry out commissions for other stud-farm owners such as Prince Oginsky, Count Pototsky and Count Stroganov. Jobs well done for such leading owners certainly spread his fame, but in the end it was the visits to Russia of a swaggering, pontificating English officer called Captain Dalgleish which lifted him onto a higher plane. Every time Dalgleish came over, he brought with him one or more animals which he had sold in advance to Russian buyers, and he went from one cavalry barracks to another giving demonstrations of breaking and handling. As he toured studs and military establishments, he lost no opportunity of telling his hosts what to do, but his enthusiasm and expertise were infectious, rather than irritating, and it was when he brought two Irish mares to Yarskoye that Joseph fell under his spell.

Count Scherbatov was hugely impressed, not just with his new mares, but with the skill of the English officer. So was Joseph. He learnt many new tricks during a few days and became so friendly with the visitor that when, in 1909, on a later trip, Dalgleish heard that

General Moerder, Director-in-Chief of the Government's horse-breeding department, was looking for a manager to take charge of the Imperial Stud at Krasnoe Seloe, near Petersburg, he recommended Joseph, who got the job.

The appointment, carrying a salary of 10,000 roubles, put Joseph on a new level. Not only did he now have a definite status, a small house of his own and a cook: he was also in frequent contact with senior cavalry officers and even with members of the royal family. Krasnoe Seloe – literally the Red Village – was an attractive place, essentially a military training area, but also a resort favoured by the inhabitants of St Petersburg, many of whom had villas there. Like the village, the stud was set on gently rolling hills, ideal for cavalry manoeuvres.

Living and working forty minutes' train ride from the capital, Joseph came to know Petersburg well. In summer the city seemed to float on its maze of shimmering waterways, and for weeks on end no proper darkness fell; even at midnight the sky remained a deep, luminous turquoise, as if light were being reflected into it from the Arctic ice cap to the north, and after a few hours of twilight, shades of pink and grey would steal into it again, so that the days were never-ending. Yet it was winter, when the place lay frozen beneath a mantle of snow and ice, which gripped Joseph's imagination most strongly. He grew to love the way in which pale sunlight scintillated off fresh snow on the roofs of the palaces, and the dash with which people skated through the heart of the city, along tracks created by pouring water on to paths, even up and down little hills. He never tired of watching the continuous activity on the ice-bound Neva: people walking across the river, either on the makeshift bridges or on the ice itself; Lapps camping in their sealskin tents on its frozen surface, and above all the races, for which the horses wore specially studded shoes. In winter, Joseph found, the crispness and sparkle in the air of the capital gave him tremendous energy.

For the first time since he had arrived in Russia, he ran across other English immigrants, and he was astonished at the scale on which they lived. Many sprang from origins nearly as humble as his own, being the sons of mill workers who had come out when British capital poured into the Russian textile industry; yet they all seemed to have immense houses, armies of servants, aggressive private coachmen who plied their whips ruthlessly on anyone in their way. They all belonged to the golf club, the tennis club, and the Krestoffsky pigeon-shooting club out on one of the islands in the gulf, and they had their own shop, the English Magazine, the only place in Russia where it was possible to buy good shoes. Above all they had the new English Club in the Moyskayia. Known to the Russians as *barins*, or gentlemen, they gave themselves the airs of the nobility; and the natives, not knowing how real English lords behaved, treated them as though they were the genuine article.

Joseph did not care for the kind of ostentation which they practised, and he was never tempted to ape it. Even so, he himself became a *barin* of sorts; he joined the New English Club and enjoyed going there occasionally. The grandiose pillared hall made him uneasy, but he could relax in the deep leather armchairs of the library to read the week-old newspapers, and in the restaurant the lunchtime menu usually included a dish called Irish stew, which the Russian chef valiantly tried to make resemble an original that he himself had never tasted or seen. At one stage, for six months, he went so far as to rent a small apartment on the Admiralty Quay, overlooking the Neva, so that he had somewhere of his own in which to stay after going to a concert or the theatre. Yet a trip into the city remained a luxury, rather than a routine, and if Joseph managed one visit a year to the famous gipsy singers and dancers of Novaya Deresvniya, he reckoned he was doing well. The gypsies' tribal life reminded him of his days in the circus: their dark complexions and garish clothes spoke to him of far places, and made him think of Wales.

It was during an evening at the gypsies that he picked up – or rather was picked up by – a Cossack girl called Shura. Short and slight, dark as a raven, with glossy black hair, violently red lipstick and a face that was striking rather than beautiful, she came from nowhere to nestle beside Joseph, and within five minutes she was addressing him as *rodnenkiy* – the peasant for sweetheart. Fuelled by lemon vodka and *blinis*, she poured out the story of her love life in a bewildering, torrential mixture of narrative, sarcastic jokes and self-pity. The gist of it was that she had run away from home, in the far south, got married in Moscow, and then run away from her husband, who beat her. Now he had followed her to St Petersburg and was trying to kill her. Everything about her seemed exaggerated – from her cheekbones to her sense of drama. 'Protect me, *rodnenkiy*, save me from him!' she cried, with tears pouring down her cheeks, and she buried her dark head on Joseph's shoulder. At that first meeting he found her attractive and amusing – and he weakened to the extent of allowing her to return to the flat with him.

It was a serious mistake. Though lithe and voluptuous in bed, out of it she was a disaster. She refused to cook anything, even a boiled egg; her idea of housework was to sit admiring herself in a mirror; and she was wildly extravagant, instantly spending any money that Joseph gave her on clothes. Her life was so highly charged with drama that merely being with her was exhausting: always some disaster had struck, or was about to strike, and she demanded constant support. After a few glasses of wine or vodka she would become maudlin and sing lugubrious Cossack songs, frequently bursting into tears. Joseph forbad her to visit the stud at Krasnoe Selo, for he feared that if she appeared there, his reputation would plummet; so she stayed at the flat in the city, and was all over him whenever he went there. After a couple of months he could stand it no longer; but the only way he could get rid of her was by giving up the lease of the apartment, and forcing her to move out. The entanglement made him wary of starting any other relationship.

For anyone who worked on the land or in any enterprise connected with it, those were years of plenty. After the uncertainties of 1905, a series of good harvests put new heart into the peasant farmers, and in 1909 - just as Joseph moved to the Imperial Stud – a new Prime Minister, Pyotr Stolypin, introduced a plan which made it possible for the *muzhiks* to own land outright. This fundamental innovation brought about immediate improvements in productivity: suddenly men took a pride in their land and worked hard so that they could earn enough money to increase their holdings. Within five years over five million peasant families had settled on their own property, and Stolypin – helped by the favourable growing seasons – had created a new class of peasant landowner, almost single-handed.

Joseph, who saw how well the new arrangement worked, was appalled when Stolypin was murdered in Kiev during September 1911. There was something particularly sinister about the fact that the Emperor had been with him, in the opera house, when he was shot down: obviously the murderer intended not only to kill the Prime Minister but to defy the entire Tsarist regime. With his newly-awakened political sense, Joseph felt the old order beginning to tremble.

The fragility of the whole structure, the feeling that volcanic forces of hatred and resentment were pent up beneath a crust of authoritarianism, was brought home to him violently one afternoon that same month, when he was riding across country scarcely an hour out of St Petersburg, on his way home from a meeting at a farm. The area contained many straggling, scattered birchwoods, with heathland between, and as his horse came silently down a sandy track towards a hollow, he began to hear faint cries of terror or pain. A few moments later he was close enough to hear the swish and crack of whips or sticks – and suddenly he stopped. A man had been hung up between two birch trees, suspended by his ankles, with his legs wide apart. Three other men – the coarsest kind of *muzhiks* – were beating him to death. Yet it was the manner of their assault that was so nauseating. With maniacal fury they had rained the blows of their birch rods into the man's spreadeagled crutch, until the whole of the middle of his body had been cut into shreds and reduced to a bloody pulp. Streams of blood had run down his chest and face and spattered the ground beneath him as he jerked in agony. When Joseph arrived, he was on the point of expiring. He uttered a feeble, gurgling groan, gave one convulsive shudder, and hung limp. '*Sdokh*,' said one of the peasants with satisfaction, using the word normally applied to animals only. 'It's dead.'

The executioners were much put out by the sudden appearance of a stranger: as they scowled at him shiftily from under their mops of hair, Joseph realised his own danger.

'Good riddance,' he said heartily. 'What was he – a thief?'

'Worse than that,' growled the tallest of the peasants. 'He came maiming our cattle, on orders from one of the Red gang-leaders.'

'Did he! Well, he won't maim any more. Good work, lads. Keep up the struggle.' Joseph lifted a hand, dug in his heels and burst past the group at a canter. The *muzhiks*, unable to place him, uncertain even as to what kind of person he was, raised hands to forelocks as he disappeared. He made a clean getaway; but when he had gone half a verst he began to shake with reaction at the horror of what he had seen, and the sight of the mutilated victim haunted him for months.

Another incident, less violent but deeply sinister, reinforced his fears. One afternoon in St Petersburg he came out of the huge warren of shops known as Gostinny Dvor and stood on the pavement of the Nevski Prospekt debating which way to go. Suddenly two men grabbed him by the arms and frog-marched him away to a building down a side street, where they bundled him into a smoke-filled office, shoved him up against a wall, searched him roughly and began to interrogate him in a loutish, bullying manner. He yelled back at them, in his best stable language, asking who the hell they were and what they thought they were doing. After a few exchanges it emerged that they were agents of the Okhrana, or Tsarist secret police, and had mistaken him for a Finnish anarchist whom they believed to be in the city. Discovering that Joseph worked in an imperial establishment, they became apologetic and obsequious, offering money to compensate for his wrongful arrest. He rejected it angrily and demanded their names, which they refused to give; then he walked out – but this glimpse of the arbitrary and ruthless methods thought necessary to keep the Tsar on his throne reinforced his unease.

In the English Club, talk turned more and more to the possibility of revolution. Most of the members thought it would come, but not for several years. One or two decided to go home before real trouble set in, yet trade was so good that the merchants and businessmen were naturally reluctant to leave. Instead, they circumvented the financial controls by various devices and surreptitiously moved as much money as they could afford overseas. Joseph, unsettled by nervous chatter, thought hard about his own future. He did not want to go. He was enjoying life in Russia, and in purely financial terms doing well. If he did return to England, what would he do? No home or job awaited him. It was sixteen years since he had emigrated. He could, he supposed, go back to Newmarket and look for work, but nobody there would know his capabilities, so that he would have to start again from scratch, at the age of thirty-four. Besides, to clear out would be to throw away the position and reputation which he had built up in Russia.

On the whole he was inclined to stay – until, every few weeks, some fresh anarchist outrage set new worries gnawing at his confidence. His financial uncertainties were equally hard to resolve. Should he get one of the merchants to smuggle his savings back to England – perhaps by buying up a consignment of steel or cotton in London, paying for it, and selling it there again? Or was it not safer to keep the money where it was, on deposit in the bank?

Then, in the spring of 1912, as he havered, his life was transformed by a momentous invitation, a new opportunity, whose repercussions proved so drastic that they removed all question of his going home.

FIVE

Nikolsk: 1912

T HE LETTER came from Prince Alexei Ivanovitch Mironov. Joseph had never heard of him, but a few minutes' research among his staff revealed that he was a distant cousin of the Tsar, and this meant that his overture was not so much an invitation as a command. The Prince wrote to say that he would be pleased if Mr Clements would come and spend a couple of months on his estate at Nikolsk, in the province of Novgorod, to advise him on the layout and construction of a new stud. First-class train tickets would of course be provided to the nearest halt, and if Clements would just send word about the time of his arrival, a carriage would meet him at the station. The Prince hoped he could be at Nikolsk in the first week of June.

Naturally Joseph sought permission to take two months' leave, but because of the nature of the Prince's summons, he knew it would be a formality. Sure enough, the answer came that he might go as soon as he had made satisfactory arrangements to cover his absence; and on the last day of May he headed for the south.

Four hours out of St Petersburg, the train deposited him at the wayside halt of Dedovichi, the only passenger to descend on to the wooden platform. At five o'clock on a soft, clear evening, there was no one to collect his ticket, but outside the station palings a troika was waiting, and the driver – a lively-looking young fellow with straight fair hair hanging down all round his head – bustled to stow his two pieces of luggage on the shelf beneath the seat. In a moment he had the horses trotting briskly along the dirt road that led out of the village towards low, wooded hills in the distance.

The drive took nearly two hours. The boy did not seem disposed to talk, and after he had only grunted in answer to a couple of questions, Joseph realised that he was deaf. Content to look about him, Joseph saw that here the crops of wheat and rye were more advanced, but thinner, and there were more fields of potatoes just starting to sprout: evidently the land was sandier, except in the shallow river valleys. Down there cattle grazed in lush meadows, and stands of good-looking oak testified to the strength of the clay. The trees were still not fully in leaf, but had that buttery yellow look of unfurling buds which precedes the green. A colony of storks, nesting in elms beside a lake, gave off a great creaking and honking as the troika went by. They passed through two or three hamlets, consisting of a dozen *izbas* – primitive houses made of wood, with window frames painted bright red and blue – and here and there they came across peasants walking home from the fields in little groups; again, as on his first few days in Russia, Joseph felt powerfully the impression of a vast land sparsely inhabited.

At last, with the sun low over the horizon, the boy drove down a gentle hill, with fields of rye on their left running up to a belt of forest. Ahead of them a few more wooden hovels appeared on either side of the road, and then, flickering between the specimen trees of a park, the facade of a two-storey white house nestling on a slope that rose behind the village. Square-fronted wings flanked a central block with a shallow dome, and a pillared portico with a shallow pediment framed the front entrance.

From the moment he set eyes on it, Joseph liked the place. An avenue of acacia led off the public road, and the drive between the trees was freshly sanded, the grass on either side neatly mown. The fences were in good repair. Several young trees had been planted recently to replace older ones lost in some gale. Hereford cattle, still shedding their winter coats, grazed in one of the fields. Lilac was in bloom, both white and purple. Behind the house stood barns and granaries, trimly thatched. Everything looked in good order.

As they came up towards the house from the flank, he waited to see if he would be deposited at the front door or the back. Seeing that the place was much grander than Yarskoye, he felt pretty sure he knew the answer – and in the middle of the shrubbery, where the drive divided, his driver swung the horses to the right, sweeping into a cobbled yard, with barns and stables facing the back of the house. A servant in grey livery, emerging from a door at one end, took his modest pieces of luggage and carried them up an outside wooden staircase which led to a loft over the coach house. There, some rooms had been converted into accommodation of a sort. Joseph's was panelled in natural pine; it contained a bed, a chair, a chest of drawers and a wash-stand with a large blue and white china bowl set into the top, and a matching ewer of cold water beside it: that was all. The window, on the side away from the house, looked out over an orchard, with long grass beneath the trees.

'There is supper for you in the kitchen, *barin*,' said the servant. 'Whenever you are ready. Go in by the door I came out of, at this end of the yard. When you have eaten, the Prince will see you.'

'Thank you. I'll just have a wash and come across. By the way, where's the lavatory?'

'Downstairs, at the back.'

'Good. I'll find it.'

With the man gone, Joseph went exploring. The arrangements made for him seemed similar to those at Yarskoye, at any rate so far as accommodation went; but there, as a newcomer to Russia, he had felt very tentative and cautious. Now, arriving at Nikolsk, he knew how Russian country houses worked. Besides, he liked the country people, and could get on with them better than with the inhabitants of towns.

He found the lavatory soon enough: an earth closet in a lean-to shed, built out into another yard, much overgrown by grass and stinging nettles – a forgotten area, quite different from the neatly-kept front approaches. Back on the upper floor, he looked into three other rooms. All were as bare as his, but at least they were not in use: he always preferred to have space about him and to be on his own. Although his room looked clean, it had a musty smell, so he opened the window and let in a cool breeze from the orchard. He had had the wit to bring soap and towel with him, so he scrubbed his hands, face and neck vigorously before putting on a clean shirt.

Not for many days did he discover how many retainers lurked in or around the nether regions of Nikolsk. Every time he thought he had met them all, another would appear. There were house men, house maids, a butler, a head cook and under-cooks, scullery maids, dairy maids, an old nannie, and, outside, gardeners, under-gardeners, foresters, farm-hands. That first night, however, though he looked eagerly for buxom peasant girls, the only other servant he met was the housekeeper, who rose from an armchair beside the stove as he entered the kitchen, a mountainous figure clad in rustling black satin, with her grey hair done up in a bun and a dozen or more keys clinking from a ring on her belt.

'Welcome to Nikolsk!' she said, in a thick country accent. 'I am Martha Alexandrovna. You must be hungry. Here – take a seat.'

A place had been laid at the deal table in the middle of the room, and she put before him a generous plateful of cold pork, cold roast potatoes and spiced red cabbage. As he set to, she sat down opposite, regarding him with a kind of inquisitive amusement and playing with a string of black beads; but hardly had she begun to ask her first question when a door swung violently open and a tall, silver-haired man in a plum-coloured velvet smoking jacket burst into the room, letting off exclamations like a firework.

'Cha!' he cried. 'I knew it! They never told me you'd come, damn them.'

Joseph swallowed hastily, put down his knife and fork and pushed back his bench. The old housekeeper also stood up and bobbed a curtsy, fluttering her small hands in front of her, as if to make excuses, and vanished backwards though another doorway.

'Our new recruit!'

'Yes, sir.'

'Pleased to meet you. Mironov.' The Prince stuck out his hand. Joseph shook it, then added a little bow.

'Never thought you'd be so tall.' The Prince glared out from under bushy grey eyebrows, but hardly at him, more downwards and to one side. 'Hell of a height for a jockey. Well – sit down, sit down.' He crumpled his own tall frame on to the chair vacated by Martha. 'Eat. I expect the food's filthy. It usually is. What is it?' He leaned over, peering at Joseph's plate. 'Pork? Is it disgusting?'

'No, sir. Far from it.'

'Rubbish. The cook's always trying to poison us. I expect you're pretty tough, though. You'll survive.'

Joseph felt something rub against his leg. He looked down and saw an elderly springer-spaniel, black and white, fawning against his knee.

'Minnie, get out!' barked Mironov, making no move or effort to enforce his order. 'The bitch isn't allowed in here. Must have slipped in with me. Something to drink. Kvass?'

Unnerved by the staccato bombardment, and wondering if he should have addressed his host as 'your highness' or 'your excellency', Joseph resumed his meal. After only a couple of mouthfuls the Prince opened up again, this time in good but heavily-accented English. 'What is going to win the Derby, then?'

'In Moscow?'

'No, no, man. Epsom. Who cares about Moscow? Epsom, of course. D'you fancy Tracery? Jaeger might be worth backing. Or what about Pintadeau?'

Joseph's grasp of English racing form had dwindled almost to nothing; but he did know that Pintadeau belonged to the King, and fastened on to that straw of knowledge. Soon he saw that his ignorance hardly mattered: the Prince was longing to talk horses, but he was also happy to keep up a monologue supported by occasional rejoinders. As he talked, Joseph had time to wonder how on earth anyone could follow Epsom form from a place as remote as this; he also had a chance to observe his host, whose long, lean, distinguished face had the ruddy, weatherbeaten complexion of a man who spent much time out of doors. His lank silver hair, parted low on the left, was swept over the top of his head in a smooth curve, and his whole aspect was a touch lopsided, his right eyebrow being higher than his left – perhaps raised by his habit of cramming a monocle in beneath it whenever he wanted to scrutinise something close to him. The general effect was lively, if unnerving.

'More!' he said abruptly as Joseph finished, glaring into the fire-place. 'Have something else. Cheese. Fruit.'

'No, thank you.'

'Watching your weight, eh? Don't blame you. Come on, then. Meet the family.'

The Prince led the way down a dingy, stone-flagged corridor and out into the hall, from which a splendid double staircase, balustraded in white and gold, rose towards the first-floor landing and the domed roof. From a door on the right came the sound of a piano, which stopped as they entered the room – a large, light sitting room, full of flower-patterned chair covers, with bright rugs on the polished boards. Two boys of about thirteen and eleven, dressed in identical sailor suits, were playing chess on the floor, and a severe-looking, middle-aged woman in a grey dress sat at the piano.

'This is our new recruit from England,' announced the Prince to the room in general. 'My sister, Princess Yelena.' The piano-player smiled stiffly, with a rustle of starched linen, and Joseph bowed in her direction. 'And these are my sons, Dmitri and Ivan.' The boys scrambled to their feet and shook hands, bashfully saying 'How do you do?' in English. Dmitri was fair-haired, blue eyed and very handsome, though nervous-looking, his brother darker and less striking, but more positive.

'You speak English?' Joseph asked.

'A little,' the dark boy replied carefully.

'Good!'

'I'm sorry my daughter isn't here,' the Prince was saying. 'She'll be back on Thursday. Take a seat.' He pointed to one of the arm-chairs and demanded, 'Tell us what goes on in Petersburg. Is it true that the horses in the stud are coughing? And who do they say will win the Emperor's Cup?'

The boys resumed their game, the Princess drifted to a seat in the window, and the men began serious horse talk. Joseph perched on the front of the proffered chair. He wondered briefly where the children's mother was, but had no time to follow the thought through, so insistent was the quick fire of his host's questions. Dark fell as they chatted, and presently the boys were sent off to bed. It surprised Joseph that no servant came to light the oil lamps (the Prince did it himself), and that it was the Princess who then drew the curtains. After Joseph had twice politely refused the offer of a nightcap, the Prince helped himself to a whisky and soda from a tray on a big chest of drawers at one side of the room.

Every now and then Joseph managed to slip in a question about the estate. He discovered that it extended to 3,000 *desyatins*, or 8,000 acres, half of which was forest. Fifteen rangers, working under a qualified forester, looked after the woodland, and combined their silvicultural duties with game-keeping. The woods contained wild boar, red deer, wolves and a few bears. Of the farmland, half was arable, growing wheat, oats, buckwheat, millet and potatoes, and the rest grassland, which supported a herd of pedigree Friesians, and on which hay was being made at that moment. In other words, the enterprise was a sizeable one. The Prince seemed pleased by his interest and suddenly barked, 'Like to ride out in the morning? See the land?'

'Thank you, sir. I'd enjoy that.' In truth he was much looking forward to the next day, but his eyelids were starting to close and he stifled yawns with difficulty.

At last the Prince noticed his exhaustion and, gruffly but kindly, ordered him to bed. 'Off you go,' he said.

Joseph bowed to the Princess, who, if not quite asleep in her chair, was very close to it. The Prince gave him a lamp and escorted him out through the kitchen to the back door. 'Sleep well,' he said.

'Thank you, sir. I'm sure I will.'

Normally Joseph passed out when his head touched the pillow, but not that night. He spent hours fretfully turning back and forth, for a simple reason: rats. The coach house was alive with them – hence the musty smell which had assailed him when he arrived. As soon as he went back up the outside staircase, he heard them squeaking and scuttling in the roof. Inside his room, the noise was irregular but incessant, rising and falling as they scampered and drummed along above the ceiling. If he thumped his fist on the boards, they fell silent for a few seconds, only to start again; and every few minutes an outburst of squeals proclaimed some feud or sexual assault. There were more beneath the floorboards: grindings and scrapings suggested that they were trying to gnaw their way through. Joseph hated rats. A careful inspection of room showed that walls, floor, wainscot and ceiling were intact: even so, he could not relax.

Morning brought another glorious summer day. Hollow from lack of sleep, he rose early and explored behind the farm buildings. Among the primitive, horse-drawn ploughs and hay-rakes he was surprised to find a brand-new threshing-machine, of the latest type, made by the American firm Harvester. It was the kind that would be drawn up alongside a rick and driven by belt, the power coming from a separate steam engine; but the idea of bringing a monster that size all the way from America to Nikolsk amazed him. Poking about, he was brought up short by the sound of a horn, which rose and fell melodiously in the distance. When he heard answering bellows, he realised that it was calling the cows in to be milked; but its golden notes seemed such a perfect match for the early sunlight filtering through the trees that they haunted him all day.

At seven he ventured into the kitchen for a can of hot water, which was given him by a tousled and monosyllabic boy whose duty seemed to be to get the stove going. Then, having shaved and dressed, he found his way to breakfast in the servants' hall, where a dozen men and women looked up from the long table and eyed him with unconcealed curiosity. Besides black bread and tea, there was a large dish of *kasha* – dark-grey buckwheat porridge laced with salt and garlic.

Promptly at 8.30 a groom walked into the yard leading two saddled horses, a grey gelding and a chestnut mare, both about sixteen hands, and Joseph had only chatted to him for a moment, admiring them, when the Prince appeared. He was dressed casually but immaculately, in an open-necked shirt of thick blue cotton with a white silk scarf knotted round his throat, breeches of the finest yellow suede, and highly-polished brown riding boots.

'Morning, morning!' he said abruptly as he strode up, looking at the horses rather than the humans. 'Sleep well?'

Joseph took a quick decision and said, 'No, sir!'

'What? Bed no good?'

'It's the rats, sir.'

'Rats?'

'Yes, sir. The coach house is full of them. In the roof especially.'

'Well, well. Better do something about that. Pyotr – tell Ivan Petrovitch, will you?'

'Yes, your highness.' The groom touched his cap.

'If you don't mind, sir . . .' Joseph tried not to sound too forward. 'I think I can deal with them. I have a special method . . . with your permission.'

'A rat-catcher, eh? Next thing, you'll be cooking the dinner.'

Joseph forebore to say that he could do that, too. The groom handed him the chestnut mare's bridle and led the grey to a mounting block, where the Prince climbed carefully aboard, with movements rather stiff and arthritic. Joseph followed his example, and the pair of them set off to see the estate.

They rode for a couple of hours, sometimes trotting a short distance, occasionally cantering, but mostly walking, with the Prince holding forth about the land, the crops, the forest and his methods of management. His manner gradually grew more relaxed, his utterances less abrupt: it was clear that he loved the estate, and Joseph warmed to him. Whenever he approached a group of men or women at work, the leader of the party would straighten up and offer a formal bow.

There was plenty to see and talk about. The estate produced not only corn, pigs and sheep, as well as its own milk and butter, but also potatoes in great quantity. These, the Prince said, went to the vodka distillery in the village, which was now run by the state but had once belonged to his father. In the autumn, when the potatoes were ripe, most of the local community would turn out to lift the crop and carry it off by the cartload to the distillery, where they were paid according to the weight they brought in. Most of the labour, in fact, was seasonal. Early in the summer many of the men migrated south to work on the hay crop in the Ukraine, where the seasons always ran at least six weeks ahead; and, having started cutting there, they would scythe their way back towards home, arriving late in May, with their faces deeply bronzed and the muscles in their forearms prodigiously developed. For the corn harvest in July and August a team of fifteen or twenty girls came out from Novgorod, forty miles away, chaperoned by two or three older women known as aunts. Ferociously guarded by these harridans, the girls lived in outlying barns, were banned from entering the village, and were supposed to have no contact with the locals. During the summer, all those working on the land were not only paid but also fed by the estate: fresh meat and fish, butter, milk, flour and vegetables were all provided. The system seemed to work well, although it was weighed down by the privileges granted since time immemorial to families who laboured all the year round.

'Trouble is, every family's got its own wretched cow,' the Prince said testily. 'That's their right – to pasture it with ours. We have a herd of sixty pedigree Friesians, but there's a horde of a hundred half-bred cattle running with them, devouring half the grass and trampling the rest.'

Little mechanisation had reached Nikolsk. Power was furnished by oxen or horses, and although the estate did possess the threshing machine, and two Ransome horse-drawn harvesters for cutting and binding sheaves of corn, the men were reluctant to use them, fearing that anything which made as much noise as they did could only be a product of the devil. As a result, most of the work was still done by hand. To overcome the suspicion of centuries and persuade men to use machinery, an elaborate system of bribes was needed.

Catholic though his concerns might be, the Prince's main interest lay in horses. Already his stables were extensive, for he kept sixty working horses, twenty brood mares and two stallions purely for the farm. Now, however, he proposed to establish a thoroughbred stud, and it was for this project that he sought Joseph's advice. The site was a good one, level and well drained, about quarter of a mile from the house; an architect had drawn up plans, and work had already begun on some of the foundations. The roofs were to be of corrugated iron, but all the other materials came from the surrounding area: bricks made out of clay from pits on the estate, oak beams, pine joists and timber cut from the forest and seasoned for several years in open-sided barns.

As soon as he saw the plans, Joseph intervened to modify them. Politely but firmly, he pointed out a number of details which seemed to him wrong. 'Excuse my asking,' he said to the Prince, 'but does your architect know much about horses?' – and he was not surprised when the answer was a gruff 'Not a damn thing.' For a start, he had not specified any enclosure in which the mares would be covered, either forgetting that vital activity, or assuming it would take place outside. Joseph insisted that there must be a large covering box, at least ten yards square, with a roof, which could be used in all weathers. Next, he found the stallion boxes too small and too low: even points such as the way the top halves of the stable doors abutted on to the bottoms needed attention. He specified a bigger overlap, of a different shape. He deemed the ventilation to be inadequate as well, and insisted that proper air-shafts were built into the roof-pitches. So it went on. Far from being annoyed, the Prince was grateful, and sent for the architect to come to the farm next day. Meanwhile, work could go forward on the range of foaling boxes, which was separate, so that the labourers were not standing idle.

What with the ride, the planning, and introductions to the bailiff and the under-managers, most of that first day was gone in a flash. Not until five o'clock did Joseph have a chance to address himself to the construction of a patent rat-trap. Already he had identified its main constituent – a cylindrical rainwater tank, made of metal and about five feet deep, which he had found standing disused in a yard. He got two men to set it up on a base of bricks so that its top was level with the floor of the old granary, and then, in the carpenter's shop, he devised a wooden frame to fit on the top.

Hearing what he was at, the two boys came rushing out to watch him. As he worked, and they stared at what he was doing, he could observe their faces: Dmitri, the elder and fairer, unnervingly handsome in his features, but with a slightly wild look in his eyes which made Joseph think he must be highly strung; and Ivan, though less arresting, a more solid character. Both of them were lively, inquisitive, not in the least shy. 'How does it *work*, though?' Ivan demanded.

'We make them walk the plank.' Joseph saw the boy look puzzled. 'You don't know that expression? It's what pirates do to their victims – they send them over the side of the ship. Look. We put some bait here, out in the middle. The only way a rat can reach it is by running along the plank. All right? So what do we do? Put in a pivot, so that the plank will tip up when it has weight on the end of it – like that. Here comes the rat, towards the bait. The plank feels quite safe to him, because this end and the middle are on solid supports. But then, the moment he's beyond the point of balance – flip! Down he goes.'

'Then what happens?' Ivan's eyes were shining with excitement.

'He falls into the tank. We've caught him. What's more, the plank falls back into place under its own weight, so that in a minute we can catch another.'

'Yes, but what about the rats you've caught?'

'We could put water in the tank, so that they'd drown. But that would be a bit cruel, because it might take ages. It's better just to

99

leave them in there, and come and hit them on the head in the morning.'

'Who'll do that, though?' asked Dmitri.

'I expect it'll have to be me.'

'Oh!'

Joseph worked on for a bit, smoothing the sockets in which the pivot – a length of broom-handle – had to rotate. Then he asked, 'Could you do something for me?'

'Not kill the rats!' Dmitri made a face.

'No, no! Get some bait from the cook. A piece of bread would do, but cheese would be better.'

The boys ran off, and by the time they came back, he was ready. Together they took the apparatus into the barn and settled it on top of the cylinder. 'There.' Joseph pushed the lump of hard, white cheese down on to a spike in the centre. 'How many do you bet we catch?'

'One,' said Ivan.

'Four,' said Dmitri.

'Oh no,' said Joseph. 'We'll get more than that. I bet you we get twenty.'

In fact he got twenty-nine. The killing of them, as they rushed frantically round the bottom of the cylinder, was an unpleasant job, and he was glad the boys were closeted with their German tutor, Herr Koch, so that they could not witness it. But the spectacular haul greatly accelerated the rate at which he was accepted by the resident staff: several of them regarded him as a magician, a latter-day pied piper, and bombarded him with bizarre requests for help against wasps, ants, mice and sundry other pests. They also freely imparted information which they might otherwise have withheld, so that on his second day he learnt a good deal about the establishment.

The boys' mother, Nadezhda Fyodorovna, had died five years earlier, they thought of a heart attack. With her gone, the Prince's sister Yelena – never married – had come to live in the house and had taken charge, but nobody liked her, since she was vain and foolish, as well as bossy, and gave pointless orders simply to exercise her authority. Everyone was looking forward to the day when the Prince's daughter managed to wrest control from her. It was only a matter of time, they thought: Princess Yekaterina Alexeievna was eighteen, and gaining in confidence and authority all the time. People referred to her affectionately as *Knyazhna* – the Little Princess – or even as Princess Katya.

The Prince's chief eccentricity was that he could not bear the sight of servants in or around the house. He did not mind them in the open, on the farm, where he could hardly help coming across them. Indoors, though, they made him so nervous that he had had parts of the house reconstructed – extra doors cut through walls, screens built to form passages – so that they could move about unseen. At meals, nobody waited on the family: food and drink were put on the sideboard, and the servants withdrew before the meal began. Beneath the courtyard at the back of the house two tunnels had been excavated so that retainers could enter or leave the building and come and go from their homes in the village unobserved.

Before his first full day at Nikolsk was over, Joseph sensed the benevolent spirit of the place. People bickered, of course. Fyodor, the head gardener, a querulous old man with drooping, white walrus moustache, complained constantly that demands from the labourers (whom he was obliged to supply with vegetables) were outrageous, and Monsieur Grenache, the French cook, was the butt of many jokes. But on the whole good nature prevailed, and Joseph's euphoria sprang from the feeling that the men and women working on the estate seemed devoted to the family: it was as if the villagers were all members of the same large tribe, united by their successful efforts to wrest a living from the land. He realised that the glorious weather had something to do with the carefree atmosphere; he felt instinctively that cheerfulness and energy were concentrated and brought out by the shortness of the Russian summer. Everybody seemed to sense that twelve months of labour had to be accomplished in a few brief weeks while the sun blazed down, the cut hay turned colour as you watched it, the corn began to ear up, the potatoes burst into white flower, and the great trees along the river cast pools of deep green shade.

For Joseph, this heady feeling of urgency, this summer excitement, found perfect expression in the making of the jam. This was a ritual, an annual event of the first importance. The scale of the operation was such that it could not take place in the kitchen, but had to be conducted outside in the courtyard. Returning dusty and sunburnt at the end of his second day, he found the yard bustling with activity. Lined up along the side nearest the house were four immense cauldrons, set on tripods over charcoal fires. Ranged alongside them on the ground stood large cones of sugar, each weighing a pood, or nearly thirty pounds, and wrapped in bright blue paper. Bare-footed girls in white smocks were stirring vigorously at the cauldrons with wooden batons, and more girls sat at trestle tables beyond the far end of the line, hulling mounds of strawberries. Most of the workers had decked themselves out in their best ribbons, hoping thereby to attract the attention of the young bloods staying in the house, who might saunter out to sample the brew. At a separate table peasant children in rags were queueing to hand in little bags of wild strawberries which they had picked in the forest: these were highly prized, because they gave a special tang to the jam, and, after scrupulous weighing, they were paid for in kopeks.

Up and down the line, like a schoolmistress supervising an exam, stalked the disapproving figure of Princess Yelena, glaring, sniffing, prodding, testing the contents of each cauldron by getting the girl to put a small dab of boiling mixture on a white plate which she carried with her and tipping the plate on edge to test the jam's viscosity. The entire courtyard was filled by a phenomenal smell of strawberries: the scent of ripe fruit alone was sharp on the air, but when reinforced by the dense aroma of jam cooking, its effect became almost over-powering. Joseph was seized by the idea of making love to one of these girls, whose skin, whose whole body, would have been infused by the smell of strawberries.

Just as that notion crossed his mind, the Princess decided that the first cauldronful had reached setting-point: the trial dab did not drip or even run when she tilted her plate sideways, and she gave orders for the contents to be ladled into the first of the wide-mouthed earthenware pots which were drawn up in regiments behind the fires. Glistening and steaming, ladlefuls of ruby-red jam sank down one after another into the depths of the jars; as soon as each was full, a girl sealed the neck with a layer of molten wax, and then tied a circle of white cloth tightly down over it.

That night in the servants' hall, gossip hummed. 'What about this *barin*, then?' said Malanya, one of the housemaids, mischievously. 'Not bad looking, is he?'

'Depends what you like,' sniffed Natasha, on the opposite side of the long table. 'I'm not struck on all those curls, myself.'

'Curls?' said Malanya incredulously. 'What do you mean?'

'His hair's curly, isn't it?'

'Well – yes. But it's short – not like yours.'

'Please yourself.' Natasha shook her chestnut coils self-consciously.

'At least he's polite.' Malanya seemed determined to stand up for the newcomer.

'Oh! So you've been talking to him, have you?'

'I only met him in the yard. He lifted a bucket of water for me.'

'Did he just! Next thing, he'll be asking you to marry him.'

'Rubbish!' Martha Alexandrovna, the old housekeeper, suddenly boomed out in her deep voice. 'If he marries anyone here, he'll marry the *Knyazhna*.'

'Course he won't!' said someone else cantankerously. 'You know quite well she's engaged. And anyway, he's only come for a few weeks.'

'You mark my words,' Martha insisted.

'Probably he's married already,' said Malanya wistfully. 'I expect he's got a wife in Petersburg.'

'Or even in London,' piped up Fedya, an effeminate young foot-man, in what he supposed was an English accent.

'It's a wonder you didn't ask him that yourself,' said Natasha across the table, at Malanya. 'During your conversation.'

There was a pause as the girls glared at each other. Then someone asked, 'How old is he, anyway?'

'How should I know?' Malanya bridled.

'He's thirty, at least,' said Martha, not unkindly. 'Could be more. But if *I* had a daughter, and he wanted to marry her, I wouldn't try to stop him.'

Next day, the weather was again gloriously fine, and morning brought no intimation of triumph or disaster. Joseph's catch of rats was down to eleven, but already his offensive had made serious inroads on the population of the coach house, and the night had been much quieter. After despatching and burying his latest victims, he was continuously occupied on the site of the new stables, and in beginning to break a batch of young horses. Not until evening did he come back to the big house, looking forward to a swim and a meal in the servants' hall.

In the courtyard the jam-making was again in full swing, the smell just as overpowering; but the instant he set eyes on the line of cauldrons and tables, he saw that something was different. The supervisor had changed. In place of the stout and frowsty figure of Princess Yelena, there was a sylph of a girl: a tall, elegant, lithe figure clad in a long white cotton dress, tight-waisted and full-skirted. Because he had come through the arch at the corner of the yard, he was already close when he first set eyes on her. For a moment she did not see him, as she was talking to one of the jam-stirrers – and perhaps it was just as well, for he stopped dead in his tracks.

She was not merely beautiful. She was obviously, immediately, intensely alive. She had long, fair hair, brushed up off her forehead so that it cascaded over at the sides to frame her provocatively high cheekbones. Her eyes were large and her mouth generously wide. It was the mobility of her face, as much as its shape, that seized his attention: as she talked, her eyes flashed and widened, her lips parted, and her cheeks creased into dimples until her whole face seemed to radiate amusement.

The sight of her pierced Joseph like an arrow. He knew who it was straight away – the *Knyazhna*, the young Princess. Although clearly of aristocratic lineage, she had a perfectly natural air. Like a highly-bred animal, she looked beautiful and good-tempered, but absolutely without affectation. To Joseph, it seemed as if an unearthly sound was coming from a great distance – the hoot of a train or the howl of a wolf floating from the steppe. He leant against the pillar of the archway, momentarily breathless.

Then she noticed him. She disengaged herself from the production line and came towards him, wiping her hands on a cloth with graceful, long-fingered movements, smiling.

'Hello!' She spoke in English. 'I am Katya Mironov. You must be Mr Clements?'

She held out a slender hand. Overcome with confusion, he took it and at the same time bobbed his head in a kind of bow. 'Yes, ma'am,' he stammered. 'Thank you. I mean, how do you do?'

'Welcome to Nikolsk! I am sorry I was not here to greet you. I hope my father has made you feel at home?' She had to search for her words, choosing them carefully, but her grammar was good, and even if it had not been, her low and musical voice would have made it perfect. Through the haze of his agitation Joseph saw that her eyes were grey-green, with flecks of hazel in them.

'Thank you, ma'am,' he repeated. 'He has been very kind. In fact, everybody has been very kind.'

She smiled again. Her eyes were on his, not challenging, but very direct. He felt some powerful current coming from her, and groped for ordinary words to mask his excitement.

'Your English is very good,' he said in Russian.

'Oh no! I never get the practice.'

'But it is. Really.'

'Well – thank you!'

'Where did you learn it?'

'Here – from our English teacher, Mr Simmonds. He is dead now, I'm afraid, but he was a very good teacher.' She looked round. 'And what do you think of our jam factory?'

'It's wonderful. You must be making enough for an army.'

'Yes – it has to last all year. Have you tried it? Here.' With a quick movement she slipped back round the tables, picked up her testing-plate and held it out to him. He looked doubtfully at his hands, which were encrusted with dust and dried earth. Seeing him hesitate, she ran a forefinger across the plate until a lump of jam had accumulated on the end of it, then held it out to him. He in turn offered his bare forearm, as a repository, but she said eagerly, 'No – eat it! Take it in your mouth.'

As delicately as possible, he closed his teeth on it. In spite of his care, his upper lip touched her finger.

'Magnificent!' he said. 'Solid strawberries.'

'That's what it is, strawberries and sugar. That's all.'

A shriek from the far end of the line attracted her attention. One of the girls had dropped her stirring-rod into the cauldron, and as the Princess hurried to help her recover it, Joseph backed away.

In his room, lying on his bed, he began to think he had got sunstroke. His whole being was on fire, fizzing from head to foot. Yet he knew quite well that it was not sunshine which had set him alight. It was the girl, the Princess, with her high cheekbones and slanting green eyes, her extraordinary combination of aristocratic looks and practical ability, her natural grace, her ease of manner, her directness. He lay on his back, staring at the pine planks of the ceiling, until dark began to fall. He had meant to swim, but the idea faded from his mind. He had meant to go to the servants' hall for supper, but his hunger had evaporated, and when at last one of the housemaids came to fetch him, he said that he had got a touch of the sun, and would not bother.

Long into the night he lay there, still dressed in his working clothes, ignoring the rats overhead and reliving every second of the encounter, again and again. What had she said? Practically nothing. But why had she had let her eyes rest on him in that fashion? Was it a way of hers, a look she gave everyone she met? Or had she felt something special about him? Why had she held out the jam for him to eat? Was that a sign of favour, or would she have done it for anyone? And why, above all, had he eaten it, just like that, without the slightest embarrassment? How could he have licked the fingers of a princess within minutes of meeting her, and done it so shamelessly? He had no explanation, except that it had seemed the most natural act in the world: her eyes had been alight with merriment, and the jam had been right in front of his face. Besides, she had not spoken to him as if to a retainer. She had addressed him as an equal human being. But then, that was how she spoke to the servants, who really were in her employ.

Whatever her intentions had been, he could not banish from his mind the shape and colour of her eyes, the texture of her face and arms. Unlike that of most high-born Russian ladies, who took care to keep their complexions milk white, her skin was tanned by exposure to the sun, and a fine down of fair hair showed up against the brown of her forearm. Even when he eventually fell asleep, feverish visions of her came to him in dreams.

Morning brought him to his senses. What was he thinking of? How could he be anything to her but one more servant? Nevertheless, at breakfast, at work, in the course of casual encounters, he made apparently non-committal inquiries of other members of the staff, not least Trofim, a young under-gardener, with whom he had struck up a friendship. Oh yes, Trofim said: they all loved the young princess, and were sad that they were going to lose her so soon.

'How come?' asked Joseph.

'Didn't you hear? She is to be married to an officer in the Cavalier Guards.'

'When?'

'Next spring, I believe.'

Joseph's fantasies withered at this news, only to revive when he fell into conversation with Anna Petrovna, the Mironov children's old nanny, a crusty, dumpy figure, always in black, with grey hair drawn tightly back round her head, who reminded him of Queen Victoria. 'That girl's got a brain,' she muttered. 'She ought to use it, not just marry some ox of an army officer. What's the point of travelling all the way to France if she goes and gets married straight afterwards?'

'She's going to France?'

'To the university, in Paris. To become civilised!' Anna enunciated the words with biting cynicism. 'As if we hadn't made her civilised enough, with our rough Russian methods.'

'When does she go?'

'In the autumn, for the winter.'

'And then she gets married in the spring? Here?'

'Yes, and a grand occasion it'll be. Half Petersburg will have to venture out into the wilds.'

As he went about his work, Joseph tried not to think of her. The hot weather continued, but jam-making had finished for the time being – until the raspberries were ripe – so that she did not come into the courtyard, and for one whole day he did not see her at all. But then, the next evening, as he walked back along the grass path from the river, there she was, hatless again, in a dress of pale cornflower blue, coming towards him with the boys, on their way to swim. Each lad carried a rolled-up towel.

'Oh,' she said in Russian. 'Here's Mr Clements! Good! Now we can practise our English on him.' She smiled at Joseph and said in English, 'You've met my brothers, Dmitri, or usually Mitya, and Ivan, or Vanya?'

'Indeed!' He made a little bow to her, grinned at the boys, and was disconcerted by the close resemblance between her and Dmitri. 'They helped me make a rat-trap.'

'Of course. I heard all about it.'

'How many have you catched?' asked Ivan.

'Caught. Forty-six, by this morning.'

The boy whistled. 'You won the bet, then.'

'I'm afraid so.'

'Well,' said Katya. 'Come and talk to me while they swim.'

'I ought to get back, really.'

'We'll only be a few minutes. You can tell me about England. Please!' She inclined her head slightly to the left, as if in supplication, and her smile of appeal was irresistible.

'All right, then.' He fell in behind the boys, wondering at the fact that, like a peasant girl, she was walking bare-foot. For a few strides he watched the easy sway of her body, thinking that she must have very long legs.

'Why don't you swim as well?' she asked over her shoulder.

'I just have,' he answered. 'That's what I was doing.'

'Oh, I see. Is the water cold?'

'Not at all. It's like a bath.'

The boys ran ahead, skipping and kicking at the long grass on either side of the mown path, and presently they all turned in through a green-painted, cast-iron gate which led to the family's private beach. The gate was only latched, and presented no real physical barrier: anyone could have walked through it. Respect for the family was apparently enough to ensure their privacy.

The path came out on the bank above a spectacular round pool about thirty yards across. A crescent-shaped spit of sand curved out into the river on its lower side, so that the stream, entering on the left as they looked, swung round in a lazy curve of deep, inviting water. Under tall chestnuts stood a wooden changing hut, and in front of it a plank had been fixed across the top of two posts to make a simple seat. Late sun, filtering through the leaves, dappled the grass and the dark water with light and shade. The boys, not waiting for any instruction or permission, threw off their clothes and rushed out to the end of the spit stark naked before paddling into the water. Katya sat on one end of the bench and by holding out her hand, palm uppermost, suggested that Joseph should take the other.

He perched beside her, acutely aware of her proximity. She gave off a faint smell of lavender.

'What a beautiful place!' he said.

'Yes – we're lucky. The village people won't come near it.'

'Why not?'

'They're convinced it's haunted by the water sprite.'

'Who's she?'

'He. It's supposed to be a thin little man, with a thin little voice, like a snipe. You know a snipe? Yes, of course. Well, the sprite calls out in his little voice from the depths of the water, trying to lure people in.'

'And if they listen?'

'They drown.'

'Has anyone been drowned here?'

'I don't think so. In the mill ponds, further downstream, yes. But not here. You hardly could drown here. If the worst happened, you'd float out of the pool into shallow water. It's all superstition.' She laughed and tossed her hair back.

Wanting to look at her profile, he forced himself to stare straight ahead, down into the water. 'Are there fish?'

'Oh yes. The crayfish are delicious.'

'How big?'

She held up her hands, a foot apart. 'Easy to catch, too.'

'How do you get them?'

'The men net them. But there are always some in holes under the bank. You dangle your arm in the water, and they grab you by the finger. Ouch!' She laughed, and shook her hand about as though it had been bitten. He laughed too, and, unable to stop himself, glanced sideways at her. She returned his look steadily.

'You're going to Paris?'

'Heavens! How did you know that?'

'Someone in the servants' hall mentioned it.'

She sighed and said, 'In September. I'm supposed to study civilisation, whatever that means, at the Sorbonne University. I'd much rather go to England. Cambridge. I would love that. Tell me about England. Tell me about Newmarket. Isn't that near Cambridge? My father never stops talking about it.'

'Well . . . please remember, I haven't been there for nearly twenty years. It must have changed a lot.'

'But is it all horses – the whole town horses?'

'Nothing else.'

'Tell me about it. And speak in English, please.'

Suddenly on home ground, he began to tell her about the Heath, the race meetings, the town, the pubs, Lordship Stud and Egerton House, the Prince of Wales and his party arriving for the Derby trial. Anxiety assailed him as he thought of Cherry Green, but he kept on, sticking to horses, races, jockeys. He hardly noticed when she steered him round on to his own career, and before he knew what he was doing he had started to describe his summer with the circus. Abruptly he stopped and said, 'But you don't want to hear about that. I'm sure Russian family circuses are just the same.'

'No – go on. I enjoy hearing you talk.'

'It was those sailor suits the boys wear,' he said. 'They reminded me. I used to wear something just like that to walk the rolling globe.'

He explained what he meant, and went on to describe the act with the untameable lion. When he came to the climax – the clash of the steel door as the lion sprang – she gave a little cry and put her hand on his arm.

'It's all right,' he said quickly. 'Nobody ever got hurt. The lion was playing the game, as much as everyone else.'

'And did *you* ever go in the cage?'

'Oh no. I was only a boy, you see. Not much older than Dmitri. What is he – twelve?'

'Thirteen.'

'Yes – I was thirteen exactly.'

'Of course.' She smiled at him with the dreamy yet direct look that he found so disturbing. His arm seemed to burn where her hand had touched it. He felt that in some mysterious way he was connected to her – but by what? Shared reminiscences? Curiosity about the other person? The desire to know more?

With loud cries the boys came running back. The spell was broken. Joseph stared at their skinny bodies, comparing them, in spite of himself, with the body of their sister who sat beside him. Ivan had caught a crayfish as long as his forearm, and held the poor, translucent creature aloft, with its pincers waving feebly, for them to admire. But because both boys were shuddering with cold, Katya enveloped them in their towels, rubbed them briskly and told them to get dressed.

By the time they had walked back to the house, dusk was falling. At the fork of the drive Joseph stopped and solemnly thanked Dmitri for letting him join the expedition. He was about to set off towards the courtyard when Katya said, 'It can't be very comfortable over there. You should stay in the house, with us.'

'Oh no, ma'am.' Joseph found himself awkwardly reverting to a formal mode. 'That wouldn't do at all.' He gave a little bow, smiled at the boys and walked away.

In the small hours of the night he tried to analyse the encounter's hidden meanings. That she had met him on her way to the river was a fluke: she could not have known he was there. Yet it was emphatically not a fluke that she had invited him to return with her party and asked him to hold forth about England. What elated and alarmed him was the way in which he felt so at ease in her company. With the Prince or his sister, he was usually uncomfortable, being neither one of the family nor an ordinary servant, but something in between. Mironov, he noticed, never addressed him as 'Mr Clements' – or indeed as anything at all. It was as if he, Joseph, were an unclassifiable being, and when the Prince had to refer to him in front of someone else, he called him 'our Englishman' or 'our new recruit'. Between Joseph and Katya, on the other hand, there seemed to be no barrier; he felt certain that if he had taken her hand in his when she touched him, she would not have pushed him away. And yet, thoughts of that kind were madness.

*

Another week passed, during which he saw her fleetingly. Then came what the Prince for some time had been calling his Big Day – an equestrian *fête champêtre*, held every year, to which he invited a number of cavalry officers. In fact they stayed for three days, arriving on the first and leaving on the third, but all attention was focused on the day of pageantry and manoeuvres in the middle. Word filtered down through the staff that Princess Katya's fiancé, Prince Pavel Pavlovitch Viasemski, would be among the guests, making his first visit to Nikolsk: eager though they were to set eyes on him, half of them dismissed him as inadequate before he had even arrived.

The equestrian events had settled into a well-established pattern: a musical ride, a couple of races, a children's fancy-dress parade (in which the ponies also had to be disguised), and some formalised cavalry manoeuvres. This year, however, as an extra entertainment, the Prince had announced that the celebrated English jockey Mr Joseph Clements would demonstrate his unique method of breaking and handling difficult horses. Left to himself, Joseph would never have thrust himself forward in such a fashion; as it was, he could hardly decline his host's invitation to perform. For one thing, the Prince was genuinely interested in spreading word of new techniques, and for another, he had a harmless desire to show off his own cleverness in securing the services of an unusual Englishman.

It was sheer bad luck that at the last moment the weather broke. For day after day the heat had built up relentlessly, but the morning of the fête dawned grey and heavy, the air so oppressively thick that breathing became difficult: and by mid-morning thunder was starting to rumble round the horizon. Nevertheless, the show went on. In the main arena – a large, level stretch of the park from which the hay had been cleared – elaborate arrangements had been made for the comfort of the guests: tents had been erected, white, cast-iron tables and chairs set out, and umbrellas hoisted above them.

Joseph had been asked to appear at mid-day, and when he walked out on to the field a few minutes early, the party was already going well. Some twenty young officers were eating caviar sandwiches and drinking champagne, many of them in the white tunics and red-banded service caps of the Cavalier Guards; which one was Prince Viasemski, he did not want to know. Closer to him, the ladies had disposed themselves elegantly on the white furniture, and when he furtively scanned the line of faces, he got a surprise: instead of a long dress and broad-brimmed hat, Katya was wearing peasant costume – a blue velvet cap, like a peaked beret, a white blouse with embroidered sleeves which ended at the elbow, and a beautifully embroidered apron of white lace over a blue dress that matched her cap. With her fair hair piled up inside the blue velvet, and a string of plain wooden beads round her neck, she looked perfect.

Joseph tore his gaze away. A cavalry soldier was riding towards him on a white troop horse, obviously of a certain age. As he approached, Prince Mironov came out of the tent and briefly addressed his audience. This horse, he said, was quiet enough in the stable, but it had one serious foible: it refused to be bridled, saddled or mounted in the open. 'What does it do, your highness?' came a voice from the back. 'You'll see,' the Prince replied, and he signalled to the soldier, who jumped off and drew the reins over his mount's head. Until that moment the grey had seemed perfectly quiet; but suddenly it was transformed into a devil. Whenever the soldier made the slightest attempt to lay a hand on its mane or saddle, it pulled back violently to the full extent of the reins and struck out at him with its front feet. Had he dodged less smartly, he would have been knocked down.

After five minutes the Prince called a halt. 'Now,' he announced. 'Let us see what our English guest can do with him.'

With a slight bow towards the spectators, Joseph took the taut reins and asked the soldier to retire. Then he began to flick the grey on the chest with the end of his whip. For a minute or two the horse continued to pull back, stamping and rolling its eyes; then, finding it could not escape the irritating flutter on its chest, it suddenly gave in and came forward. Quickly Joseph took a short rope from his pocket, slipped it over the horse's neck and round its upper lip, tightening the loop to form a twitch. With this lock in position on head and neck, he began to stroke the grey, running his hand over head, neck, shoulders and forelegs, all the time repeating the word 'steady'. After ten minutes, feeling the horse relax, he removed the rope and stood still, keeping up a quiet flow of words. Then he turned to the audience and said, 'Now the animal has its confidence back, it will stand being saddled or mounted like any other.'

'Oh, rubbish!' called a loud and slightly inebriated voice from among the young officers. 'Just you try it.'

Joseph held himself in check. He could not see who had made the remark, and in any case did not want to lose concentration, so he made no reply but turned back to the grey and murmured more soothing phrases to him. Then, running a hand along its back, he raised the flap of the saddle, undid the girth, slipped the saddle off and laid it on the ground. Next he did the same with the bridle, holding the horse only with a rope loosely tied round its neck. Joseph heard a rustle of surprise go through the watchers as the grey stood without moving. After a few moments he put bridle and saddle back on, without difficulty, and called the horse's normal rider, the soldier, who had been looking on from a distance.

'Up you get,' Joseph told him. 'You'll have no trouble now.'

As the man put a foot in the stirrup and swung up into the saddle, with an incredulous grin, Joseph did not even hold the bridle. A ripple of applause ran through the audience, and one or two cries of 'Bravo!' rang out.

'Take him once round the field,' Joseph said to the soldier. 'Wake him up a bit. Then we'll try again.'

Round went the pair at a hand gallop. Thunder was rumbling nearer. A flash of lightning split the murk beyond the river, and the answering crash reached them in only a few seconds. Back came horse and rider. They drew up in front of Joseph, and the soldier vaulted to the ground. The grey stood like a statue, not pulling at all. His rider remounted, came down again, went back up, removed the saddle, replaced it. Then he saluted the audience and began to move off.

Again, applause broke out – but this time it erupted in a disturbance. A young officer was on his feet, not quite steady perhaps, but heading out into the arena. A plump, florid fellow, with a black moustache and an arrogant tilt to his head, he went right up to Joseph, poked him in the chest and called out: 'Anyone can do that. What makes you think you're so clever? We can manage our own horses, thank you very much. Why don't you go back to England, where you belong? We don't need foreigners like you here.'

Joseph was so taken aback that he did not know what to say. Before he could react, the officer made an exaggerated gesture at the departing grey and shouted, 'Here! Come back!' The soldier turned his horse, looking doubtful; clearly, he did not want to come near this drunk, but equally, he could not easily disobey an order. He wheeled and trotted back.

'Dismount!' the officer ordered. 'Immediately.'

'No – please!' Joseph tried to intervene. 'It would be better to let the horse settle down with his normal rider. Then the lesson will sink in.'

The young man turned his flushed face to Joseph and said scathingly, 'When I want advice from a *barin*, I'll ask for it.' Then again he faced the soldier and cried, 'Dismount!'

No sooner was the soldier on the ground than he seized the horse's bridle, brought the reins forward over its head and gave them a good flap. 'Now!' he shouted. 'I'll show you. Anybody can play that game.'

Before anyone could move, before Joseph could intervene, he had given the reins another violent shake. The grey, alarmed, instantly reverted to its old ways and pulled back. The lieutenant hung on and shouted again. The horse's response was quick and effective: it reared and struck out with both front feet. A sober man might have evaded the flashing hooves. This one was too full of champagne and of his own importance. One hoof knocked off his cap, scraped past his right cheekbone and caught him full on the shoulder. A second later he was on the ground, pouring blood from a cut on the jaw; ladies were screaming, and the horse had taken off in a wild charge across the field. At the same instant thunder burst overhead with a reverberating crash, and rain came hissing down.

So the fête ended in sudden chaos and cataclysm. Champagne glasses toppled and shattered as people leapt to their feet. Several of the ladies became hysterical. Some skittered for the shelter of the marquee; the rest cowered from the deluge under their umbrellas, and tried to comfort the ones in tears. Two or three young officers rushed forward to pick up their felled comrade, who turned out to be unscathed, except for his cut chin, a torn ear and some heavy bruises. Others went after the runaway horse, trying in vain to herd it into an enclosure of wattle fencing, and by the time they eventually caught it, twenty minutes later, they were all soaked to the skin. So was Joseph, wearing only a shirt and breeches; yet he insisted on going through his gentling routine once more, so that the value of the first session should not be lost. Again, at the end of it, the horse stood like a lamb.

'*Spasibo*,' said the cavalryman who rode it. 'You've made him a different animal.'

'He'll be all right now.' Joseph gave the grey a pat on the neck and walked away.

Only when he got back to his room did he feel his anger rising. Until then he had been too preoccupied with catching the horse and repeating its lesson. Now, as he stripped off and towelled himself dry, he became furious. Not only had the arrogant young lout insulted him, for no reason: he had also put a perfectly good horse at risk.

At lunch the servants' hall was alive with gossip. 'Well,' said Joseph to Marusia, the under-cook, as she filled his plate. '*He* won't get invited here again.'

She gave him a quizzical look. 'I'm not so sure.'

'What d'you mean?'

'Surely you realise – that was *the* young man – the fiancé.'

'*Bozhe moi*! I don't believe it.'

'Oh yes it was. Nice manners for a prince. No wonder the *Knyazhna* doesn't want to marry him.'

'I thought she'd chosen him.'

'Oh no – it was all arranged by the parents.'

The news confirmed what Joseph had instinctively felt all along – that Katya's spirit was not in thrall to another man. Why should that make any difference to him? He could hardly say; but he went about on fire with a mixture of elation and anxiety – and the flames were fanned still higher when, returning to his room in the evening, he found a book lying on the table beside his bed. It was an edition of Shakespeare's plays, in English, handsomely bound in blue leather. His heart jumped. Who else could have put it there? The moment he picked it up, he saw a sheet of white paper protruding slightly from between the pages. The writing was big and bold: 'I am so sorry. I look for a chance to talk. K.' Again he had the sensation that some invisible but irresistible force was reaching out at him from miles away.

Next morning the Prince sent for him. Joseph, arriving in his book-lined study, was reminded of the day when Harry Maguire had taken him to see Richard Marsh at Lordship: he had the same feeling of being in the presence of the headmaster. This time, however, there was no inquisition – only an apology.

'Don't know what got into the fellow,' said Mironov abruptly. 'Too much champagne, I'm afraid. Apart from that, he was all right. But I told him it wouldn't do. Sent him home. You'll be hearing from him presently. Meanwhile, please accept my apologies, on his behalf.'

'Thank you, sir. I appreciate that.'

'Good. *We* appreciated the way you handled the horse. Most impressive. And now – something more amusing. Weather's cheered up.' He turned stiffly in his chair and craned his head to look out of the window. 'My daughter wondered if you would like to go with them for a picnic in the forest?'

'Well! Thank you. When?'

'Today. They'll be leaving about 11.30. It'll give you a chance to see the area we call the Barrel Factory – where the best oaks grow.'

'Thank you. I'd like that very much.'

'Good. They'll be glad to have you with them, in case they get stuck or anything, after the rain. Outside the front of the house at 11.30, then.'

The storm had cleared the air and brought in fresher, more invigorating weather: fleecy clouds rode high in the sky, and a breeze tempered the sun's heat. Just after 11.20 Joseph came round the front of the house to find three carriages standing ready in line-ahead formation, each drawn by two horses. The first vehicle was the most elaborate, with a roof over the passenger compartment, and was obviously for the ladies. The second was also for passengers, but the third was already loaded with servants and their gear: one of the assistant cooks, with wicker baskets full of plates and cutlery, and great hampers of food, and two of the kitchen boys to build the fires. Joseph chatted idly with them for a few minutes, but his mind was on someone else. What would she wear? How would she look? Who would come with her?

His heart sank when the front door of the house opened and out came Princess Yelena in a tight fawn riding habit, radiating disapproval. A few seconds later there was a boisterous rush, and a mass of children poured out into the drive: the two Mironov boys, in pale green blouses and trousers, and three female cousins, about their age, who had come to stay, swathed like their elders in long dresses of white cotton. With them, dragged half off his feet, came Herr Koch, the German tutor, a pale, myopic young man, with wiry black hair already receding from his forehead, clad in an ill-fitting dark suit and pointed black shoes. Finally, at the back, carrying a white parasol, came Katya, cool as a lily in a pink-and-white striped dress and a broad-brimmed straw hat, with a ribbon of the same two colours round the crown. Whereas her aunt had climbed straight into the front carriage, she greeted the drivers with a smile and a word before she herself stepped aboard.

'Let's go to the Climbing Tree!' shouted Ivan, dancing round the carriages.

'No! The Tree with Three Feet!' cried Dmitri. 'And the Seven Dials. And the Round Pond.'

'We can't go everywhere,' said the leading driver respectfully. 'Which is it to be?'

'The Climbing Tree area's got the best mushrooms,' said Katya. 'I vote for that.'

After more clamour, those in favour of the Climbing Tree prevailed. The ladies and two of the girls rode in the first carriage, the third girl, the boys and Herr Koch in the second. Because there was most space there, Joseph climbed in with them, and off they went, out of the park, past the field in which the *fête champêtre* had taken place, and into the dappled green world of the forest.

The boys were merciless in harrassing their tutor. '*Achtung*, Herr Koch!' Ivan cried, in English edged with a creditable German accent. 'Ze wolves vill eat you!'

'Ent ze bears!' Dmitri chipped in. 'Zey are very dengerous!'

'Then you must guard me, please,' said Koch, also in English. His tone suggested that he was well used to being teased, and did not mind it. 'I see we have a gun, at least,' he added, pointing at a rifle which stood upright in a deep leather holster behind the driver.

'What's the Climbing Tree?' Joseph asked.

'It's a huge oak with hundreds of branches you can climb right to the top,' said Ivan. 'And from the top you can see for miles.'

'What about the Tree with Three Roots?'

'That's nothing special,' said Ivan dismissively.

'Rubbish!' Dmitri threatened him with a mock punch on the ear. 'It's got three terrific roots, with a space underneath them as big as a house.'

'Not *our* house,' Ivan corrected him.

'No, but an *izba*.'

'Oh well, an *izba*.'

'We have a camp there, anyway, and in the winter the bears come and live in it. At least, we think they do, because it always looks different when we go back in the spring.'

The sandy track, flanked by wide grass verges, wound deep into the forest. Puddles left by the storm splashed up round the carriage wheels; the horses' legs became spattered with mud. Trees and undergrowth glistened with moisture, and the spiders' webs slung from bushes were spangled with drops of water. It was as if the rain, in washing the whole wood, had left it bathed in primeval freshness. The only sounds were the jingling of the horses' bells, the creak of the carriages and occasional bird-calls.

'*Wunderschön!*' exclaimed Koch, surprising Joseph, who thought that the professor had no time for the country.

'You like the forest?' he asked.

'*Aber nein!*' said Koch sharply. 'To be alone in it would make me *ganz nervös*. But I see that it is beautiful.'

Joseph's spirits were as high as those of the boys, if for a different reason. As always, his status in the party was undefined: certainly not one of the family, yet not quite a servant, he was hovering somewhere in between. He recognised that his invitation to the picnic was a form of redress for the insult he had suffered, but the knowledge did not quell his conviction that it had been Katya's idea to ask him. No one else would have thought of it – certainly not the Prince, still less his sister.

Every now and then the travellers came to a junction of tracks, with grassy rides leading off to right and left between the trees, which were mainly birch and larch. Here and there a pile of logs stacked beside the track showed where the estate foresters had been at work, but mostly there was nothing that Joseph could see to distinguish one ride from the next. Then the ground began to fall. The track led down to a ford, where a river ran fast but shallow over a stony bed, and beyond it the forest changed into one of oak and beech. Here the trees were older, larger, more stately, spreading their branches widely, with grassy glades between. At last Ivan gave a shout of 'There it is!' and leapt to the ground, with the carriage still moving, to run the last hundred yards.

The Climbing Tree was a colossal oak, set on a slope, and must have been hundreds of years old. Its trunk was at least ten feet thick near the base, and its lower limbs were as massive as the trunks of ordinary trees. Some twelve feet above the ground, where the stem divided into three, dozens of smaller branches, growing out horizontally from the uprights, made a perfect aerial maze for human monkeys.

'Look – I'll show you,' cried Ivan, running up the hill to a spot where one of the lower boughs rested its extremity on the ground. All he had to do was step on to it and, steadying himself with a hand on another branch at the level of his head, walk straight along it to the main fork. This, he announced from on high, was the tribe's headquarters. Within seconds, all five children were aloft, shrieking contradictory instructions at each other. Even the girls, constricted as they were by their long dresses and frilly underwear, could easily reach the fork; and though forbidden to go any higher by Princess Yelena, on the grounds that they would spoil their clothes, they nevertheless began to wriggle and filter their way upwards.

On the ground the servants unharnessed the horses and staked them out on tethers to graze. Then they bustled about to spread rugs, set out chairs and tables, and, at a discreet distance downwind, light fires for cooking. Herr Koch, resisting the boys' attempts to lure him into the tree, settled down on a rug with a volume of Pushkin's *Eugene Onegin*, keeping up occasional polite conversation with Princess

Yelena, who had brought out her crochet work and made continuous but ineffective efforts to stop the boys climbing higher. Katya took a basket and wandered away out of sight along the hillside in search of mushrooms.

Watching her pink-and-white striped form disappear among the trees, Joseph wished fervently that he could think of some excuse for going with her, or after her. As it was, he had had an idea which would be of interest to the boys. From the trunk of his carriage he fetched a coil of thick hemp rope, carried in case one team of horses had to pull another from the mud. With it slung round his neck, he climbed rapidly to a certain high branch which, he had noticed, overhung an open space, and wriggled out along it on his belly. Above the middle of the gap he made one end of the rope secure and let the rest fall, so that it hung with its end just reaching the ground. After testing his knots by yanking at them, he went down hand-over-hand, to the great alarm of Princess Yelena, who was convinced that he must fall. On the ground again, he tied the rope in two big knots, one on top of the other, so that they made a bulge on which a child could sit, about two feet from the ground, with a tail of rope hanging below it.

Ivan, immediately spotting what he was at, scrambled down to the main fork and demanded first use of the swing.

'You'll have to hold on tight,' Joseph warned him. 'Unless you *want* to fly off at the other end. In which case, just let go when you start coming up again.'

'I'll fly,' said Ivan. 'Give me the rope, quick.'

Holding the tail end, Joseph walked to the base of the tree and flicked the rope upwards so that the boy could catch it.

'Pass the end over the branch and give it back to me,' he instructed. Then, once he had hold of it again, he said, 'Take a good grip on the rope, pull yourself up, and sit on the knot, with one leg on either side.'

Ivan was agile enough to accomplish the movement without difficulty. 'Let go! Let go!' he shouted.

'All right – and when I call *now, you* let go. Ready . . . steady . . . *fly!*'

Down went the boy in a sweeping arc, brushing the grass with his feet and curving up again; but when Joseph called *Now!*, he merely gave a loud yell and hung on tight, so that he swung backwards and then forwards again, like a giant pendulum.

At once the swing became immensely popular, and Joseph was

high aloft, adjusting the anchor-point slightly, when he heard a call below and saw a pink-and-white figure come running under the tree.

'Where's Mr Clements?' Katya cried.

'Here,' he called. 'What's the matter?'

'Quick! There's a bird with a broken wing. A jay. We must catch it or put it out of its misery.'

'Just a minute.'

He was down the tree in a flash, to find her flushed and panting.

'Don't be too long,' said Princess Yelena. 'Lunch is nearly ready.'

Joseph deputed Herr Koch to take charge of the swing, and a minute later he was where he passionately longed to be: alone with Katya in the middle of a wood. For as long as they were in sight, she hurried, holding up her skirt in one hand to skip lightly over the grass; but then, as they came round the side of the hill and entered a dense thicket of hazel, she suddenly stopped and turned to face him with a curious expression – half amused, half anxious – on her face.

'There's no bird,' she said. 'I invented it, so that we could have a talk.'

'Oh!' Joseph felt himself blushing as anticipation surged up through him.

'Yesterday was terrible,' she said. 'I've never been so ashamed in my life. I couldn't be more sorry.'

'You've nothing to apologise for. It wasn't your fault.'

'It was, in a way. I felt for you dreadfully.'

She stood looking up at him, only a couple of feet away. In the shade of the wood her eyes looked greener, her teeth whiter than ever. Before he knew what he was doing, as if something outside him was guiding his arm, he had taken her chin in his right hand and lifted her face towards him. A moment later he kissed her on the mouth.

A shudder ran through her body, coming up from below. She gave a tiny cry, half smothered. But she did not pull away. Far from it: she opened her lips wider and pushed towards him. The basket fell from her hand on to the grass. Her hands came round his shoulders, and he drew her hard against him, one hand in the small of her back, one on her behind. Her hat was in the way, digging into his ear. He reached up and pushed it off, so that her hair fell free. Still her mouth was pressed in his, her tongue flickering across his teeth. He had the impression that he was falling: an actual, physical sensation of dropping into a void. The forest, the birds, the picnic, the other humans

– everything had vanished. When he opened his eyes, all he could see was soft fair hair and one small ear, about an inch away.

At last she drew off and half fell against his chest, shuddering. He held her tight with one hand, and stroked her hair. He too was shaking. 'Don't cry,' he whispered. 'It's all right.'

'I'm not crying,' she gasped. 'It's relief. Shock. Dear God! What's happening to us?'

'It started the first day I saw you, making jam.'

'I know.' She raised her head and looked into his eyes with a combination of incredulity and longing that made him breathless. He kissed her again, harder, longer, lifting her clear off the ground. Under the cotton dress, her body felt wonderfully pliant. Again, she was shuddering when they drew apart.

'What can we do?' His voice sounded hoarse.

'God knows. Nothing now. We must go back.'

'I can't come back with you. It would be too obvious. I'd give us away.'

'Go on then. Be looking for the bird. You've seen it, but you can't catch it.' She smiled, lifting her eyebrows so that her forehead wrinkled.

'You've dropped your mushrooms.'

'Oh!'

The basket had rolled over and spilt half its contents on the grass. He went down on his knees, facing her, and began to pick the little yellow mushrooms up, one at a time. Since he could not take his eyes off her face, his fingers were not very efficient at locating the fallen treasure. Then, as she stood up and replaced her hat, she said in a low, thick voice, 'Tonight.'

'What about it?'

'Come to the swimming hut at midnight.'

He stared at her. 'You mean it?'

'Of course.'

SIX

Lost in the Snow: December 1919

THE MOMENT he passed into the lee of that blessed wood, the temperature rose and the force went out of the wind. Now: plough on and risk disaster, or stop and make some sort of bivouac among the trees? Neither alternative was alluring – but a decision was needed. 'It's horrible, boys,' he said, 'but we've got to stop.'

What with the snow, the cold, the oncoming darkness and the lack of comforts or facilities, his struggle to establish camp tested him severely. Because he had no enclosure in which to confine the stallions, he was forced to tether each to a separate tree while he unpacked the stores from their backs – itself no easy task, for the animals bumped and blundered against each other in the gloom. As quickly as he could, working by feel, he loosened their girths, left their saddles in place, got their rugs on top and put on their leg-bandages.

Most of the trees were young spruce, growing close together, and Joseph saw that if he could strip two or three of them of their lower branches, he would open out a kind of hollow cavern in which the horses could stand, protected from the worst of wind and snow; so he felt in his haversack for his folding saw and began to cut away the small branches, hard against the trunk. At least the work kept him warm – and it also gave him firewood, for most of the branches had died from lack of light, and the twigs at the end were brittle enough for him to break up by the handful. Occasional cascades of snow came filtering down from above, but the forest floor was still mostly dry, and when he put a match to his little pile of tinder, it flared immediately. Carefully, methodically, he fed the infant fire with twigs until it had a proper hold, then gave it bigger branches. As it spat and crackled, Boy began to snort, and in the leaping shafts of light Joseph saw the stallion's eyes rolling, so he got up and went to stand at his head and talk him into accepting this outlandish camp as a delightful open-air stable.

At first the fire gave out scarcely any heat, but its light enabled Joseph to see to enlarge his cavern until it was big enough for him to lead the horses in, turn them round and tether them on either side of two central trees. Then he set about the laborious process of melting snow in his billycan to provide all three of them with a drink. He packed his one canvas bucket with snow from a drift out in the open and then poured into it the water he had already heated over the fire. The amount of liquid produced was pitifully small, but by repeating the process several times he eventually managed to give each horse a gallon or more. Then he pulled out the bag of oats which Lubin had given him and half-filled the bucket. Boy, to whom he offered it first, just stood with his head hanging. 'Come on, lad,' said Joseph gently. '*Yesh! Yesh!* – Eat! Eat!' When he would not, he passed the bucket to Min, who tucked in with his usual enthusiasm.

Mundane tasks kept him absorbed for a couple of hours. Then waves of exhaustion started to sweep over him again, and he realised he must devise some shelter of his own. Branches seemed the best answer. He cut several green boughs from nearby trees, shook the snow off their thick, glossy needles and laid them in a heap beside the fire. Then at last he dug out the remains of Lubin's food and slowly ate it. Never had rancid balls of meat and soggy dough tasted better; he could have done with five times the amount, but washed down what he had with a few mouthfuls of smoky warm water. Then he checked the horses once more and found that they felt surprisingly warm: generating their own heat beneath their rugs, they were gently warming the air beneath the hollowed-out trees.

Outside the canopy snowflakes were still filtering down, but less heavily than before. For a while Joseph dried his sodden boots by holding his feet out to the fire; then he rolled himself in his own blanket and burrowed into his heap of resiny spruce branches, with some below him for insulation from the ground and some above for protection from the air. Inside, only just able to see out to the firelight flickering round the glade, he felt like a hedgehog settling down to hibernate for the winter; but at least he was a hedgehog with a loaded Luger within reach. A sense of security enveloped him, and although he had been in many beds more comfortable than this one, it was not long before he fell asleep.

*

Dawn found him stiff and cold. He had turned often, trying to curl ever tighter into a ball as he searched semi-consciously for warmth; and once during the night he had come wide awake when one of the horses whinnied. Emerging rapidly from his lair, he had poked up the fire to make a light, in case a wolf or a bear was on the prowl; but the stallions settled again without further alarm, and eventually he had gone back to sleep.

He struggled out of his lair, calling to the horses, stamped his feet and swung his arms round his body. His breath smoked in the air and caught in his throat, so low had the temperature fallen. But his spirits rose when he saw that the paling sky was clear and pricked with stars: as the snow clouds rolled away, frost had cracked down. He found the horses shivering under their rugs; by the look of the ground, they had hardly moved all night. He must get them moving. First, though, he fed them the remains of the oats and went through the tedious routine of creating water. The stallions flinched as he tightened the icy girths round their stomachs; for the moment he left their rugs in place over their saddles, kicked the fire apart, checked that he had left nothing behind, and moved out into the open.

A new world greeted him, a world coloured pearly grey from edge to edge. Snow lay in an unbroken blanket as far as he could see. The sky – pale blue-grey, like the shell of hoopoe's egg – brightened as he watched it, and a gigantic red glow flared up over the horizon ahead of him. A few moments later the rim of the sun appeared, blazing crimson, and the snow all round him, turning from grey to pink and white, began to sparkle as if scattered with thousands of diamonds. The sight was stupendous, but it gave him pause, for the line of his previous day's advance lay straight towards the rising sun, and he realised that for the last two hours at least he had been heading due east. Nor – he could now see – did the wood which had sheltered him correspond in any way to the one which Lubin had described.

Should he return to the river and search again for the elusive Wolf's Cairn? Or should he carry on along the path he had followed this far, and whenever a chance presented itself, turn right, towards the south? Reason told him that the first would be the safer, but he knew it was psychologically impossible: any form of retreat was bad for morale. He had to go forward.

Even on level stretches, the snow lay a foot thick, and where the wind had piled it into hollows, the drifts were deep enough to swallow a man. At every step it creaked like leather beneath his weight.

Progress was slow and difficult, and his morale fluctuated sharply: at first the beauty and brilliance of the morning sent it sky-high, and he was able to keep his hunger at bay by eating handfuls of snow. The best moment of the day came after about two hours, when he saw some slender, man-made object on the skyline ahead and discovered that it was a wooden sign-post, or the remains of one. Wind and rain had long since erased whatever writing it once had borne, but two of its four grey arms were still in place, and one of them pointed to the south, the direction which instinct told him to take.

Thereafter the day became steadily more of an ordeal. The horses were listless after their meagre rations and their night in the open, and needed frequent coaxing. Joseph himself felt increasingly tired; his eyes watered from the glare and his head ached. Although the sun shone continuously as it wheeled in its low arc across the sky, the temperature never rose above freezing-point, and the crust on the snow never softened. Later, as he looked back on that endless day, he found that its hours blurred into each other and that most of its details had vanished. At one point in the afternoon a moment of excitement cleared his head. As he came up a long slope, he saw an animal padding downhill towards them over the snow. '*Volk!*' he exclaimed out loud, 'wolf!' – as if to warn the horses, only to realise that his sense of perspective had become distorted, and that the creature, far from being a wolf several hundred yards off, was nothing but a fox fewer than fifty paces away. At the sound of his voice it stopped and stood looking, before wheeling round and cantering away. The sight of its russet coat, glowing ruddily against the snow, set Joseph wondering about how wild animals could survive in such a climate. He realised that carrion-eaters like foxes and wolves were relatively well off, since creatures such as birds, rats and mice were liable to succumb first, and their bodies would offer food to the scavengers.

Another facet of that day which he never forgot was the way the snows turned blue late in the afternoon. When the sun went down, an astonishing transformation came over the steppe, as if the whole landscape had been overlaid with a film of gunmetal: hollows darkened into pools of pewter, and smooth crests gleamed dully as though clad in unpolished steel. He had seen something similar at St Petersburg, in the far north, often enough; but there the landscape was variegated by buildings and bridges and islands, and the expanse of snow was broken up; here it stretched for ever, like a dead and frozen sea. The effect was one of terrible cold and loneliness, and

Joseph – already close to despair at the thought of another night in the open – felt ready to lie down and die.

Then everything changed. All day he had urged the horses to the next crest by pretending that when they came over it, they would find salvation in the next valley. Now he did the same thing once more – and by God, as they came over one more broad-backed hill, there below them, in the next shallow declivity, lay a farm.

'Manino!' he croaked. 'Come on, boys. We're there.'

The crust on the snow was tougher now, but he crunched through it joyously as he went down the hill at a spanking pace. Soon he could see that the wooden buildings below him were set out round three sides of a yard, much as at Lubin's, with the house at the far end, and a two-storey barn nearest to him. Around them were three or four paddocks, whose post-and-rail fences stood out clearly against the blanket of snow. Away to his left, some two or three hundred yards from the farm, was a triangular patch of forest, set in a corner of the valley, which looked from its straight edges as if it had been planted to furnish firewood and timber.

Not until he was almost at the first fence did he realise that something was amiss. Already he had seen that there were no horses or cattle in the fields, but this seemed normal: with snow lying deep, he would have expected them all to be under cover. Then, at the last moment, he noticed something else: no smoke was rising from either of the house's two squat chimneys. A stab of alarm half-checked him: he suddenly felt sure that the place was deserted – an impression reinforced by the unmarked surface of the snow.

All the same, he approached with care, wary of an attack by dogs such as young Lubin had prevented two nights before. Having tied the stallions to the fence, he went cautiously ahead to explore. Dusk was closing in: already the light was thick. But he saw that the snow in the farmyard *had* been disturbed, scuffed about, though not much trodden down.

A door of the two-storey barn stood open. He went across to it and was about to look in when a sudden movement inside made him jump back. Out fluttered a flock of black chickens, which ran all round his feet, skidding on the snow, with their heads turned on one side and their bright little eyes looking up at him expectantly. At once he saw that they were frantic with hunger. How long had they been abandoned? And why had their owners gone away?

A few quick strides took him to the door of the house. Virgin snow showed that no one had been in or out since the blizzard. Although sure that it was a useless formality, he thumped on the wooden boards, waited a moment, then pushed his way in. No gust of warmth came out to meet him – only a sickening smell: mostly the normal stink of a *hata*, made up of sweat and smoke and old cabbage-cookery, but with something sweet and sinister superimposed on it. Inside, the hovel was almost completely dark. He needed a light. Leaving the door ajar, he returned to the barn and found some straw, which he twisted into a brand. Back on the porch, he lit one end of it, and advanced into the single room with the makeshift torch held in front of him.

As individual straws flared, died down and ignited neighbours, tongues of light flickered randomly over furniture, walls and ceiling. In the middle of the room he made out a rough wooden table, with a samovar standing on it, and a home-made bench along one side. Across the far right-hand corner, at chest height, was a shelf bearing several icons, whose surrounds of gold-leaf and coloured glass flashed light back at him. Beside them, strings of onions were suspended from nails. In the right-hand wall was an open fireplace, and beside it a blackened kettle, suspended on a swinging arm. Yet it was the left-hand back corner of the room that caught and held his attention. In it loomed the bulk of the stove, the most important feature of the household. Its sides were not tiled, as in grander dwellings, but finished in plain mud-plaster, and from the bottom of it, at one side, projected the wide shelf on which the family must have slept.

There was something lying on that platform: a long, bulky object, or several. To see them properly, Joseph had to go closer. His brand flickered and almost went out. Cursing quietly, he opened the bunch of straw out slightly and waited for it to flare again. Then at last he could see, all too clearly. From the grey-brown bedclothes protruded a hand, two hands; a face; another hand; a smaller face; the top of a third head – an entire family, dead.

With hand clapped over his nose and mouth, he scuttled back across the room and slammed the door. Outside he waited till he was clear of the house before gasping in lungfuls of clean, frosty air. *Tif,* he thought in sudden terror. Typhus. Or was it what the peasants called the Black Death? Those terrible faces were black, and grotesquely swollen. One was certainly that of a child. One, he was pretty sure, belonged to a woman, the third to a man. That was the sweet and filthy smell – the smell of death. How long had the bodies lain there, for God's sake? A few days, anyway. Not that many, for the chickens were surviving. But had some member of the family escaped and gone for help? It looked like that, because there was evidently no horse on the place? And was this farm Manino, or somewhere else?

Joseph felt weak and indecisive, afraid that merely by entering that house of death he had exposed himself to some lethal infection. With an effort he pulled himself together. Typhus, he knew, was carried by lice, and in any case, at Katya's insistence, he had had an inoculation against it. Spotted or black fever he was less sure about; but surely he could not have been contaminated so long after the victims had died?

Whatever the risk, he had no option but to spend the night in the farm. Daylight had almost gone. The stallions were still shivering on the paddock fence. He went to bring them in. Lack of light hampered him. Having opened the big doors of the barn, he led the horses inside, but then had to grope about for something to which he could tie them. Undoubtedly there were lamps in the house, but he had no intention of going back in. Might not the people have left one out here? He struck a match and peered about. Yes! One simple lamp made of black metal hung on a nail near the door. He took it down, shook it, felt that it contained oil, and a moment later had it burning.

The barn made an excellent stable. Two wide stalls, separated by a wooden partition, with hay-racks and mangers at the end, served perfectly as quarters for Min and Boy. Still better, there was plenty for them to eat. In an iron bin with a hinged lid, Joseph found a store of good-looking oats. Beside the bin stood an old-fashioned, hand-cranked roller-mill, and it took him only a few minutes to process two handsome feeds. The loft above the stalls turned out to be half-full of good hay, made that summer by the smell of it, and he filled the racks by throwing armfuls down. Water he got from a well in the centre of the yard: he pulled several feet of line off the roller, took the wooden bucket, turned it upside-down and dropped it rim-first down the pitch-black shaft. It fell many feet before, with a rich smack, it hit the surface, and the water which he wound to the surface was several degrees warmer than the air. As he worked, he was haunted by the thought that either he was stealing from the dead or trespassing on the property of people still alive.

Suddenly, from further down the yard, came a loud bellow. He stood rooted. The horses whipped up their heads. What in God's name was that? A cow, of course, he told himself: calm down. The poor brute must be starving: better see to her too.

He found her tethered in the end building, gaunt, brown and white, apparently a Hereford cross, with the earth floor around her back-end covered in dung. Loose at her side was a little calf the same colours, only a few weeks old. At least it had been suckling her, so that she was not bursting with milk, but she looked hollow with hunger and thirst, and when he brought her water, she drained the bucket at one draught. To eat, he gave her the same as the horses, for there was no alternative that he could see.

Back in the barn, he got another surprise. He was peering up into the rafters, trying to see where the chickens had gone to roost, when from somewhere high up he heard a faint miaow, and there on a beam he spotted a furry, silver-grey cat with a white shirt-front, staring down at him. His heart and mind took another of those backward leaps which he was powerless to prevent. All at once he heard Katya telling him how she had gone into the kitchen at Nikolsk and found their grey cat Morka sitting on the stove: that, she had told him solemnly, was the infallible sign of an important stranger arriving – and a few days later he – Joseph – had come to stay. He certainly did not mock her superstitions, but he did not subscribe to them either, and now he did not take the appearance of another grey cat to indicate anything except that one more animal had been left behind. As he tried to coax it down, it opened its mouth silently in a wide, pink gape, but it declined to respond to his overtures, and he left it while he saw to his own affairs.

The horses were fed, watered, rugged-up and comfortable: so comfortable, in fact, that Boy had already lain down – something Joseph had hardly ever seen him do. They needed no more attention until the morning. He, on the other hand, urgently needed food. The thought of those onions hanging in the house was almost irresistible – yet he held out against it, and against the idea of getting any other form of food from the house, repelled by fear of contamination. Hunger turned his thoughts to the chickens: if he caught one, he could cut it into joints and boil the pieces in a billy-can of water. Then he reflected that, unless rats had eaten them, there should be eggs about the buildings. Maybe the cat had eaten the rats first. A search with the lamp soon proved him right; in odd corners he found three nests, of four, five and nine eggs. Boiling eggs would be quicker than boiling chicken. A fire, then. Finding an old plank, he smashed it into splinters and quickly had a blaze going in the threshold of the barn. Another search revealed a store of firewood in a shed at one side of the house, and, joy of joys, a sack of potatoes. Water from the well seemed to take a long time to boil, but at last it began to seethe and tumble, and in not much more than half an hour he was scorching his mouth on potatoes with soft-boiled eggs broken over them. Salt, he needed: salt, pepper, butter, bread, and a good many other things – but he ate till he could eat no more, and washed his hands and his bristly face. Then, as he sat by the fire on an upturned wooden bucket, recovering, he felt something brush against his hip, and, looking round, found the grey cat polishing its coat against him.

'So you came down after all,' he said, lifting it on to his lap, where it stood with its tail straight up, rubbing one ear against the front of his wolfskin waistcoat and purring loudly. 'I reckon you've done a good job on the rats, whatever.'

The cat was a female, so he called her Moorka. Since he reckoned that, no matter how many rats she had killed, she must be hungry, he milked one of the cow's teats into a bowl and set it before her. The result was that she became his inseparable companion, following in his footsteps about the farmyard and curling up to sleep on top of him when he lay down in the hay.

A full belly, the warmth of the barn, his exertions during the day, temporary release from anxiety – all combined to overpower him with drowsiness. Even so, he lay awake with his mind turning on the macabre scene in the house. He could not make out what had happened. Had all three of the family died simultaneously? Had someone gone for help? And if so, why had he taken all the horses with him? How long had be been gone? Would he come back?

Morning left most of the mysteries unsolved. Again dawn came up clear, with a crunching frost, and from the state of the snow Joseph confirmed that nobody had left the farm since the onset of the blizzard. In the stable barn the freshest alien horse-droppings were at least three or four days old. The chickens, when he fed them oats, ate like birds possessed. From all the signs he reckoned that catastrophe must have struck at least five days before.

The lapse of time made him loath to re-enter the stricken house; for all he knew, the bodies might be releasing toxic emissions or lethal germs. He cursed his own medical ignorance; he did not even know, for instance, whether it would be safe for him to go in to find salt with a wet handkerchief tied over his nose and mouth. Why had he never questioned Katya more closely on such subjects?

In the end he remained out of doors and eschewed salt, onions, sugar, tea and all the other comforts which the *khata* might have afforded him. For breakfast he brewed up what the peasants called *mamalyga* – coarse-ground maize boiled in water; without any season ing, it tasted like paper or glue, but at least it filled him. He also boiled another eight eggs, of which he ate two and kept six. With a heavy heart he killed, skinned and boiled one of the chickens, an inquisitive brown bird which was all too trusting and came right up to his feet. As at Lubin's, he was tempted to stay put for another night and give the horses a rest, for when he took their rugs off to groom them, he was shocked to find how much condition they had lost. Boy, the more highly strung, looked worst, and was showing all his ribs; but even Min appeared to have shed half a pood – an English stone. Yet he dared not linger: he had to put distance between himself and the advancing Reds, and also, still more urgently, between himself and the three putrescent corpses.

Even in the bright morning sun his map was almost useless, since it did not mark individual farms or country tracks. The line of the main road slanted seductively away south-eastwards, bold and straight to Izyum, Artyomovsk and the massed towns of the coal-producing Donetz area, beyond which lay his destination, Taganrog. But on either side of the highway huge open spaces were marked only by rivers wandering vaguely and cloud-like puffs that indicated hills. Two days lost in the steppe had been enough to convince him that his attempt to move across country was misconceived; after that experience, he decided that, no matter what the state of the roads, he must return to them – otherwise he and the horses would not survive the winter, let alone the Bolshevik advance. His aim, now, was to regain the main road. He knew that it must lie to the east or north-east, and in clear weather he could navigate by the sun; but to make worthwhile progress, he needed a track that led in the right direction. The sole indication of any path leaving the farm was a line of trees which led away to the south: he decided to start in that direction and try his luck.

His own preparations for departure were simple. He loaded up all the oats the horses could carry, including two small extra sackfuls, and let them go on eating hay until the last moment. He stowed maize flour, boiled eggs and the chicken, now cooling, into his pack. He did not like to be helping himself in this way, for it amounted to stealing. Or could one steal from the dead? Equally, there seemed no point in leaving money: the next people into that stricken household might be Bolsheviks, and he had no intention of giving anything to them.

Yet as he worked, he became haunted by fear that the farm might lie unvisited for months, with the snow building round it, locked in the grip of winter. What, then, should he do about the animals? How could he leave the cow and her charming calf to a slow death from hunger and thirst? How could he abandon Morka the cat or leave the chickens to starve? Should he shoot the cow and her calf, hit the cat on the head and strangle the fowls, to make sure that none of them suffered? Should he set fire to the buildings and purify the site?

The worry delayed him, sitting on a block of stone beside the well. He hated the idea of animals being left to die; and yet he could not kill them. Rousing himself, he drew bucket after bucket of water from the well and filled every receptacle he could find, stationing them all round the wall of the building in which the cow was tethered. Then he brought armfuls of hay from the loft and banked it up so that she was almost hemmed in by it. Finally he released her tether, so that she was free to move about. There was no point in letting her out, for she would find nothing to eat outside, and the wolves would get her calf if she wandered away from the buildings. He had given her provisions for a week at least. If people returned within that time, she would survive. Otherwise, she would die. He had given her a chance, and there was nothing else he could do. For the chickens, he dumped all the remaining oats in heaps round the stable barn, and set them troughs full of water. For the cat, he killed one more of the chickens and split it open with his knife: how long that would last her, he could not tell; but at least she could supplement it with rats and mice.

Still heavy-hearted, he prepared to leave. The horses moved stiffly as he led them out; but there was already some warmth in the sun, and they seemed glad to be on the move. Before he passed the house for the last time, he crossed himself, touching Katya's figure of St Nicholas with his other hand, and said a prayer for the dead souls inside. Then he walked away.

After perhaps two minutes, when he turned for a final look at the buildings, he was startled to see a movement close behind him. Something dark appeared, disappeared and appeared again in the track that he had beaten through the snow. Stopping the horses, he was amazed to find the cat come bounding neatly after them.

He considered bombarding her with snowballs, to make her turn back, but she ran straight to him and with loud purrs began to rub herself against his boots. 'Sorry, my love,' he said. 'Your legs are too short for this job. You'll have to stay.' But even as he spoke he bent down and picked her up, and a second later she was on his left shoulder, balancing precariously, bush tail in the air. When he put her down again and started to walk once more, she followed, at some peril to herself, dodging in and out of the hoofs of Boy, who was leading. Twice more Joseph tried to shake her off, and when he saw he could not, he lifted her on to Minoru's back, where she crouched, sphinx-like, on top of the sack of oats.

The horse appeared not to mind in the least. 'Of course,' Joseph said to him. 'You always used to fool about with Matilda, the tabby at Lordship.' Minoru was a cat-fancier at heart. So they went on, with the party improbably increased from three to four.

SEVEN

By the River: Summer 1912

H E HAD CREPT down from his room at 11.30, wearing blue jersey and trousers, and soft-soled shoes. The sky was overcast, the air soft and still; with the moon hidden behind clouds, the night was very black. Down in the yard he paused, looking at the house. One light still burned in the servants' quarters on the top floor, but otherwise the place was dark. That was a measure of how little he knew about her: he had no idea where her bedroom was, what it was like, or how it lay in relation to the other rooms. How would she come downstairs? Through which door would she emerge? Would she use one of the servants' tunnels? If she did, or if she came from the front of the house, he would not see her, so there was no point in waiting there.

He slipped away, under the arch, through the shrubbery. Before he came out on to the open park land, he paused in the blackness under the trees and let his eyes accustom themselves to the faint night light. Nothing moved in the park, and presently he went on along the mown grass path. In less than ten minutes he was at the green-painted iron gate. Holding the latch in both hands to muffle any click, he gently disengaged it and went through.

Under the old trees on the river bank, it was again intensely dark, and he had to wait a minute before he could see anything at all. Then he made out the square shape of the hut, and the angular outline of the plank bench. He went and sat on it to wait. He was at least ten minutes early – an eternity. Reason kept warning him that he was playing with fire. The consequences of discovery scarcely bore thinking about. He would certainly be sent away by Mironov. He might well lose his job at the Imperial Stud. Prince Viasemski, though temporarily disgraced, would probably challenge him to a duel – indeed, perhaps it had been some telepathic intuition about what Joseph was feeling that had made the fiancé insult him. All this was obvious – yet it weighed nothing against the fact that she had kissed him.

From time to time the river let out small, liquid noises, ripples and gurgles, and once an owl made him start by giving its dry screech in a tree right over his head. Now and then a fish jumped, smacking back into the water with a splash. An occasional, wandering breath of air moved up or down the stream.

He sat with his back to the river, facing the path, willing her to come. Yet when she did, she took him by surprise. So used was he to seeing her wear white or some pastel colour that he expected a pale shape to materialise out of the night. Instead, without a sound, there was suddenly something dark right beside him – a presence, a scent of lavender, a quick, quiet exclamation. He leapt up and reached out for her. His left hand landed on her shoulder, and in an instant she was in his arms, passionately returning his embrace.

'You came!'

She did not answer, but nodded her head against him, rubbing her cheek up and down on his chest. He could feel that she was wearing a scarf over her head, and a dress of thin, dark wool. There was something hanging over her left shoulder – a bundle.

'What's this?'

'A rug. Come.' She moved away, leading him by the hand to the deepest shadows of all, beside the changing hut. There she laid her bundle on the ground and took off her headscarf.

Suddenly she demanded in a low whisper, 'Make love to me!'

'Here?'

'Yes.' With a sudden rustling, swirling movement, she wriggled out of her dress, pulling it up over her head and letting it fall to the ground. From being an invisible presence, she was transformed into a living ivory statue, pale and slender as marble, yet hot to his touch. A few seconds later his own clothes were on the grass and he had pinned her to the rug beneath him.

Her hunger was as great as his, but at first she did not know how to satisfy it. Sensing this, he silently guided her hands, lifted and spread her limbs, gave her all the time he could. Yet inevitably it was he who reached a climax first; the tightness and perfection of her young body were more than he could resist.

She clung to him tightly until his shudders died away, then whispered in his ear, 'That was nice. Do it again.'

'In a minute.'

'No – now!'

'I can't. Have to wait a minute.'

'Why?'

He lifted his head and looked down at her face, barely visible in the dark, then laughed. 'Oh my love! Nobody can do it twice running, just like that. The system takes time to recover. You'll see.' Again he guided her hand, kissing her as he did so. 'Give it a minute. Am I squashing you?'

'Not at all.'

'Wait, then.'

In the event he was surprised by the speed of his own recovery – and this time he was relaxed enough to carry her with him. Presently she began to writhe and groan, calling out 'More! More!', softly at first, but then quite loud. For a few moments he smothered her cries by kissing her on the mouth, responding ever more vigorously to her arousal, but then suddenly a great surge convulsed her whole body and she twisted her head sideways to give a hoarse roar, right beside his ear. The sound was so raw, so intense, so animal-like that it jolted him out of all control and care.

For a long time neither of them moved. Then she said, very slow and drawn-out, 'How extra-or-dinary! How un-be-lievable!'

'Yes,' he whispered. 'You are un-be-lievable.' Moving very gently, he turned her on one side and drew her back against him, so that her head rested on his left arm and her body was cuddled against his. With his right hand he began to stroke her face. Presently she murmured: 'Not me. You.'

'What?'

'It's you who's unbelievable.'

'Nonsense,' he said. 'I'm nobody.'

'That's not true. You're the most complete man I've ever met.'

'What d'you mean? I've got nothing. I'm no good at anything except horses.'

'Oh yes you are. You're absolutely natural. You react in the right way. You're in harmony with life.'

No one had ever said such things to Joseph before. 'But you're a princess,' he whispered. 'You live in a different world.'

'A princess!' The words came out hot with scorn. 'Just because my father's a prince – what does that mean?'

'It means you live in a big house, with lots of servants, and go to balls in St Petersburg, and get sent to be civilised in Paris.'

'Yes, but that doesn't make *me* any different – the real me.'

'No, thank God. The real you is perfect.'

'Petersburg!' She made the place sound as if it were hell. 'The artificiality is impossible. All people want is to be noticed, to cause a stir, to show off.'

For a while they lay quiet. Thoughts too big to be expressed whirled in Joseph's mind. Then he said, 'What shall I call you?'

'Katya. Katyusha, if you like.'

'No – I need a special name.'

She twisted onto her back and lay looking up at him. He craved brighter light, to see her properly, and as if in answer to his longing the moon crept out through a gap in the clouds.

'*Bozhe moi*,' he whispered, tracing the lines of her eyebrows outwards with one finger. 'You are *beautiful*.'

A mischievous smile puckered her face. 'I know what I shall call you,' she said. '*Martyshka*.'

'What does that mean?'

'*Martyshka* is a marmoset, a little monkey. Your face is a bit like a monkey.'

'Thank you!' He kissed her again. 'Shall I tell you a secret?'

'Please.'

'You're not the first to think that. It's what they used to call me in Newmarket: Monkey Clements.'

She chuckled, so that her flat stomach fluttered up and down. 'Good. Then you are my Martyshka.'

He waited and said, 'I have an extraordinary feeling.'

'What?'

'That in finding you I've *come home*.' He paused. 'It's the only way I can describe it. Perhaps it's because I've never had much of a home of my own. I've always been a bit of a nomad. But that's how I feel now: as if I've always known you. This is where I want to be. May I stay for a bit?'

'For ever. Don't ever go away.'

'Oh God! If only that were possible!' After a while he said, 'I'm nearly old enough to be your father.'

'How old is that?'

'Thirty-five.'

'You poor old thing!'

'I know. But when I'm with you, now, I don't feel any age. Neither old nor young. I just feel whole. I feel right.'

All she said was 'Yes,' but the word came out like a shudder of her heart.

'Are you cold?'

'No – hot. It's just that I feel the same. You described it exactly.'

He shifted his arm, which was getting cramp. 'Shouldn't you wash? I'm worried you might start a baby.'

'No! I shall never have children.'

'How d'you know?'

'It is fated.'

'How can you tell?'

'I feel it. But I will wash, anyway. At least, you wash me.'

He picked her up in his arms, carried her out along the grass spit and walked into the river. The water was even warmer than the air, a delicious, tepid swirl. Gleams of phosphorescence flashed and darted as his shins broke the surface. When he was chest-deep he let her legs down, holding her tight to him with one arm, and began to run his spare hand up and down her back, over her behind, her thighs and calves.

'Inside, too,' she said in a whisper as low as the ripple of the current.

As he obeyed, reacting strongly, he felt her take him with both hands and guide him into her again.

'Quick!' she hissed. 'Go on.' Her legs came round his waist and she bobbed against him, almost weightless in the water, with her small breasts flattening on his chest. Closing his eyes, he had the sensation of rising rapidly in a black void, up and up, borne on a swirling, inky flood, higher and higher, until he tumbled over the edge of the world and began to fall.

He *was* falling, too. They were both rolling over sideways. He just had time to hiss '*Hold your breath!*' before they plunged beneath the surface. As they rolled over underwater, she clung to him fiercely. They tumbled in gloriously abandoned slow motion, creatures of the river. Then his feet came back on to the gravelly bottom; he stood up, with water cascading off him, and staggered ashore, where they lay on the grass gasping like stranded fish.

Recovering, he carried her across to the hut and gently dried her with the towel, rubbing her hair and smoothing it back; then he laid her on the rug, dried himself, pulled the spare half of the rug over them and nestled beside her.

'Now I know what to call you,' he whispered.

'What?'

'Rusalka.'

'A mermaid?'

'Why not? It'll remind me of what happened in the river.'

He saw her smile, and knew that the name would stick. 'Bet that gave the water sprite something to think about,' he murmured. 'I hope he isn't jealous.'

'He's talking to me,' she said, so faintly that Joseph could hardly hear.

'What's he saying?'

'Mm?'

'What's he saying, the sprite?'

She did not answer. Her lovely face had softened in sleep, and her breath blew sweet and even on his cheek as he lay beside her.

All too fast, the eight weeks of his assignment to Nikolsk flashed away in a bewildering mixture of exultation and despair. Released by love into a new dimension, he had yet to conceal his excitement and carry on with his work as if nothing had happened. Relief came after dark, when Katya slipped out of the house and across to his room in the coach house: there they made love ecstatically, with only a few remaining rats for company, and talked until the sky began to lighten. Almost always she wore the same dark dress, for camouflage. Seeing at last, in the light of a candle, that the garment was made of dark-green wool, Joseph conceived an obsession with that colour, for it brought back searing erotic memories of how she had materialised beside him on the river bank.

Katya managed her life with extraordinary discretion, never by the slightest lapse betraying her feelings, never showing Joseph undue favours, never (apparently) changing in the least from her normal, easygoing self. Occasionally she appeared tired – something for which Joseph could always account directly – but in general she looked wonderful. 'Blooming' was the word that members of the household staff kept using, and they attributed her glowing health to the fact that she had found some new young man. Joseph, knowing how near the mark the gossips were, agreed that she was a credit to the family; he found that he could derive secret delight from discussing her in the superficial terms of the servants' hall, joining in general conversation about her as though she was a decorative stranger, while simultaneously rejoicing at his own secret knowledge.

Sometimes they could meet legitimately – as when he gave her and the boys riding instruction. She already rode well – sidesaddle, as all girls did – and there was not much he could teach her; but the boys had done less, and benefited from his tuition. As he expected, Ivan was the bolder and more natural horseman, Dmitri more nervous and tense. Spurred on by a desire that they should become tough young men, rather than flabby idlers like most cavalry officers, he pushed them to the limits of their endurance. Sometimes all four of them would go off for long rides through the forest, and twice he organised paperchases, himself acting as the hare.

Whenever they met by chance in public, she treated him with perfect formality, addressing him and referring to him as 'Mr Clements', always asking what job he was doing or about to do, and enquiring as to whether he was comfortably housed or needed anything. Even so, every time their paths crossed she would contrive to send him at least one glance so cool yet conspiratorial, so intensely inviting and private, that he would treasure it all day. At night, things were utterly different. They became indivisibly close. She told him which her bedroom was – the one with two windows on the south-east corner of the first floor – and once he visited her there, climbing a ladder left behind by the gardeners, who had been cutting back trees near the house. But in general the risk was too great, partly because old Andrew, the nightwatchman, did occasionally potter round that part of the garden, and partly because one or other of the boys would sometimes come to her room in the middle of the night when woken by a bad dream. That, in fact, was the closest they came to disaster – a night when Ivan ran to her room for comfort after a nightmare, only to find her gone: luckily she returned as he was still looking for her, and managed to persuade him that she had gone out to get some fresh air because she had a headache.

In spite of this scare, she continued to come to him, twice, three times or even four times a week. By circling out through the shrubbery and through the farm buildings, she avoided the front of the house, where Andrew had his base, and came to the coach house from the orchard side, avoiding the courtyard altogether. Lying in bed, rigid with anticipation, Joseph would listen for the tell-tale creak of the stairs, then leap up to take her in his arms.

For the first half hour they would scarcely speak. Then, as they relaxed, they would talk and talk until sleep overcame them. Joseph was moved to find that Katya's mother, who came from the far north, on the Gulf of Finland, had not died of a heart attack, as rumoured, but that she had committed suicide by swallowing poison, the victim of long-term depression. At one stage doctors thought they had detected signs of the same condition in Dmitri, and Katya had conceived it her duty to take charge of the boys until they were old enough to look after themselves.

'That's the main reason why I didn't want to marry Viasemski,' she said one night as they lay naked on top of Joseph's narrow bed. 'Apart from the fact I couldn't stand him, I didn't want to leave home while the boys are still so young. Thank God you arrived. Thank God you finished it off. At least, no: that's wrong. Thank *you* for finishing it off.'

'It was a pleasure. Buy why did they all try to make you go through with it?'

'It was Aunt Yelena. She wants to get me out of the way so that she can run the house. I love Father, as you can see – but you know how she dominates him. He's so easygoing, he's inclined to go along with what she suggests.'

'You are going to Paris, though?'

'Yes, but I want to do that. And it will only be for a few months.'

'Then what?'

'I'll come back here.'

The dread of not seeing her came flooding over Joseph like a black wave. Though he did not move, Katya felt his despair.

'Don't!' she whispered fiercely. 'Don't think like that.'

'I can't help it. Everything looks so hopeless.'

'*Nothing*'s hopeless – not if you want it enough.'

'You can't ever marry *me*.'

'Why not? Perhaps one day in England. If I went to England, nobody here would know what had happened to me. At least, they wouldn't be able to control what happened. Maybe when Mitya's eighteen or so . . .'

'It'll be 1917 by then. Besides, I've got no house, or anything, there.'

'We wouldn't need much. A cottage would do. One of those black-and-white cottages I've seen in photographs . . .'

Although Joseph could not match her optimism, he gradually came to realise that he shared her instinctive belief that he, she and all other humans were in the grip of some power which was shaping their destinies. What else could have caused him to fall victim to the wiles of Cherry Green, to be sent to Russia, to find a princess of his own?

They shared many jokes about mermaids, and Joseph told her that, were she a true *rusalka*, like the one he had looked after in the circus, she would have a scaly bottom. But one night she turned serious and said, 'Men shouldn't have affairs with mermaids. It always ends in tears.'

'Why?'

'Don't you know the story of the Princess from the Sea? There's a poem by Lermontov . . . A mortal prince falls in love with the Sea King's daughter, and pulls her from the waves by her hair. Listen!'

Her voice sank to a murmur as she recited:

> He saw, on the golden sand asleep
> A green-tailed wonder out of the deep:
> A maid with snaky scales for gown,
> Trembling, writhing, sinking down,
> Cold drops upon her forehead's rise,
> A mortal shadow in her eyes . . .

Katya's voice faltered.

'Then what?' Joseph prompted.

'She died. But he never forgot her.'

Time passed. At last Katya said, 'Do you believe in God?'

'I never know.'

'You *must* believe. Otherwise life's pointless.'

'What do you mean?'

'There must be something higher than just eating and drinking and sleeping . . . animals do all that. Who gave us intelligence if it wasn't God?'

'But if He exists, where is He? And what does He look like? Is He the same as fate?'

'I'm not sure where He is. Not in heaven. Not straight up there.' She raised an arm towards the ceiling. 'More in our minds. But I do know what He looks like – and one day I'll show you.'

As the time of Joseph's departure from Nikolsk approached, the idea of not seeing Katya, of having no definite plan to meet again, grew almost insupportable. By then work on the new stud was well advanced; some of the buildings already had roofs, and all the major points of construction had been settled, so that Joseph's advice was no longer needed. The Prince congratulated him generously on what he had achieved. He had at last overcome his phobia about using names, and now belatedly addressed him as 'Joseph Petrovitch' – a mark of approval and acceptance vouchsafed to few strangers.

The wheat harvest was at its height; in the golden, burnished fields the horse-drawn reaper-binders were clacking away, frequently breaking down, and behind them, piling the sheaves into stooks or binding them by hand, advanced the small army of girls from Novgorod, who had come out to live on the estate for the duration. With their skirts tucked up and the stubble scratching their bare brown ankles, with white handkerchiefs folded into little caps, they worked steadily from the moment the dew went off the corn in the morning until dusk brought it down again. Yet now, even though some of them were good-looking enough in their sturdy fashion, Joseph had no eyes for them.

The family considered asking him to have supper with them on his last full day; but after secret discussions he got Katya to kill the plan, on some spurious grounds, because he could not face making polite conversation in her presence while being unable to communicate with her. Instead, she arranged a plan which held greater promise. 'We can't let Joseph Petrovitch go back to St Petersburg without seeing Novgorod,' she said to her father, when she came into the study, as if by accident, while the two men were checking stud records. 'That would be too much of a waste. If I go in with him, I can show him some of the churches and buy the material we need for the new curtains.'

'You can't get there and back in a day,' said her father moodily.

'No, but I can stay a night with the Antonovs, and Joseph Petrovitch can catch the evening train for Petersburg.'

So it was arranged, with perfect propriety. At 9 a.m. on the morning of 8 August, the troika drew up outside the front door of the house, with Grigor, the deaf boy, driving. A footman brought out Katya's blue travelling valise and loaded it into the carriage's box-space. Joseph's modest leather satchel looked insignificant beside it. He himself was ready and waiting, freshly shaved and dressed in his best white shirt, before any of the family came out.

He was sad to leave Nikolsk. Although he had never come to like Princess Yelena, he had grown fond of the eccentric old Prince, and very fond of Ivan. About Dmitri he had reservations. He felt that the elder boy did not like him, and had always held something back. Many times Joseph had wondered whether, by some sixth sense, he had divined what was going on between his sister and the visiting Englishman. Was he, in some barely conscious way, jealous of the stranger? Joseph had done his best for both boys, teaching them how to make whistles out of elder sticks, how to imitate a stricken rabbit's squeals with a blade of grass stretched between one's thumbs, how to skin a fox's brush with a split stick, how to demonstrate centrifugal force by swinging a bucket of water over one's head, and a dozen other useful tricks. In their presence he had been friendliness and discretion personified. Anyway, it was too late now.

The whole family came out to see him off. The Prince had already paid him two hundred roubles extra, as a bonus. Now he shook hands and thanked him again. Princess Yelena managed a frosty smile. The boys presented him with a thumb-stick which Ivan had cut from the forest – a fine, straight stem of hazel, with a fork at the top, neatly trimmed and pared smooth over the knots. The finding and preparation of it, Joseph could see, represented a major effort, and a lump rose in his throat as he received it. Finally, out came Katya, in a dove-grey travelling suit: a jacket with wide lapels and padded shoulders, a full-length skirt and a matching hat.

He waited awkwardly as the Prince handed her up on to the seat. Then he climbed up beside her. This is how we would leave if we had just been married, he kept thinking: a grander carriage, of course, but the circumstances much the same. He imagined the chaos which would result if, even now, at the fifty-ninth minute of the eleventh hour, he were to lean over and murmur graciously, 'Princess Yelena – you might like to know that since I came to Nikolsk I have made love to your niece fifty-seven times.' He saw the starched, beaky figure falling prone in a faint, the servants rushing to revive her with smelling-salts ... But of course he said nothing of the kind. After more farewells, Grigor shook up the horses, wheels scrunched on gravel, and in a minute or two the handsome white facade of the house had disappeared behind them among the trees.

It was early afternoon when they reached their destination. In spite of repeated instruction, Joseph hardly knew what to expect. Katya had told him that Novgorod was an ancient city, one of the oldest in Russia, and that its particular glory was its numerous wooden churches; but so preoccupied had he been with thoughts of leaving her that he had not paid much attention to what she said. Then suddenly, as they drove away from the station in a cab, he saw what she meant: the whole skyline was full of onion domes, some gilded, some blue, some silvery, some clad in scalloped tiles, and everywhere little white churches rose from patches of grass, their walls and towers outstripping the houses, but not by much. The city had a comfortable, small-scale feel, quite different from the barbaric splendour of Moscow or the regimented grandeur of St Petersburg.

'Those towers with pointed roofs, in the high red wall – that's the Detinetz, or Kremlin,' said Katya, pointing. 'We ought to visit that. It's nearly a thousand years old. But there's something else I want you to see first.'

She had given the driver instructions, and presently he pulled up outside a square white church, bigger and more ornate than most. It had a single large dome on a central tower, a complicated eight-pitch roof and elaborate ornamentation on its facades, with narrow, pointed slits of windows and crosses raised in relief on the stonework. 'This is the Church of Our Saviour of the Transfiguration-in-Elijah-Street,' Katya announced as they walked towards it.

'You sound like an official guide,' said Joseph lightly; but she turned her big, grey-green eyes on him with a solemn look and said, 'Martyshka, please: I'm not joking.'

He felt abashed as she went on: 'It dates from the fourteenth century. But it's not the building that matters. It's something inside.'

Taking his arm, she guided him through the doorway and into a cavernous, dim interior, which struck damp and cool after the heat outside. The building was deserted and perfectly silent: even though she whispered, her voice echoed within the bare stone walls. She led him to the centre of the floor, beneath the dome, and then said, 'Look up.'

He tilted his head back, gazed upwards, and gasped. Staring down at him from the murky heights, glaring out of the shadows, was a pair of fearsomely powerful eyes, like those of some tremendous owl. He was aware of white circles round the sockets, a brown face, dark hair framing a long and noble face, the whole surrounded by the halo of a saintly figure. But it was those glaring, hypnotic eyes which struck down at him and filled him with awe.

'Who is it?' he whispered.

'It is Christ Pantocrator.' She took his hand in hers.

He looked at her, then back at the overpowering fresco above. The hair on his neck crawled as he understood that she was trying to give him strength by letting him share her faith. Together they sat in a pew, remaining there in silence for many minutes. Although she came back to the station with him to say goodbye, it was there, in the cool shadows of the church, that he remembered her: in a dim light, looking at him slightly sideways with a mixture of hope and yearning, and high above them both, in the dome, the face of God.

EIGHT

Epsom: 1913

ONLY ONE letter came from her before she left for Paris: the postman was the biggest gossip in the village (she wrote) and would immediately spread rumours if another envelope addressed to Tovarich Klementz went through his hands. Once she had arrived in France, however, she could write freely, and she sent loving messages, laced by accounts of her life at the Sorbonne. She was living with her cousins, the Volkonskys, and said little about what went on at home, but always had news of the university. Normally she wrote in Russian, sometimes in English, and she had a knack of telling a story economically in either language – as when she wrote: 'Today the Professor's trousers caught fire and he was put out with a bucket of water, but as that hit the electricity there was something called a short circuit which plunged the whole school into darkness & we all had to go home.'

That winter, for the first time in his life, Joseph felt lonely. He missed Katya acutely, and tried to keep the image of her before him by writing her long letters. But it was not until the spring of 1913 that he had any real news.

Then once again he felt like a tuft of thistledown borne on the great winds that sweep the universe. In the middle of May he was summoned to see Grand Duke Dimitri Pavlovitch, the Tsar's nephew, who had been put in overall charge of the Imperial Stud. A tall and elegantly dressed young man, he received Joseph with the easy charm of an aristocrat whose manners had been polished by foreign travel. Waving him to a chair, he addressed him in elaborately perfect English.

'I wonder if you would feel able to undertake a special mission for me?' he began, as if about to beg a favour of an equal or superior.

'Certainly, sir.'

'Good! In fact, without wishing to make too much of a mystery of it, I must – for the moment – ask you to regard it as a *secret* mission. Some rather delicate negotiations are in progress, and until they are concluded, I would rather that nobody knew about them . . .'

Joseph was about to say, 'Of course,' when the Grand Duke went on: 'All I require you to do is to travel to England and present yourself to a certain gentleman, a trainer of repute, who will tell you what else has to be done.'

'May I ask who the gentleman is, sir?'

'His name . . .' the Grand Duke shuffled some papers on his desk and found the correct sheet ' . . . his name is Marsh. Mr Richard Marsh, of Lordship Stud, Newmarket.'

'Oh!' Joseph exclaimed. 'But I know him.'

'You do? How is that?'

'I worked for him, for nearly five years, before I came to Russia. He trains the King's horses.'

'Exactly. Well then, you will have no difficulty finding your way to Newmarket. Perhaps you will enjoy going back. To your old haunts, you say? The journey, of course, will cost you nothing, either way.'

'I am to return to Russia, then?'

'But yes! That is the whole point. You will, I hope, come back with a particular . . . shall we say, trophy. Excellent! I should like you to go as soon as possible – and I will send Mr Marsh a telegram to say that you are on your way.'

His old haunts! The prospect of seeing them again filled Joseph with delight. Within a week he was off, and the three-day journey passed in a haze of anticipation. As the train rumbled westwards from Warsaw, he had wild thoughts of making a detour to Paris; but his sense of duty won, and he allowed himself to be carried on towards England.

Landing at Harwich early one morning, he took a train for Newmarket, and as he watched the flat fields of Suffolk flicker past the windows, the last seventeen years seemed to roll away. Here the horse-chestnuts were in bloom and the hay harvest was in progress, as in northern Russia: in some fields the crop had already been carried, in others it still lay drying in neat rows. But everything was slightly different: the shades of green were more intense, the cottages better built and surrounded by neat gardens, the fields smaller and bounded by thick hedgerows, the whole landscape more intimate. Everything seemed immensely familiar. The sight of Guernsey cows waiting in a yard to be milked struck a chord deep inside him. As the train waited in a station, he heard a cuckoo call, and saw the bird fly hunched and hawk-like up the line of a hedge. He was surprised to find how deeply the old images were ingrained in his memory; he had the comfortable feeling of being on home ground, and a sudden rush of homesickness seized him. Why did he not stay here, rather than return to the great open wastes of Russia?

There were two short, sharp answers to the question. One was money. He had wired £200 ahead of him to Hammond's Bank in Newmarket, for expenses while he was in England, but the rest of his life's savings, amounting to the very substantial sum of almost £30,000, were reposing in the Imperial Bank in St Petersburg, and currency restrictions prevented him removing them in one lump. The second answer to his question was even more easily expressed: Katya.

The sight of the level East Anglian fields moved him to wonder where the Maguire family circus might be at that moment: on the road, no doubt. To his sorrow, he had long since lost touch with them. And what about the fair Rosaleen? Married, for sure. He felt a pang for those far-off days.

In Newmarket many surprises greeted him. Strings of horses were out at exercise, of course, but new buildings had sprung up, and old ones had gone, among them the Greyhound Inn. It was a shock to see motor cars and lorries parked along with the horse brakes in the High Street, and as his cab went up out of town towards Lordship, he was amazed to find a tall, open structure, with a small dome supported on two pillars, near the brow of the hill, right beside the London Road.

'Whatever's that?' he asked the driver.

'That? The Cooper Memorial Fountain, innit?' the man replied.

'How long's it been there?'

'Two or three years. Why?'

'It wasn't there when I last came this way.'

It was just after nine when they reached the lodge at the end of Lordship's drive: by then, Joseph reckoned, Marsh would be in his office at Egerton, so he told the driver to go on down to the yards. Here the changes were still more obvious. The avenues and hedges – in their infancy when he last saw them – had grown so much as to alter the face of the land. Now they were big enough to give the paddocks proper shelter and create leafy lanes down which one could ride. The effect was both practical and attractive. The place had matured almost out of recognition.

When he came in sight of the buildings, with their black clapboard walls, green doors and steep roofs of scalloped red tiles, a wave of nostalgia swept over him. He stopped the driver short of the main entrance arch and paid him off, so that he could walk, carrying his bag, the last few yards.

Then he strode through the archway and stood looking round. The scene was absolutely familiar: some stable doors standing open, horses' heads protruding over others, men with barrows, men with brooms, wallflowers in the beds, the grass in the centre of the yard immaculately mown. Suddenly a voice from his left cried 'Blimey! If it ain't old Monkey Clements!' He looked round and saw a stocky middle-aged man advancing on him with a great grin. Panic threatened. Who was this? Then, inside the wide contours of the ruddy face and greying sidewhiskers, he recognised the face of Basher Brown.

'Basher!' he cried. 'Well I'm damned!'

They had hardly shaken hands before the cry went up, 'Look who's here!', and in a few seconds Joseph was surrounded. For a moment he was confused: expecting to meet the boys he once knew, he found himself hemmed in by men whose faces were vaguely familiar. But of course, he knew them all: Tiny Morrison (now over six feet tall), Big Bill Alley, Dusty Smith, Jem Johnson, Horry Norman with his big black eyebrows and greased-down black hair. The air was filled with a babel of questions, most of them ribald. 'What – not married? ... had any dusky Russkis? ... Too cold for it out there, then, is it? ... Come back for a bit of instruction, have you? ... Where's your droshky, Jossky? ...' and so on. He waited till the noise died down and then said: '*Ubiraites von!*'

Whistles and cries of derision greeted the Russian. 'What's it mean?' someone demanded.

'Give or take the odd syllable, that you can all sugar off.'

A roar of delighted abuse broke out. They pushed off his cap, tousled his hair, thumped him on the back, shook hands. In the middle of the hubbub he heard a familiar deep voice call out his name – and there was Marsh advancing on him, over sixty now, a little greyer, perhaps a little thicker-set, limping slightly, but scarcely changed.

'Clements!' he said as he bore down on the group. 'I heard such a devil of a racket that I knew something was up. How are you, me lad?'

Joseph, on the point of bowing, as he would have done to a prince or a grand duke, made an awkward movement with his feet, as if coming to attention, and shook the proffered hand. 'Very well, sir, thank you,' he said.

'By Jove you've worn well,' said Marsh. 'Hasn't he, lads?'

'It's a bloody disgrace,' said somebody. 'Hasn't done a stroke of work since he left here.'

'Well, I've got a job for him now.' Marsh looked at his watch, gave Joseph a conspiratorial glance and said, 'We might as well go. Got some breeches with you?'

'Yes, sir.'

'Get 'em on, then.'

Evidently Marsh had been planning this surprise. By the time Joseph had changed, junior lads had led out two hacks ready saddled, one of them Marsh's own chestnut gelding and the other a bay. A minute later both men were trotting up the grassy lime avenue that led to Lordship Stud. In a few minutes they crossed the London Road, then turned right and left down beautifully mown alleyways of grass between tall hedges. Immediately after one more right turn Marsh reined in and said, 'There he is.'

In a paddock to their left, surrounded by a high fence of four wooden rails, stood the most splendid stallion that Joseph had ever seen. A bay with dark points, and ideally proportioned, with a splendid crest developed by his career at stud, he stood side-on to them, gleaming with health, and as their hacks drew up he turned his beautiful head in their direction.

'Know who he is?'

'Not a clue, sir.'

'Minoru. He won the Derby for the old King four years ago. And now he's yours.'

'He's *what*?'

'He's yours. They've sold him to the Imperial Stud, and I want you to take him to Russia.'

'*Bozhe moi!*'

'Excuse me?'

'Sorry, sir . . .'

'He's the gamest bit of horseflesh that ever was shod – and one of the gentlest, too.'

'He's a clipper to look at, anyway.' Joseph agreed. 'Not by Persimmon, though? I don't see Percy in him.'

'No, no. He's by Cyllene – no lack of blood, as you can see. He

150

came from Ireland as a colt, one of six we got from the Tully Stud in Kildare. Property of Lord Wavertree, who leased him to the old King. People thought he *belonged* to the King, because he carried the royal colours, but that was wrong. He went back to stand in Ireland for a couple of years, then came here. And now Wavertree's sold him to your people.'

Joseph whistled. 'What's he like with the mares?'

'Perfect. No vices, and very high fertility so far. One filly of his in particular looks bound for great things – Serenissima.'

'How about in the stable?'

'Perfect again. A real gentleman, and one of the best tempered horses I've ever had. Now look – you'll see.'

A groom appeared at the gate in one corner of the field and called. The stallion gave a whinny and trotted over. Joseph watched the man go into the paddock, put a bucket on the ground and slip a head-collar on to the horse as he nuzzled at it. With many stallions, no groom would dream of doing that: even for the man who looked after him, it was potentially dangerous to intrude on a horse's own territory.

'No vices whatever,' Marsh repeated. 'He'll give you no trouble. When he first came to us, he was a bit nervous: always seemed to be on the alert, as if expecting a clout, and I decided the only thing to do was to change his lad. I didn't like taking the first one away, as he'd done nothing wrong, but he did tend to be noisy and excitable, so I put in someone quieter. The result was excellent. Minoru settled down like a lamb.

'He's got a lovely stride, too – very free. Works hard. I hardly had to train him. Not that he did much as a two-year-old. He was late coming into his strength. As a three-year-old, though – that's another story. Until the spring of that year, 1909, I never thought of him as a Derby winner. But then he came through a trial so well that I realised he was better than I'd thought. So we put him in for the Greenham Stakes at Newbury, and he won in capital style by a length and a half from the odds-on favourite.

'He was entered for the 2,000 Guineas, against Bayardo, unbeaten as a two-year-old. Nobody gave Minoru a chance against him, but our fellow came through to win by two lengths. Come the Derby, Bayardo again looked the big threat, but we heard that he still wasn't right, and I was more afraid of the American colt, St Martin.' Marsh cocked an eyebrow. 'But you heard what happened to him.'

'No, sir. I'm afraid I didn't. We're pretty cut off out there.'

'Came down at Tattenham Corner. Either he was struck into, or he hit someone's heels, and that was the finish of his chances. After a terrific battle over the last furlong, Minoru won by a short head from Louviers. Great excitement, of course. When the King led the winner in, the whole crowd went wild, singing the national anthem . . .'

The groom had led the stallion out of the paddock and was bringing him towards them.

Marsh cleared his throat and said, 'Go and have a word with him. Give me your reins.'

Joseph dismounted, handed over his horse and received in exchange a carrot which Marsh had produced from his pocket. Then he walked across to the stallion and came up slowly, nodding to the groom. He felt Marsh's eyes on him as he began to address the horse in a quiet, murmuring voice. Out of habit he spoke in Russian: the groom looked baffled, but Minoru understood perfectly the hypnotic flow of pleasantries. Joseph spoke of his success in the Derby, his prowess at stud, his equable nature: after a few moments he produced the carrot, which Minoru accepted gratefully, and as he scrunched it between his teeth Joseph ran a hand down his shoulder.

'Nice manners,' he said to the groom. 'You've done him proud.'

'Not me, sir. It's him. He's like that.'

'Is it official, that he's going to Russia?' he asked Marsh as they hacked back to Egerton. 'In St Petersburg I was told to keep it secret.'

'The price hadn't been agreed.' Marsh gave him a wink. 'All settled now, and the news will be out in a couple of days.'

'Can you say how much?'

'No!'

'How will we travel?'

'By boat. Easiest for the horse. You can go from Hull straight to St Petersburg on the Wilson line.'

'And when are we to go?'

'Not before the end of June. Minoru's still got some mares to cover. That'll give you time to get to know him.' He smiled. 'You can have a busman's holiday, too. Go to the Derby.'

That night, over pints of Greene King Abbot ale in the back bar of The Bushel, they caught up greedily on past gossip. Joseph's beloved Persimmon had died of a fractured pelvis five years before, when he was sixteen. His mentor, Prince Soltykoff, who had sent him to Russia, was also dead, and it was a shock to learn that his own friend Wilf Collyer had been killed in a gale when a tree fell on him one January night. More cheerful were the accounts of how the old King, Edward VII, had taken to visiting Egerton in his 40-horsepower Mercedes, and how he would order his chauffeur, Stamper, to drive like Jehu, in defiance of the overall speed limit of twenty miles per hour.

'Didn't that bugger go!' chortled Horry. 'In the middle of the night? No matter what time he left on his way back to London, there'd be a dozen other motorists, all tucked into side turnings, waiting for the royal car to pass. Soon as it came by, they'd whip out and get on the tail of the convoy, hoping to dodge the police and their speed traps. But the law would come out after them like the devil, and nip them off the back of the convoy, one by one.'

Apparently a crisis had threatened in 1908, when things were not going well for the royal stable, and Edward decided to cut costs by transferring his horses from Egerton to Blackwell's stables, in the centre of Newmarket. But Marsh, almost in despair, had the brilliant idea of seeking help from the actress Lily Langtry, who invited the King to Regal Lodge in Newmarket, where she was staying for the July meeting, and talked him round.

Everyone seemed to regret the death of the old King, who had been so closely connected with Egerton, and even though it had happened three years ago, they remembered it like yesterday. 'Friday, the sixth of May, it was,' said Basher Brown. 'I was with the Guv'nor at Kempton Park, when we won the Two-Year-Old Plate with the King's Witch of the Air. Marshy telegraphed the news to Buckingham Palace, and it was just about the last message the poor old sod understood. He got it at five o'clock and died at midnight.'

His son, George V, had kept the royal horses on at Egerton, and had showed an encouraging amount of interest in them; but although he had a still better eye for a horse than his father, he could not quite equal him in the fervour of his enthusiasm for the turf. So the atmosphere in the stables had changed.

One subject which produced heated controversy was the new American style of riding, which had begun to creep in at the end of the century, not long after Joseph's departure, when American jockeys took to riding with their stirrups very short. The man who first made it fashionable was Tod Sloan, who came to England in 1897: brilliant in the saddle, but so tactless and conceited that everyone hated him. In spite of this, the American crouch had caught on and been widely adopted. Reactionaries like Marsh claimed that it deprived a man of any control of the horse from his hips downward, and he refused to allow Herbie Jones, Egerton's leading jockey of the moment, to use it; but most thought it produced greater speed, and took it up.

Only when he had three pints of Abbot inside him did Joseph venture on to the subject of Cherry Green. 'Cherry!' snorted somebody in a mixture of hilarity and derision. 'Too late, mate. Like the old grey mare – ain't what she used to be.'

Joseph considered the implications of this remark. 'What's happened to her, then?' he asked carefully.

'Nothing,' said Horry. 'She had a nipper by Ginger Harris, and more or less had to marry him. But then she settled down and had a couple more, right as ninepence. Now she's the most respectable housewife you could imagine. Mrs Ginger Harris.'

Nodding sagely into his beer, Joseph resolved to go and see her before he left.

Derby Day proved cloudless and hot. Together with two of his old cronies, Joseph travelled down to London by train, and then on to Epsom by one the specials run every ten minutes by the Brighton & South Coast Railway. Although not a betting man, he studied the form during the journey, determined to celebrate the fact that the birthday of the King – 3 June – now coincided with his own. He did not fancy the favourite, Craganour, whose odds of 6–4 were too short to interest him, and settled for backing the royal horse, Amner. He, as it happened, had not been trained at Egerton, but he was being ridden by Herbie Jones, and his starting price of 50–1 seemed a good enough challenge, so Joseph decided to support him with a pound each way.

The scene at Epsom took his mind straight to Persimmon's great year of 1896. Back it all came with a roar – the immense crowd, the brilliant colours of the ladies' dresses, the sea of marquees, the noise, the commotion, the raucous clamour of the bookies, the palpable excitement, far surpassing anything that Russia could contrive: a thrilling atmosphere engendered partly by the traditions of the occasion and partly by the presence of the King and Queen. Again Joseph thought, 'This is where I should be'; but the moment passed, and he settled down to enjoy himself. Before the big race he separated from his companions, who wanted to position themselves on Tattenham Corner for a close scrutiny of the tactical riding on that notorious downhill bend which had unbalanced so many good horses. He himself, eager to see the finish, made for the public enclosure opposite the stands.

It was from Horry, who had a place on the rails, that he heard of the drama at Tattenham Corner. 'The field was right on top of us, when out of the crowd burst this wild creature of a woman in a long pale coat. Out under the rail she popped, right beside me. I could have grabbed her, only she moved so quick. She knew what she was doing all right, because she ducked under Agadir's neck, raise her arms above her head, gave this horrible scream and flung herself straight at Amner. Poor old Herbie couldn't do a thing to avoid her. Came a horrible thud – next thing, the woman's flattened, Amner's gone arse over tip, and Herbie's being dragged along by one stirrup. Then the horse is up again, and the rest of the field is clean gone, leaving Herbie and the woman unconscious on the turf. I reckon the crowd would have finished her off there and then, only the police were out round her in a flash. They knew her, of course, and word came across that it was Emily Davison, the mad suffragette.'

None of this was immediately apparent to the crowd at the finish. All they saw was a pack of horses driving towards them up the straight, with a disgraceful amount of barging and bumping in progress. At one stage it looked as though the Hulton horse, Shogun, would take it, but he became caught up in a tussle with Day Comet, and then the favourite Craganour crashed into the 100-1 outsider Aboyeur, who was thrown to his left and headed Shogun. In the end Craganour passed the post a head in front of Aboyeur, with the well-fancied Louvois third.

After such rough stuff, everyone expected objections to be lodged, and a great gasp of relief went up when Craganour's number was hoisted into the winner's frame. A loud voice boomed out 'All right' – the traditional signal that formalities had been completed – and bookies began to pay out. Then suddenly someone else shouted, 'Stop! Bring the horse back!' Craganour, about to pass out of the gate, was led in again, the word went round that the stewards had ordered an inquiry on their own account, without any objection being lodged. Sure enough, the dark blue objection flag was run up the pole, and a breathless wait ensued as it flapped aloft. While the officials deliberated, Herbie Jones was carried into the jockeys' dressing-room unconscious on a stretcher, with his purple-and-gold shirt torn open and blood oozing from a V-shaped cut on his left cheek. At the same time, word of the suffragette's desperate action filtered through the crowd. Then, to almost everyone's consternation, the stewards announced that they objected to the winner on the grounds of jostling: Craganour was disqualified, and the race awarded to Aboyeur.

Rumour and gossip sizzled through the crowd like a forest fire, fuelled by anger that Craganour had been ridden by the American jockey Johnny Reiff, rather than by his normal partner, Bill Saxby. People said that Reiff had started the trouble on the straight, and that he deserved to lose the prize; others claimed the race had been fixed, and that backers of Aboyeur had won £40,000 in bets; others still spread word that one of the stewards, Major Loder, could not stand Craganour's owner, Mr Ismay, and had influenced the inquiry for personal reasons. Ismay himself attracted many vicious rumours. The mere fact that he had survived the *Titanic* disaster the year before became a black mark against him: how was it, when so many women had died, that he had escaped? Again, everybody knew that Tom Coulthwaite, who trained Ismay's jumpers, had been temporarily suspended – another shadow over Craganour's owner.

Back in Newmarket, discussion seethed for days, especially when, at the weekend, it was announced that Emily Davison had died of her injuries. Most people said 'Good riddance'. Had she not hidden in air-shafts at the House of Commons, attacked a Baptist minister in mistake for the Prime Minister, chained herself to railings and taken part in protest marches, been arrested and, when she went on hunger strike, force-fed, all in pursuit of her grand political aim – to win the vote for women? But whatever you thought of her methods, no one could say she lacked guts. Horry Norman was haunted by the image of her flying at the King's horse. 'There was something mad just in the way she went at him,' he repeated. 'Her hands were up in the air, like claws, and she was screaming something horrible.'

Joseph settled back into Lordship as though he had never been away, riding out on the Heath in the mornings, handling difficult horses, generally making himself useful about the stud and training stables. Since his main purpose was to get to know Minoru, he spent hours in the stallion's company, with or without his regular lad. Everything Marsh had said about him proved true: his manners were faultless, both in the box and in the covering-yard, and he even had a sense of humour: whenever Matilda, the stable's tortoiseshell cat, ventured across his paddock with her tail waving in the air, he would stalk after her, lower his nose close to her heels and exhale so violently that he almost blew her into the air. The cat seemed to like the joke, and flaunted herself shamelessly, apparently in the hope of having it repeated.

Then a rumour reached Lordship that Aboyeur also had been sold to Russia. 'If it's true,' Marsh told Joseph, 'you'll probably end up taking him as well. We'd better find out something about him.'

The results of their research were not reassuring. Aboyeur had been bred in Ireland; he was by Desmond, descendant of the great St Simon, but his form was undistinguished. As a two-year-old he had won only one race, the Champagne Stakes at Salisbury; he had come second once, third once, and failed three times. In 1913, before the Derby, he had run once and come nowhere. He was also reputed to have inherited a bad temper from his maternal grandsire Morion.

Before long the rumours were confirmed. Aboyeur had been sold for £13,000 to the Imperial Racing Club of St Petersburg, and he was to be sent out later that summer. When his owners realised that Minoru was about to travel the same road, and moreover that Joseph Clements had come from Russia to fetch him, they made contact with Marsh and asked if the two horses could be despatched together. So it was that, in August 1913, Joseph took charge of two valuable exports.

With Aboyeur came the lad who had been doing him, Ernie Forrest, and soon it was apparent that the horse's reputation was well-earned. Almost the first words that Ernie addressed to Joseph were, 'Just watch him, or he'll bloody have yer. Don't go into his box, whatever you do,' and he regaled his new listeners with the story of how the horse had bitten the thumb of a predecessor clean off. Soon he was known about the stud as 'Muley', in memory of the notorious biter Muley Edris, who had once seized Fred Archer by the arm after a gallop on the Heath, carried him off, flung him to the ground and knelt on him. The one thing that seemed to scare Aboyeur, Ernie said, was an umbrella: you had only to put one up to cow him into docility.

Joseph was content to take his time and get to know Aboyeur slowly, chatting to him over the door of his box – which was next to Minoru's – and offering him the odd carrot. The first time he did go in, he was responding to urgent yells for help. Rushing to the door, he found that the stallion had got Ernie pinned in one corner, underneath the manger, and was striking at him with both front feet. Remembering the remark about umbrellas, he seized a bucket, hung it upside-down on the handle of a fork and went in holding it in his hand. Having bolted the door behind him, he walked straight up to the horse, not shouting, but addressing him in a loud, firm voice. 'Come off it, you bloody fool. Stop playing the idiot, or I won't take you to Russia after all.' Aboyeur bared his teeth and swung his head menacingly, but Joseph pushed the bucket/umbrella towards him, and, before he could bite, grabbed the head collar, dropped the bucket into the straw and got his other hand on the horse's neck. In a moment he felt his tension drain away, and he led the animal across to another corner of the box so that Ernie could scramble out, shaken but unhurt. Whether or not the bucket had helped, he could not tell, but the incident taught them all to be more careful.

In retrospect, the violent introduction seemed to have been just what was needed. Aboyeur started to tolerate Joseph's presence in the box; Joseph, for his part, began to like his awkward charge, and his tendency to see the good in any animal made him defend Aboyeur against human detractors, who said there was little point in taking him all the way to Russia, as he had never been any use on the race course anyway. 'Rubbish,' Joseph told them. 'Even if he did win the Derby on a disqualification, he was still within half a head of Craganour at the finish, and he must have run pretty fast to be there. He'll throw some clinking foals – you'll see.'

Another discovery, which pleased Joseph as much as it surprised him, was that Minoru and Aboyeur became friends. 'Talk about chalk and cheese,' he said to Ernie one day. In his experience friendships between stallions were rare: normally, grooms took trouble to make sure that horses were kept well apart, since if they came together there was every chance that they would fight. These two were different, and Joseph soon found that they could be walked out together for exercise without fear of a dust-up. Even so, he did not feel confident that he could handle both of them on the complicated journey to Petersburg, and insisted that Ernie should travel with him.

The delays in completing formalities seemed endless. Weeks ticked past, and it was not until the beginning of September that the necessary papers were in order. At last definite bookings could be made, and the party was scheduled to take an afternoon train to Hull on the fifth. The day before that, Joseph went to call on Cherry.

She and Ginger were living beyond the railway at Hungry Hill Farm, which they had taken over from his father when he retired. As

Joseph rode out to the farm through the lanes, he saw her clearly, looking just as she had on that far-off evening when she had lain in wait for him, with her black hair and even white teeth. He doubted if she knew that he was in England, for Ginger no longer had connections with the racing world.

The whitewashed house and its timber-clad barns, lying in a hollow, came into sight from a distance. He was disconcerted to find the place poorly looked-after: the hedges were untrimmed, the grass fields scruffy, the garden a wilderness. A wooden gate, once painted white, hung awry, and although a few zinnias straggled under the front window, the path leading to the door was overgrown with weeds.

Having tethered his horse to the gatepost, Joseph hesitated before setting out up the path; the squalor offended him, and he began to hope that there would be nobody at home, so that he could slip away unseen. But at that moment the door opened, and out came a hulking, copper-haired lad of about seventeen. As Joseph set eyes on the boy, he felt a wave of relief sweep over him. Beyond any shadow of doubt, this was Ginger's son; except that he was bigger, he resembled his father in every particular. The knowledge flushed any last traces of guilt from Joseph's mind, and he said confidently, 'Evening, me lad: is your Mum at home?'

'Ar,' came the answer. 'She be in the kitchen.'

So Joseph went on, and knocked at the half-open door, and called out, 'Are you there, Cherry?'

'Come in,' she called. 'Who is it?' In he went, and there she was, wiping her hands on her apron. It would be hard to say whose surprise was the greater. 'Well, heavens! If it isn't Joseph!' she cried, whipping a hand up to her mouth, as if in fear. 'Wherever have you been all these years?'

'I went to Russia,' he said.

'So you did! I remember now. But you're back.'

'Yes. Just for a while. I'm going away again tomorrow.' He smiled – but it was an effort to do so, because the girl after whom he once lusted had turned into a coarse and dowdy woman. Her face had broadened and roughened; her teeth were discoloured; her hair, once so shiny and neat, was dishevelled and streaked with grey. Her body bulged inside a loose black dress. Even as he looked at her, he had a vision of Katya's sylph-like grace and saw her flitting through shadows by the river at Nikolsk.

'I just wanted to make sure you were all right,' he began awkwardly.

'Course I'm all right. Why shouldn't I be?'

'Well – if you remember, the last time I saw you, you were going to have a baby.'

'Oh, that!' She flicked a strip of peel into the sink. 'Ginger and I got married, so it was put to rights, and the baby come next February. That was him you saw go out, Daniel.'

'I know. But you told your Mum I was the father.'

'Never!'

'That was what she told Marsh.'

'Get away with you!'

Cherry's tone was easy, bantering, but she kept her eyes averted. Joseph could not make out if she had forgotten her attempt to involve him, or whether she was covering up. He decided that he did not care. He had come meaning to tell her that, in precipitating his departure for Russia, she had changed his life, and to thank her for doing him a service. Now, belatedly, he saw how selective his memory had been: recalling only her velvety eyes and seductive physical charm, he had forgotten how sly and sluttish and thick-witted she was. Now that he perceived her clearly, he did not want to bother with her. Instead, he recounted a few harmless details of his career, made small talk about her family – all boys – accepted a cup of tea, and rode away.

Back at Lordship, he found that Marsh had one more surprise for him. 'The King's coming to see you off,' he announced casually.

'*What?*'

'The King. Wants to say goodbye to Minoru, so he's coming over from Sandringham in the morning.' Marsh smiled and added: 'I don't want to disappoint you, but in fact he was coming anyway, to see his other horses, and I told him you happened to be leaving.'

'Blimey!' said Joseph.

Next morning, in a fever of anticipation, not knowing what form the royal inspection would take, he got up in riding gear, changed into his one and only suit, then went back into riding gear again. He need hardly have worried. The visit was as informal as a royal visit could be, and the King, accompanied only by his racing manager, Lord Francis Beresford, was in genial mood. Joseph, waiting with Ernie by the stallion boxes, saw the big black Daimler slide up to the front of the house and watched the party go inside. 'Coffee-housing,' he said to Minoru. 'That's what they're up to. If it hadn't been for them coming, you'd have been out in your paddock by now, chasing that ruddy cat. Not to worry. It isn't every day you see the King.

Mind you don't bite the old bugger, either.' He turned to Ernie and added, 'You might tell yours that, as well.'

After a short wait, he saw the visitors coming, the King dressed for the country in light-coloured suit, brilliantly polished brown shoes, tan-coloured spats, a high white collar and a straw hat. At his approach, Joseph drew himself up as if on parade, and stood rigidly to attention, staring straight ahead. Then he heard Marsh saying, 'Your Majesty, may I present Mr Clements, who will be taking Minoru to Russia.'

'I am very glad to meet you, Mr Clements,' said the King gravely.

'Thank you, sir.' Joseph managed a bow.

'And how is Minoru?'

'Capital, sir. Never been better.' Whatever protocol might dictate, Joseph felt he had to move. He turned sideways, so as to bring the stallion into the conversation. Minoru, caring nothing for royalty, fluttered his nostrils in a gentle whinny at some mare passing in the distance. The King produced a carrot from behind his back.

'Handsome fellow,' he said as Minoru munched.

'Shall I bring him out, sir?'

'Please do.'

Joseph clipped a rope onto the horse's head collar and led him out, bringing him round in a circle. Then, at Marsh's suggestion, the whole party walked the short distance to Minoru's paddock, and Joseph turned him loose – whereupon he cantered away, reared, lay down, rolled, and generally showed off.

'No wonder he was a favourite of my father's,' said the King. 'He admired him more than any other horse that carried his colours, except perhaps Persimmon.'

'He's a cracker, sir,' said Joseph with unforced loyalty. 'No doubt about that.'

'Perhaps you would like to take this with you, for good luck.' The King pulled a small, dark blue leather case from his jacket pocket and held it out. For a moment Joseph hesitated, but then he noticed that behind the monarch's shoulder Marsh was nodding vigorously. He reached out, took the offering, and gave another little bow.

'Open it!'

Inside the case, cradled in light blue silk, was a substantial gold medallion, with an embossed representation of a horse's head in the centre, and the words MINORU – EPSOM – 26 MAY 1909 round the perimeter. At the top was a small ring, mounted on a swivel, so that the medallion could be fastened to a chain.

Joseph struggled for words. 'How beautiful!' he said.

'Wear it as a talisman,' the King told him gruffly.

'I will, your majesty. Thank you. Thank you very much indeed.'

'And look after the horse on my behalf.' He turned to the trainer. 'I'm glad I came today, Marsh,' he said. 'I can see he's in good hands.'

The journey passed off without incident, and the horses soon settled down in their new environment; but when, in the middle of 1914, Joseph was posted to the Imperial Stud at Kharkov, in the Ukraine, he was dismayed, for even though the move was part of a general reorganisation of the government's horse-breeding programme, and the stallions went with him, he felt he was being sent into exile. A thousand miles to the south – five hundred miles beyond Moscow, even – Kharkov seemed like the end of the world, and he feared that, once buried in such remote country, he might never see Katya again.

It was the outbreak of hostilities in August 1914 which came to their rescue. When war started, Katya at last persuaded her father to let her do what she wanted: train for a career. Germany's attack on Russia gave her the opportunity which she had long sought. Nurses were urgently needed: the cry went up for more. Instead of remaining idle and useless at Nikolsk, she would train as a nurse and serve her country. By then Dmitri was fifteen, Ivan thirteen, and both were developing strong wills of their own; Aunt Yelena, debilitated by a mild stroke, showed less inclination to push the boys around, so that Katya no longer felt obliged to remain at home. The Prince accepted her proposal with good grace, and she further managed to convince him that the best medical school open to women was the newly-founded one in the University of Kharkov. So, in September, she too travelled south, and a joyous reunion took place. Even in the Ukraine the lovers had to behave with circumspection, for the trainee-nurses lived in a hostel and were strictly chaperoned; nevertheless, they were allowed, within certain limits, to go about the town, and Joseph solved the problem by renting an apartment in which they could meet without arousing suspicion.

Under the stress of war, nurses' training was shortened from the normal two years to one; at the end of 1915 Katya was sent to the

Western Front on a tour of duty which lasted eighteen months and exposed her to horrors and privations such as she had never imagined. Frozen in winter, baked in summer, sleeping in cellars, in carts, in the woods, living on the meagrest rations, and all the time overwhelmed by floods of hideously-wounded casualties, she had been put to a savage test, but somehow, in spite of the carnage and acute personal discomfort, she found positive exhilaration in doing a fearful job as well as it could be done.

When she returned to Kharkov in 1917, Joseph found her astonishingly unchanged. He feared she might have become tough and cynical, but to his delight she was exactly the same, able to talk about the horrors she had been through, yet no less fresh and spontaneous in herself. When she described to him the wounds with which she had been faced – heads smashed open, limbs blown off, stomachs ripped out, private parts shot away – and told him how dying men clamoured at her for mercy and relief, he felt proud and humbled by her strength. Back in Kharkov, she worked for a while in the hospital, then returned for a second tour at the front, this time in the northern sector.

If anything, it was Joseph who changed, for as the war dragged on he became increasingly uncomfortable about the fact that he was contributing nothing to the struggle against the Germans, either on behalf of Russia, or for England. News from overseas reached him intermittently, all of it bad. When he heard of the slaughter in the trenches of the Marne and the Somme, and thought of all the young Englishmen being killed there, guilt plagued him. Even though, by 1916, he himself was thirty-eight, he felt he should somehow have made his way home and volunteered for the armed forces: at his age, he realised, he would probably not have been sent to the front, but he could at least have given some kind of a hand in the crisis.

Once the war started, it became difficult to travel inside Russia, and impossible to reach England by train. When he inquired about sea passages, he was told that they were available only for military personnel and officials in government service. In accepting this as a fact, he knew he was being feeble, and the knowledge rankled: he was left with the uncomfortable certainty that if he had made a determined effort, he could have reached England. In seeking to justify his decision to stay, he told himself that he was doing a good job where he was, that he owed it to the old Russian regime to carry on, and that if he left the stud, at best its standards would fall, and at worst the whole place would disintegrate. This was true enough –

but how could one weigh the breeding and welfare of thoroughbred horses against the needs of human beings in a world at war?

Behind his practical reasoning, he knew perfectly well, lay his overpowering desire to remain within reach of Katya; and when she herself went off to the front, his feelings of guilt and inadequacy burned. The longer he let things drift, the more remote grew the possibility of escape, for the vast, sprawling country to which he had committed himself was not only enmeshed in the toils of a debilitating foreign war, but crippled internally by the spreading poison of Bolshevik revolution. As law and order broke down, and news spread of ever more frightful atrocities, Joseph became increasingly determined to preserve order and decency in the one small part of Russia over which he exercised control. As society disintegrated, he found fulfilment in organising the defence of the stud farm and resisting attempts at takeover.

Early in 1918, when representatives of the Ukraine made their own peace with the Kaiser, and German forces of occupation arrived, his task became easier for a while, since the troops supported the status quo and reinforced the flimsy structure which he had devised at the stud. Then, in the middle of their stay, came news that the entire Imperial family had been murdered at Yekaterinburg, in the Urals. Joseph was incensed. He cared nothing for the Tsaritsa, and not much for the Tsar; but he felt pity for their daughters, the three Grand Duchesses, and still more for their young son Alexis, the Tsarevitch, whose pain-racked life had come to an end at the age of only fourteen. 'What sort of beasts would murder a child like that?' he said angrily to one of the lads at the stud. 'At least, no – I shouldn't call them beasts, because animals don't behave like that. They don't kill except for food. They don't murder each other out of jealousy and spite. These people are monsters, and I loathe them.'

NINE

The Train: December 1919

H E WAS far gone with exhaustion and hunger when at last he found the train. For two days, with another night in the open between, he had struggled on through the snow, blinded by a freezing mist that never dispersed and never let him glimpse the sun. With all sense of direction gone, he could only crawl towards what he hoped was the south. By the second afternoon both he and Boy were lame, he from twisting his right ankle in an ice-bound hole, the horse from cracks in his heels, caused by immersion in snow and slush. They had long since eaten their food. The only member of the party who seemed undistressed was Moorka, who spent most of her time riding on the horses' backs, a miniature, sphinx-like jockey, with excellent balance, hunched comfortably in front of the saddle, on the base of the neck. Joseph was surprised that Boy allowed her to take such a liberty, but he appeared to enjoy having her as a passenger.

They seemed to be heading for yet another night out in the steppe; the light was already failing, and the mist had taken on that sulphurous colour which presages the fall of a winter dusk. Then, from the murk ahead, came a familiar sound. Joseph stopped to listen. It came again. Beyond any doubt, it was the hoot of a railway engine – not the long-drawn-out wail of a train at speed, but the staccato toot of an engine manoeuvring in a siding or station.

'By God, boys, the railway!' He urged the horses forward. 'Where we are, your guess is as good as mine. But we're somewhere.'

A couple of minutes later, square shapes loomed out of the mist. At first he took them for a row of buildings; then he realised they were the box-coaches of a freight train. For some reason it was at a standstill, though not apparently in a station or a town. Immediately he was seized by the fear that it was about to move on, that after his luck in walking on to it, he would miss the chance of a lift. It occurred to him that the train might be a Bolshevik one, but then he thought,

No: we're too far south. He clicked his tongue at the stallions and broke into a shuffling trot.

A shout stopped him. He recognised that the yell was a challenge, but it seemed to be in a foreign language, and he did not understand it. All the same, he came to a halt. Another shout, this time quite clear: 'Stand still or I shoot.'

Dimly Joseph comprehended that the words were English. He raised both hands. A figure detached itself from the corner of one wagon and came towards him – a man in long, khaki greatcoat and peaked service cap, with a rifle at the ready. 'This is a military train,' he shouted. 'Keep away.'

'English?' Joseph faltered, weak with fatigue and astonishment. 'So am I.'

'Who the hell are you?'

'My name's Clements. Where is this?'

'Never mind.'

More men appeared between the wagons, alerted by the shouts. With his confidence returning, Joseph said firmly, 'Where's your commanding officer?'

'Who are you?' the guard repeated. 'Military or civilian?'

'Civilian. Who are you?'

'None of your business.'

'Fair enough – but fetch an officer.'

There was no need for the guard to move, as a tall man in a tan greatcoat and peaked cap came forward and said quietly, 'All right, Ellis. I'll handle this.'

'Sir!' replied the guard, not lowering his rifle.

The officer was young – in his late twenties – dark, clean-shaven, except for a moustache, and had a long, lean, humorous face. 'What are these horses?' he asked.

'Stallions from the former Imperial Stud at Kharkov,' Joseph answered. 'Both winners of the English Derby.'

The officer shot him a look. 'And I suppose your name's Charlie Chaplin.'

'I'm Joseph Clements. I was manager of the stud.'

'And what are you trying to do?'

'Save the horses, of course.'

'You've walked from Kharkov?'

'Yes.'

'Good God! What are they called, then, these fellows?'

'This is Aboyeur – won in 1913 – and that's Minoru, 1909.'

By then the officer was staring at him. 'Are you serious?'

'Absolutely.'

'Minoru – the King's horse.'

'That's right.'

'Well I'm damned!' The long face creased into a smile. The man held out his hand and said, 'Sam Kinkead, Royal Air Force.'

'How d'you do.' Joseph shook the hand, suddenly close to tears with relief. 'I'm sorry to inflict myself on you, but I need help.'

'Shelter? Food?'

'If you can.'

'Will the horses go into one of them?' The officer indicated the box-cars behind him.

'Provided there's a platform more or less level with the floor.'

Kinkead looked at his watch and whistled. 'You nearly missed us. We're leaving in forty minutes.' He looked round, spotted a young, red-headed aircraftman, and said, 'Atkins: nip and tell the driver I want him to move forward so that number seven's on the platform.'

'Very good, sir.' Atkins ran off along the train, disappearing into the fog.

'We're in a siding,' Kinkead explained. 'But the engine's fired up, ready to go.'

Joseph asked, 'Where are we?'

'Outside Kubyansk.'

'Kubyansk!' Joseph was astounded. The place was almost due east of Kharkov, miles from where he had hoped to be.

'You seem surprised.'

'I thought I was near Balakleya.'

'No – that's on the other line.'

'But you're heading south?'

'Very much so. The Bolshies are less than twenty miles to the north. There's nothing but a few miles of blown-up track separating them and us.'

Out of the fog came a couple of gentle toots from the engine, and the trucks began to squeal forward at a walking pace. Joseph led the horses alongside them, so stunned by the sudden turn of events that it did not immediately occur to him to wonder how it was that the RAF came to be here, in the middle of nowhere. Kinkead, walking beside him, said, 'The cat beats everything. Where in hell did *that* come from?'

'She joined us on the way.'

Kinkead began to ask questions about the journey, but Joseph was so tired, and so preoccupied by the problem of finding forage, that he gave only monosyllabic answers. Then he asked, 'Do you know of a farm near here?'

'Yes – there's one only half a mile a way. The boys were up there after eggs this morning. You're thinking of food for the horses – oats? Hay?'

'Either. Beans. Anything they've got. I can pay for it.'

'Don't worry about that. We've traded them enough bully beef to feed them for the whole winter.' He looked at his watch again. 'There's time for someone to pop out there again.'

In a moment he had despatched two other aircraftmen, with a sledge. 'Whatever you manage to get, be back in half an hour,' he told them. 'At the outside.'

Joseph could hardly believe it. After the privations and anxieties of his solitary passage across the steppe, it seemed an unbelievable luxury to have fallen into the hands of somebody so sympathetic, so capable, so quick to see what he needed, and in command of such resources. He tried to thank Kinkead, but the officer merely grinned and said, 'We've been stuck here for a week, so any event's welcome. But this – this is amazing. In the nick of time, too.'

Car number seven was no palace – just a steel box on wheels, with double doors which slid apart to open up half one wall. As he came alongside the entrance on the platform, Joseph's mind flew back twenty years to the day when Persimmon had refused to enter the special train at Newmarket on his way to the Derby. Suddenly he heard Marsh's loud voice offering a guinea to any man who managed to persuade the horse to go aboard, and saw again the swarm of helpers struggling to hoist the animal bodily through the door. Now, he would have bet, they were in for a performance of that calibre, especially as they were in a hurry. True to form, although Min began to march in confidently, the clang of his shoes on the steel floor was too much for Boy, who threw up his head and pulled backwards, feet skidding all over the snowy platform. When Kinkead moved to take hold of his bridle, Joseph said sharply, 'No! Leave him, please, or he'll be worse. Is there anything we can use as litter on the floor?'

Again Kinkead had an answer. In the end wagon were a whole lot of empty packing cases made of cardboard and paper. Though due to be burnt, they had so far escaped the flames, and now could be torn up. Word had already gone round the unit that something unusual was happening: willing helpers appeared, and a dozen pairs of hands quickly created a passable form of litter, which deadened sound as well as giving a better grip. Snow began to fall again as Joseph waited anxiously on the platform; then, for the second attempt, he handed Min to Kinkead and led Boy in alone. Whatever the reason – whether because the cat had gone in to investigate, and was prowling round the van, or because he did not like the snow outside – Boy went in like an angel, Min followed, and soon both were safely tied up, with buckets of water against the wall beneath them. Hardly had Joseph secured them, unsaddled them and put their rugs on than the scavenging party returned with a sledgeload of hay – not of the finest quality, but in those circumstances a miracle of its own.

'I ought to put some grease on Boy's heels,' said Joseph, half to himself, as he watched them eating. 'But, God, I think they can wait till morning.'

'Bring your own kit, then,' said Kinkead.

'I was planning to sleep here with them.'

'Please yourself. But there's a sleeping compartment you can have all your own. We can lock these doors. No harm can come to the horses . . .' He saw Joseph weakening. 'You must be starving, anyway.'

'Yes. Well – thanks. I'll come.'

'What about the cat?'

'I think she'll stay here. Perhaps I can bring her something to eat later. There's just one thing . . .'

'What's that?'

'Warn your men that this fellow kicks.' He indicated Boy. 'Nobody ought to come in here except me.'

As they hurried towards the front of the train in quickly-gathering darkness, Joseph saw that fighter aircraft, with their wings dismantled, were strapped to flat cars. He learnt that he had landed among B Flight of 47 Squadron, Royal Air Force, but that, for political reasons, to calm the anti-interventionist faction in London, the unit was now known simply as 'B Squadron', and all its men were officially classed as 'advisers' or 'instructors'. Equipped with Sopwith Camels, they were attached to the White Army – part of the British Military Mission – and had already flown numerous sorties against the Red forces, mainly above the Volga in the area of Tsaritsyn, some 500 miles to the south-east. Ten days ago they had been ordered northwards in the hope that they could bomb and strafe the Bolshevik forces closing in on Kharkov; but Kupyansk, a hundred miles short of Kharkhov, was the furthest point their train had been able to reach, for the lines beyond it had been destroyed, and ever since their arrival the aircraft had been grounded by fog, able to do nothing except wait for better weather and listen to wireless reports of the Red forces gaining ground. Now they had been ordered south again. Their first destination was Debaltsevo, a junction some 150 miles to the south, and then Taganrog.

Joseph was amazed when he saw the style in which the airmen were living. Admittedly, this train had been their home for months; even so, it seemed extraordinarily opulent. The pilots' quarters were in two Pullman cars, with separate sleeping compartments giving off a corridor, the whole done out in dark, polished wood and red plush. The dining-car was the same – a spacious saloon with a long table down the middle, and chairs ranged either side. Halfway along one wall stood a grandiose fireplace, looted from some house, complete with fluted pilasters, plaster cherubs and a log fire burning in a the grate. Next door was a lounge and bar, equally spacious and well-appointed.

To Joseph's confusion, the car was full of officers, in various kinds and mixtures of uniform, but all trim and neatly turned out – in absolute contrast with him. Unshaven, dishevelled, sodden, exhausted, he felt unable to cope with all these strange people and fervently wished he were back in the horse-van. Worse still, he heard Kinkead excusing himself on the grounds that he was duty officer and had to supervise the departure of the train.

'Let me introduce you to our CO,' he said. 'Colonel Raymond Collishaw.'

Joseph found himself shaking hands with a big, fair-haired man of about his own age. 'Welcome to 47 Squadron,' he said. 'At least, welcome to B Squadron. Bit of a crash landing, I gather.'

Joseph grinned. In the heat of the saloon car his brain did not seem to be functioning too well, and he couldn't quite see what the Colonel meant. But Collishaw said, 'You look to me as though you could do with some refreshment. When did you last eat?'

Joseph tried to answer, but could not. The lights began to sway, then to revolve, and finally they all seemed to fly up into the air.

He came round lying on the floor and saw a ring of faces above him. Someone had taken off his shuba and his waistcoat. Beneath his back the floor was shuddering and bumping: the train was on its way. He felt better – clear-headed again – and began trying to sit up.

'Gently does it,' said a voice. A hand came down. He grasped it and allowed himself to be pulled upright, then sat on a chair.

'Sorry,' he muttered. 'Must have been the heat. Change of temperature.'

'Get that inside you.' His helper indicated a steaming glass that stood on a table beside him. Thinking it was tea, Joseph took a sip, only to find that it was powerfully alcoholic.

'A Petersburg pony,' said the officer. 'Made with rum. A speciality of our cook, the one and only Cowderdrill.'

Behind him hovered an awkward, gangling scarecrow of a man, with red hair standing straight up and freckles all over his face. When he spoke, his long, yellow horse teeth waggled and clicked as though they might fall out. 'Is it all right, sir?' he asked anxiously.

'Yes!' said Joseph emphatically, having just swallowed a mouthful. 'It's very much all right.'

All night the train trundled on. Sometimes it slowed to a halt as it came up behind the next one in the queue, sometimes it waited, occasionally it reversed, for the line was choked with traffic, most of it coaches loaded with refugees. Joseph slept heavily but intermittently in a comfortable, broad bunk. Every time he half-woke, his thoughts went to the horses in their van; he became obsessed by the fear that during one of the enforced halts a saboteur might creep up to the train and sever the couplings, so that the freight trucks would be left behind. At every stop he came fully awake and lay tense with worry until movement began again.

Morning reassured him. The mist was thinner, and only a faint haze shrouded the snowbound steppe. During a halt he slipped back along the track and scrambled up through the sliding doors of box car number seven. Both stallions whinnied softly as they saw him, making him wish that he had something better for them than the crusts of grey bread which Cowderdrill had given him after breakfast. The horses ate them gladly, but he thought wistfully of the good oats buried in barrels at the Kharkov stud, of his carrots so carefully stored in sand. After the bread, all he could offer was more of the musty hay. 'Never mind,' he said to Boy as he rubbed him down. 'It's better than walking.' He checked his sore feet carefully and was relieved to find them no worse. Having nothing with which to treat the cracks, he could only hope that they would heal up naturally if the horse spent a day or two on a dry footing. Considering what they had been through, Min seemed in surprisingly good condition.

As he worked, the train began to move again, and suddenly from outside came the noise of shots. In a second he was at the narrow slit of door which he had left open. Out in the snow, less than a hundred yards off, a troop of Cossack cavalry was galloping parallel with the train, an impromptu escort. Steam spurted from the horses' nostrils; snow flew from their hooves. The men wore short, conical black hats of Persian lamb; their long grey coats were belted in at the waist and criss-crossed by bandoliers of ammunition. They held their rifles high and vertical in their right hands. With a mixture of joy and envy Joseph marvelled at the sheer beauty of their style: they rode low and loose in the saddle, in typical Cossack fashion, apparently not bothering about their horses but perfectly in tune with them, with such control that they were free to fire their rifles into the air, reload and fire again, without the slightest change of pace or direction. After a minute the leader made a signal and wheeled to his left, away from the line of the track, so that in a few seconds he and his followers had vanished into the mist.

That was the last friendly guerrilla force the travelling airmen saw: thereafter they had to fight off attacks all the way. Inside the officers' accommodation, Joseph found himself quickly accepted. The pilots had been welded into a close-knit group by their experiences in the war, but they opened ranks to admit a stranger – especially one with such an unusual background. Kinkead, in particular, was a keen punter in civilian life, and welcomed Joseph warmly. 'Listen, fellers,' he said on the second evening. 'You realise we've got a famous jockey in our midst? Twice won the Russian Derby – what about that!'

'Only the Warsaw Derby,' said Joseph deprecatingly. 'The one in Moscow's the big race.'

'Never mind! A Derby's a Derby. Let's drink to it.'

Kinkead questioned Joseph closely about his background. In the easy, informal atmosphere, the officers addressed each other by Christian names or nicknames: apart from Tommy and Bill and John, Collishaw was known as Colly, Kinkead as Kink, a man called Aten as Bunny. Joseph was surprised that so few of them were English. Collishaw and Aten were Canadians, and Kinkead South African; then he realised that all were volunteers, united by their love of flying dangerously. Even though almost two years had passed since the official formation of the Royal Air Force, they still clung to their army ranks and uniforms. They spoke of their own exploits in the most casual terms, but it became clear that in their operations over the Volga they had shown extraordinary skill and courage, and won several medals.

Had not Wrangel himself given them a banquet out of gratitude – an immense meal, washed down with vodka and champagne, in a castle overlooking the river, during which Cossack officers smashed their glasses, made passionate speeches, sang lugubrious songs and danced their wild knife-dances which ended with them all hurling their *kinshals*, or daggers, into the floor? Had Wrangel not called the RAF pilots 'my Cossacks of the air'? They described him in terms that brought the power of his personality vividly alive: with his tall, spare frame, his gaunt face and hollow cheeks and shaven head, his ice-blue eyes, he had impressed every one of them with his strength and competence. Had *he* been commander-in-chief, rather than Denikin, they said, the Whites might by now be in Moscow; as it was, Wrangel had fallen out ever more bitterly with the Admiral, and the White counter-attack had become bogged down in the quicksand of their disagreements. The pilots speculated endlessly on the possible outcome of events; but they rated the Red Cavalry General Semyon Budenny almost as highly as Wrangel, and were pessimistic to a man.

About noon on the first day, when the train pulled into a small town called Zagryzovo, their fears seemed all too well justified. They heard from the station master that Kharkov had fallen to the Bolsheviks, and that Denikin's central forces were pulling back in disorder. Budenny was driving southwards. Volunteers who had fought for the Whites were deserting to him by the thousand. The Whites' next line of defence – people thought – would be in the Taganrog area. This meant that B Flight was caught in a mass retreat, a rout, even. Joseph felt cold inside. Kharkov captured! Pray God the hospital and its staff had simply switched sides, as Katya had predicted they would. He could not imagine what she would be doing, except working: he knew that she would go on ministering to the wounded and dying, no matter whose side they were on. Pray God the stud and the remaining horses were intact. Pray God, especially, that the fat, black-bearded man who led the raiding-party had been diverted to some other sector of the front, and that a less vindictive Communist had come to claim the stud in the name of the Revolution. Had anybody realised that two of the best stallions were missing?

The station and sidings at Zagryzovo were in chaos, every line jammed with trains, every train stuffed with people desperate to escape: regimental trains carrying the shattered remains of White units, hospital trains crammed with wounded, one or two civilian trains, all packed to the windows and festooned with hangers-on outside. Soldiers in uniform lay on the roofs of the coaches, many incapably drunk, yet still pouring vodka down their throats from bottles and flasks; how they stayed in place when their trains were moving, Joseph could not imagine, but the sight of them, frozen on the very edge of life and death, stabbed him with guilt when he thought how his horses had taken over a box-car which could accommodate at least fifty humans. 'Forget it,' said one of the pilots. 'We're under strict orders not to pick up anyone except our own personnel. And even if we did, it would make no difference: fifty, five hundred, five thousand – there'd still be millions out there.'

The press of humanity made it impossible for Joseph to bring the stallions into the open. During one of the innumerable stops, when the box-car happened to be alongside a platform, he longed to lead them out and walk them up and down, even if only for a few minutes, to get their circulations going; but, quite apart from the risk that pressure from other drivers would force the train forward at the wrong moment, he knew that the sight of privileged animals appearing from inside a military train would constitute an intolerable provocation. Even though the regime to which he had been driven – four days of prolonged exertion and exposure, followed by complete inactivity – was one that he much disliked, he had no alternative but to keep them in. Merely to move between their van and the rest of the train was a risky operation: once during the first day he was caught out by a sudden departure, and had to remain with them for the next three hours, until another halt allowed him to move forward again.

At least B Flight's train was well armed. During any alert members of the ground staff manned nests of Lewis machine-guns, deployed at intervals down the train, and all ranks (including Joseph) were issued with .303 Lee Enfield rifles. Even the four *plennys*, or prisoners-of-war, who had been taken on as officers' servants, were given weapons. Unlike other prisoners in less favoured circumstances, who were marked out by their black overalls with yellow crescents on the back, these men wore bits and pieces of ill-fitting British army uniform, and showed a dog-like devotion to their new masters: indeed, a vast, black-bearded man called Ivan kept professing his eagerness to slaughter Bolsheviks by the train-load – even though, as he grasped his rifle by the woodwork a few inches down from the muzzle, he looked as though he intended to use the weapon as a club rather than as a firearm.

His chance came soon enough. At about eight o'clock on the second night, as the train trundled on at twenty miles per hour and the pilots sat in the lounge with rum toddies, the alarm suddenly went up. Out in the night green and red flares looped high into the air and floated down. Rifle shots rang out. Bullets began to slam into the side of the coach, making it boom like a gong. A window shattered with a crash of breaking glass. 'Green attack!' somebody shouted. 'Action stations! Get the lights out!'

Officers and servants dashed to take up pre-arranged defensive positions. Joseph, who had never in his life done serious bodily harm to anyone, loaded his rifle and crouched at a half-opened window. For the moment everything was dark. Then another red flare illuminated a line of four or five horsemen galloping parallel with the train. The snow glowed pink all round them, but bright sparks spurted from their rifles as they fired at the coaches. Bullets clanged against the steel walls, whined off in ricochets. From Joseph's left came a heavy rattle as the nearest machine-gun opened up. The leading rider crumpled, fell backwards and slid over the tail of his horse. Joseph aimed at the new leader and fired. Getting no result, he loaded and fired again. This time not the new leader but the second in line slumped in his saddle and toppled to his left. Joseph could not tell whether it was his own bullet which had fallen behind the moving target and done the damage, or someone else's. Horrified but excited, motivated purely by the instinct to survive, he loaded and fired until his barrel was too hot to touch.

The attack lasted twenty minutes. By the end of it the defenders reckoned they had killed at least fifteen of the bandits, but the battle left the saloon car in a poor way, with three of the eight windows shot out and the panelling splintered. Nevertheless, the pilots were exhilarated: they called for a round of Cowderdrill's best Petrograd ponies and eagerly swapped details of the fight, claiming kills as if they had been shooting at a fairground. 'Who got that guy on the grey?' demanded Kink. 'That was a great shot! We sure thinned the bastards, anyway.' Joseph, as he cooled down, became sickened by the thought of horses being shot almost for fun, and then started to worry about his own two. Bunny reassured him. The Greens never bothered to attack freight wagons, but concentrated their fire on personnel, and in any case the box-cars were made of such heavy sheet steel that they would easily withstand rifle-bullets.

So it proved. Morning revealed that the box-cars had sustained a few stray hits, but that none of the bullets had penetrated, and the horses were unharmed. Daylight also showed how essential it was for trains to be well defended. Again and again the RAF contingent passed wrecks lying on their sides or burnt out, apparently turned over and off the tracks by sheer numbers of human assailants. What had happened to all the passengers, it was impossible to say. A few bodies lay by the track, first charred and later frozen, but thousands more humans had disappeared. The further they went, the more Joseph felt that they were being sucked into a vortex of madness and destruction, in which civilised values no longer played any part, and from which only the fittest and most ruthless would emerge. Get tougher, he told himself; and he seemed to feel his own moral fibre coarsening.

Only in the evenings did a little cheerfulness creep into the company of travellers. After supper, with a round or two of Petrograd ponies inside them, the pilots became boisterous as they swapped yarns and sang songs, accompanied erratically by Bunny Aten on a balalaika. With only a smattering of Russian, they nevertheless laced their own conversation with Russian words, and although they tended to mock Russian habits and customs, they reserved their real scorn for the Bolsheviks. Their favourite song – called for at least once a night – was a ridiculous music-hall ditty:

I've just come back from Moscow. You must go to Moscow,
For it's where they keep the Bolshevism,
And you get cold feet and rheumatism.
I landed from my yachtsky. Young Olga Petrovotsky
Took me for a jolly good trotsky, and very, very soon . . .
Olga Petrovotsky used to squatsky on my knee.
Did we care a jotsky for a trotsky? No, not we!
Oh my baby doll she, was a proper Bolshie – yes,
Upon my life she put me in a whirl.
Nightly in the snowsky my poor noseky would get frozesky,
Froseky to the noseky of my pretty little Bolshie girl.
Ta-ra-ra, ta-ra-ra, ta-ra-ra, ta-ra.
Beneath the Russian moonsky we'd kissky and spoonsky,
And the wolves all round would howlovitch, and prowlovitch,
    and growlovitch.

Her husband in a droshky drove up, and Oh by goshky!
He didn't 'alf want to washsky. He shouted 'Ha! My vife!'
He said, 'With this knifesky, I will take your lifesky.
That you kiss my wifesky, I have evidence.'
Then he roared like two bulls, 'Pay me 50,000 roubles!'
50,000 roubles? English money eighteen pence!
Ta-ra-ra, ta-ra-ra, ta-ra-ra, ta-ra.

For most of one morning they ran close beside a road, which lay parallel to the railway, a few yards off on their right. Along that road struggled the most wretched procession imaginable: men, women and children trudged head-down through the snow with scarcely enough energy to turn and look at the train beside them. Starving horses, with ribs and hip bones threatening to burst through the skin, listlessly pulled carts and sledges piled with household effects. Countless refugees had already succumbed to raiders and the bitter cold. Human bodies lay scattered along the roadsides, many almost naked from the attentions of looters. Nor had the dead horses, frozen though they were into grotesque attitudes, escaped the knives of scavengers: meat had been hacked from their quarters so that their thigh bones shone white among tatters of black flesh. Joseph thanked God that he was not out there, among the living or the dead. It was a relief for everyone on board when the railway turned away from the road and there was nothing to look out on but an expanse of frozen water.

On the third day the weather cleared and the landscape began to change. The long swell of the steppe gave way to shorter, steeper country, to hills clad in pine forests, which themselves were clad in snow: for the eye, a welcome change after so much monotonous open space. Joseph found himself sizing the hills up in terms of the difficulties they would present to someone trying to trek through them. In spite of their friendlier appearance, they might easily prove worse than the steppe, for in those steep woods and valleys the snow-drifts would be deep, the chances of losing one's way high. And here he was, not floundering through the snow on his own feet, but travelling in an absurd degree of comfort, with the stallions secure, with caviar at every meal, unlimited rum in the evenings, and a hot shower-bath at the end of the carriage. The worst disadvantage was that he had far too much time to think and brood.

On the fourth day they reached Debaltsevo, only to find that the

177

chaos in the marshalling yards surpassed anything they had seen so far. Not only did every train in the Ukraine seem to have reached the junction simultaneously: engines had burst their boilers or suffered other mechanical failures, drivers had taken to drink and deserted. The result was indescribable congestion. B Flight's train crept into a siding and stopped. When word came from the station-master that there was no chance of them being shunted onto the main line south until next day, gloom spread among the pilots and ground crews. For Joseph, however, it was a chance to give the horses much-needed exercise and muck out their box. By luck the train had drawn up on the outermost line in the sidings: the platform beside it was flanked by a high wall, so that it was unusually private, especially with an armed guard set at either end to repel refugees. Joseph saw this secluded space as a God-given exercise arena, narrow, but about three hundred yards long.

By then, after four days' immobility, the stallions were pent-up and ready to go. In a way it was lucky that they had had no better food, for oats would have made them almost impossible to handle. As it was, Boy took a swing with his teeth when Joseph went to inspect his foot; but Joseph, expecting trouble, took care to keep out of range. As far as he could tell without trotting him out, the horse was sound again: with the help of a fitter, Leading Aircraftman Billy Bond, who had worked in racing stables before the war, he had worked half a tin of butter into the cracked heels, and that seemed to have done the trick. Bond was a godsend to him: a young, fair-haired Yorkshireman from Wetherby, he was both horse-mad and under-employed. Not only did he drill holes in the floor of the box-car to give it drainage and cut slots high up in the walls for ventilation: he was also proud of having such celebrated animals on board. At Debaltsevo he helped by leading out Min, who had got to know him over the past few days.

'I'll go first,' said Joseph, having clipped a leading-rope to Boy's head collar. 'You follow close behind.'

The snow on the platform, several inches deep, had not yet been packed down hard, so that it offered the horses' hoofs a good grip. As Joseph had expected, Boy played up at first, rearing, kicking and squealing, and he came down once on his haunches; but after he had trotted four lengths of the platform, with Joseph running beside him, he calmed down and began to take an interest in his surroundings. Brief as it was, the break did the animals good.

Joseph took advantage of the enforced delay to go foraging. Unlike the railway yards, the streets were almost empty, because so many people had already gone. Inquiries revealed that a cavalry regiment had recently pulled out of a barracks on the western fringe of the town, leaving behind many of its stores. He made his way there in an *izvozchik* on runners, and told the driver to wait while he went to barter with an armed sentry on the gate. At first the man claimed that nothing had been left behind; then, at the sight of a gold rouble in the palm of his visitor, he changed tune and asked what he could offer. Joseph came away with one sack of maize, one of oats, some beans, a truss of good hay, and – wonder of wonders – a few carrots. It took the *izvozchik* two journeys to ferry his loot back to the train, and Joseph made sure that the driver kept his cargo hidden under wraps, so as not to excite the cupidity of other horse-owners on the way.

Back in the siding, he found that the train had two new passengers, taken on against the rules, and against the better instincts, of the RAF officers. As he came into the lounge car, Bunny Aten got up from one of the banquettes and motioned him towards a man and woman sitting opposite, both – he guessed – in their forties, and immensely aristocratic in their appearance. 'May I introduce Count and Countess Orlov, of Novgorod?' said Bunny. 'This is Joseph Clements.'

Novgorod! Joseph stepped forward smiling and shook hands. The woman remained seated, but the man stood up to greet him – a tall, slim figure dressed in a coat of luxurious grey fur, with an ascetic, emaciated face made to look positively gaunt by a pair of rimless spectacles. The woman's coat was even more sumptuous: full-length, jet-black mink, with a high collar turned up round her ears, it dramatically set off her own dark colouring.

'You're travelling with us?' Joseph asked in Russian.

'Yes,' said the Count. 'Thanks to the kindness of your commanding officer, we have been taken into the bosom of the Royal Air Force.' His accent and form of expression were old-fashioned and patrician: they reminded Joseph of Katya's father.

'And you come from Novgorod?'

'Originally, yes. But immediately, from Kharkov.'

'Kharkov! What's happening there?'

'Today, I cannot tell you. All I can say is that when we escaped from the back door of our house two days ago, the Bolsheviks were shooting out the windows at the front.'

'I'm sorry. Did you save anything?'

'Only this.' The Count pointed to a small black leather attaché case on the floor beside him. 'And the clothes we stand up in. You are interested in Kharkov?'

'I worked there.'

'That is how you speak Russian so well?'

'Thank you – yes.'

There was a pause. Then Joseph said, 'You come from Novgorod – so perhaps you know Prince Mironov?'

'Indeed. I knew him well.'

'Knew him? Is he dead?'

'Alas, yes. He was shot last month.'

'Oh God! And the house – Nikolsk?'

'Burnt to the ground.'

'Oh! The rest of the family?'

'I believe the old Princess is still alive. She went to St Petersburg. But about the children, I don't know.'

'How could they do that?' asked Joseph in a dazed whisper. 'What could they have against a harmless eccentric like the Prince?'

'That is typical of the Bolsheviks,' said Orlov unemotionally. 'You heard what they did in Kharkov?'

'No?'

'They surrounded the hospital and set fire to it, with 300 people inside.'

The news made Joseph silently frantic. Unable to explain his anxiety to anyone on the train, he left Billy Bond in charge of the horses and went back into town on the faint chance that the telephone line to Kharkov might be open. His hopes were soon dashed. Having fought his way through a mass of people in the central telegraph office, he found that there was no communication of any kind with the north.

He withdrew to a cheap *traktir*, crowded with a mixture of towns-people and refugees, and full of tobacco smoke. There was almost nothing to eat, and in any case he was not hungry, so he bought a glass of tea and sat at a table in the corner. Should he go back? Leave the horses on the train? But even if he did, what good could he do? All he wanted was to find her.

Across the dimly-lit room a queue moved jerkily forward along the counter. As the people shuffled, Joseph began staring at a particular face in the line – a tall young man in an army greatcoat, bareheaded, with his fair hair cut short at the back and sides, standing side-on, so that his finely-drawn profile showed against the light. Joseph was puzzled: the face was familiar, yet strange. Then, as the boy moved forward and turned slightly towards him, he felt his heart start thudding. The youth bore an astonishing resemblance to Katya. Of course: it was Dmitri, her brother Dmitri, Mitya, whom he had last seen at the age of twelve, during that golden summer seven years ago.

Impulsively, Joseph stood up, wove his way between the tables and touched the boy on the elbow. Dmitri turned – and Joseph never forgot the series of expressions that chased each other across that handsome but disturbing face. For a second he looked quite blank. Then recognition lit up his blue eyes, but just for an instant, as if sunlight had swept quickly over a snowfield, only for a cloud to chase away the gleam and darken the landscape again.

'Dmitri!' Joseph held out his hand, but the youth said coldly, 'No – you've mistaken me for someone else. My name is Pyotr.'

Joseph, astounded, said, 'But you know me. I worked for your father at Nikolsk. I used to give you riding lessons . . .'

'Wait.' The boy turned to the old woman behind the counter and paid for his tea. Then, holding the glass in one hand, he said tersely, 'Let's sit down.'

Back at the table in the corner, Joseph stared at him. The face was unmistakable, for it was a heavier form of Katya's, from the same mould. A fuzz of downy fair hair covered upper lip and chin, and there was something unsettling about the eyes, which had a distant, cold look. Back it all came – the boy's latent animosity towards him, his reserve, his tendency to sulk. Now his clothes – a mixture of uniform and civilian garments – were dirty and torn. His hands and fingernails were filthy and stained yellow with nicotine. Joseph was about to protest and give his own name as evidence when the youth held up a hand and said, very low: 'Yes, I remember you, Mr Clements. But please don't draw attention to my identity here. I'm sure you'll understand why I've changed my name.'

'Of course.' Joseph swallowed with relief at finding that he had not taken leave of his senses. 'I didn't mean to embarrass you. I'm sorry.'

'*Nichevo*. Nobody noticed. But what brings you to a dump like Debaltsevo, and at a time like this?'

'I'm on my way south with some horses.'

'Horses? Really! What horses?'

'Stallions from the former Imperial Stud at Kharkov. I didn't want the Bolsheviks to get them.'

'I see. And you've come this far on foot?'

'No – part of the way by train. I got a lift from the RAF – the British air force. They've been flying in support of Wrangel.'

There was something going on behind the cold blue eyes, but Joseph could not tell what. 'I heard bad news of your father,' he said. 'I'm very sorry.'

'Who told you?'

'Count Orlov. Your old neighbour.'

'Orlov? You saw Orlov? Where?' The questions came out quick as whiplashes.

'Here, on the . . .' Suddenly Joseph sensed danger, like a gust of cold air, and corrected himself to say, 'In Debaltsevo.'

Dmitri looked down at the table and said, 'Yes – poor father.'

'The house, as well.'

'I know.'

There was a pause. Joseph noticed that Dmitri's left hand was turned downwards from the wrist at an unnatural angle. Just as there was something wrong with that joint, so, in the boy's brief answers there was something amiss – an unnatural distance, a lack of genuine feeling. But he went on, 'What about your sister?'

'I'm sorry?'

'Your sister – Katya.'

'What about her?'

'Where is she now?'

'How should I know?'

This was overtly antagonistic. Had Dmitri known about their liaison all along? Joseph said more warily, 'You've been away, then?'

'Yes.' The blue eyes regarded him steadily. 'I ran away from home three years ago to join the army.'

'Good for you! But you must have been under-age.'

'I pretended I was a year older than I am and enlisted as a private soldier.'

'Where were you sent?'

'To the Western Front. Where else? To Poland. That's where I got this.' He held up his damaged left wrist.

Joseph looked at it sympathetically. 'Rifle bullet?'

'No – shrapnel from a shell.'

'So you were invalided out?'

'For a while. Then I went back – until things fell to pieces around us.'

'How was that?'

'Everyone ran away. The officers first, then most of the men.'

'And now?'

'Now?' Dmitri hesitated. Until then his answers had been fluent enough, but now he seemed uncertain. In the end he said, 'Well – like you, I'm heading south.'

'Have a lift, then.'

'I beg your pardon?'

'Come on the train. There's plenty of room. I'm sure I can get them to take you.'

'Oh no. I'm all right, thanks.' He hesitated again and asked, 'At least, if I wanted to, how would I find it?'

'It's in the sidings at the station. Grey Pullman coaches and box-cars. The engine's number 607.'

'When's it leaving?'

'As soon as it can. But not before tomorrow morning.'

'Well . . .' Dmitri smiled fleetingly. 'It's good of you. But I can't go yet. I'm waiting for a friend to catch me up.'

'Are you sure? How will you travel?'

'We'll be all right.'

'Have you got money?'

'Oh, yes.'

'Well, then.'

Joseph saw there was no point in pressing him. He longed to talk about Katya, to ask about her again, even to reveal that he loved her – anything to bring her into the conversation. But he suppressed the urge and said, 'What news of Vanya?'

Dmitri shrugged. 'As far as I know, he is in Petrograd, with some cousins.'

You don't care, do you? Joseph thought. You've broken with the family. But all he said was, 'Oh well. I suppose I'd better be going. Good to see you, anyway.' He stood up and put a hand on Dmitri's shoulder. 'Remember the rat-trap?' he asked.

The boy nodded, but he neither stood up nor looked up, and when he said 'Do svidaniya', it was in such a cold, absent voice that Joseph went out into the street wondering what the hell was wrong with him.

*

An hour later, as the light was failing, Pyotr Lysenko, formerly Prince Dmitri Mironov, arrived unobtrusively at the back door of a mill that had once ground various types of flour and corn. There were still sacks in the front window, which faced on to the street, but iron bars had been padlocked across it, and a notice proclaimed that the establishment had closed until further notice. At the back, however, activity of a different kind had started up. To the revolutionary cell, the attraction of the building was its height: its four-storey tower, which housed the hoists for raising sacks of grain, made a perfect vantage-point for a radio transmitter and its aerial. A pleasant, old-fashioned smell of flour and grain still emanated from the old wooden walls and floors.

Pyotr had not wasted any time. Already he had made a discreet reconnaissance of the marshalling yards and checked the position of train 607. He had even considered going straight to the nearest guard, asking for Clements, and taking up his offer of a lift. In that way he would at least have put himself within striking distance of his quarry. But it would need more than one man to overpower him and the Countess, make sure of the valuables, and escape. Besides, now there was this extra business of the horses.

As Pyotr entered the ground floor of the mill from the alleyway and ran up the wooden stairs, he could hear the drumming of the generator which powered the radio. Excellent, he thought: transmission was in progress. He had already written out the text of his message for headquarters, in capital letters, and it only needed to be turned into Morse code. Slava would do that in a flash: he was a genius at encoding and decoding messages.

At the door on the stairs he paused and gave the complicated double knock: one, one-two, one, one-two. After a short wait he heard the bolt slide back, and as the door opened he slipped through the opening. Inside the tower-room, the smell of flour and corn was even stronger. 'Thanks, Comrade,' he said into the dark, and the deep voice of Vladimir greeted him. 'Any luck?'

'Very much so. He's here.'

'*Razve*! In town?'

'On a train.'

'Stuck?'

'Yes, but unfortunately it's well guarded. Too strong for us. He's got in with some British airmen. We'll have to wait till they're more in the open. There are some racehorses on the train as well. I found the box-car that they're in from the smell.'

He followed Vladimir up the creaking, ladder-like staircase to the loft which housed the transmitter. There, in a glare of harsh yellow lamplight, Slava was ensconced in a corner like a great black bear, hunched over a table, earphones almost buried in his sooty hair and beard. He raised a paw in greeting, but continued to write rapidly as a message came in. Presently he stopped, transmitted a few words and sat back.

'Admirable, No 21!' he said as he read Pyotr's message. 'Commissar Trotsky will like this.'

'Where is he?'

'At the other end. He's there now.'

At once Slava began to send, and after only two or three minutes an answer came clicking back. 'First class. Agree wait till target in open. Strong interest horses. Capture if possible. Otherwise liquidate. Show no mercy reactionary enemies of revolution. Greetings. Trotsky.'

On board the train Joseph checked the horses, rubbed them down, gave them small extra feeds and clean water, and put down a saucer of bully-beef for Morka, who had temporarily gone absent through the small hole which Billy Bond had cut for her in one corner. Then, having double-checked the padlock on the box-car door, he went forward and sought out Count Orlov.

The Count, as usual, was in his sleeping compartment. A reserved and fastidious man, he did all he could to avoid inflicting himself on his hosts, and kept out of their way with an almost embarrassing degree of self-effacement. His wife was the same, scarcely venturing into the saloon or dining-cars except at meal-times, and then always late, so that contact with the airmen was reduced to a minimum. Now Joseph knocked on their door, himself embarrassed. The Count appeared immediately, fully dressed, except for a hat. As always, he looked strained.

'Excuse me,' Joseph began. 'I'm sorry to disturb you, but I want to ask you something.'

'Come in!' Orlov stepped back, ushering Joseph into the cramped compartment. A smell of stale scent filled the cold air. The Countess was lying full-length in the upper bunk, also fully dressed, wrapped in her magnificent mink. At his entrance she levered herself on to one elbow and smiled bleakly down. Awkward as it was, at such close quarters, with nowhere to sit, Joseph forced himself to explain.

He described how he had just met Dmitri in the *traktir*: how there was something odd about the boy's manner, how the account he gave of his movements had been unsatisfactory, and how he had showed a peculiar interest in the fact that Orlov was in Debaltsevo.

'I may be wrong,' Joseph went on, 'but I got the impression he's working for the Reds. I reckon he's become a Bolshevik agent. If I'm right, is there any particular reason why he should be after *you*?'

Orlov looked quickly up at his wife, then said, 'Yes. There is every reason. First, I am a prominent White Russian, and second, I am carrying one of the most valuable jewels in the world – the Orlov diamond.'

When Joseph merely stared at him, he went on: 'My great-grandfather bought it from a ship's captain more than a hundred years ago, but it came originally from the eye of the idol in the Brahmin temple at Mysore. It weighs nearly two hundred carats. It is one of the most famous diamonds in the world. But the point now is hardly its worth: after the Revolution, it has become one of the most potent symbols of the old regime. That was why they raided our house in Kharkov: no doubt it was the diamond they were after.'

'And where is it now?'

'There.' The Count pointed at his briefcase, which lay on his bunk. 'Along with other family heirlooms. I am sorry to inflict my personal problems on you – but because our family is well known in the Ukraine, you can see why we could hardly travel on an ordinary train.' He gave a wan, apologetic smile.

'No wonder they're looking for you,' said Joseph. 'The sooner we all get out of here, the better.'

Kinkead agreed. Extra guards were set; but a special plea to the station-master's office, accompanied by five of Joseph's gold roubles, produced a magical improvement in the state of the traffic. The station-master himself had disappeared, and his deputy seemed altogether more effective. First, word came that a track would be cleared for them to join the main line at midnight; then, at 11 p.m., came another message saying that a route was already open. The engine-driver had got up steam in preparation, and they moved out immediately, with the wheels squealing and groaning over successive sets of points.

TEN

In Bolshevik Hands: December 1919

WHEN THE Bolsheviks reached the hospital at Kharkov at three in the afternoon, Katya was in the operating theatre on the first floor, helping Dr Mikhailov. On the table lay a young soldier whose right leg had been shattered below the knee; someone had applied a tourniquet made from strips of dark-red cloth, but the bandage had been put on too tight, and the foot looked blue and lifeless.

'It'll have to come off,' said the surgeon flatly, as he picked chips of bone from the shredded flesh with his pincettes. Like everyone else in the building, he was half-deadened by fatigue, working on in a fog of exhaustion far beyond the point at which he should have stopped to rest, but impelled by the ever-increasing flow of casualties. The only wounds he refused to dress were those obviously self-inflicted: anyone whose shattered hand showed burn-marks, revealing that the owner had shot himself from close range, he rejected angrily.

His present casualty was clearly genuine. 'Be ready to staunch the artery when I let this go, sister,' he said. Yet when he cut through the tourniquet with a pair of scissors, blood did not spurt out as he had expected. 'Ah!' he said, with a sudden lift in his voice. 'One little piece of luck. The artery wasn't severed, after all. Look at that.' Even as he spoke, signs of life began to show again in the ankle and foot. 'Perhaps we can save it, even now. Once I've got this cleaned up, all we'll need is a splint and some bandages.'

He went to work again. At that moment the fire-bell in the passage began to clang in short, irregular bursts. Taking it for the usual false alarm, caused by surges in the faltering electricity supply, doctor and nurse carried on; but then there came a pounding of boots on the bare concrete floor of the corridor, the door burst open and a soldier

187

– one of their own guard regiment – burst in. '*Skoro!*' he shouted. 'Outside! They're going to set the hospital on fire.'

'Who?' said Mikhailov, not looking up.

'The Reds. They've got the place surrounded. They gave us five minutes, at least a minute ago.'

Mikhailov swore under his breath. Looking at his haggard face, Katya felt a surge of despair: the doctor, a good man, was done in. Normally he would have shouted defiance, issued orders, organised the evacuation of the patients. Now he had no strength left. His body sagged and buckled, so that he had to catch hold of the edge of the operating table to stop himself falling to the floor.

'Doctor!' she came round and took his arm. 'You'd better go.'

'What about my patients?' he asked dully. 'What about *him*?'

The man on the table moved slightly under the anaesthetic.

'Leave him,' said Katya. 'They may not carry out the threat. He'll have to take his chance.' The sound of her own voice appalled her. She had never said anything so brutal in her life – but for the moment practical commonsense overruled her natural instincts. In the three minutes or so that remained, there was no chance of evacuating the sick and injured. Those who could walk or crawl or drag themselves – they might escape. But if the worst happened, and the Reds went ahead, there was no point in the staff committing suicide.

'Come!' She took Mikhailov by the elbow and propelled him towards the door. The corridors were full of people running. Shouts of '*Prochj Otsyuda!*' – 'Outside!' – battled with the alarm-bell. Some women had started to scream incomprehensibly. A patient who had lost both legs was dragging himself frantically towards the main staircase, bumping along on hands and stumps, tripping up the runners. The sight of his bloodstained bandages trailing behind him on the floor was almost more than Katya could bear. She stopped and stared at him aghast, but forced herself on to the dormitory which she had shared with the other nurses. There she grabbed her cloak, threw a few things into a handbag and darted out on to the emergency iron staircase which went down outside the building into the back yard.

The big wooden gates, and the street beyond, were blocked by a throng of soldiers. Too late, she realised they were the enemy. In a second a man had grabbed her by the arm and jerked her to a standstill. 'Not so fast, my beauty,' he said. 'Get over there with your friends' – and he propelled her roughly sideways to the spot where a group of other nurses and orderlies had already been apprehended.

'Like rats deserting a sinking ship,' said another soldier. 'Just about in time, too, because there she goes.'

From the front of the building, out of their sight, came the *whumph*! of petrol suddenly igniting, followed by a tremendous cheer. Black smoke billowed up immediately, and after a few seconds flames began to appear inside the first-floor windows. The armed mob around and behind the nurses cheered too, and when desperate, white-faced, white-clad figures appeared at the hospital windows, they opened up on them with their rifles, as if shooting rabbits bolted by a ferret. The sight was too much for Olga, one of Katya's colleagues. A small, red-headed girl, she suddenly went berserk and with a piercing shriek of 'Murderers!' launched herself at the soldier nearest to her. The man, caught in the act of firing at the windows, was taken by surprise, so that Olga's nails raked down his face and he pulled the trigger of his rifle involuntarily. The bullet caught a comrade, only two or three yards off, in the back of the neck and hurled him bodily forward, dead before he hit the ground. Another soldier clubbed Olga to the ground with the butt of his rifle, whereupon the man whose face she had lacerated wiped the blood from his eyes, put his own reloaded rifle to the side of her head and blew her brains all over the trampled snow.

For Katya, that was only the start of the horror which ruled her next two days. How she found the mental reserves to survive it, she never knew. She liked to think that it was her talisman, the Minoru medal, which preserved her – and certainly, when things became really bad, she helped keep her sanity by thinking of Joseph, his equable temperament, his love of animals, his normality, his absolute difference from the lunacy raging all round her. But really, she knew, the saving factor was that under extreme stress she went emotionally dead: surrounded by unspeakably revolting sights and actions, threatened with rape and murder, she became like a living corpse without thoughts or fears or feelings, but with a brain that continued to function.

The hospital burnt like a firework before it collapsed in ruins. At least three hundred people died in the inferno, many of them patients whose lives she had fought to save. She remembered particularly one small boy, about six, whose back had been broken by falling masonry after his home had been hit by a shell: she was haunted by the thought of his big brown eyes, like chestnuts, beseeching her to relieve his pain. Yet all she could do was to thank God that his sufferings, and those of everyone else in the building, were at an end. So hardened had she become that she even felt glad for those whom the snipers had picked off at the windows: at least their torment had ended that much more quickly.

Thereafter, she remembered events only as a blur. As dusk was falling the surviving staff – doctors, nurses and orderlies – were brought together and herded into lorries. After a drive of about twenty minutes under armed guard, with shots and heavier explosions going off intermittently on all sides, they were taken out into an empty, dimly-lit warehouse and sorted into three lots, so many doctors and nurses in each, as if they had been teams in some competition. Word went round that they would be transferred to Red Army hospitals; but the next thing Katya knew, an obscenely fat general with one foot swathed in bandages came hobbling along the line of her section and stopped opposite her. He leered at her closely, told her to turn so that he could see her profile, and then said to the two junior officers following behind him. 'This one will do. Take her to the house.'

The men hustled her away, this time in a motor van with a closed back. Again the drive lasted about twenty minutes, but the journey was punctuated by two stops at which the driver was challenged before being allowed to continue. Evidently General Denisov was a powerful figure, for they continued with minimal delays, and their destination turned out to be a palatial villa somewhere in the city suburbs, no doubt taken over that very day. A couple of windows had been shot out, and the electricity supply had failed; but otherwise the place seemed to be intact, even down to its fine Tartar furnishings – painted wooden chests and chairs, brilliantly-coloured carpets and cushions. The stove was burning, so that the house was warm, and oil-lamps glowed in all the rooms; the nether regions of the building had been taken over by the general's staff, and a guard had established strongposts in the grounds.

A pretence was made that the general had been wounded in the ankle by bomb-splinters and needed skilled nursing: hence his appropriation of Katya. When she arrived, she thought that he really must have been injured, for an orderly directed her to a large chest full of drugs, bandages and surgical instruments which had evidently been looted from some hospital or dispensary. She chose a few things that she might need and laid them on a tray – yet her first confrontation with the patient made it all too clear that his alleged wound was merely a cover for a more basic need. When he sent for her, she found him reclining with his tunic unbuttoned and his injured foot up on a chaise longue in the master-bedroom, with pale green silk drapes framing the bed alcove. Without his service cap on, he looked even less preposessing. His square head was shaven to the skull, and creased rolls down the back of his neck sprouted dark bristles. His wide cheekbones, slanting eyes and thick lips proclaimed his eastern origins. A bottle of red wine stood on a table at his elbow, and he held a full glass in his right hand.

'Ah, sister,' he said as she came in. 'You will dress my foot, please.' He raised the glass and drained it at one gulp.

'Certainly,' she said, setting her tray on a chair. To herself she said, 'Anyone who drinks wine like that is a barbarian.' Carefully she took off the dirty outer bandages, aware that he was looking directly at her; but when she removed the last of the coverings, she was outraged to find that the ankle was no more than swollen, and that the injury was nothing but a sprain. Mastering her instinct to tell him that he was malingering, she said, 'Well – it doesn't look too bad. The best thing would be to soak it in hot water.'

He did not seem to have heard what she said. He was staring at her with naked lust. 'Sister,' he said thickly. 'You have other duties to perform.' Suddenly he grabbed her right wrist and put her hand down on the crutch of his breeches, which were lifting tautly away from his body. With a gasp Katya snatched her hand away.

'Oh!' he said lightly, pretending to be amused. 'It won't bite you. Look – I'll show you.' In an instant his stubby fingers had undone his fly and brought out his penis, which was thick and purple and three-quarters erect.

'Comrade General!' Katya leapt up. 'Come to your senses. I'm a nurse, not a whore.'

'So!' With surprising agility he rose to his feet, crossed the room, turned the key and put it in his pocket. 'Now. Perhaps we can teach one of these prissy ladies of Kharkov a little discipline.' He advanced on her, penis lolling and swinging in front of him as he limped. Katya backed until she was against the wall and could go no farther. She tried to outstare him by glaring into his yellow eyes, but had to look away. Suddenly he had both hands on her shoulders, pushing her down.

'Kneel!' he ordered.

'No!'

'Kneel, damn you, and take it in your mouth.'

'Never!'

With a violent twist of her torso she broke his grip, wriggled away from him and dashed to the other side of the room. He lumbered after her, breathing heavily, but swung away to pick up a short, straight whip of plaited leather which stood against one wall. 'I see you need to be taught manners,' he said. 'It would be a pity if I had to have you tied down. Much more civilised if we just arrange things between ourselves.'

'Civilised!' She spat the word out. 'How can you call yourself civilised when you stand there exposing yourself to a perfect stranger? I shall report you!'

'Will you!' He advanced on her with the whip. 'Who to, I wonder?' He laid the tip of the whip on her right breast, drew a ring round it and ran the point down to her fork, where he suddenly drove it forward hard. Katya's skirt took the force of the jab, but even so she gasped and bent forward, bringing herself disgustingly close to that swaying, tumescent organ.

She looked desperately round for a weapon. The wine-bottle. One good bang on the head with that . . . But almost certainly he would overpower her. Before she could decide, he made a lunge at her. Instinct or luck made her step sharply to her right. So swiftly did she move that the general missed her, tripped over the edge of a rug and fell headlong, knocking over the oil lamp, whose glass chimney shattered.

In an instant the whole position changed. Instead of being brightly and steadily illuminated, the room was lit by flickering flames. Burning oil ran across the floor and set fire to the lace curtains. In seconds tongues of flame were climbing the window. With a roar of fury the general hauled himself to his feet. Clearly he, as much as Katya, was in danger. Yet such was his frustration that before he unlocked the door he made another grab for her. Catching her by surprise, he seized the front of her blouse, ripped it open, got his hand round her left breast and pulled it out. Before she could move he had dragged her towards him and sunk his teeth into her flesh. She screamed with pain and lifted her knee hard into his crutch. With a grunt he let her go. Then, looking round, he saw that if he delayed any longer, the whole house would be ablaze; so he rapidly did up his trousers, got out the key, flung open the door and roared down the stairs, 'Fire! Fire!'

For Katya, the next day was torment. A prisoner, she was confined to the room which had been allocated her – a former servant's bedroom at the back of the house. The staff gave her food and allowed her to wash, but she found it humiliating to be dependent on them, especially as they regarded her with open contempt – the general's plaything. Her room was cold and cheerless, and she had nothing to do but brood on the destruction of the hospital and her own predicament. Her breast ached wretchedly: although the skin had not been broken, it bore two lines of blue-red teeth-marks, and beneath them the flesh had been severely bruised. From the contusions, she was afraid that permanent damage might have been done.

Above all, she dreaded the evening. The fire of the night before had been put out before it did too much damage, but it caused much chaos and disruption, and she was not sent for again. In the morning, however, the general had made it clear that when he returned from his day's rounds, he would expect her to come to heel and perform any role or act that he demanded. She prayed fervently that a sniper's bullet, or doom in some other form, would strike him down before nightfall, but she knew that the chances of that were remote, and that somehow she would have to fight him on her own.

The idea came suddenly, from nowhere. She was lying on her bed, eyes on the ceiling, when it arrived. Hope welled up in her. It would be so simple, so easily done. The only trouble was that she would have to dissemble at first, to act willing for as long as necessary, until the right moment presented itself. Again she prayed, this time that she could avoid physical contact with her master. Often in the course of the war wounded soldiers had tried to make advances and pestered her with lecherous remarks – but never had anyone behaved with the gross coarseness of General Denisov.

Everything depended on one requirement: that he would again be drinking wine. He was! The scene bore a nightmarishly close resemblance to that of the night before. Again, the general was stretched out on the chaise longue, with his bandaged foot up. Again, there was a bottle at his elbow and a glass of deep red-purple wine in his hand. A new lamp had been installed, it was true, and a length of plain white cotton – a sheet, perhaps – had been hung up in place of the burnt curtains; but by far the greatest difference was in the demeanour of Katya herself. Fighting to control the tremor in her hands, she forced a smile on to her face as she went into the room.

'Good evening, general! How is the foot?'

'Better, thanks. Ah, my dear!' He raised his glass in a gesture of nauseating false bonhomie and tossed half its contents down his throat. 'I see you are in better spirits tonight.'

'Yes – I'm afraid I was very tired yesterday. It was the shock of seeing the hospital burn down. I apologise.'

'I understand. And tonight you are more relaxed.'

'I hope so. Shall I look at your ankle ... first?' Katya felt sick inside as she gave that deliberate pause, loaded with innuendo.

'Please go ahead.'

She went through the motions of taking off the bandages and, rubbing in some liniment. When the general reached down and began to fondle the hair on the back of her neck, she held herself rigid but carried on. Then she sat back on her heels and said, 'Perhaps we should leave it like that for a few minutes. It'll help the circulation.'

'Certainly, my dear. You have a perfect touch. And now perhaps you would like to take some clothes off.'

She made herself throw him a coquettish leer. 'In a minute,' she said. 'But could I ask a favour?'

'What is it?'

'A glass of wine!' She pointed at the bottle. 'It would put me in the mood. I haven't tasted wine for months – years, even.'

'But of course! Help yourself. There are more glasses in the cabinet behind me. It is Tsinandali Reserve, from Georgia – 1909, and very drinkable. How considerate of the former owner to leave it behind!'

Now she had to move with absolute precision and control. By the time she was behind the general she had the cyanide capsule ready in her right hand. She found another glass and with trembling fingers took it from the shelf. To her amazement she heard herself say, 'You're very well organised here, I must say.' As the general made some banal reply she crushed the capsule into the glass, holding it well away from herself. To cover the slight delay, and to let any gas go upwards, she put that glass back on the shelf and rearranged the others, clinking them against each other. Then she turned and made herself run the back of her hand down the man's bristly, fat jowl before she picked up the bottle and filled her glass.

'Shall I give you some more, too?' she asked innocently.

'Please do.'

Again she brushed that loathsome cheek as she reached for his glass and withdrew it. Then she put the bottle down and came round in front of him with a glass in either hand. Only a supreme effort of self-control kept her hands steady. 'Now!' She beamed as she handed him one. 'Let's have fun!'

She raised hers and drained it straight down.

'*Bozhe moi*!' he exclaimed. 'I can see you know how to drink. Let's see if you can make love as well.'

Those were the last words that General Denisov spoke. He too threw back the contents of his glass. Katya, watching him warily, was poised to spring out of reach if he reacted aggressively. She thought that he detected something odd in the taste, for his face took on a momentarily inward look and he gave a slight grunt. But then, an instant later, the glass fell on to the floor beside him and he doubled forward with a groan.

Katya leapt back, terrified that he would go for her in his death throes. But the poison struck so swiftly that he had no time to pick any target. In a moment he was writhing and roaring on the carpet, already purple in the face. Katya jumped over him, snatched a cushion from the chaise longue and crammed it over his face to deaden his cries. Every time his body heaved she had to change her grip and apply pressure in a different direction. His moribund hands seemed to reach and claw at her. Very soon, however, his struggles subsided and he died with his head bent back, his mouth open, his face the colour of the Tsinandali Reserve. For a minute or two she listened with her breath held for the sound of approaching footsteps, but the staff were two floors below, and nobody came.

Shaking violently now, she stood up. She could feel alcohol working in her blood. Collect your wits, she told herself. She had not really planned beyond this point. What was her best chance? To say he had had a heart attack. That was it. She picked up the glass which had contained the cyanide, put it away in her medical bag and left her own glass with its dregs of untreated wine on the floor. She tried to pull the general's face into a less tortured expression, and for good measure ripped open the front of his breeches. Then she went to the door and ran down the stairs, calling loudly for help.

Her stratagem worked with the staff, but not with the doctor hastily summoned from some nearby unit. He took one look at the dead man, one cautious sniff near his face, and instantly said, 'Poison! Arrest the nurse.' Within an hour Katya was driven to the nearest headquarters. She received no sort of a trial or hearing: she was taken between two soldiers and made to stand before a grey-haired colonel, who sat on duty at a table in a makeshift, ill-lit guardroom.

'Murder of an officer of the revolutionary army,' he said mechanically, as he stared at a note on his desk. 'Do you deny it?'

Katya, numbed beyond words, shook her head.

'Then you are sentenced to death. There is no appeal.' He looked up at her two escorts. 'Put her in cell number three, with the other women. They are all to be shot at dawn.'

ELEVEN

Destination Rostov: New Year
1920

O NCE MORE the train could only crawl through the freezing mist and snow. Occasional glimpses of pithead winding gear and factory chimneys told the travellers that they were passing through the Donetsk coalfields; otherwise, they lived in a vacuum made steadily more disagreeable by the scraps of news that filtered down to them as they passed through stations. Former White positions behind them were crumbling like sandcastles before an incoming tide. In the far west Kiev and Poltava had fallen. On all fronts General Budenny's cavalry was rampaging towards the south. Taganrog – once the farthest target of Joseph's ambition – had already been abandoned by the British Military Mission, the remnants of which were retreating towards Rostov-on-the-Don. The RAF officers spoke ruefully about how comfortable the base at Taganrog had been only last summer, with its tennis court and swimming pool, its yacht club and theatre, and Admiral Denikin's own orchestra, which gave concerts during the hot southern evenings. Now the best hope of the White commanders was to hold the river crossing at Rostov and to consolidate their forces beyond it. 'Beyond the Don'! The phrase should have had a fine, romantic ring about it: it should have spoken of Cossacks riding like fiends on fiery horses; but now it signified a position grown desperate, a last redoubt. If anything, the dissent between the White leaders seemed to have become worse. Denikin, determined not to lose touch with his fighting Cossacks, planned to hold the Don crossing, come what might; but Wrangel proposed that all White forces should withdraw westwards into the natural redoubt of the Crimea, which, being a peninsula, would protect them while they reorganised.

The atmosphere aboard Train 607 matched the frozen gloom

outside. Typhus – the dreaded *tif* – was rife in the refugee trains, and had gained access to the servicemen, two of whom were down with high fevers and the telltale red-brown rash. They needed hospital treatment, but had no chance of getting it before Taganrog – and that, at their dismal rate of progress, was three or four days away. The rum was holding out and Cowderdrill's hot toddies were as good as ever; but rations had become deadly monotonous: there was corned beef, Maconnachie's meat-and-two-veg stew, pilchards in tomato sauce and hard-tack biscuits: nothing else. The only variation was the order in which those staples came round. Vegetables, fruit, eggs, fresh bread – these were things of the past. 'What wouldn't I give for a couple of *piroshkis!*' groaned Kinkead one morning as they stared down at a platform solid with grey-faced would-be escapers. In peacetime the station would have been alive with women peddling little hot pastries full of cabbage, and their delicious, greasy smell would have come wafting into the train. Other vendors would have been selling sunflower seeds, roasted nuts, sweetmeats, tea. Now there was nothing to eat, nothing to buy, nothing to smell; and in any case they kept the windows shut for fear of admitting lethal germs.

Of all Joseph's anxieties, the keenest was naturally about Katya: whenever he thought about her – most of the time – he felt cold with fear. But he also worried much about her wretched brother. What had turned Dmitri into a Red? When he confided in Kinkead, the officer gave him a typically robust answer: 'It isn't just your friend. Thousands of young men have gone over to the Reds. They think it's the new dawn. But I can tell them now: red sky in the morning is shepherd's warning. It'll piss with rain on them before night.'

'But I went and told him about Orlov.'

'So what?' Kinkead remained unmoved. 'Count or no count, we'll throw him off if things get too uncomfortable.'

For the moment the horses were the least of Joseph's problems. They badly needed exercise, it was true; but with Billy Bond helping him, and by keeping their rations low, he was able to maintain them in a reasonable state. Billy had commandeered a small iron stove and fitted it up with a makeshift smokestack which poked up through the roof of the box-car; and this, slowly burning coal filched from bunkers alongside the track, kept the van at a comfortable temperature. Either Joseph or Billy rode in it for most of the day, moving up and down the train during the interminable halts. Anther invaluable improvisation was a ramp made of timber picked up along the railway.

This lay on the floor while the box-car was in motion, but could be quickly fitted into position during a halt, so that the stallions could go out even if the train was not standing at a platform.

On the second day out, at Makayevka, Joseph made the mistake of setting forth in search of news. The most hopeful source seemed to be a hospital train which had come in after them and was parked on another track a few hundred yards behind, so he stumbled towards it over sleepers and banks of frozen snow, ducking beneath the couplings of stationary wagons.

The coaches were white, with red crosses painted on the sides. It puzzled Joseph that the engine which had pulled them was no longer in position – but he soon saw why. Pulling himself up on a vertical hand-rail, he climbed a set of steel steps and grasped the handle of one of the doors. It turned easily enough, and a moment later he was in the corridor, greeted by an all-too-familiar stench, faintly overlaid with disinfectant. He clapped his handkerchief over his nose before proceeding – and then one glance into the first compartment was enough. Three of the four bunks were occupied by corpses. The fourth was empty, but only because its body had fallen to the floor, where it lay frozen, clad in nothing but a grey hospital gown.

Joseph recoiled, slammed the door, jumped down on to the track and walked on, feeling numb. Not until the fourth coach did he detect signs of life within. This time he was met by a nurse, a dark, tall girl, white-faced, defensive. Her Red Cross uniform – black smock and cap, with red arm-bands – was so familiar that it made him hesitate. 'Who are you, and what do you want?' she demanded.

'*Pozhaluista*, can you help? I'm looking for a friend.'

'Well?'

'She's a nurse. Sister Mironov.'

'I've never heard of her. What unit is she with?'

'I don't know. The last I heard of her, she was in Kharkov.'

'Kharkov! You know what happened there.'

'They burnt the hospital.'

'Yes.'

'Did anyone escape? Were there survivors?'

'How am I supposed to know? I wasn't there.'

'I thought perhaps you'd come that way.'

'No – from Poltava.'

'Oh well – *spasibo*. Thanks anyway.'

The nurse watched frostily as Joseph backed down the steps and closed the door. He felt crushed by the futility of his quest. How, with an entire society disintegrating, would he ever find the one member of it whom he longed to see? Back at 607, another shock awaited him. The service train was besieged by refugees begging, clamouring, screaming for a passage south. Armed sentries guarded every door to deny them access even to the outside of the carriages. When Joseph forced his way through the crowd from the back and appeared beside the line, a pocket of silence developed round him as people realised that he was about to go on board. Then a menacing whisper started. Mutterings of '*He*'s not in uniform' and 'Look – a civilian' began to fly. Joseph felt himself surrounded by barely-contained aggression; but then, as he turned round for a moment, back to the train, he was confronted by a young woman in a full-length black fur coat, with a hat to match. Everything about her proclaimed her class. Her face was strong and dark – Jewish, he thought – and very good-looking. Her bearing was aristocratic. Among that ragamuffin throng, she cut a striking figure: in the sea of tattered sheepskins, threadbare padded-cotton jackets and cloaks of felt or hessian sacking, all browny-grey with age and dirt, her coat made her stand out like a raven among a flock of dowdy pigeons.

Before Joseph could scramble up the nearest ladder, she seized him by the shoulder and said in thickly-accented English, 'Dahling, take me with you.'

'I'm sorry,' he answered in Russian. 'This is a military train – no civilians allowed on board.'

'That doesn't matter,' she answered, also in Russian, with an upper-class accent, 'I am no ordinary civilian. I can pay my way. Look.' With a flourish she flung open her magnificent coat, to reveal that beneath it she was wearing nothing but jewels. Ropes of pearls, necklaces of diamonds, strings of coloured stones cascaded between and over her splendid breasts. More jewels, slung round her waist, hung over her crutch, so that her dark pubic hair seemed to be full of rubies. Since her body matched her coat in its magnificence, she would have made a sensation in any setting, be it Turkish harem or St Petersburg nightclub: in that scene of snow and destitution and death, her exhibitionism was horrifying. Joseph saw at once that, in return for a lift, she was offering not only the jewels but herself as well.

'For God's sake!' he said sharply, pulling her hands together to close the coat. 'Cover yourself up. Think where you are.'

'You don't like me?' she snapped. 'You don't think I'm beautiful? Have you no balls?'

'Of course you're beautiful. But we can't take you.'

With a scream of *'Merzavets!'* – 'Bastard!' – she went for him, striking out at his face with both hands. When he grabbed her wrists and held her off, she began to kick, so that her coat swung open again, and her nudity was exposed for all to see. After a short, incredulous pause, there was a surge towards her, a swell of noise from the nearest section of the crowd. Joseph saw that she and he were both in dire danger. He could not afford to let go of her wrists, for fear of the damage she might to do his face or eyes. He could not even reach for his Luger, to keep the crowd at bay. By screaming and spitting and kicking and exposing herself, she rapidly raised the nearest men to a fever of rapacity and lust. In a few seconds not only she, but probably he too, would be torn to pieces.

To his unspeakable relief he heard the train door behind him open. There came a tremendous yell of, 'Clear off, the lot of you!' He half-turned, to see Sergeant Cowderdrill poised in the opening, teeth waving, rifle levelled. Next second, the weapon went off with a shattering report. Joseph flung the woman's wrists from him, turned and snaked up the ladder, to dive headlong on to the floor of the corridor. Behind him the door slammed shut. Immediately Cowderdrill ran the window down and fired another couple of shots. By the time Joseph looked out, the scene below was like something in a medieval painting of hell. Bodies were heaving face-down in a pile, every human a maggot struggling to reach the carrion at the bottom. Whether the woman was being raped or merely looted, it was impossible to tell, such was the weight of flesh on top of her. Either way, there could be only one outcome, for nobody could stand pressure of that kind, especially as the men on top of the heap were savagely striking out at those below with fists, saucepans, sticks and any other weapon that came to hand, oblivious of the fact that it was physically impossible for them to come anywhere near their target.

Mercifully for the onlookers, the train began to move, leaving Joseph nauseated with disgust. That people in danger of their lives should descend to such depths seemed a dreadful indictment of the human condition. He was appalled that greed, carnal and material, could overpower even the instinct for self-preservation – for not only the supplicant woman, but several of the men fighting for her body or her jewels, must certainly have been killed in the maelstrom.

'If I live to be a hundred, I'll never see nothing like that again,' declared Cowderdrill. 'At least, I hopes I don't. She didn't half ask for it, though, did she? Fair thrust it at you, sir.'

'I know. But thank God you were there. If it hadn't been for you, I reckon I'd have been under that pile as well.'

They gave themselves tots of rum to recover; but as Joseph stood at the window, looking out into the fog, he could not help brooding over the incident. Who was the woman? When and where had she decided on that desperate step, of trying to sell her body to someone on the train? How far had she travelled in that state? At some stage she must have undressed, deliberately. Where had she abandoned the rest of her clothes? He found it unnerving to realise that his memories of the incident were disturbingly erotic. In both face and body the woman had reminded him of Shura: she had been taller – nearly his own height – but built on similar lines. Even though she had been *in extremis*, the sight of her body had excited him, and suddenly he realised how near erotic feelings were to sadistic ones, how closely the instinct of the male to serve the female was linked with his desire to mutilate and kill. He thought how in some species things worked the other way round: how, after she has been mated, the female scorpion eats the male to increase her supply of protein . . . He shuddered, and turned back to the foetid interior of the train.

Next morning dawned fine and almost clear: instead of fog, only a faint haze hung in the air. 'Flying weather!' said Bunny Aten jovially as he came to breakfast.

'You'll be lucky,' muttered Kinkead through a mouthful of pilchards – but for once he was wrong.

The train had halted in open country, and for the first time its inmates could see snowfields and pinewoods on either side of the line. Hills rose at a distance, but close to the track the ground was level and open, and because there was a long curve in the line, other stationary trains were visible fore and aft. It was a surprise to the RAF men to see only one set of coaches behind their own: beyond that, the line was clear. The servicemen noticed, of course, that they were at a standstill, and had not moved for a couple of hours: yet such delays had become so common that no one paid special attention or said much about it. The only real difference from earlier hold-ups – and a very welcome one – was that this halt had occurred away from any town, village or road, with the result that the landscape, instead of being crowded with refugees, was empty.

The alarm went up after breakfast. A messenger on foot came back along the track, floundering through the snow. There had been a derailment ahead, he announced. Engineers were working to get the engine back on the rails, but there was no chance of any forward movement for at least the next three hours. Meanwhile, a report from the north, which had come down the line by telephone to the next station ahead, and then been passed back by word of mouth, revealed that the Red forces had managed to shunt a *bronevik*, or armoured train, on to the main line, and that this was bearing down on the stationary convoy from the rear.

B Flight's pilots held a quick conference in the lounge-car. 'Blow up the line,' suggested one. 'We've got explosive galore.'

'Where?' said Aten. 'Unless we hump all the gear a mile back, the *bronevik* will shoot hell out of us from the other side of that curve.'

They could see what he meant. The line behind them swung so gently that it was visible a mile away. A four-inch gun mounted in the forward turret of an armoured train could easily engage them across the curve. There might not be time to carry explosives out beyond the point at which the line disappeared and rig them up. Besides, there was no bridge or culvert where a decisive break could be engineered.

'Bombs, then,' said Kinkead. 'They're the answer. We'll launch a couple of planes and blow the bastards off the line. Take the two Camels that have skids fitted already. No problem with navigation – just follow the line back. No air opposition, either, I don't reckon. The Reds can't have any aircraft this far south yet. No time to waste, though. Who's going to fly? Bunny? Rick?'

There was no shortage of volunteers. The whole train came alive as mechanics hustled to unlimber two of the Camels and prepare them for the sortie. The fragile aircraft were lowered off the flat-cars on derricks. As some men bolted their wings into position on the centre sections, others lit acetylene lamps beneath their engines to dispel the frost. Armourers loaded belts of ammunition into the Vickers .303 machine-guns – two belts of 800 rounds per plane – and then slung two 56lb bombs, painted bright yellow, one beneath each inner wing. Everybody not otherwise employed – Joseph included – was detailed to trample a runway in the virgin snow. The joy of being outside on a crisp, sunny morning went to the heads of the young aircraftmen, who spent the first couple of minutes racing about and throwing snowballs; then a sergeant had them in line-abreast, trotting up and down at the double to flatten a strip some three hundred yards long on the outside of the railway curve. Joseph ran with them, exulting in the exercise and release from the stale, cold confines of the train. The snow lay six inches deep, but it was light and powdery, and packed down under their boots to a layer less than half that thick. Count and Countess Orlov did not emerge, but everyone else took advantage of the break.

Tension mounted as the two pilots appeared in their leather flying suits, goggles, gloves and helmets. Kinkead gave them a final briefing. 'Good hunting,' he said. 'Give the *bronevik* a roasting. And if all goes well, take a sweep to the south when you come back, to see what the problem is up ahead of us.'

With that they scrambled into the cockpits and ran through their checks. Mechanics swung the wooden propellors to fire the engines, which coughed and spluttered into life, then roared up to full revolutions. As the anchor ropes came off, the aircraft trundled forward over the snow and took up position at the end of the makeshift runway. Then Bunny Aten, in the lead, raised his right hand, opened his throttle wide, roared forward over the snow and lifted off, closely followed by his companion. Climbing heavily, weighted down by their bomb loads, the two little biplanes were quickly lost among the hills to the north.

As the pilots soon found, they had only a short way to go. Following the railway, they cruised at a height of five hundred feet, and sighted their objective after no more than ten minutes. Sure enough, an armoured train was trundling down the track to meet them. Bunny, in the lead, waggled his wings to show that he had seen it, but there was hardly any need, for the grey, slug-like beast was sending up a thick column of smoke as it crawled towards them, and in that white, open landscape nobody could have missed it. Leading the train was a heavily-armoured truck, with, fore and aft, truncated, conical turrets, each housing a four-inch gun. Machine-gun nests bristled from it amidships. Behind that came the engine, itself armoured right down to ground level. Behind that was a munitions wagon, and at the back another fighting unit the same as the one in the lead. Altogether, it looked a formidable proposition.

The B Flight pilots, however, had had experience of *broneviks* during their campaign over the Volga, and had evolved tactics to deal with them. A mile out, in a prearranged manoeuvre, the aircraft separated. As Bunny climbed and flew straight on, preparing to pass high over the train and dive at it from behind, his partner peeled away to the right, made a wide turn and began to run back in low, at right angles to the track. With the rising sun behind him, the Bolshevik gunners would be dazzled as well as distracted when he came at them from their flank – and in any case, he would keep them busy with bursts from his machine-guns.

Rolling on to the line of the track at 1,000 feet, Bunny watched till he saw Rick start his run almost at ground level. From his vantage-point the other Camel looked like a brown dragonfly speeding in above an endless white blanket. In it came, from his left, with spurts of fire showing through its propeller as its machine-guns opened up. He loitered till it was within seconds of the track, then started his own dive.

The note of the wind, whining past wires and struts, rose to a scream as his speed increased. At five hundred feet he levelled out, coming up fast on the train. He saw Rick skim low over the wagons and climb away. Now flashes were spurting from the armoured carriages. Out of the corner of his left eye he saw fabric fly up as a bullet went through his lower wing. This was the time for absolute concentration: he placed the twin crosses of his bomb sight on the munitions wagon and held them steady until the centre of the train filled the hollow square. Then he pulled the bomb-release lever.

Nothing happened. The aircraft should have jumped, with the sudden loss of weight, but it flew straight on. Cursing, he turned away right-handed, made a wide sweep and came in again. Rick, seeing him go round, put in a second low-level, diversionary run.

Bunny's second pass was exactly the same. He lined himself up precisely, took perfect aim, pulled ... Nothing. This time he dived away to his left and descended to low level, showing Rick that his turn had come. The two Camels changed roles. As Rick prepared to bomb, Bunny came in a few feet above the snow, firing short bursts. From the increase in black smoke pouring out of its funnel, he could see that the engine had put on speed, and he sharpened the angle of his approach to allow for its forward movement. As he roared close over the roof of the tender, he saw white faces peering anxiously from the slits of the gun turrets. Then he was clear, and climbing away as Rick made his run.

Both bombs fell wide, to the right. White puffs of snow and vapour erupted into the air, but the *bronevik* continued unharmed. Anxiety stepped up the flow of Bunny's adrenalin. They had been airborne for twenty-five minutes, and over the train for nearly half that. By now its speed must have built up to thirty miles per hour. At that rate – unless they stopped it – it would reach the stationary convoy in less than half an hour.

What the hell was wrong with his bomb-release mechanism? Ice, he supposed: moisture must have frozen in the locking catches. All he could do was try again.

Once more he climbed, dived and ran in. But this time, instead of levelling out, he continued his dive until the last possible moment, so that he could haul back on the stick at the same instant as he released the bombs, and thereby augment their own weight with a sudden snatch of gravity. The manoeuvre demanded absolute precision of control and timing. Bunny calculated that a sudden pull-up would throw the bombs further forward than normal: he therefore set his sights on the rear half of the train and dived for it all-out.

Again the wind howled past his struts and wires. The air-speed indicator went up almost to the 200 mph mark, but he ignored it and kept his eyes glued to the target. Even when he knew he was close enough, he gave it one more second – and then yanked hard with both hands. The little aircraft jumped and shuddered violently. Bunny let out a yell. 'Eggs away!' he roared, into the rush of air. Turning hard to his right, he was just in time to see the impact.

The first bomb burst a fraction to the left of its target and flung out a blast of snow; but the second was perfectly placed – better even than a direct hit on one of the wagons, which might have bounced off – for it exploded right against the *bronevik*'s wheels.

'Bull's eye!' he yelled exultantly. He saw the train buckle sideways as it sustained a crippling blow in the midriff. The back of the engine and the front of its tender were flung bodily to their right, so that their wheels left the rails and ploughed into the ground; but the momentum of the wagons, with their tons of armour, was such that they churned on for more than a hundred yards: by the time they stopped, the whole train had folded together like a pocket-knife, and it came to rest with the leading armoured car lying on its side across the line.

Figures in rough brown uniforms crawled out of the wreck like ants and started to run away from it, clearly afraid that its store of ammunition would explode. The main objective had been achieved. No matter, thought Bunny: we'll give them as much hell as we can – and he wheeled to dive again, hammering at the ant heap of men and tangled machinery until his ammunition had gone. He saw three or four men collapse and pitch into the snow, but he was over and past them too quickly for any accurate assessment of casualties. Then he waggled his wings and set out for base, along the line. In spite of the cold, he was soaked with sweat inside his flying suit, and his mouth was parched. He shuddered and wriggled in his seat, uncomfortably aware, once again, of how war changed everyone, even him. On the ground he was a quiet and peaceable citizen, not given to fighting; but when he took to the air on an armed sortie, he seemed to leave his feelings behind. Instead of a human being, he became part of his war machine, able and willing to kill as many Bolsheviks as his bombs and bullets would account for.

When the Camels took off on their mission, and silence fell on Train 607, Joseph suddenly decided not merely to bring the horses out, but to ride them. 'It'll do them more good than just leading them about,' he told Billy. So they saddled up Min and Boy and led them down the steep ramp. Moorka also decided that the time had come for an excursion; but the deep snow did not appeal to her, and after executing a few high jumps and pounces, each of which ended with her disappearing beneath the surface in a flurry, she thought better of it and returned to the van.

The horses had different ideas. 'For God's sake keep a grip of him,' Joseph told Billy as he saw Min preparing to take hold of his bit. 'Otherwise you'll finish up in the Crimea.'

He himself had enough trouble on Boy, who began jigging and bouncing as soon as they set out. On the trampled runway Min tried a couple of bucks, but Billy, good rider that he was, sat down tight and drove the animal forward with his legs, so that he had no option but to keep moving. Joseph was afraid that snow would ball in the horses' hoofs and make them stumble, but it turned out to be so powdery that it did not stick at all. Emboldened by this discovery, he struck out across the unmarked expanse at a canter.

It was a glorious moment. Boy, responding to the bright sunshine as strongly as his rider, strode out powerfully, sending up a bow-wave of powdered snow, whose crystals flashed with every colour of the rainbow. The stallion's breath spurted white in the frosty air, and his ears were pricked as if he had heard the roar of a race crowd ahead of him. Joseph felt liberated from the deadening tedium and anxiety of the train. His eyes watered from the rush of icy air, but he had no need to see details, and felt nothing but exhilaration.

'Does he pull!' shouted Billy as he went past, holding Min as best he could.

'Start turning right!' Joseph yelled back. 'Ease him round gently.'

Both horses came round in a grand, sweeping arc. Then for a while they settled into a steady canter, side by side, and when they turned again to face back towards the train, they were nearly a mile from it, so that the carriages looked like a row of shallow bricks dotted along the valley. 'Now,' said Joseph mischievously. 'Why don't we let them go? Race you back.'

Even if home is only a train, horses need no urging when they go towards it. The stallions took off as if they were back at Epsom – and memories of actual races, not least his second Warsaw Derby, poured through Joseph's mind as he crouched up Boy's neck and flew over the snow. For a couple of furlongs, it was neck and neck. Then Boy began to draw away – as he should have, with four years' advantage. By then some of the aircraftmen had seen what was happening, and set up a cheer as the ball of flying snow drew near them. 'Looked like a bloody egg whisk, you did,' said one of the mechanics as they came in, wiping snow from their hair and eyes. Joseph felt exhilarated: his face stung and glowed with the cold, though he knew that in galloping over that strange ground he had taken an unwarrantable risk. The horses could easily have lamed themselves on hidden rocks or in unseen holes.

No sooner had they put the stallions back in the box than they heard the faint *boom-boom* of a double explosion in the distance. 'By jiminy, they've found it,' said Billy. 'Hark at that.' A couple of minutes later the sound came again, slightly louder. 'Moving this way,' Billy observed. 'That's all their bombs gone. I hope they got the blighter.' An anxious wait ensued, but at last the Camels came into view again, and as they flew past, to make a quick reconnaissance of the line to the south, the leader waggled his wings twice to indicate success.

The marshalling yards at Taganrog were at a standstill. Again the fog had come down, and beneath its icy shroud the lost and helpless living mingled with the unburied dead. On the spaces between tracks, on the triangular corners between junctions, frozen corpses were stacked in piles, like cordwood. Some of the heaps were neat and tidy, but others were tumbled in confusion, and the bodies had been stripped of their clothes, so that blue-grey limbs and torsos stuck out at all angles.

Round these piles and between the stationary trains wandered a ceaseless tide of refugees, dazed by cold, hunger and exhaustion. Such was the log-jam of traffic, so little chance did there seem that any of the trains would ever move again, that many people abandoned the wagons on to which they had fought their way earlier and started to walk. Yet still some begged and shouted for lifts, or tried to bribe their way on board.

'This is bloody dangerous,' said Kinkead as they stood looking out from the lounge-car into the dusk. 'The Bolshies are supposed to be just outside the town. If they infiltrate the yards in search of sodding Orlov, we're a sitting duck. I wish I'd never let the wretched fellow on board. Him *or* his damned diamond.'

Everyone knew that the Count's presence had made Train 607 a special Bolshevik target. Not only had the *bronevik* somehow been filtered on to the main line directly behind them; they had already, in open country, beaten off a cavalry assault which was clearly directed at them, rather than at the refugee convoy in general. The horsemen, constantly wheeling and turning, had tried to stage a diversion and cover the approach of a boarding party, but at the last moment, providentially, the line had cleared, so that the train could move on. Now, as they stood becalmed in the suburbs of the town, the airmen reckoned another assault inevitable.

Gunfire broke out, as expected, just when the light was fading. Rifle bullets began to clang against the sides of the train. A window in the lounge-car exploded inwards. The guards posted in the vestibules started to fire back, even though their view was limited and their chance of identifying the attackers minimal. Suddenly a cry went up that a man had been seen crawling underneath the train. 'Outside!' somebody yelled. 'Tackle them on the ground. Otherwise we'll be blown up.'

A second later Joseph found himself crouching on sleepers beneath one of the Pullman coaches, loaded Luger in hand. He waited motionless until his eyes grew accustomed to the gloom. Then suddenly he saw a dark figure slip in between the wheels, two bogeys along, only a few yards away. Quick movements betrayed the fact that he was trying to attach something to the train. Joseph raised his pistol, steadied it with both hands and fired. The man gave a grunt and slumped down, disappearing between the wheels. With the Luger reloaded and levelled, Joseph crawled stealthily towards the spot. Before he could react, a brilliant flash and explosion split the murk ahead of him. He felt the wind as a bullet passed his left ear. He too fell flat, but with his head turned so that he could still see forward, and the pistol still levelled in his right hand. Feign dead, he told himself. Let him move first. He waited, chin in the frozen snow of the rail bed. All round him the noise of battle raged: shots, impacts, explosions, yells; but down there under the train he could hear his own breathing, and he tried to slow it to the point of inaudibility.

Presently he began to hear another noise, very very close: low grunts, heavy intakes of breath, the scrape of cloth over wooden sleepers. His man was wounded, but dragging himself back into action. Joseph held his breath as he saw something bulky rise slowly up in front of him, not six feet away. Was that a back or a chest? Which way was the saboteur facing? Where was his head? A moment later the flash of an explosion from outside gave his attitude away. He had his back to Joseph, and was leaning to his right, with his shoulder propped against a wheel. Raising himself with infinite care, Joseph took aim at the point where head must meet body and fired again. This time the man went down flat on his face and lay motionless. Still wary, Joseph crawled forward and gave the torso another bullet from point-blank range. White wires, protruding from beneath the body, led to a bundle bound with string. Joseph peered at it: an explosive device, but not primed yet. With his pocket-knife he cut the string and ripped the bundle apart, scattering the pieces up and down the line. He crept still closer, until he could see that the dead man was young, dark, bearded, and wore a khaki battledress top with red stars on the epaulettes. Arching over him, he felt in the snow until his fingers closed over the cold metal of a revolver. The weapon was no use to him, and everyone on the train was heavily armed; so he broke it, shook out the five unspent cartridges from the drum, and hung it over the rail immediately under the leading edge of a wheel, so that it would be crushed as soon as the train moved forward.

That done, he waited silently behind the sheltering wheels. It crossed his mind that effluent from train lavatories must pour down on to this track, loaded with germs of every conceivable nature, and that he must be lying on top of it. Thank God, everything was frozen, and there was not even any smell – so he remained where he was, in ambush, feeling safer and more useful there than in the open.

The battle was flaring intermittently: a volley of shots, some yells, then a minute's silence, followed by an explosion and the heavy rattle of a Lewis gun. Anybody moving in the open, away from the train, was in mortal peril, for the defending gunners were firing blind into the murk whenever they saw a flash or a movement. He jumped as a scream burst out just to his right. He turned to face the sound, but before he could bring his pistol to bear a body landed on the ground not two yards off with a loud slap and thud. A Cockney voice cried, 'Gotcha, yer fuckin' Red bastard!' and Joseph heard a squelch as the Englishman yanked his rifle bayonet back out of the dead bandit's ribs.

To minimise the chance of being accidentally bayoneted or shot, Joseph called firmly, 'Great stuff!'

'Who the hell's that?' snapped the Cockney voice from above.

'Jo Clements, the stallion man.'

'Where are you, for Christ's sake?'

'Under the wheels.'

'Watch yourself, sir. The sods are all over the place. I'd stop there for a bit if I were you. I'm going back along the train.'

'Thanks. I'll stay.'

Very soon his tactics were rewarded. Fires in buildings had by then created some background light, and against the glow he spotted another figure advancing. The man came first at a crouch, then dropped on to hands and knees, half carrying something, half pushing it in front of him. Another bomber. Whether by chance or design, he headed straight for Joseph's hiding place.

Joseph's nerves were steady now. He planned not to fire prematurely, but to let the intruder come within two yards and shoot him dead. To aim, he had no need to move: he already had the Luger levelled, and resting on his left forearm, firm as a rock. The man was five yards off, four. Another couple of seconds would do it. He would get the bullet just below the jawbone, where neck and head joined . . .

Then an extra bright flash cast a moment's clear illumination over the whole scene, and in it Joseph saw the intruder's face. His resolution faltered, his hand shook – for the man he had almost shot was Dmitri Mironov. He hesitated; then he silently let down the hammer of the pistol and swivelled the gun in his hand so that he could use the butt as a bludgeon. When Dmitri's head came over the rail, in front of the wheel, Joseph swung a short backhander to his temple and knocked him cold.

In a flash he dragged the body under the train and sat on top of it, face down. In a holster under the coat he found another revolver, which he unloaded and threw away, scattering the bullets. The burden which he had seen turned out to be another primitive bomb, like the first one, in a canvas bag. That too he destroyed. Then he turned the body face-upward and continued to sit astride it.

The boy stirred and began to come round. Joseph, by then in an icy rage, slapped his face back and forth to accelerate his recovery, and as soon as he saw the eyes focus he hissed, 'Dmitri Mironov. Do you want to die?'

The boy shook his head but did not speak.

'I could have killed you then,' Joseph went on. 'I can kill you now. Just tell me one thing. Why did you go over to the Reds?'

A lazy, contemptuous smile spread over Dmitri's face. 'You poor old man,' he said slowly. 'You should stick to looking after horses. You've backed the wrong side in this war.'

Joseph struck him again. He saw that his prisoner was zombified – as near as made no difference, mad. Yet still he could not kill the brother of the woman he loved. Instead he relaxed his knee grip, got off and crouched over him. 'Fuck off,' he said bitterly. 'And if you ever come near this train again, die you most certainly will.'

Dmitri was not so far gone as to rush straight out into the open. First, he looked out cautiously, then scuttled like a rabbit into the drifting fog.

As the fighting moved away, Joseph crawled out and stood up. He slipped into the gap between two carriages and waited, listening. He heard someone call his name from inside the train, and he was on the point of calling back when, through all the other hubbub, he caught the sound of a horse's whinny. Minoru's alarm call. 'Oh God!' he thought. 'They're going for the stallions.'

He went fast towards the box-cars, moving crabwise, with his back to the carriages. Because the door of the horse-box was on the other side of the train, he dived under the coupling between two carriages and came out beyond. Some building – a warehouse or equipment shed – had caught fire and was blazing about a hundred yards off. A ruddy, leaping glow lit up the patchy fog and illuminated the train itself.

As fast as he could, he edged past the carriages and flats to the first of the box-cars. To his horror he saw that the doors of the horse wagon – padlocked when he left them – were open. There was a flurry of movement in the opening. Again, a roar of a whinny reached him, but this time it was Boy's. He began to run, tripped and came down heavily. As he stood up, a bullet slammed into the steel within inches of his face. The impact knocked him down. At least, he went down, perhaps out of shock. He felt blood on his forehead, but he could not tell where he had been hit. He felt nothing. The wound did not seem to be serious. He came up on one knee for a second, breathing hard, making sure that his limbs still worked. When he found they did, he got up and ran, made fearless by rage and anxiety about his horses.

He reached the open doorway, scrambled up on to the floor and tried to dive to the left, behind the steel wall, but slipped and went down flat in a slimy, warm puddle on the floor. In a second he had scrabbled his way into cover. Thank God! Both horses were still there. But Boy was loose. Someone had untied him, or he had broken free. He stood with his quarters jammed into the left-hand back corner, weaving his head wildly from side to side. His eyes flashed and his teeth gleamed in the flickering red glow of the fire. His flanks were heaving. Angular, horse-shaped shadows, exaggerating the shape of his head and ears, flew about the walls. In the other corner stood Min, still tied, but straining back on his head-rope.

'Steady, boys, steady!' gasped Joseph. 'Boy! Min! Take it easy, lads.' He stood up and took a step towards Boy, but the horse rolled white-rimmed eyes and threatened murderously with his teeth. Get the doors shut, Joseph thought: he stepped back and pushed the nearer door away from him, across the opening. To reach the other one he would have to expose himself by crossing the gap. He looked down, measuring the distance, and saw that the liquid in which he had slipped was a great pool of blood, which had flooded the litter inside the door and glinted dark-red in the firelight. Following the stain with his eyes, he saw that it ran back across the car towards where Boy stood at bay.

'God almighty,' he breathed. 'What's happened to you?'

He saw no blood on the horse. He could be wounded on his near side, which was turned to the back wall, but he showed no sign of any disability. Again Joseph moved slowly forward, drawn by dread of what he might find. Then he saw something in the litter just short of the stallion's front feet. Keeping up an automatic, soothing flow of sound, he inched forward.

The horse was calming down, but not enough for any liberty to be taken with him. Retreating, Joseph reached down the broom which he kept hanging in one corner and fished the alien object forward. For the first time in the fight he felt faint. What he had in his hands was a human arm, torn off its body at the shoulder, but still clad in the sleeves of a shirt and grey flannel jacket. That was grisly enough; still worse, he knew straightaway whose arm it was. Nausea overwhelmed him as he recognised the curled-down, clawlike fingers of Dmitri Mironov.

Crouched on his haunches, Joseph laid his head back against the wall of the box-car and closed his eyes. He could see exactly what had happened. Mitya, leading the raid on the horses, had gone up to Boy and untied him. The stallion, in fear and anger, had seized him by the arm in his teeth and swung him round with such force as to tear him apart. Or perhaps he had struck him down with his forefeet and then, kneeling on his victim, snatched his arm upwards. With an injury like that, the boy must have bled to death. Probably within a few yards of the van.

Joseph leant against the cold steel wall, utterly drained. When he looked down, he found that the whole of the front of his wolfskin waistcoat was smeared with blood. His mind flew to the river at Nikolsk, to the skinny, undeveloped boys running back with their captured crayfish. 'Oh, Rusalka, Rusalka, Rusalka,' he whispered. 'Forgive him. Forgive me. But, oh *God* this is a horrible war.'

The firing and explosions had died away. The blaze was still burning, but the attack seemed to have been beaten off. He struggled stiffly to his feet, threw the arm out into the snow, closed the second door and lit the oil lamp which hung beneath the roof. Then, after more coaxing, he got a hand on Boy's neck, soothed away his stress, and retied his head rope. Miraculously, he seemed uninjured. Min also needed reassurance, but settled down. A feed of oats helped steady both stallions, but Joseph did not want to leave them alone again.

He was reaching for the lamp so that he could inspect the door catches when he heard a movement outside. Automatically he drew his Luger and covered the door before calling, 'Who's there?'

'Only me,' came the voice of Billy Bond. 'You all right, sir?'

'More or less.' Joseph opened up and said, 'Watch out – there's blood all over the place.' He pulled his faithful assistant up by one hand and told him what had happened. Billy was distraught that he had not been there to guard the horses – but he had been detailed to man one of the machine-gun nests. 'Don't worry,' Joseph told him. 'It turned out all right. But we've got a body to find.'

'You don't think he's still alive, then?'

'Hardly, with an artery bleeding like that. But watch yourself.'

They did not have far to look. Blood, flowing freely, had melted the snow in an unbroken trail, which led them straight to the back of the horse-box. There it turned inwards, on to the track – but that was as far as the dying man had gone. He lay face-down on the sleepers, neatly stretched out in the direction of the rails.

'Hold that a minute.' Joseph gave Billy the lamp and crawled in beneath the coupling to turn the body over. All colour had gone from Dmitri's face, which was like putty. His eyes were closed and peaceful, but the trace of a smile seemed to play at the corners of the mouth. Joseph could hardly look at it.

'Who is he?' Billy asked.

'I'll see if he's wearing any identification.' Joseph pulled open the collar and felt down inside, over Dmitri's throat and chest until his fingers found a metal disc hanging on a fine chain. This he broke and handed the disc up to Billy. 'There,' he said. 'What does that say?'

'Sorry, sir. Can't read Russian.'

Joseph took the disc back and himself read out, 'Lysenko, Pyotr Nikolaivitch.'

'Well – whoever he was, RIP.'

They left the body where it lay and made an examination of the box-car. The padlock had been shot off the door catches, or perhaps blown off – there were scorch marks on the steel – but the catches themselves were intact, and a new lock would make them secure again. 'Funny, that,' thought Joseph. 'I took his gun off him – unless he had another that I missed. Or maybe he had someone with him.' Still more puzzling was a tuft of grey hairs which they found clinging to one of the roof girders. At first sight Joseph feared it had come from Moorka the cat, of whom there was no sign; then he found that it was not cat hair, but a bunch of fibres wrenched from some garment.

'My God!' he said. 'I know what it is. It came from his boots. The dead man. Did you notice – he was wearing felt boots this colour.'

'You mean Boy swung him right upside-down?'

'Must have. Whirled him round like a rag doll.'

Billy whistled softly.

It was Taganrog that finished Joseph's patience with the train. Claustrophobia, growing with every day of frustration and immobility, gradually poisoned his peace of mind and made him determined to seek his own fortune once more. It was claustrophobia, also, that frayed Boy's nerves to an intolerable degree: after the attack on the box-car his mood grew steadily worse, and Joseph saw that if he did not get the horse into the open air, he was going to lose him.

From the air reconnaissance carried out by Bunny and Rick, everyone knew what to expect. The pilots reported not only that the lines approaching the town were choked with traffic, but also that the track beyond it, along the coast to Rostov, was similarly blocked solid. From Taganrog to Rostov was only forty miles – in normal times, an hour and a half's journey. Now it might take them four or five days, even a week.

'You'll all be glad to know that the Emperor Alexander the First died here on 1 December 1825,' announced Kinkead, with a show of exuberance, as he came in to the inevitable breakfast of pilchards, hard-tack biscuits and tea. A keen amateur historian, he had spent many an idle hour during the past few weeks reading such works of reference as he had been able to lay his hands on, and enjoyed bringing out odd facts to annoy his colleagues.

'Lucky bugger!' growled somebody. 'At least it saved him hanging about.'

'Now then! The Tsar of all the Russias? No jokes, please!'

'This place'd be enough to kill anyone.' Bunny Aten stared out of the window at the leaden Sea of Azov.

'Oh,' said Kinkead airily. 'In summer it's lovely.'

But even his moment of ebullience could not lift the others' spirits. They were too bored, too worn-down and too apprehensive about the future. They knew that with every hour that passed their chances of crossing the Don were diminishing: every intelligence report confirmed that the Red army was driving powerfully towards Rostov from the north, and that they, approaching now from the west, along the coast, might well be beaten in the race to the river bridge. Nor was there any way of circumventing that bottleneck: either they reached the Don in time and crossed it, or – if it was still possible – they would have to turn tail and flee westwards for the Crimea. Yet even that last resort might, in the end, prove beyond them: if the Reds reached the sea behind them, their retreat would be cut off, and they would be in a trap.

The one cheerful piece of news was that the Orlovs had left the train. In Taganrog itself they had slipped away unobserved, leaving a brief note of thanks. 'Miserable bastard!' stormed Aten. 'Couldn't even face us to say thank you.' Somebody suggested facetiously that they should sport a large notice proclaiming COUNT AND COUNTESS ORLOV HAVE LEFT THE TRAIN, but it was generally agreed that any such device might prove counter-productive.

One whole day out of Taganrog, they had advanced no more than five or six miles, for although one line of the railway was kept clear for hospital trains coming westwards from Rostov, and patrolled regularly by two White *broneviks*, the east-going line was at a standstill with retreating traffic. At that point the railway followed the coast, a couple of hundred yards from the sea, which on the right merged indivisibly with the leaden, misty sky. On the landward side of the tracks ran a main road, choked with traffic: horse-carts, ox-carts, sleighs, people on foot pulling sledges or pushing hand-carts. Bodies of men and horses were strewn along it. But at least the traffic was moving, and for most of the time it was manifestly going faster than the trains.

Eventually the sight of it pushed Joseph to a decision. He pretended that it was solely the deterioration in the condition of the horses that drove him to it: he said truthfully enough that they had been cooped up in the box-car for far too long. But he knew quite well that another factor was his own restlessness. The erratic nature of their progress kept making him postpone his decision: time and again, just as he had screwed up courage to announce his disembarkation, the train would move forward, causing him to change his mind and give the railway one more try.

In this fashion Christmas Day came and went, uncelebrated. Three days later Joseph finally brought himself to form up to Kinkead like an aircraftman asking some special permission. 'Flight Lieutenant,' he began. 'You may think I'm mad, but I wonder if you'd mind if I took the horses off?'

Kinkead blinked at him. 'You mean you want to walk?'

'Or ride. We must be less than twenty miles from Rostov now. I reckon I could do that in a day.'

'Well – it's up to you. I know we're making zero progress, and I won't try to stop you.'

'Thanks. I don't want to seem ungrateful. You've done such a hell of a lot . . .'

'Don't mention it.' Kinkead waved away his attempt to express gratitude. 'We've enjoyed having you along.'

Joseph took a deep breath. 'There is one other thing . . .'

'Fire away.'

'May I borrow LAC Bond until we cross the bridge at Rostov?'

'Borrow him?' Kinkead raised his eyebrows.

'Have him to help me.'

'Borrow him!' Kinkead repeated with a touch of indignation. 'That would be highly irregular. I've never heard of a civilian *borrowing* Royal Air Force personnel.'

'You could have him back when we get to Rostov.'

'Thank you! And what will you do on the other side of the river?'

'Find somebody I can hand the horses over to, I hope.'

'From what we've been hearing, I reckon you'll be lucky to find anyone prepared to take them. But that's your lookout.' He stood up and walked about. 'There's not a lot Bond can do on board the train, I must admit. What does *he* say about it?'

'I haven't asked him yet. I wanted to clear it with you first.'

'Let's find out, then.'

Billy Bond was sent for, came in, saluted, and, when he heard the proposition, jumped at it. Kinkead himself, suddenly entering into the spirit of the venture, declared, 'It's outrageous, but I'm damned if I refuse permission. And if anyone asks me why I did it, I'll know nothing about it.'

So it was that at mid-morning on 29 December Joseph opened the doors of the box-car, fixed the makeshift ramp in position and led Boy down on to the snowy ground. Billy followed with Min, and in a very short time they were both in the saddle and on their way. This time Moorka travelled in a special box which Billy had built for her. Made of wood, with holes drilled through the lid to let in air, and padded with straw, it was shaped so that it would sit on Min's withers, and secured to the rest of his tack by straps threaded through slots.

Joseph felt like a swimmer who has dived into cold water. Waiting for the moment of departure, he could scarcely imagine why he had chosen to leave the security of the train and the companionship of the pilots; he had dreaded the moment at which he would have to join that straggling mass of refugees outside. Yet once he had taken the plunge, it was not so bad. Just as the swimmer's body grows used to the temperature of the water, so he adjusted to the sensations of being on the road again.

The terrible human suffering along the way no longer shocked him. He observed it, and knew that it was dreadful, but his soul seemed to have grown a carapace. The living outnumbered the dead, but often it seemed that the scores were rapidly drawing level. Every few yards some human being had come to the end of his or her particular road. People had simply stopped and died in every conceivable attitude – lying down, sitting, propped against rocks, curled up, stretched out. One young woman had expired sitting in the corner of a ruined building, with a tiny baby frozen on to her bare breast. Passers-by, driven beyond decency and respect by their own desperation, had torn off most of her clothes and carried them away.

At least the dead were beyond suffering. The living were in

atrocious misery and pain. Many were barefoot, or shod only with bundles of rags. Their feet were blue, and split by hideous sores. Hundreds were stricken with typhus, debilitated by fever and ravaged by the dreaded red-brown rash. Dysentery and measles had also exacted a fearful toll. Yet easily the greatest single agent of wretchedness was hunger: almost everybody Joseph saw was emaciated and on the verge of starvation. Their horses were the same – gaunt skeletons burning out their last reserves of energy. Many were saddled but riderless: either their owners had died on the road, or they had simply turned their mounts loose because they had no food to give them, and were themselves too far gone to remove their tack. Joseph's impulse was to share what food he carried with the starving creatures round him, but the hardness which had developed in his heart made him easily able to withstand the temptation and to hoard what he had for his own party.

His progress was far slower than he had hoped. Some stretches of the road had been churned into slush, but on most the mud, snow and ice remained frozen into hard ridges, which made the horses slip and stumble. The other hazard was the sheer number of people on the move. Again and again he and Billy were blocked by slow-moving traffic – ox-carts with their wooden wheels squealing under heavy loads, ancient *babushkas* pushing or dragging their prams. Many primitive vehicles had collapsed with the strain of the journey, so that wrecks dotted the fairway like rocks in a tide-race, forcing the current to flow round them.

Through all these obstacles Joseph and Billy threaded their way at the best pace they could manage. The stallions, though physically not what they had been, nevertheless stood out like super-horses, dangerously conspicuous among the broken-down nags that could barely drag themselves and their burdens along. Often people shot them challenging or envious glances, and several demanded to know who they were – to which Joseph replied that the horses belonged to the British Army headquarters in Rostov, to which he was returning with important documents. With his tan greatcoat, his RAF duty cap and his rifle slung on his back, Billy certainly looked every inch a despatch rider. What people made of Joseph, he could not tell, for his own appearance had been satisfactorily roughened by a growth of curly brown beard and by a slanting scar on his right temple, legacy of the steel splinter that had knocked him down in the fight along the train. Whatever they thought, his stock answer was accepted readily enough: the British were still held in high esteem, and casual inquirers, unable to distinguish Billy's duty cap and badge, supposed he was Joseph's military escort.

Now and then, as they manoeuvred to overtake a straggler, they would elicit an angry shout of '*Ne gonite!*' – slow down! – or you'll kill someone.' But one or two of the travellers had enough resilience to greet them with jokes. 'Don't you know there's a speed limit?' yelled one young man.

'What is it?' asked Joseph.

'A hundred versts an hour.'

'*Chepukha!*' called somebody else. 'Nonsense! It's one verst a month.'

Soon it became clear that they would not reach Rostov, or anywhere near it, that day. Joseph knew they were ahead of Train 607, for they had overtaken many other steel caterpillars crawling in front of it; he therefore felt justified in his decision to strike out. Yet when dark began to fall, and he was confronted with the need to find shelter for the night, doubts came piling on him. For the hundredth time that day he thanked God that he had Billy with him: trying to manage two horses in that maelstrom would have been a nightmare – especially when, as happened twice, they passed a mare and the stallions began to squeal out amorous messages.

As dusk came on, Joseph's instinct was to leave the teeming rat-run and ride inland until he found a farmer who might give them shelter. 'Let's try this,' he said as they came to a small junction, and a track which led off towards the hills. There was no signpost to say where it went, but marks in the snow made it clear that a horse and sleigh had been up it during the afternoon. Their luck was in: the farmer, though hostile at first, gradually thawed, and not only allowed them to sleep in the barn, but sold them a truss of hay for the horses.

From that point, the dangers and difficulties increased sharply. Next day not only the trains but pedestrian traffic also came to a halt when a troop of Red cavalry appeared on the low hills inland and swept down in a series of raids, firing indiscriminately at the defenceless civilians. The refugees' only escape from the bullets lay in diving between coaches and sheltering behind them on the seaward side of the track. Horses, of course, could not dodge through so easily, and after Joseph had seen two animals cut down in the shafts of a cart on the road, he kept on the far side of the line of trains, even though the going – up and down banks, in and out of ditches – was much harder. Still greater alarm spread among the refugee horde when a tank crawled into view on top of a hill and blew open one of the stationary carriages with a shell: the wagon caught fire, and screams from the wounded rang along the line. That, however, was the extent of the tank's success, for the White forces' *bronevik*, coming up on patrol, at once scored a direct hit with its four-inch gun and incinerated the vehicle's crew.

The noise, the cold, the constant anxiety, exacerbated by lack of sound sleep, had started to wear both Englishmen down. In spite of his deliberate efforts to stay cheerful, Joseph grew irritable and depressed. Billy was debilitated by a fever, which he fervently hoped was nothing worse than influenza. Like the humans, the horses showed signs of stress. In spite of continuous harassment, Min remained more or less his normal calm self, although even he played up from time to time. Boy, on the other hand, grew more and more jittery, especially during the frequent enforced halts, and Joseph had a job to control him. One of his rear shoes was working loose and made a faint clink whenever it came down on anything hard: hoping it would last for another day or two, Joseph nursed it along by trying to keep the horse on snow rather than on bare ground.

Rostov, so near in terms of miles, began to seem impossibly far away. The desirability of the place grew hourly in Joseph's mind: he saw it as his ultimate destination, the place at which he could hand over responsibility, the haven in which his troubles would come to an end. When finally they reached its outskirts, as dawn broke for the last time in 1919, reality brought savage disillusionment. The trouble was not that the suburbs of the town were ugly and heavily industrialised: far more shattering was the fact that the Reds had reached them first.

The long winter darkness still hung over the land as Joseph and Billy, hugging the trains for shelter, rode into the marshalling yards; but already they could hear small-arms fire and the boom of artillery ahead. As the light came up, a scene of utter desolation greeted them. At first sight everything seemed grey-white. The yards, which were carpeted with fresh snow, lay on the high north bank of the river. Immediately above them ran a line of low, snow-covered hills. Down to the right was the Don; but because the river had burst its banks and flooded the low-lying land on the south side, it had spread into an immense expanse of ice. Across the middle of it, not quarter of a mile away, ran every traveller's goal – the bridge.

Daylight, growing stronger, revealed that traffic was crawling cease-lessly across the viaduct, whose stumpy arches stood rooted in the ice. Trains moved on one side, pedestrians, horses and carts on the other, one way only, north to south. Between the yards and the nearer end of the bridge, however, there seemed to be a block: although refugees poured out of stranded trains by the hundred, they were piling up in the lee of the wagons and not moving forward. Joseph, hustling through their massed ranks, soon found the cause of the trouble.

Red machine-gunners had established themselves on the snowy heights to his left, and from their commanding eminence had begun to pour down lethal fire. The outer half of the yards lay in dead ground, covered from the gunners by an intervening bank, but the inner half, closer to the bridge, was in direct line of shot. Up there, the trains rang like gongs as they were struck by bullets, and the air sang with the evil whine of ricochets. People in the open kept toppling to the ground, suddenly cut down.

Joseph, having recklessly led Billy across an open space, pulled up in the shelter of a burnt-out engine. 'This is getting too bloody hot,' he said. 'Let's wait here for a bit to see if things cool off.'

The opposite happened. Even as they watched, a full-scale battle developed. Red artillery opened up from the bluffs on their left and began to lob shells over the river, into the area where the White forces were trying to redeploy. The bridge, with its crawling traffic, must have presented an almost irresistible target, but the Bolsheviks let it alone, anxious not to damage or destroy their own next means of advance. Soon the odd shell started to whistle back overhead and explode with a crump in the hills. Talk of encirclement by Red forces spread panic among the massed refugees, whose fears were redoubled by other rumours emanating from the Whites: that the bridge was to be blown up as soon as the last of the British Military Mission's trains was across, and that an ice-breaker was on its way down-river, smashing open a channel so that the Bolsheviks should not be able to walk over.

Long, reverberant hoots began to boom out through the rattle and thump of gunfire. '*Ledokol!* The ice-breaker!' people cried. Word went round that the vessel was already in sight. The news set off a stampede, straight down the banks of the river and on to the ice. Had the surface been smooth, more might have managed the crossing; but because the frost had set in on a windy night, gusts had frozen the surface of the river into a petrified sea of waves, peaks, troughs and banks almost impossible for humans to negotiate, completely impossible for horses. For those who remained on the north bank, it was horrible to watch horses and men stumble, slide, fall, and slither on with broken limbs. Yet those who somehow kept going were the lucky ones. The Red machine-gunners, scenting helpless prey, turned their sights on to anybody trapped on that treacherous waste and mowed them down relentlessly. Body after body toppled into hollows, and blood ran out in scarlet glaciers across the ice.

Joseph's hopes rose when he heard the hammer of heavy machine-guns answer the Bolshevik fire from within the yards: evidently a military train armed with Lewis guns had come in. But the Red barrage continued unabated, and amid the incessant noise the sensation of being trapped built up inexorably. The hoots of the ice-breaker grew steadily louder, answered by the whistles of engines still crossing the bridge. The first time Billy shouted, 'I can't stand this much longer', Joseph told him not to be so stupid; but the second time he made the remark, the only answer seemed to be to move.

'We'll go up a bit, anyway,' Joseph told him. 'But for God's sake watch yourself.'

The instruction was superfluous: Billy was by nature as careful as anyone could be. But by then the confusion was such that their salvation or damnation appeared to lie as much in the hands of fate as in their own resourcefulness. Joseph remembered Katya's fatalistic approach to life. If a bullet was going to find him, it was going to find him. Even so, he was damned if he would make things easier for that bullet by exposing himself unnecessarily.

The sights that greeted them at the neck of the yards were enough to turn the most hardened stomach. They found that although cover of a kind continued almost all the way to the start of the bridge, there was a gap about fifty yards wide between two trains which had broken down and been abandoned. To cross that gap was death, for the Bolsheviks had zeroed their machine-guns on it, opening up the instant anyone tried to cross. Bodies lay everywhere, and if the gunners had nothing live to fire at, they would put a burst into a corpse, lifting it bodily into the air, shoving it sideways over the trampled snow, blowing pieces of flesh off it, cutting it into bits. Even that sight did not stop people, so desperate had they become. An army officer, already wounded so badly that he had lost the use of both legs, dragged himself forward on his hands, roaring obscenities in the direction of the Red positions. His protest was over within ten yards. Hit in the body, he flopped down, then forced his torso up again with blood gushing from his mouth, only for a bullet to blow his head to pieces. Before he had stopped twitching, a young woman with a baby swaddled in grey clothes suddenly rushed forward out of shelter. People near her screamed and grabbed at her coat to stop her, but she was too quick for them. Nimble as a deer, she darted forward. Five seconds later she was dead, flung bodily sideways to the ground. The baby pitched forward out of her arms and rolled on like a ball. Hardly had it come to rest before the marksmen found it: a hail of bullets sent it skidding sideways, and a pathetic trickle of blood seeped out of its grey bandages.

The slight was too much for Billy. 'Hold Min a moment,' he said grimly as he shoved the reins at Joseph and unshipped his rifle. 'I'm going to give the bastards a couple.'

Joseph saw that he was too angry for argument, so he let him go, and watched him worm his way into a firing position between the wheels. Billy emptied his magazine twice – five carefully aimed shots each time – in the direction of the flashes which flickered from the machine-gun nest on the bluff, and claimed at least one victim. Yet his act of defiance, much though it had to commend it, was not what saved him, Joseph and hundreds of others.

As he crawled back from his firing point, a general shout went up. People were pointing over the river, and there, rolling in across the ice, was a blanket of mist. In two or three minutes the dense grey wall reached the yards, engulfed them and blotted out the bluffs. The Red gunners fired a few more rounds but then fell silent, blinded. In one mass, with scarcely a word or a sound, the crowd surged forward across the gap, over the crumpled bodies in their pools of blood.

'Get up! Get up!' Joseph cried as Billy rejoined him. 'Ride like hell. The Reds may be down among us any second.'

Back in the saddle, they drove forward, barging pedestrians out of their way. At the end of the bridge, they found that curved stone walls formed a funnel, into which a solid mass of people was trying to force its way. Between its low parapets the bridge carried a double railway track, a road and a footpath. Two trains stood half on the bridge, half on land: their engines had steam up, about to depart. Joseph noticed that both were guarded by British soldiers, who were repelling would-be boarders with fixed bayonets. No use looking to them for help *now*, he thought. Even if there was a box-car empty, Boy would never go into it. He was bad enough on the ground, swerving, barging into people, half-rearing and trampling on their feet.

Joseph cursed him steadily in a ferocious undertone. 'Get on, get on, you stupid sod,' he growled as he drove him forward. 'Stop mucking about or you'll kill us all.'

At last they gained the bridge, wedged in a slow-moving mass of bodies. Earlier, looking over the river, Joseph had reckoned that the bridge was only three hundred yards long. But as they started on that desperate crossing, the trains beside them began to move, and although they went at only a gentle pace, they drew away from the pedestrians. Quickly people looked back down the line and saw that no more trains were coming: at least, none was coming within the limit of visibility. So they flowed over on to the tracks and hurried after the receding wagons. 'God!' shouted a man beside Min. 'Now they'll blow the bridge and we'll all be killed.' This cowardly cry spread further panic. Many of those who had transferred on to the railway tripped over the sleepers and were trampled underfoot. The rest surged blindly on, counting the seconds. From close on their left the ice-breaker's siren boomed out its warning. Joseph looked over his shoulder and saw that Billy had become separated from him by a few yards, but was making good enough progress.

At last something solid loomed in the murk ahead: buildings. They were across. Released from the constraint of the bridge, the crowd spread out and accelerated. 'Keep going!' shouted Joseph. 'Get as far into the town as we can.' His positive tone masked deep misgivings. Even though the relief of escape was exhilarating, it was undermined almost at once by the realisation that he had no idea what to do next. Rostov was not in the least as he had expected or hoped. Somehow he had imagined an orderly retreat, with the road policed by British servicemen, and friendly soldiers on hand to direct him to the headquarters of the British Military Mission. This would be ensconced in a secure compound equipped with stables to accommodate the horses, and in the yard some genial general would take charge of Min and Boy in the name of the King of England – for it was to him, now, that Joseph supposed the stallions should be returned.

Of this comfortable picture, no single facet existed. It was not even as if a jigsaw puzzle of the picture had been taken apart and the pieces scattered about. Joseph could not discern any piece of it. Groping through the fog, he saw neither soldiers nor military vehicles nor any evidence of British occupation. The shops were closed and barred. Ruined buildings gaped open, some of them still on fire from the impact of shells. Far from treating the town as a safe retreat, the inhabitants were hurrying to escape.

Gradually the awful realisation came over Joseph that instead of ending, his journey had scarcely begun. Hunger and exhaustion threatened to overwhelm him. The excitement of the crossing had kept them at bay for a while, but now the fact that he had had no sleep or breakfast became a crushing weight. He glanced at Billy and saw that he felt the same. Both horses looked wretched, and from inside her box Moorka was giving piteous yowls.

'We've got to stop,' said Joseph dully. 'Have something to eat.'

Hardly had he spoken when the ground shook as an immense explosion thundered out from behind them. 'There goes the bridge,' he said. 'Just in time, we were.'

Billy nodded, too drained to speak. By then both men had dismounted, to save the horses, and they walked on, leading them, until they came to a wooden gate set in a high brick wall. The gate had been knocked off its hinges and was only propped in position. On impulse Joseph pushed one end of it open and looked through the gap. Inside was a timber yard, with piles of planks stacked here and there, covered with snow, and down one side a line of open-fronted sheds. At least the place offered shelter, fuel and a temporary refuge.

A minute later they were all inside, with the gate back in position behind them. 'If anyone tries to turn us out, we'll bribe him or shoot him,' Joseph announced. But nobody appeared. The yard was deserted, and in the sheds they made themselves at home. They unsaddled the stallions, rugged them up and gave them the last of the oats. Then, on a fire made from shavings and odd bits of timber, they melted snow to make water, brewed tea, and heated a couple of tins of stew. Moorka, released from her travelling box, ate some stew and went on a prowl round her new surroundings.

With food inside him, Joseph felt stronger. 'You stay here,' he told Billy. 'I'm going to find out what's happening. What is it now? Midday. I'll be back by two at the latest.'

He set out on his own. It felt very strange to be without the stallions, but he was able to move more quickly, without attracting attention. His instinct was to return to the railway, for he reckoned that someone on a military train would surely direct him to the British high command. With any luck, he might even meet his old chums from B flight.

But he never reached the railway. He was standing on a street corner, considering which way to go, when he heard the whistle of an incoming shell. He just had time to realise that the build-up of sound was ominously rapid before the house on the corner opposite seemed to disintegrate bodily and come hurtling at him with a blast of air that turned the whole sky black.

TWELVE

Beyond the Don: January–March
1920

ANTISEPTIC. DISINFECTANT. Those were the first things of which he became aware. As he tried to open his eyes, he realised that something was covering his head. Above him a woman's voice said in Russian, 'He's coming round.' He tried to speak, but found he could only croak. A hand came down on to his shoulder, and the same voice said, 'Don't worry. You're all right.' Then the nurse turned and said to someone else, 'Tell Sister Mironov he's regained consciousness.'

The name drove into his brain, clearing his mind and freeing his vocal cords. 'Sister Mironov!' he gasped. 'Where is she?'

He tried to sit up, but felt too weak. The effort sent pains shooting through his head, and in any case a hand restrained him.

'She is here,' said the nurse. 'She will be back soon.'

'Are we in Kharkov, then?'

'Kharkov! No, thank heaven. We're at Kuschevskaya, eighty versts south of Rostov.'

'Rostov! Of course.' Everything came back: the marshalling yards, the bloodstained ice on the river, the bridge. He disengaged a hand from the bedclothes and felt bandages on his head.

'*Bozhe moi!!*' he cried suddenly. 'Where are my horses?'

'What horses?'

'The ones I was taking south.'

'I don't know. You'll have to ask the sister.'

He felt numb with helplessness. 'Am I in hospital?'

'No – this is a hospital train.'

'What happened to me?'

'We're not sure. You were brought in with a head wound by some British soldiers.'

He lay still as the information sank in. Feeling under the bed-clothes, he found that he was clad in rough woollen pyjamas. Katya's ikon still hung round his throat, but his money belt had gone. He remembered nothing after crossing the bridge. 'I was with someone,' he said. 'What day is it?'

'January the fourth, 1920.'

The information meant nothing. 'These bandages. Can you take them off?'

'When the sister comes.'

'Are my eyes hurt?'

'We don't think so. You've got a scalp wound – that's all.'

'I feel cold.'

'The train is very cold. The heating is not functioning any more.'

'When will Sister Mironov come?'

'Soon. She's only gone into the village.'

The idea of seeing her was so immense that he could hardly grasp it. His hold on the world seemed very feeble. In fact, he could feel himself drifting off again ... But when he next came round, a soft hand was holding his, and as he stirred, he felt the grip tighten. 'Rusalka!' he whispered.

Warm, soft lips came down on his. 'Martyshka!'

Tears welled up as he held her. In a choked whisper he said, 'Take off the bandages. I must see you.'

'Wait, then.' She went to work with quick, deft fingers, unpinning and unwrapping. In a minute he was blinking at the light, at the bright, white walls of the cubicle that reflected snow-glare from outside. First he saw her hand, wrist and forearm, deliciously familiar; then, removing the last of bandages, but leaving a pad over the wound itself, she turned and perched on the edge of his bunk.

'Oh, my love!' Her appearance shocked him. He had expected her to be thin and tired, but not so worn as this. Stress and exhaustion had etched lines across her forehead and deepened the creases that ran down from her nose to the corners of her mouth. In three weeks she seemed to have aged ten years. Seeing that she must have suffered greatly, he could not speak.

She sat and held his hand, and presently there stole over her face that look of faintly mocking amusement which bewitched him. 'I hardly recognised you with that beard,' she said, 'Never mind. I think you'll live.'

'Did you think I'd die?'

'We weren't sure at first. You had a bad bang on the head from a piece of wood. We took out a lot of splinters, and by the time we got our hands on you, you'd lost a good deal of blood.'

A party of soldiers had found him lying unconscious in the road, she said, in the southern outskirts of Rostov, near a building set on fire by a shell. Because of the Union Jack on the sleeves of his overcoat, they had picked him up and taken him to the nearest hospital train. 'They took you to another train first, but then I heard about you, and got you transferred.'

Now, two days later, they were stranded in a siding at Kuschevskaya, the boiler of their engine burnt out . . .

As Katya talked, one idea kept forcing itself to the front of Joseph's mind: he must tell her that Mitya was dead. But how? As he wrestled with the problem, he hardly took in what she was saying, until he caught the words 'At least the horses are all right.'

'Thank God! Where are they?'

'Here, in a farm on the edge of the village. Your friend Billy Bond brought them from Rostov – but now he's been ordered to rejoin his unit.'

'I remember now. I was with Billy. I left the horses with him in a little yard. Where is he?'

'On his way to Novorossisk. The retreat's continuing. Everyone's heading for the coast of the Black Sea.'

'I thought Rostov was supposed to be the place where the tide turned.'

'It was. But the Bolsheviks crossed the river and kept on.'

'So we have to go on, too?'

'As soon as you're well enough – yes.'

The idea of further travel seemed impossibly exhausting. In his state of debility, Joseph could not face the idea of more days on the road. 'Perhaps I could leave the horses where they are,' he said weakly. 'If they're in a farm, they'll probably be all right.'

'No!' The fierceness of Katya's retort jolted him. 'Don't say that. Don't think any such thought. After bringing them all this way! We'll take them together. I'm coming with you.'

Joseph stared at her. 'But . . . your patients?'

'To hell with them. Most of them are dead from *tif*. The rest will have to take their chances. This train is going to be evacuated anyway. It's finished. I've looked after dying men for long enough.'

The ferocity of her answers was astounding. Joseph had never heard her speak so brutally, never seen her nostrils pinch in or her lips tighten with such harsh feeling. Her anger scared him, but at the same time fired him with new hope.

'You'll come with *me*?' he said incredulously. 'That would be a miracle.'

The anger melted from her face, and she smiled. 'Yes. We'll go together – and this is what I've arranged. This evening, after dark, an *izvozchik* is coming to take us to the farm. You shouldn't be moved, I know, but anything would be better than this morgue of a train. The owner of the farm, Kozlov, is an old Tartar: he says he can put us up for a night or two.'

Joseph was in no state to argue; and when the time came, he managed the short trip somehow. Katya dressed him and then, with the help of the sleigh-driver, supported him from the train. The drive through snowy streets seemed to take for ever: his head throbbed, and he shivered beneath his mound of rugs. Yet when they reached the farmhouse, everything changed.

Kozlov and his wife Anna Yegorovna greeted them like children – and indeed they were old enough to have been Joseph's parents, Katya's grandparents. Kozlov must once have been strikingly dark and handsome: now his hair, which stood straight up like a brush, was iron grey, though his long moustache still had black shadows in it. Anna Yegorovna was small and buxom, her rotundity emphasised by the way she wore her silvery hair, pulled tightly back in a bun. The house was modest but well constructed, of thick, dressed logs lined with planks. Apart from a cramped hall, it had two rooms, the main *izba*, dominated by a tiled stove in one corner, with the family's sleeping platform next to it, and the smaller *gornitsa*, or parlour, which had a stove of its own and a proper bed – even if its base was only a board, without springs. Built on to the back of the house was a simple but effective *bania*.

A hot bath – the first that either of them had had for weeks – and a meal of chicken stew with potatoes seemed like miracles from another world. Clean, comfortable and replete, they withdrew early to their little room and went to bed, where they clung to each other silently. They did not make love, for neither was in a state to do so; yet in that snug lair, with an oil lamp flickering on the table, they were able to let loose their pent-up emotions.

When Joseph told the story of Mitya's death, Katya lay silently beside him, clutching his arm. Guilt lay heavily on him. 'What could I have done?' he asked helplessly. 'I let him go, and yet he came back.'

'Nothing.' Her voice was steady. 'His trouble started long ago. I blame myself for going away to the war in 1915. But even if I'd stayed at Nikolsk, I don't think it would have made any difference. Mitya was fated to go that way. I believe it was he who burnt the house.'

'No!'

'Yes – and shot our father.'

'God! How could he?'

'The devil was in him.'

'But how did he – how did the devil get there?'

'Martyshka – I don't know.'

'This war – it's made everyone mad.'

'Except you and me.' She leant over and kissed his cheek.

'What about Vanya?' he asked.

'I've heard nothing of him for more than two years. At least I haven't heard that he's dead.'

When she came to describe the burning of the hospital in Kharkov, and her experience with the Bolshevik general, her voice went strained and jerky, and her body shook. She spoke in short bursts, pausing often and breathing hard. At first Joseph was horrified. Then he grew so angry that his head began to throb.

'I killed him!' Katya gasped through her shudders. 'My profession is to save men, but I killed one. God forgive me.'

'Don't worry.' Joseph clenched his teeth against the pain. 'I'd have killed him, ten times over. I'd have cut him in little pieces.' He waited before asking, 'How did you escape?'

'I was dumped in a cell with other women. A terrible night. All of them shrieking and crying. Freezing cold. No lavatory. Rats on the floor. Nobody slept. Then, before dawn, there was a terrific commotion. Shots went off outside. There was a heavy explosion. Our door burst open, and somebody shouted, "Outside, all of you!" We thought our end had come – but the next thing we knew, we were taken into a big canteen and given breakfast. It turned out that a squadron of White cavalry had counter-attacked and recaptured the barracks just as the sky was growing light. They didn't look any less rough than the Reds, but because we'd been prisoners of the Bolsheviks, they made much of us: they gave us this breakfast – tea and black bread – and put us on a southbound train.'

'Perhaps, if you hadn't poisoned the general, he'd have been killed in the attack anyway.'

'No, because he would have been in his villa, not the barracks.'

'Oh – of course.'

'I tried to persuade myself something like that: that if I hadn't killed him, somebody else would have. But I did it.'

They lay quiet for several minutes. Then Katya said, 'I keep thinking of a man who came to me from the front, mortally wounded, in 1916. His insides had been destroyed by shell splinters – liver, stomach, everything. We gave him morphia, but otherwise we could do nothing for him. It was just after noon on a brilliant summer's day, near Chernovitz. "*Sestritsa!*" he kept crying. "Don't let it get dark." I told him not to worry. I said that evening was coming on. But he did not believe me. "No," he said. "It's growing dark because I'm dying. For the love of God, Sister, give me light!" Then, just before the end, he went quiet and added calmly. "We are born once, and we must die once. We are in God's hands. It is His will." Then he passed away.'

Joseph asked softly, 'Are *you* afraid of the dark?'

'Not really. Pain I'm frightened of, yes. But not dying. Especially if I'm with you.'

'Put out the lamp, then, and we'll go to sleep.'

For two days Joseph lay low in that blessed retreat. His wound was a long gouge, slanting up across his left temple from the corner of his eyebrow into his hair, caused by the impact of a piece of timber, which had evidently hit him edge-on. A doctor had sewn the edges of the gash together, and it was healing well, but Katya's fear was that germs would enter the cut, so she disinfected it meticulously with iodine and insisted that Joseph kept it bandaged. 'Now I'll have two scars,' he said. 'One on each side.'

Under her care, and nourished by Anna Yegorovna's good food, his strength quickly returned. By the first afternoon he was well enough to go out and see the horses. To his joy, they were not put off by his bandages, and whinnied warm greetings. He embraced them in turn, but when he went down to look at Boy's loose shoe, his head felt as if it would burst, and he had to straighten up quickly. To his surprise and delight, he found that both horses had been completely reshod, with the shoes which he had carried all the way from Kharkov. Somebody had made a good job of them, too. Then, to his still greater astonishment, he saw a cat sitting on Min's back. *A* cat! It was *his* cat, Moorka. 'How in heaven did you get as far as this?' he asked. He had thought that she must have been killed in the explosion, but then he realised that she had not even been with him when the shell landed. She must have come on with Billy. 'If ever I see that man again,' Joseph told her, 'I shall give him all the money I've got.'

That night they did make love, gently and slowly. The act brought them infinite release, and after it Katya said dreamily, 'I feel as if I'm on honeymoon. From now on, let's pretend we're married. After all, we are, in body and soul.'

'We've got no papers to prove it,' said Joseph sleepily.

'Who wants papers? We've lost them all. That's our answer. They've been stolen. Everything's in such chaos that nobody will know any better. From now on I shall be Mrs Joseph Clements.'

'Who are we, then?' Joseph took up her fantasy.

'We're country people from somewhere north of Rostov . . . from near Taganrog. You can be what you are – manager of a stud. The place was burnt down. Horses stolen. I'm your wife. But I come from the far north, on the Gulf of Finland. That's why I have fair hair, and a northern accent. The horses are our own – all that we managed to save.'

'Whose stud was it?' Joseph thought for a moment. 'I know – Leon Mantachev's. Everyone's heard of him. And I know for a fact that his place was raided by the Bolsheviks.'

Their euphoria was shaken, in the morning, by news that the Red forces had broken through the barrier with which the White army had sought to contain them south of Rostov, and were advancing again. It was no time for delay. Katya, anticipating just such a development, had made a plan of action.

'I've bought a sleigh,' she announced after breakfast, 'and I've hired a man to help with the horses. In fact it was him who shod them. He's a farrier by trade. I got some harness, too. I'm afraid I've spent rather a lot of your money.'

'A sleigh? What's going to pull it?'

'Min.'

'Min?'

'Didn't you say you'd broken him to harness?'

'Yes – but that was with a cart.'

'Well – what's the difference? Can't he get used to a sleigh? Especially if we take off the bells.'

Her vitality and enthusiasm swept difficulties aside. The hired help, Arkady, a swarthy young man with a long, heavy face, was Kozlov's nephew. Beyond doubt he had a gift for handling horses: that was immediately apparent when he dealt with the stallions. Min was at ease with him from the first, and even Boy, though wary, allowed him to make friends. Yet Joseph did not like him, and felt suspicious of his motives. Why was he so keen to go south? He claimed to have a girl friend in Abynsk, a small town near Novorossisk; but there was something about him that made Joseph uneasy.

When he and Katya were alone, Joseph asked, 'You didn't let him see my money belt, did you?'

'Heavens, no.'

'Or tell him anything about who the horses really are?'

'Of course not.'

'Why's he so keen to come with us, then?'

Katya could not say – yet this was clearly no time for argument, and anyway Joseph, in his weakened state, lacked the energy to thrash the matter out. The rest of that day passed in making preparations. Katya washed their spare clothes and draped them over the big stove in the *izba* to dry. She also helped Anna Yegorovna bake bread and do other household chores. Joseph and Arkady turned their attention to matters of transport. The sleigh was a simple one, with a curved-over front to break the wind, a padded seat with room for two and a generous space behind it for luggage. Min accepted the harness, with its heavy collar, readily enough, but when they first brought the sleigh up behind him, with the shafts along his flanks, he began to fidget. Joseph, head aching from any exertion, several times had to sit down on an upturned wooden bucket and wait for the pain in his temples to subside. Gradually, however, the horse accepted his new role, and after a few jerks and plunges during the first trials across a field, settled down to pull steadily.

They left early next morning. Joseph and Katya both wore *burkas*, or cloaks of thick grey felt, which she had bought in the town, and she sported a muffin-like hat of light grey fur which was big enough to be pulled right down over her ears. As they climbed into the sleigh, the garments settled round them like tents and insulated them perfectly from the cold. The Kozlovs, refusing any payment, waved them off with pathetic cries of '*Do svidaniya*, children.' Joseph, with one look round to make sure that Arkady had a good hold of Boy, shook the reins and set Min in motion. The sleigh glided forward, and icy air began to flow past their faces. After a minute Katya turned, and saw the old couple standing like pillars of grey-topped stone in front of their little house. She waved and called a last farewell. When she faced forward again, Joseph saw tears in her eyes.

'Cheer up!' he put his arm round her shoulders. 'We're off! And I feel miles better.'

'Good! It's just that they were so kind.'

'Everybody's kind to you, thank God. *You* look better, too. A different person from the one on the train.' He kissed a tear off her cheek. 'Now – where are we going?'

'Novorossisk, of course.' She gave him the sideways look that had first captivated him in the courtyard at Nikolsk. 'Unless you'd like to drop in at Petersburg on the way.'

'Yes, please. Let's have a night at the Astoria.'

'Certainly, sir.'

'But where shall we go first?' When he turned to look at her, laughing, she stuck out her tongue and said, 'Don't ask me. Follow everyone else.'

That was a good enough precept. The road to the south was full of other travellers – people on foot, in sleighs, in horse-drawn *telegas* and *furgons* and squealing, wooden-wheeled ox-carts. Another human flood was in motion, but this one was less frantic than the torrent which had poured down towards Rostov. Partly because the road was straight and level, partly because the danger from behind was less pressing, people had the time and spirit to exchange greetings, ask about plans and swap experiences. Everybody had some story of disaster or narrow escape to tell, and Joseph became adept at saying, 'Everything! We lost everything. Just got away with ourselves and the horses.' His wound lent authority to his story of an attack in the night: he said he had been hit by a club or rifle butt that some half-seen assailant had swung at him.

He spent most of the first day perched in the sleigh, nursing his strength, and getting out to walk only when he felt cold. Katya put in more time on her feet, partly for the sake of exercise, partly to give Min a lighter burden. Already a competent driver, she soon had Min going kindly. In the afternoon she rode Boy for half an hour; it was the first time she had ever ridden astride, and she found it highly uncomfortable; but, with Arkady leading the horse, things went smoothly enough.

They spent that night in a farmhouse belonging to friends of the Kozlovs. From there they went on to another farm suggested by their latest hosts – and so they continued down a chain of stepping-stones, moving from one friendly rendezvous to the next. The weather remained cold and fine, and Joseph gained steadily in strength. He could not tell how far they went each day, but he supposed about thirty versts, or twenty miles. His notion of topography was extremely vague: without his map, which had disappeared in Rostov, he had only the haziest idea of what lay ahead, but he knew that they were on the easiest stretch of the journey to the coast. Here, on the Kuban steppe, the land was even flatter than in the Ukraine, and a snowy plain stretched as far ahead as eye could see. They knew from talking to local farmers that this was part of the black soil belt – and every now and then they saw evidence of its fertility in the skeletons of sunflowers and maize which stuck up spikily through the snow. Orchards and vineyards spoke of hot summers.

Between them and the sea, however, lay the northern spurs of the Caucasus massif, and they would have to climb to a pass 3,000 feet high. Fellow travellers variously estimated the distance to Novorossisk at 300 and 400 versts. If they kept up their present rate of progress, they might do it in two weeks ...

As they approached a town called Pavlovskaya, the main railway line swung in to run parallel with the road, and the sight of stationary trains standing nose to tail sent Joseph's mind back with a lurch to the hellish days of inactivity between Taganrog and Rostov. 'Thank God we're in the open,' he said as they overtook snake after snake of stranded wagons. He described how Boy had developed claustrophobia from being so long in the box-car, and how he had come out like a jack-in-a-box when finally released. 'That's one thing I'm sure of,' he told Katya. 'He'll never go into another wagon like that.' In spite of his revulsion for the railway, Joseph looked eagerly for the military train bearing his friends in the RAF, in case he might snatch a chance to thank Billy Bond; but there was no sign of it, and then, after Pavlovskaya, rail and road went their separate ways again.

To Joseph those few, precious days seemed a true honeymoon. Pale sun shone. The sledge rode easily over crisp snow. He himself was almost back to full strength. Katya's face had shed its deathly pallor, and her cheeks glowed from the cold. He had never known her more lively, never loved her more. 'I can hardly believe this!' he exclaimed one morning. 'When I left Kharkov, I thought I'd never see you again.'

'Not really?' She gazed at him searchingly. 'You underestimate my tenacity. I knew I'd catch up with you somewhere.'

As always, her supersitions both delighted and alarmed him. One evening, after supper in an *izba*, she started forward and said, 'Oh! Quick! Don't sit like that. It'll bring you seven years without love.' He had perched on the bench at a corner of the table, with one knee on either side of the leg. 'Move!' she cried, not joking. 'Do!' And to humour her, or to keep safe (he was not sure which), he shifted so that his knees were together. Two days later, in the morning, they were about to leave another small homestead when a girl came round a corner of the cowshed with two wooden pails hanging from a yoke across her shoulders. At the sight of her Katya turned snow-white and crossed herself.

'Whatever's the matter?' said Joseph quickly.

'The buckets are empty!' she groaned in a voice of doom. 'That is a sign of misfortune.'

'But she's only going to the well to fill them.'

'It makes no difference.'

At the last moment before their departure this evil omen was to some extent mitigated by the discovery that the farm girl was also called Katya. Finding two girls with the same name was a sign of good luck, and it cheered Joseph's Katya a little; yet the incident weighed on his mind.

On the road, life seemed extraordinarily good. They had enough food for themselves and the horses. The stallions were no longer so conspicuous as they had been. In a month of travel their winter coats had grown shaggier; they had lost a lot of condition, and their aristocratic outlines were to some extent disguised by saddles, panniers, rolled rugs and tattered leg-bandages: even so, they attracted many favourable comments, and some envious ones. Katya fell in love with both of them, especially Boy, who seemed to reciprocate her affection. 'It's nothing to do with you,' said Joseph, teasing. 'He's worn down by the journey – that's all. Otherwise he'd never let you near him.' But he had to admit that he had never known the horse so amenable. As for Moorka - Katya could scarcely contain her delight at having a silver cat in the party. The little creature rode for some of the way in the sleigh, and whenever they stopped she dashed about in the snow, batting lumps into the air with her paws; but she also spent much time crouched on Min's withers, strengthening the impression that the party were survivors of a household, travelling with all they had been able to salvage. Arkady made a dour but efficient assistant, and Joseph had to admit that his reservations seemed ill-founded.

The sight of Min pulling the sledge delighted him. 'If word of this ever gets to Newmarket,' he said, 'the lads'll die laughing. A Derby-winner in the shafts, in the snow! Who ever heard of such a thing? The King's horse, as well!'

Blithely ignoring such trivial difficulties as might confront them on the rest of the journey, they had eager discussions about what they would do when they reached England. Katya longed to see London, but Newmarket was always their final target. They would find a cottage outside the town and settle down in it. Katya would consult a specialist to see if she could bear children, and when that problem had been dealt with, they would bring up a family in the English countryside. Later, when the Bolshevik menace had been suppressed, they would return to Russia, at least for a holiday, if not for longer, and show their children whatever was left of the estate at Nikolsk.

Day by day, like the needle of a barometer moving up towards 'fair', Joseph's spirits lifted. Excitement about the journey's end gave him fresh energy – even though nobody on the road had any clear idea of what that end might be. Some rumours claimed that ships brought in by the Allies were evacuating refugees to the Crimea, others that their destination would be Constantinople. Joseph hoped for the second alternative: his ambition remained to escort the stallions off Russian soil and into British hands. Even if the Whites still held the Crimea, it remained part of Russia, and he felt that Turkey would make a safer haven.

'What we need is an aeroplane,' he announced one morning. 'A really big one, so that we could all get into it and fly straight to England.'

'What about the horses? We couldn't leave them now.'

'Oh no – they'd come too.'

'But they'd never fit into an aeroplane.' Katya, having never seen a flying-machine, had only a vague idea of how big one might be; but she thought of it carrying one or two men at the most.

'I'm joking,' said Joseph lightly. 'It's impossible, of course. But just an idea. Think of covering a hundred versts in an hour. That's what they can do.'

For days, as they passed slowly across the Kuban steppe, they had noticed low mounds rising here and there from the level plain, but they had taken the bumps for natural phenomena and thought nothing of them. One afternoon, as they came to the largest mound they had seen, they found an old man sitting on a bank beside the road with his gaze fixed on it. His clothes hung from him in filthy tatters, and his fur hat sat beside him on the bundle that contained his belongings;

but with his gaunt face, hollow cheeks and long, unkempt grey hair and beard, he looked like a prophet. At first Joseph took him for a *staretz*, or wandering priest, and called out to him, 'Good day, Little Father. Do you need help?'

The old man gave a start before he focused on the newcomers.

'No, thank you,' he answered in a surprisingly well-educated voice. 'I am happy enough.'

'Not much to be happy about, these days,' said Joseph. 'What makes you so content?'

'It is this tomb, and the thought of what lies inside it.'

'A tomb, is it?' Joseph looked out across the white plain for others. 'Are all these little hills tombs, then?'

'Of course. They are the burial mounds of the Scythian nomad kings.' The old man stood up, pointing a shaky arm. His voice rose in excitement. 'In there lies not only a king, but also his horse. A horse nearly as fine as yours, I daresay. And all round it, in a circle at the edges, are the skeletons of his bodyguard. Perhaps as many as thirty good men.'

Joseph, who had been leading Min, handed the rein to Arkady and went closer. 'How do you know?' he asked.

'Because I am an archaeologist. Or at least, I was, before all this started.' He gave a wry smile and made a quick, irritable gesture towards the north, as if to indicate the whole menace of the Bolsheviks and the civil war. 'I have excavated several of the mounds. Most have been looted, but some still contain wonderful treasures.'

'Why should the king bury his horse?' asked Katya.

'It was his most important possession. He venerated it. It carried him over the steppe in this world, and he needed it to carry him in the next.' The old man paused, with his eyes boring into the mound. 'All animals were sacred to the Scythians. That was why they made such wonderful figures: lions, snakes, lizards, all in gold. If this mound has never been looted, there will be gold deep inside it.'

'But how could all his bodyguard be killed at once . . . at the same time as the horse?'

Keen blue eyes regarded her from under shaggy grey tufts of brow. 'They weren't killed in battle. When the king died, they were sacrificed, for his benefit, and buried round him to protect him in the afterlife. The horse the same.'

Katya had a hand at the throat of her *burka*. 'Wasn't that rather expensive in men?'

'Very. But to those people it was essential. And the result? That their remains are still there, for us to see, two thousand years later. Whereas these barbarians who are smashing our civilisation now – in one century the earth will bear no trace of them.'

The old man spoke not so much with bitterness as with the certainty of absolute knowledge. Joseph was fascinated. 'Where do you come from?' he asked.

'I was born in Yaroslavl, but I lived and worked in Moscow, with expeditions in this part of the world. When the revolution came I was in Rostov.'

'And where are you going?'

'To the sea. As you are, I expect.'

'Yes – we're heading for the sea. Would you like to ride in the sleigh for a while?'

'Thank you, but no. Your beautiful wife must ride. I can manage.'

'But where will you spend the night?'

'In a hovel, I expect, as usual.'

'And have you anything to eat?'

'Enough.'

So they left him, once again sitting, lost in thought. The encounter lingered in Joseph's mind. Himself a nomad at heart, and now more dependent on horses than ever, he felt drawn to the mysterious kings whose bones still lay in the mounds. He thought of Persimmon – his own charge, Percy – who had ended his days stuffed in a museum. Joseph did not like the idea of that: better to be buried than stuffed, he thought, and glorious to be buried in state, with golden ornaments all round. He had a vision of Minoru's skeleton being found a thousand years hence, and among its bones the medallion which King George had given him.

It was during the next morning, as they approached the provincial capital, Yekaterinodar, that Katya burst into tears and admitted to having been feverish since dawn. 'I'm sorry,' she sobbed. 'I don't want to slow you down.'

Joseph helped her down off Boy and tucked her warmly into the sleigh. 'We'll stop somewhere so that you can lie up for a day or two,' he said firmly. 'Then, as soon as you're better, we'll carry on. Lucky we're coming to a town.'

He felt none of the confidence which he forced into his voice: he greatly feared she had typhus. In spite of all their efforts to keep clean, their clothes and bodies were once again infested with lice, which had crept into them from bedclothes in the farmhouses or straw in the barns where they had slept. Joseph loathed being thus contaminated, but could do nothing about it until they reached a place where they could scrub themselves from head to foot, and wash their clothes or burn them.

Yekaterinodar reminded him of Kharkov in the emptiness of its streets, from which all life seemed to have departed. The town was larger than he expected, and well laid out on a grid pattern, with regular streets crossing at right angles. The very size and order of the place led him to hope that he would find medical assistance.

At the hospital – a decrepit-looking establishment, with windows boarded-up and walls pock-marked by bullet holes – a harassed junior doctor rejected him outright: the wards were already filled with wounded, far beyond their capacity, he said, and the last thing he wanted was another patient with typhus. But by persistent inquiry and a little judicious bribery Joseph found his way first to a private clinic, only to discover that it had closed, and then to a succession of doctors. The first three turned him away, and it was with increasing desperation that he came to the house of the fourth, announced by a brass plate on the door as 'Doctor of Medicine V. A. Mikhailov.' With its facade of white-painted stucco and pale blue shutters, the place had a solid and prosperous air. A cross-looking woman would have got rid of him, saying that the doctor was asleep and could not be disturbed, had not a voice behind her called out, 'Who is it?'

The man who appeared looked about forty, but it was hard to tell, for he was dishevelled and only half awake. Beneath an old house-coat of brown nankeen he wore a white shirt without collar or tie, and he blinked several times as he settled a pair of spectacles into position on his nose; but his pale face, with its high forehead, receding dark hair and beard neatly trimmed to a spade-shape, was lively and intelligent, and his first question took Joseph by surprise. Instead of asking 'What do you want?' he said, 'Where do you come from?'

'Kharkov,' said Joseph.

'But before that?'

'England.'

'I thought so!' The doctor gave a slight smile. 'Your accent . . . I know your country.' He paused, as if collecting his wits, and said in faultless English, 'I was lucky enough to study medicine at Cambridge.'

'Cambridge! So you know Newmarket?'

'Yes. I went to Newmarket. I even walked on the celebrated Heath. But I fear I have little interest in horses. Rugby was rather more my ticket. If I may say so without seeming to boast, I was quite successful as a scrum-half . . . Is there something wrong?'

'It's just that Newmarket is where I come from. You gave me a shock.'

'My apologies. What can I do for you? Is it your wound? I see you have been in the wars.'

'No – it's my wife.' Joseph struggled to keep his voice steady as he explained that she was ill, and then blurted out, 'I have money. I can pay.'

'No, no.' Mikhailov waved the offer aside. 'Money is the last thing I need. Drugs, yes. Dressings, yes. Food, yes. Fuel, yes. But money – no. I shall be delighted to repay a little of the debt I owe to my old friends in Cambridge. Where is she? Bring her in.'

Within twenty minutes Katya had been put to bed in a clean, light room at the back of the house, on the first floor, and Duniasha, the brusque but kindly housekeeper, who helped the doctor in his surgery, deputed to look after her. Mikhailov, confirming that the patient had typhus, prescribed a mixture of vodka and quinine, which Katya found almost too disgusting to choke down. Lodging for the horses was found by the sleigh-driver whom the doctor seemed to retain permanently for going about town on his rounds. The stables, in an old courtyard, were filthy and infested with rats, but the best available, and there Arkady went to ground with his charges, including Moorka, who rightly decided that the vermin-hunting would be better there than in the house.

Mikhailov was desperately overworked, both in the surgery and outside in the town. People came for help at any hour of the day or night, and he refused few appeals. A widower, with no children of his own, he seemed to devote his whole life to helping others. At home he gave Joseph the run of the house and insisted that he share meals – an invitation gladly accepted. The food was adequate, but monotonous, for it consisted mainly of *blinchiki*, or pancakes, which Duniasha served up in various forms, sometimes with fillings of cheese or spiced cabbage, occasionally with caviar. Mikhailov apologised for the lack of variety, explaining that although pancakes were traditional Kuban fare in the period before Lent, he would not have them so often if other kinds of food were available.

On the surface, Joseph's immediate problems seemed to have been solved by the kindness and generosity of this one good man. Yet as the days dragged by, he felt gripped by ever-mounting claustrophobia.

Katya's fever rose inexorably until fiery red spots glowed on her cheeks, perspiration rolled down her temples, and her whole body became covered with a brownish rash. As the disease took hold, she was tormented by thirst, and pleaded constantly for water; but whenever they gave her some, she could scarcely swallow. Joseph spent hours beside her bed, talking to her, holding her hand, all the time hoping fiercely that his presence would bolster her resistance. Then, overcome by the sight of her suffering, he would go out, walk to the stables, take the horses out for exercise, return them, groom them, talk to them, walk about the town – anything to occupy his mind and pass some time. In the evenings, when Mikhailov had come back from his rounds and seen her, he scarcely dared ask for the doctor's latest opinion. At first it was 'What do you think? Is she any worse?', but soon it was 'What are her chances? Will she come through?'

'She may.' Mikhailov looked straight at him, and Joseph was grateful. 'I can't tell. The disease is taking its normal course. The fact that she was inoculated should help her. We can only wait and see.'

Walking the streets was a form of escape; but it brought Joseph face to face with the fact that the military situation was again fast deteriorating. Every day more ragged troops came pouring through the town, remnants of Denikin's volunteer army. The fronts south of Rostov had broken, and the final retreat to the sea was underway. Some of the regiments made efforts to fortify the town's public buildings, and the barrels of field guns poked out of strategically-sited porches; yet most of the troops went straight through. Rumour proclaimed that Yekaterinodar, for months the headquarters of White resistance in the Kuban, was about to be abandoned. A Red rising was said to be imminent, with undercover cells poised to seize the station and the telephone exchange. Certainly all discipline and organisation had broken down. Riotous parties raged through the night in the town's biggest hotel, the Metropol, and drunken Cossacks lurched about the streets loosing off with their revolvers through any windows that offended them.

The febrile atmosphere unnerved everyone, not least Arkady, who became increasingly irritable and truculent. 'Why don't we go on?' he kept asking. 'What's the point of staying? If your wife gets better, she can follow. Otherwise, I'll go on my own. I'm damned if I wait any longer. It isn't safe.'

'Give it another couple of days,' said Joseph. 'She's on the mend.' But his words carried no conviction. Arkady sensed his antipathy, he knew, and he could do nothing about it. When he said he could not pay any wages until they reached the coast, the statement sounded no better than the naked threat it was.

His own dilemma was the same as ever, but more acute than at any time before. If he wanted to save the horses, the only sensible thing was to start at once for Novorossisk, which was ninety miles away. Yet he could not move Katya, and still less could he leave her.

One evening he made his way to the huge, dark cathedral whose onion domes towered above the square in the centre of the town. The door of a side-porch was open, and he slipped in, to find the cavernous church perfectly dark except for a single candle burning in front of the screen covered with icons which separated the nave from the chancel. There, soothed by the scent of incense burning, and seeing nothing but a faint glimmer of gold from the icons in their serried banks, he thought of Novgorod, of Christ Pantocrator, and prayed to Him that Katya might be spared.

That night she became delirious. When the doctor arrived, she thought he was her father. She no longer recognised Joseph, and did not respond to his questions. Instead, she began to talk wildly, launching into floods of reminiscence about her childhood. Winter scenes predominated, and she returned again and again to the great Christmas tree which the grown-ups would secretly prepare every year for the children at Nikolsk. 'They throw open the doors, and there it is!' she cried, in a hoarse, dry voice. 'All lit up with candles burning, and everyone we know from our stories is on it – the snow queen on her sledge pulled by silver reindeer . . . angels with silver wings . . . Little Red Riding Hood with her basket, the Big Bad Wolf, the beautiful fairy, the horrible witch outside her cottage, and the house standing on chickens' feet . . . everything silver and glittering with frost, ice, even the little mermaid . . .'

Mention of the mermaid was too much for Joseph. 'Oh, my love!' he cried. 'Rusalka as well!' But she ignored him and cried out, 'Why do they put the witch there? The witch, with her pointed hat and her black cat. They know how I hate her.'

On she went, in and out of reality, turning her head violently back and forth on the pillow. She began to speak in French, then to shout obscenities – the coarsest farmyard words, which shocked Joseph, well as he knew them himself. He fetched a piece of wet towel and held the damp, cool cloth to her burning forehead, but she snatched it away and flung it against the wall. He felt for it under the bed, picked it up, and left the room in tears.

'Try not to worry,' Mikhailov told him. 'The course of the disease is still normal. This always happens. We'll give her another sedative to help her through the night, and with any luck the fever will come down tomorrow.'

'But how long have we got?'

'You mean how long can she hold out?'

'No – how long till the Reds get here?'

'A good question. Three or four days, by the sound of it. Not more.'

'What will *you* do when they come?'

'Sit tight.' The doctor gave a cynical, mirthless laugh. 'They'll need me, just as much as the Whites do. And if anything bad happens ... I have the means to frustrate their designs, in the form of this.' He reached into a waistcoat pocket and held up a small grey cylinder between finger and thumb. 'This is enough,' he said. 'Cyanide is all the insurance I need.'

Later that night Joseph took his mattress and laid it out on the floor of Katya's room; but he hardly slept, for she was tormented by feverish delusions and filled the air with gibberish. Even when she lay quiet, waking nightmares crowded in on him so fiercely that the effort of fighting them off made him sweat, and he feared that he too was going down with typhus. Outside, the *bora* whined and howled against the windows, punctuated every now and then by a rattle of gunfire. Three times he got up and walked about the house, trying to throw off the feeling that a great weight had settled on his chest and was making it impossible for him to breathe. At last, not long before dawn, he did drift off, and when he woke he felt weak but calm and clear-headed.

Katya also had fallen asleep. Her breathing was short and shallow, but she looked less agonised, and he slipped out of the room to make a cup of tea down in the kitchen. Then, as soon as it was light, he pocketed two crusts of bread for the horses and headed for the stables.

The bitter wind was still blowing from the north, and already the streets were full of people on the move. Ten minutes' fast walk brought him to the stable yard. '*Dobry den!*' he called as he came to the high wooden gates – but no whinny answered his greeting. Usually both horses called back, always one. Today he got no answer at all.

Alarm stabbed at him as he reached through the hole to slide back the bar of the gate. The moment he was inside, he saw that the stable doors were open. He crossed the yard in a couple of seconds, but already he knew the worst: the stallions had gone.

He stood rooted to the spot, momentarily paralysed. He felt his heart start to pound with alarm and anger. That bastard Arkady! He had panicked and run. Or else he had deliberately stolen the horses. What was the difference? Joseph looked quickly round the yard and saw that the sleigh was still in its corner. In one stable the pulling harness still hung over a beam. Only Boy's saddle had gone. That meant that Arkady must be riding him and leading Min. The scuffed and rutted ice in the gateway bore no new marks: there was no means of telling how long ago they had left.

Joseph ran, trying to form a plan as he headed back for the doctor's house. There was only one route that Arkady could have taken – the road for the coast – and the only thing to do was to follow him down it. He burst open the door, startling Duniasha, shouted out what had happened, and ran again, this time in the direction of the bridge over the Kuban River which carried the road to Novorossisk. After a few hundred yards he slowed to a walk, realising that he would never catch the runaways on foot. He needed transport or another horse – and in a moment he saw one. He had not even reached the bridge when he spotted a dun horse, saddled but riderless, standing outside an iron gate in a wall, with its reins looped over the top of a post. Clearly its rider had gone inside to collect or deliver something.

Necessity banished any scruples that Joseph had left. Closer inspection revealed the animal to be a scrawny mare of no more than fifteen hands, in poor condition, with ribs showing and a sore patch on her withers. She did not jump when he suddenly came alongside her – a bad sign – and she made no objection when he slipped the reins back over her head, sprang into the saddle and squeezed her forward. The stirrup-leathers were too short for him, and he could tell that the girth was loose. The leather of the reins felt dry and brittle from lack of oil. But none of that mattered for the moment: his only concern was to put distance between himself and her owner.

The mare was sluggish, and unresponsive to urging, but he banged his heels into her flanks and soon had her cantering. At least she seemed sound and sure-footed, and used to the ice on the road. In a few seconds he had reached the end of the street and turned a corner. With one last glance backwards he confirmed that nobody had emerged in pursuit. Once round the end of the block, he slowed to a walk, let the leathers down three holes each side and pulled up the girth. Feeling more comfortable, he trotted again, and very soon was on the bridge.

Beyond the river, the land fell away, and even though the morning was dim and hazy, he had a long view of the road leading into the distance. The highway – a dirty grey streak between white farm land – was thickly dotted with the dark shapes of humans, horses, carts and sleighs, heading as one for the south. Since all were moving at a dogged walk, he at once began to overtake them, and one or two people shouted out ribald remarks, reminding him of the road between Taganrog and Rostov. Experiment showed that the mare's best pace was an extended trot: her canter was short and uncomfortable, and he did not dare to gallop her, for fear that she might exhaust herself too quickly or come down on the ice. Every few minutes he reined back and walked for a couple of hundred yards to give both of them a rest, but then his sense of outrage burned hot again and he drove the mare on, cursing himself for not having obeyed his instinct about Arkady in the first place.

In the first hour he overtook several hundred other refugees. Twice he stopped to ask people if they had been passed by a man riding one horse and leading another, but his inquiries produced blank responses, and it seemed a waste of time to make any more. Even if someone *had* seen the stallions, it would not make his task any easier. Sooner or later he would spot them in the distance ahead of him: but once he had them in sight, what was he to do? That was the problem which plagued him as he rode. If he tried to surprise them by galloping up from behind, Arkady might simply take off at full speed – and Joseph did not fancy his little mare's chances in a race with two former winners of the Derby. Even worse than the thought of them galloping away into the distance was that of them being brought down on the ice. *Any* form of race on that treacherous, rutted, frost-bound track would be madness.

He decided that a stealthy approach was the answer. He must spot the stallions from far off and come up to them slowly, crouched forward with his head down one side of the mare's neck so that Arkady would have no chance of recognising him, and then, when he was close enough, give him a bullet from the Luger between the shoulder blades.

It was just after ten when he spotted the renegade party. By then the flat plain had given away to gentle undulations, and just as he was starting down into a shallow valley, he saw them going up the other side; but he also saw, between him and his target, a troop of Cossack cavalry some thirty strong, riding in column three-abreast. At once he conceived a new plan: he would join the troop casually, as if by accident, and enlist the help of its leader in surrounding the runaways, who could be brought to a halt by sheer pressure of other horses encircling them. All Russians – of the old school, at any rate – regarded horse-stealing as the most despicable and reprehensible of crimes, and Joseph felt confident that the soldiers would readily assist in the recapture of a stolen mount.

The manoeuvre demanded careful timing. The Cossacks, Joseph saw as he followed them, were gradually overtaking Min and Boy. He himself had to overtake the Cossacks, without attracting the attention of Arkady, before they closed the gap. As he came nearer, he saw that the men and their horses were in a bad way. Uniforms were ripped and filthy. Bandages showed from sleeves and under fur caps. Several of the horses were lame, and their equipment was patched together or tied up with rope.

Closing on them cautiously, he came up the inside of the column, in the middle of the road. As each man turned to look at them, he was struck by the exhaustion in their faces: hollow eyes regarded him dully, and nobody so much as returned his greetings. In a few moments he was level with the leader – a young and smart-looking man, freshly shaved, with a luxuriant black moustache. Since he bore no insignia on the shoulers of his ragged blue greatcoat, Joseph could not tell his rank, so he addressed him with a general term which he hoped would not give offence.

'Officer,' he began. 'Can you help me?'

'What's the matter?' The answering inquiry was brisk, but not unfriendly.'

'You see those horses ahead – the two bays? Well – they're mine. The man riding the first one has stolen them.'

The officer seemed to grow in stature with sudden interest, rising higher in his saddle. 'Stolen?' he said sharply. 'Where from?'

'Their stable in Yekaterinodar.'

'When?'

'Early this morning.'

'Can you prove it?'

'Not from here, obviously. But if we catch up with them, yes. You'll see how well they know me.'

'What do you want me to do?'

'Stop them. Move up and surround them so that the rider can't gallop off. That's what he'll do if I go up on my own.'

By then Min and Boy were only about two hundred yards ahead. Joseph saw Arkady look back, check over the cavalry patrol and decide that it posed no threat.

'There you are,' said Joseph quietly. 'He's expecting to be followed.'

The Cossack officer had a quick word with the man beside him, then turned back to Joseph. 'What about the rider? What if he gets hurt?'

'I don't care. All I mind about is the horses.'

Word spread back through the squadron like wind riffling through the leaves of a forest. Rank by rank the men came to life: at the prospect of action their lethargy lifted, and like their leader they seemed to grow in the saddle.

Joseph felt his adrenalin rising. 'I don't want to tell you what to do,' he said, 'but perhaps if you go up on him slowly . . .'

'Yes, yes,' came the answer, quick and confident, but still not irritable. 'We know what to do. Drop back and leave it to us.'

He did as he was told. The officer uttered a couple of low orders, which were passed back from rank to rank. A few steps later the whole troop moved into a trot and drew ahead.

So anxious was Joseph not to upset the operation that he held off at a greater distance than necessary, and in consequence did not witness exactly what happened. All he saw was the troop break into a sudden gallop, divide in two and coalesce again all round his beloved stallions. Then there was a general flurry and blur of movement, with horses rearing, bumping and turning. The moment the encirclement was complete, Joseph accelerated sharply. In a few seconds he was level with the mêlée, just in time to see Arkady topple sideways from Min's back with six inches of sabre blade protruding from his chest.

His heart leapt. In a second he had slid to the ground and handed the mare's reins to the nearest soldier; then he pushed quickly between the milling horses and caught Min's bridle, talking to him above the general din, with one hand on his neck.

'I see he knows you all right.' The officer was behind Joseph, in the middle of the scrum. 'The other fellow's a bit wild, though.'

'He's always like that. But there's no harm in him really.'

'Nice horses, both. Bit of breeding in them.'

'Thank you. And thank you for stopping them. I could never have done it alone.'

The officer grinned. 'If only it was as easy to stop the Bolsheviks! Can you manage now? Are you heading for the coast?'

'Yes, thank you. But first I must return the mare. I borrowed her from someone in Yekaterinodar.'

'Good luck, then.'

'And to you. What about him?' Joseph pointed at the body.

'We'll deal with that. There are thousands more where he's just gone to.' The officer issued an order; two men dismounted, and, as the horses cleared, dragged Arkady's body to the side of the road, where they threw it into the ditch. Then, without more ado, the troop reformed and went on its way.

He started for the sea next morning, weighed down by the grimmest fears. Katya had come through her immediate crisis; the fever had left her, and she had managed to swallow some meat broth. But she was still far too ill to be moved safely. What she needed was a period of rest, warmth, good food and cosseting; what she emphatically did not need were days of bumping and shaking on a sleigh out in that ice-edged wind.

'It really is most unwise,' said Mikhailov the night before Joseph prepared to depart. 'You may easily kill her.'

'I know. But don't you agree – it's now or never?'

'Well – you may be right.'

The town was on the verge of collapse. Most of the White troops had dismantled their temporary defences and pulled out. Looting raged unchecked, and the crackle of sniper fire, no longer intermittent, continued steadily throughout the hours of daylight. Bodies lay out in the streets, frozen stiff. The spearheads of the Red forces were said to be no more than a day away to the north-east.

At least Joseph had food for all his party. With typical generosity Mikhailov had instructed Duniasha to give him everything they could get, and many good bundles were stowed into the luggage shelf of the sleigh. Thanks to the resourcefulness of the doctor's *izvozchik*, the horses were also well provided for.

Had Katya been fit, Joseph would have been more sanguine. What worried him most was her listlessness. Although, after the fever, she had obviously been pleased to see him, her reactions to everything had become alarmingly muted. When he told her that they would have to go on in the morning, she showed neither pleasure nor apprehension – only passive resignation. When he asked if she thought she could manage, she merely gave a faint smile and closed her eyes.

'My darling love,' Joseph said urgently, taking her hand. 'The last thing I want is for you to suffer any more. But our only hope is to move on.'

'Go, then,' she murmured, not opening her eyes.

'No! *I'm* not going. We're going together. That's what I mean.'

'All right.'

Her vagueness frightened him. He feared that even if she were at death's door, she would still say nothing. He seemed to be losing her – perhaps had lost her already. Perhaps her brain had been damaged by the fever, her character changed.

'Is that possible?' he asked the doctor. 'Will she ever come back?'

Mikhailov tried to reassure him. 'Again it's normal. Patients are often like this for a few days. But if they get as far as she has, most of them recover fully.'

Morning came – another grey and windy day. Katya seemed a fraction more responsive, and drank some tea with relish. When she got out of bed, she tottered and had to steady herself against the wall, but found she could walk without too much difficulty. While Joseph went to fetch the horses, Duniasha helped her dress – or rather, dressed her, wrapping her as warmly as possible in layer after layer of clothes.

At the stable, one member of the team was conspicuous by her absence: Moorka. Joseph had not seen the cat since the day before, and he could not make out what had happened to her. Whether she had tried to follow Arkady when he bolted, and had got left behind along the road, or whether she had simply gone off into the town, he could not tell. Having squeaked and called for several minutes, and got no response, he packed up and left, sick at heart with the feeling that the loss of their mascot, who had been so faithful and come so far, must bring bad luck.

By the time they were ready to leave the house, Mikhailov had already gone out on his morning round, and Joseph had missed the chance of thanking him. Instead, he left five gold sovereigns in a drawer of the doctor's desk, gave one to Duniasha, and promised that he would write in gratitude from England when the war was over.

The sight of Katya emerging from the house shocked him afresh.

She moved like a ghost, insubstantially, as if she were hardly in contact with the ground, and held her hands out sideways, as though balancing on a beam. Although not much of her face was visible between hat and collar, what did show was still dirty brown with the typhus rash. She did not greet the horses, but settled into the seat of the sleigh without a word, allowing herself to be tucked in with rugs like a child into bed. To Joseph's intense relief, she did not ask about the cat.

Looking back, he reckoned the four days that followed were the most difficult of his life. Such was the stress under which he laboured that he could remember few details; what remained with him was the sensation of being weighed down by a colossal load. Not only did he have to keep his own frail human machine going forward: he had also to galvanise two run-down horses and a stricken companion who seemed suddenly to have passed beyond the reach of his love. The feeling of helplessness which this caused compounded his physical burdens to an almost intolerable degree.

The journey alone was tough enough. For the first night they had a safe house, an address provided by Mikhailov; but after that they were on their own. Once an old woman took pity on Katya and let them sleep in her shed, but on the third night they were forced to seek refuge in a barn. The weather remained unremittingly grey and leaden; the wind never ceased to whistle past them, first on their backs, and then on their right cheeks.

Every now and then, on easy stretches, Joseph encouraged her to get out of the sleigh and walk as far as she could, in the hope that gentle exercise would prevent her becoming fatally chilled; but when he saw how severely even a slight effort taxed her, and how, after a few yards, her steps would begin to waver, he would hastily tuck her back into her seat. Whenever he asked if she was warm enough, she murmured that she was all right, but when he took off her gloves to chafe her hands, they felt as cold as ice. Most of his own effort, he felt, went into making one-sided conversation: trying to keep her interested, he poured out a stream of chatter and reminiscence – about Nikolsk, about Krasnoe Selo, about Newmarket, and even about his foster-family in Wales. Yet nothing he said seemed to get through to her: he might, he thought, as well be talking to a sack of potatoes. But at least she grew no worse: her temperature did not flare up again, her colour remained constant, and in the evenings she managed to swallow small quantities of tea, soup and bread. Nor did she ever lose her balance and topple out of the sledge – as he had feared she might – while it was in motion.

Towards evening on the first day he suddenly realised, with a prickle of excitement, that the mountains were in sight ahead. The nature of the land changed: foothills forested with oak and pine rose out of the plain, and behind them the great grey-and-white bulk of the North Caucasus massif towered away to spiky crenellations against the clouds. On the second morning the road turned westwards, to his right, following the line of the foothills, so that for the whole of that day and the next he was walking with the mountains on his left, and gradually drawing closer in beneath them.

By the fourth morning he was so drained that individual events fused into a general recollection of pain. For the first few hours they climbed steeply through hairpin bends which wound up between crags covered in pine and slim, dark cypresses. For Katya, the ascent made little difference, since she was being transported, but for Joseph and the horses it was a dour struggle. Then, as they at last drew near the pass which led to Novorossisk and the sea, Joseph suddenly found himself being shepherded and jostled by armed men in British uniform. When he expostulated angrily at being pushed around, one of them shouted back that the pass had been occupied by the breakaway revolutionaries known as the Green Guards, and that the refugees' only chance of getting through was to form up in organised parties, and for each one to proceed with an escort.

This they did, moving on in groups, like segments of a centipede. A battle was indeed in progress. Joseph heard shots and yells, and then the boom of a big gun, but such was his exhaustion that the noises seemed scarcely to concern him. All he wanted was to keep walking, gain the pass, and go down to the coast.

The higher they went, the louder the noise became. Joseph belatedly realised that in the pass itself the railway line ran beside the road, and that a *bronevik* had come up to shell the rebels who were trying to block the cutting. Now he could see them – men scrambling and sliding like monkeys among the rocks high above the line: even from some way below, the green sashes which they wore outside their coats were clearly visible. Flashes spurted from their rifles as they fired on the straggling lines below. Rifle and machine-gun fire rattled back at them. Then the four-inch gun thundered off another round, and a sizeable patch of the mountainside erupted into splinters, earth, dust, ice and snow, setting off an avalanche which swept several of the guerrillas to their doom.

'Keep going! Keep going!' an English voice was shouting. The danger and excitement cleared Joseph's head, and he took up the cry in Russian. '*Zhivo! Zhivo!*' he yelled, partly at Min and Boy, partly at anyone in earshot. Occasionally men fell as the ragged column struggled forward, but most of them kept on. Then for the lucky ones came a miraculous moment: instead of constantly rising, the ground beneath their feet began to fall. They were over the pass, and in the distance below them lay the sea.

THIRTEEN

Novorossisk: March 1920

THE SEA! There it lay, black in name, but in reality pewter grey and forbidding. Joseph's eye took in the wide horseshoe sweep of the bay, with a mole running out to protect the harbour, and a lighthouse standing on a promontory to his right. The houses of the town spilled down the western slopes; to his left, factories and docks crowded the edge of the quays, which were dominated by the tall, rectangular hulk of a grain elevator. Out in the bay a dozen ships rode at anchor, and from their angular shapes and bristling guns he could see that two of the biggest were men-of-war.

'There we are, my love!' he cried triumphantly. 'Journey's end.'

Katya gave a faint smile. The *bora* moaned over the pass, fluttering the red-and-blue striped Kuban flag that flew from a broken-off pole. 'It's far too bloody cold up here,' said Joseph, more to himself than anyone else. 'Let's get down.'

The descent proved worse than the climb. On the steep, icy road Min could not cope with the sleigh, whose weight kept pushing him forward, so that his feet skidded dangerously. Twice he almost bolted, in fright and exasperation, and in the end Joseph reluctantly decided that they would have to abandon their little transport. In a sheltered spot on one of the hairpin bends he unloaded the sleigh, re-stowed the bags in the horses' panniers, and lifted Katya up on to Boy's saddle, with the promise wthat she would not be there long. So they slithered precariously down the last leg of their journey.

Not until dusk did they reach the outskirts of the town. The place was in a far worse state than Yekaterinodar. Many buildings had had their windows shot out, their walls pock-marked with bullet-holes. Bodies lay everywhere in the streets, some alongside the houses, others stacked in piles on the corners: a few remained fully clothed, but many had lost their boots and coats to looters. Dead horses were scattered about, frozen into grotesque attitudes. Here and there the remains of a broken-down cart lay collapsed in the gutter. Joseph found it almost impossible to believe that in summer, before the revolution, this icy morgue had been a fashionable spa and watering place, with hot mud baths and thermal cures.

Through all the flotsam he picked his way with mounting apprehension. It was too late to arrange any embarkation that day, and his paramount need, as usual, was to find accommodation for the night. Soon they came to a decrepit-looking guest-house on a corner, with a signboard hanging out over the street. Its windows were boarded over, its door shut, and when Joseph hammered on it, there was no reply.

His resolve hardened. Normally he would not have dreamed of stealing, breaking and entering; but if local people had taken to the law of the jungle, he could do the same. Having heard that the town centre was overflowing with refugees, he decided to stop short, and presently, down a side road, he spotted the tall, green-painted iron gates of a villa set back in a garden. A look of general dereliction suggested that the owners had long gone. 'That'll do,' he thought. The gates were closed by a chain and padlock. He looked round. Other refugees were passing along the main road fifty yards away, but none paid him any attention.

'Get down, my love,' he said to Katya, and helped her to the ground. 'Move off a little way and hold the horses while I shoot out this padlock.'

She did as he asked stiffly and automatically, with neither interest nor resentment. As soon as she was clear, he drew his Luger and, having positioned himself so that his body was between the gate and horses, fired a round point-blank into the keyhole.

The lock disintegrated. The chain fell to the ground. 'Fancy the place for yourself, do you?' said a sharp-faced man who happened to be passing.

'Not at all,' said Joseph stiffly. 'It's mine. I lost the key.'

The stranger went on his way. Joseph brought the horses into the garden, closed the gates, slung the chain across so that it looked intact from the outside and made his way round to the back of the house. Again he asked Katya to hold the stallions while he reconnoitred the buildings. His heart sank when he saw the outhouses: there were sheds and a glasshouse, but nothing large enough to take a horse. Then his eye fell on tall french windows in the garden front of the house itself. They stood slightly open. Obviously the place had been looted. A moment later he was inside a large, high room, his boots thumping on bare wooden boards. Even in the failing light he could see that the place had been stripped. No furniture remained. Rectangles of paler colour showed where pictures had hung on the dingy yellow walls. An inner door had been torn from its hinges, the marble mantelpiece smashed.

He felt no compunction about bringing the horses into such a ruin. The noise of their own feet on the floor made them jumpy, and there was nothing to which he could tie them except two radiators; but at least they were out of the bitter wind. He shut the french windows, unsaddled the stallions and took their impedimenta through into the next room, which turned out to be the hall.

Katya, to his delight, came to life and went exploring. 'There's a kitchen,' she said, 'and what's more, there's water in the tap. I can't think why it isn't frozen.'

'Praise be!' Lack of water had been one of Joseph's main anxieties. 'Anything to put it in?'

'Yes – there's a tin bowl.'

'That'll do.'

He gave each horse a bowlful in turn, wishing fervently that he had more for them to eat than two last handfuls of oats. His own hunger seemed unimportant beside theirs. 'Don't worry, boys,' he said to them. 'I'll bloody well find you something.'

He went to look round the house. It was, or had been, a modern villa, with central heating, electric light and European bathroom. Two spacious front rooms gave off the hall, and on the upper floor were four bedrooms, one of which still contained two iron bedsteads. None of these rooms, however, seemed suitable as a refuge for the night, since their windows looked out forwards or sideways, and any light inside them might be seen by people in the street. Instead, Joseph settled on the kitchen, at the back, which faced the garden and rear yard. There he quickly had a fire blazing in the cast-iron range: by ruthlessly smashing the door of an outhouse he furnished himself with kindling wood, and then, to his delight, he discovered a small pile of coal, out in the garden, beneath a tarpaulin covered in snow. The stove had an open fire-basket in the middle, between its ovens, and soon the coal in it was burning with a ruddy glow.

Next he dismantled one of the iron beds, brought the sections down and slotted them together again beside the stove, so that Katya had something less unyielding than bare boards to lie on. As he worked, she sat on the floor, warming her hands at the fire.

'Now, Rusalka,' he said. 'Lie down and be comfortable. Your job's to keep the fire in. And see if you can boil some water for us to make tea.'

'Where are you going?'

'To find something to eat.'

'I'm not hungry.'

'I am – and so are the horses. I won't be long.' He kissed her on the forehead, pulled on his coat and hat, and went out into the freezing dark. The wind cut more viciously than ever. Inside the gates he paused to listen and make sure that there was no one nearby, then slipped out and re-slung the chain behind him. He headed for the main road, and after a quick check on the corner to fix landmarks in his mind, set out for the centre of the town.

The flow of refugees had dwindled to a trickle, and he joined the shadowy, intermittent procession unnoticed, walking as fast as the rutted ice would permit. The streets were very dark. Occasionally the glow of a lamp showed from within a house, but the main illumination came from fires lit on corners and in the recesses of buildings, where vagrants had set up makeshift camps. Huddled in little clusters round their bonfires, they crouched beneath whatever shelter they had been able to devise, so cold and wretched that they scarcely bothered to look up as Joseph went past.

Haunted by pinched, hollow faces and deep-set eyes, skirting the heaps of bodies, slipping on the ice, he at last reached what he assumed to be the middle of Novorossisk. The chances of finding food seemed negligible. Every shop he passed was shut and boarded up, every restaurant the same. When he stopped a passer-by and asked, 'Any idea where I can get something to eat?' the man gave a cynical laugh and went on his way. A commotion attracted him. As he drew near, the noise resolved itself into raucous, drunken conversation and shouts of laughter. Cold though the air was, it carried high-octane vodka fumes. In an alley light spilled from two open doorways. Glancing in, he saw that thugs had broken into a vodka distillery. Someone had fired a couple of shots into one of the large steel vats, so that jets of colourless spirit were spurting out horizontally, and the revellers were jostling each other for position so that they could apply their mouths directly to the flowing alcohol. Some were already insensible and sprawled in the flood of spirit on the floor. Others were staggering about or leaning on the walls. Poor sods, Joseph thought, they'll all be frozen to death by morning.

He moved on, but the dark and cold seemed to stifle his initiative, making it impossible to think. As he hesitated, a slender beam of light suddenly leapt out across the sky and began to sweep back and forth above the tops of the houses, angled up into the mountains behind. One of the warships in the bay was playing a searchlight on the pass. Joseph watched the wandering beam in sudden hope: what he needed was contact with the British Military Mission – army, navy or air force. But how to make it?

When, after a minute, the beam went out, another kind of light caught his attention: a ruddy glow which grew brighter as he watched. Some building was on fire: the central block of a long facade was alight from bottom to top. Firemen were doing their best to rescue the inmates, but their equipment was hopelessly inadequate to the task, and the feeble jets of water from their hoses made no impression on the flames. Screams rang out from the upper floors, and every now and then some wretch leapt for his life towards the canvas sheets which other firemen were holding stretched out to break his fall.

Joseph joined the crowd of spectators. Finding himself next to three officers in service caps and khaki greatcoats, he asked, '*Chto eto?*'

The nearest man – a narrow-faced, clean-shaven young fellow of about thirty – turned and looked at him disdainfully, but did not answer, so he repeated the question. This time he got a look of blank incomprehension, and realised that the officer was foreign. 'What is it?' he said in English.

'The Hotel Nicholas II,' came the answer in a drawling, upper-class accent. 'At least, it was.'

'You're English!' Joseph exclaimed.

Again the officer surveyed him haughtily down his thin nose. 'Matter of fact, I am.'

'I wonder if you can help. I'm looking for a passage on a ship.'

'Ha ha! So are about a hundred thousand other people.'

'Yes, but I'm British.'

'Military or civilian?'

'Civilian.'

'Not a chance, old boy. Military personnel only on British-requisitioned ships. You should see the docks. Literally solid with people. You've a job even to reach the quay. Your only hope is to bribe one of the shipping agents to sell you a civilian passage. I hope you've got plenty of money!'

The officer turned back to his companions. It crossed Joseph's mind to say, 'All right, you condescending sod, I've got two former

Derby winners with me. What about that?' But he had taken an instant dislike to the man, and wanted nothing to do with him.

Another notion slipped into his head. In normal circumstances he would have rushed to the aid of the firemen and thrown his own weight into the attempts at rescue; but now baser instincts asserted themselves. There must be food in that hotel, he reasoned. The fire at the front would have distracted attention from the back. The kitchen and storerooms might be wide open.

Two minutes later he was at the building's rear entrance. As he hoped, chaos prevailed. Men were running frantically in and out, trying to save belongings and equipment. He went in with the rush. The building was in darkness and thick with smoke, but a smell of cooking led him to the kitchen. Others had had the same idea: as someone hurried by with a lamp, he saw two men hunched over a counter in their full outdoor clothes, cramming food into their mouths with both hands.

The heat was intense, the air almost unbreathable. From above came an immense crash which made the ground shake. 'Get out! Get out!' somebody yelled hysterically. 'It's coming down.' A new flare of flames lit up the kitchen and its adjoining pantries or store rooms. On a shelf Joseph spotted a baking-tin which contained elongated lumps of dough, neatly set out. Tomorrow's bread! In a moment he had collected up seven or eight of them and stowed them inside his shirt, where they settled clammily round his stomach and flanks, held up by the waistband of his breeches. Then, on the floor beneath the shelf, he saw a row of small hessian sacks, standing open, with whitish substances inside. He licked a finger, plunged it into the first, tasted the meal that clung to him: kasha, ground buckwheat. Without waiting to try any more, he brought the neck of the sack together and swung it on to his shoulder. It weighed perhaps thirty pounds – a hefty burden, but one that he could manage. He had a craving for salt, and for a few seconds looked round the kitchen to see if he could spot any. Then, with a sharp crackle, flames burst through the wall at the other end of the room, and he scuttled out into the night.

Half an hour later he was back at the villa, faint with thirst and hunger. Many times he had had to dodge into doorways to avoid passers-by, for anyone who saw him carrying the sack on his shoulder at once became unhealthily inquisitive, and he had had to knock one drunk cold with the butt of his Luger to get rid of him.

He slipped into the garden and opened the french windows with a quiet word of greeting to the horses. In the kitchen the fire had burned low, but the air struck gloriously warm. He found Katya lying on the bed, with her head propped on his haversack.

'Here I am,' he said quietly, taking her hand. 'Have you been asleep?'

'I don't think so. The water boiled, though.'

'Good. I got some bread – or at least, some dough that we can bake, and quite a lot of kasha. I think the horses'll eat that.'

He poked up the fire with a sliver of board, gave it some wood and more coal to heat the oven, and extracted the lumps of dough from his midriff. The lack of proper utensils, or of any clean surface on which to lay things, made every task extraordinarily awkward. Finding that he had seven pieces of dough, he remodelled four of them into their original elongated shapes and laid them on the base of one oven. Then he poured three or four pounds of dry kasha into the tin bowl and took it to the horses. Boy sniffed it and turned his head away, but Min, after a cautious appraisal, began to lick it up thoughtfully, and in due course finished the lot.

A delicious smell of fresh bread filled the kitchen. To contain his hunger, Joseph made tea in the billycan and poured it into his tin mug. He could hardly wait for the scalding liquid to cool, but when he offered some to Katya, she said she was not thirsty.

He wanted her to ask where he had been, what the town was like. Her listlessness frightened him. Normally she would have helped in all his preparations – indeed, she would have taken the lead, made him sit down and sought ways of pleasing or surprising him. Now she had done nothing at all. He himself was so near the limit of his endurance that he could not find the energy to discuss things with her properly. He felt that he was pacing himself for a final effort: by throwing in all his reserves, he could last for another twenty-four hours, but then he would be finished. In the meantime, all he could do was treat her gently, like a child.

Sitting on the floor, he held his wrist out towards the fire to look at his watch, and was amazed to find that the time was only eight o'clock. He had thought it must be past midnight. 'Watched pots never boil,' he said in English. But in fact the bread was almost done, and after a few more minutes he drew out the crisp new loaves, as proud as if he had devised some unprecedented culinary masterpiece. As with the tea, he had difficulty waiting for them to cool down: then, as soon as physically possible, he ate the whole of one in three or four mouthfuls.

Sitting on the edge of the bed, he fed Katya little pieces of the second. She ate one or two absent-mindedly, but then gave him a new fright by saying, 'I shall visit Aunt Olga in the morning.'

'Aunt Olga?'

'Yes. She lives here. I remembered while you were out.'

'In Novorossisk? You've never mentioned it before.'

'No? Well, as I said, I just remembered.'

'You've never said a thing about her. Who is she?'

'My mother's sister.'

Joseph was astounded. He had never heard of any such person. 'Is she married?'

'She was. She's a widow now.'

'What's her name?'

'Smirnova. Olga Leonidovna Smirnova.'

'Where does she live?'

'Sergeievskaya, No 41.'

'Rusalka – are you sure?'

'Of course. I used to write to her here.'

'She can't still be here now. The town's in its death throes. Nothing's functioning any more. I'm sure she'll have gone. Anyway, tomorrow we've got to get the horses on board ship. Tomorrow we're sailing out of here. I'm afraid Aunt Olga will have to take her chance.'

Joseph set off as soon as the sky began to lighten. Katya seemed more herself. She had slept a good deal, said she felt rested, made tea and baked the other loaves for him before he went out. 'Whatever you do, don't leave the house,' he told her firmly. 'It'd be very dangerous for you. The place is full of drunks and murderers. You might easily get raped or killed. Besides, I'm counting on you to look after the horses till I get back. All right?' He took her by the chin and gave her a quick kiss on the lips.

'All right.' She managed a smile.

'I won't be long. As soon as I find out anything worthwhile, I'll be back. If I get a passage, we'll go straight to the boat.'

'Don't worry. I'll be good as gold.'

It made him very nervous to leave her and the horses alone, yet he could see no alternative. Had it been possible, he would have locked the house, to keep her in and intruders out. As things were, he could only hope that she would have the sense to stay put.

One pleasant surprise was that the wind had abated, even though the air was still very cold; another, that gangs of men with horses and carts were collecting dead bodies. The municipal authorities, it seemed, had not quite given up, though there was evidently nothing they could do to control the mass of humanity swarming in the town centre. The street which contained the Lloyd's shipping agency was jammed with people, wall to wall. The office itself was besieged by a crowd a hundred yards long and ten wide. Joseph joined it, and for half an hour listened to the gossip surging among the supplicants. The warships bombarding the pass were the British cruiser *Emperor of India* and the French destroyer *Waldeck-Rousseau*, but both were to sail that night. As soon as the foreign forces departed, Budenny's cavalry, which was poised in the mountains, would come sweeping down on the town. The place would be engulfed by murder, arson and rape. Already a posse of Green Guards had stolen a truckful of British army uniforms and were masquerading about the town in them, causing chaos. In particular, they were trying to gain access to the ships of the evacuation fleet, so that they could plant explosives and sabotage them. Thirty thousand Kuban Cossacks had already abandoned the town and pushed on along the coast towards Georgia, but many others had already given up hope: the harbour was full of dead horses, whose owners had driven them over the quay, rather than risk the Bolsheviks getting them. A loaf of bread could be got at such-and-such a bakery for 1,000 Kerensky roubles, but half of it would be sawdust. Only gold roubles or foreign currency could secure a passage in a ship. Ten gold roubles would get a man to Yalta, in the Crimea, fifteen to Constantinople. In London, King George had been deposed, and a socialist govenment had taken over in his place. Alexis, the Tsarevitch, had escaped the massacre in Yekaterinburg after all and had been smuggled to safety in Yalta.

Joseph, whose belt was still half-full of coins, turned to a man next to him and asked, 'How much is a gold rouble worth?'

'My God!' came the answer. 'You have one? Then why are you standing here?'

'No, no,' said Joseph quickly. 'I just wondered.'

'You get about 30,000 to one.'

The news made him change tactics. After a wait to allay possible suspicion, he slipped out of the queue, went up the side, and forced his way boldly through the front, into the office, ignoring the shouts of rage that pursued him. One middle-aged official, with an expression of terminal exasperation on his face, was trying to deal with ten frantic customers at once. Or rather, he was trying not so much to deal with them as to get rid of them.

'I repeat!' he shouted. 'I can offer no passages to anyone. I have no ship and no passages. It is as simple as that.'

'Look!' cried an attractive woman of about forty who wore an expensive black fur coat. 'I will pay fifty English gold sovereigns, and on top of that you can have my daughter. Here she is. Seventeen, and a virgin, I guarantee. She is yours. Do whatever you like with her.' She tried to force forward a slim, dark girl who stood beside her with head bowed.

'Take her away!' yelled the official. 'You disgust me! I tell you, *I have no ship*.'

The woman turned, spat on the girl, screeched some obscenity at her and cuffed her so hard round the ear that she fell down.

Joseph went out, feeling sick. His only course now was to make contact with the British military. Struggling through the crowds, he headed down towards the docks, and there an astonishing sight greeted him. Lined up on a quay, side by side, were six Sopwith Camels, exactly like the aircraft which had travelled on Train 602, except that these ones were brand-new, their markings fresh, their paint unscratched and unsullied. As he looked down from a parapet above, a tank with white stars and British markings on it came trunding along and crawled straight over the flimsy planes, grinding and smashing them to tangled wrecks of wire, fabric and matchwood. Men in uniform, moving fast, pushed the remains over the wall into the sea. Then other men ran out four more planes, larger, of a type that Joseph did not recognise, and the tank destroyed them too. Finally the driver aligned his crab-like vehicle so that it pointed over the sea-wall, climbed out, and by yanking a cord set it in motion, so that it dragged itself over the drop and plummeted into the depths below.

Joseph found a steep concrete stairway and hurried down to the dock wall, where he accosted the first serviceman he saw, a corporal. 'Are you from B Squadron?' he asked hopefully.

'No, mate. Mission HQ.'

'Any idea where B Squadron is?'

'Search me. They might have left already.'

'Hell!'

Something in his tone engaged the corporal's sympathy. 'What's the matter?' he asked.

'I need a passage, for some horses.'

'Horses! Christ Almighty! You've got a hope. The harbour's full of them. Look at that.' He pointed, and to his horror Joseph saw that at least one of the rumours was true: here and there, bodies with vastly-distended bellies were floating.

'I know,' he said. 'But what's the best bet?'

'Quay No 4,' said the corporal. 'That way. That's where passenger embarkations are being done. You'd better try there.'

As Joseph headed for the other sector of the docks, a sudden deep *boom* shook the town, followed by the *whoosh* and whistle of a shell departing overhead. A few seconds later came a fainter second explosion as the missile burst in the mountains. He had hardly walked the length of one street when the big gun fired another round. When it went off yet again, he realised that the bombardment had become regular, one round every minute. To his overstretched nerves it sounded like some monstrous bell tolling the end of imperial Russia, counting off the minutes to catastrophe. From closer at hand came the occasional crack of a rifle: snipers firing from roof tops or upper windows.

The scene on the passenger quays was like something out of hell. No square foot of space remained unoccupied. Thousands of people, dirty, dishevelled, red-eyed, had herded together, some crouched round fires, but most standing in a solid mass facing the sea. Confronting them, at point-blank range, were soldiers with fixed bayonets, on guard to prevent the crowd rushing the gang-planks of the ships drawn up alongside. Machine-guns mounted on decks and upper-works gave further cover - for such was the tide of destitute human beings that, had it flowed on board any vessel out of control, it could have sunk the ship under its own weight. From the vast swarm of bodies came a continuous angry murmur which rose at times to a roar.

Joseph needed all his physical strength, and all his moral courage, to fight a way through the crowd to the front. It was a matter of using elbows and knees ruthlessly, of trading the filthiest insults, of striking back, both physically and verbally, whenever he was struck. By the time he did burst through the human wall, he was gasping for breath and in danger of either being pushed over the edge or impaled on a bayonet by sheer pressure from behind.

He found himself face-to-face with a sergeant. 'I want to see an officer,' he said in English.

'No civilians on board,' came the stony answer.

Joseph drew himself up and said stiffly, 'Sergeant, will you please send for an officer?'

'Sir . . .' The sergeant was thrown off-balance by his accent, which might have been that of an officer. 'What do you want?'

'I need to talk to someone in authority.'

'Have you any papers?'

'No. But I am British. My name's Clements.'

'Wait one moment, sir.' The sergeant called something over his shoulder, and another soldier disappeared into a companionway. A moment later there emerged a neat, trim lieutenant, fresh-faced and fair-haired. 'Yes?' he said tersely, 'What d'you want?'

Joseph took a deep breath. This was the moment he had long dreaded. 'I've got two famous stallions,' he said. 'Both winners of the Epsom Derby. I need to get them on board a ship.'

The lieutenant blinked. 'You've got *what?*'

Joseph repeated his message.

'Two stallions!' The officer seemed dumbfounded. 'Which ones?'

'Minoru and Aboyeur. Both winners of the Derby.'

'Where are they?'

'In the town.'

'Where've you come from?'

'Kharkov.'

'Where's that, for God's sake?'

'In the Ukraine.'

'Are you sure?'

Joseph exploded. 'Of course I'm bloody well sure! I've walked for weeks to get here.' Then, as he saw the young lieutenant blench, he said, 'Sorry – I'm a bit tired.'

The officer forced a nervous smile. 'Hang on a moment,' he said. 'I'd better get the general. He's our racing expert.'

He vanished back into the ship. 'Who's the general?' Joseph asked.

'General Sir Tom Bridges,' the sergeant answered. 'Officer in charge of embarkation.'

A tense pause followed. Joseph felt poised on the edge of the world, liable to fall off either way. He was standing about a foot from the end of the gangway. Ahead of him was the security of a

British-manned ship; behind, thousands of hostile, resentful faces, the nearest ones now slightly softened by curiosity about the exchange in progress.

Out came the general, big, beefy, grey-haired, with his complexion nearly as red as the band on his hat. His boots clanked on the steel gangway, and he gave off loud exhalations, so that it seemed as if a steam train were coming ashore.

'Now then! What's all this?'

Joseph, feeling that really he should salute but could not because he had no uniform, did his best to stand to attention and said, 'Joseph Clements, sir.'

'Horses, is it?'

'Yes, sir. I've got Minoru and Aboyeur in the town.'

Bridges stood back with his head on one side. 'Could it be,' he asked heavily, 'that someone is trying to pull my leg?'

'Definitely not, sir. I've walked them about six hundred miles, just to get them this far.'

'Minoru,' said the general thoughtfully. 'A bay with black points?'

'Yes, sir.'

'Carried the King's colours, won in 1909?'

'Yes, sir.'

Bridges' dreamy tone changed to a snap. 'Who owned him?'

'Colonel Hall-Walker.'

'How's he bred?'

'By Cyllene out of Mother Siegel.'

'Grandsire?'

'Bona Vista.'

'What year did Aboyeur win?'

'1913.'

'Odds?'

'100-1.'

'What happened?'

'A mad woman brought down the King's horse – and then the favourite was disqualified. Sir, I was *there*.'

All this took only a few seconds. The general looked at him searchingly and said, 'I think you'd better come aboard.'

In the cabin that served as operations room, they gave Joseph hot, sweet tea and a bacon sandwich as he explained what he had done. Bridges was excited, and did not mind showing it. This was the best thing he had heard for weeks, he declared. If he saved the horses, it would make his whole job worthwhile. Within ten minutes he promised Joseph that if he returned at 3.30 p.m., there would be space on board for the stallions. But whatever he did, he must not be late, because the ship would sail for Constantinople at four.

'Sir, I don't know how to thank you,' Joseph began.

'It's nothing,' said the general. 'It's you who needs thanking. Amazing achievement. Amazing!'

'There's just one thing – I have my wife with me. Will there be room for her too?'

'We might squeeze her on board.'

'Thank you. I'm afraid I don't have any fodder for the horses.'

'What do you need?'

'Hay or oats. Anything to keep them going.'

He stumbled ashore feeling that a huge weight had lifted from him. The crowd, seeing him return, supposed that his pleas had been rejected, and parted to let him through. Some people even cast sympathetic glances in his direction. He braced himself for the long walk back to the villa when suddenly he spotted an *izvozchik* driving past empty. He was going to hail it when he realised he had no paper roubles, and that if he was to avoid being grossly exploited by a cab-driver, he had better get some. He therefore returned to the shipping office, again jumped the queue and boldly said to the official, 'D'you want some gold roubles?'

'Of course,' came the answer. 'How many?'

'What'll you give me for four?'

'Kerenskys? A hundred thousand.'

'Done.'

The man brought out a vast roll from a safe, and in a minute Joseph was on his way. Soon he managed to hail another sleigh, and as he was climbing in an idea struck him. If his driver had a horse, he must have food for it.

'Well,' said the cabby irritably over his shoulder, 'Where do you want to go.'

'I'll tell you in a minute. But first I want forage for horses.'

'Don't be stupid. There isn't a shred of hay in the town.'

'Oats, then. Beans.'

'Nothing like that, either.'

'Come on. This mare's not living on air. She looks well. I'll pay you a lot for a small amount.'

'How much?'

'Twenty thousand for a pood of oats.'

The driver hesitated, then said, 'Thirty'.

'Thirty, then.'

'Where's the money?'

'At home – where I want to go. But let's get the forage first.'

Muttering unintelligibly, the man drove off at a furious pace, uphill, towards the northern suburbs, by chance in the same direction as the villa. In ten minutes they pulled up outside a shabby-looking house with a ramble of outbuildings behind it. The driver, having darted round the back of the dwelling, reappeared with a dirty sack which looked about half full.

'There,' he said ungraciously. 'I shouldn't let you have it, but still. Now – where to?'

'I'm lost,' said Joseph, trying to cover up the fact that he did not know his own address, for fear that if the cabby discovered his state of utter insecurity, he would throw him out and drive off. 'Let's get back on the main road out of town.' Luckily, when they reached the highway, he recognised the crossroads and could give fluent directions thereafter.

As they drove up to the gates, he glanced at his watch and saw that it was already quarter to one. 'Just a second.' He got out and hoisted the sack on to his shoulder. 'The money's inside. I'll be back straight away.'

A powerful stink of urine and manure greeted him as he opened the french windows, and the stallions whinnied out a hungry welcome. 'Good boys!' he said. 'At last I've got something decent for you,' and he tipped out a generous pile of oats on to the floor in front of each.

'Katya!' he called through the closed door into the hall. 'Rusalka! I'm here.'

No answer greeted him. 'She's asleep,' he thought – but even as he opened the hall door, he knew that something had happened. In two steps he was at the entrance to the kitchen, and without even walking into the room he knew that she had gone.

'What's the matter?' asked the cabby. 'You look as though you'd seen a ghost.'

'It's my wife,' said Joseph tersely. 'She's been ill. She's got a bit vague in the head. Now she's wandered off somewhere. Do you know a street called Sergeievskaya?'

'Yes. In the New Town.'

'Where's that?'

'On the west side of the bay.'

'How far from here?'

'About three versts.'

'Can you take me there?'

'Of course – provided you pay.'

'Here.' Joseph brought out his huge roll of notes. 'That's fifty thousand. The money for the oats, and some more on account.'

The driver stuffed the roll down inside the front of his *shuba* and said, 'Very good, sir! I'm at your disposal. By the way, my name is Nikifor.'

Away they went. The sledge slithered and bumped ferociously in the icy ruts. Joseph found himself being flung so violently from side to side that he had to cling to the roof struts to avoid being thrown out, but he did not tell the driver to slow down. On a steadier stretch he contrived a glance at his watch. One o'clock. Time was perilously short. Given the density of the crowds round the port, it might easily take him an hour to bring the horses to the quay. That meant he must leave the villa at two, at the latest. He tried to calculate how long he had been driving: not more than five minutes. Every now and then, above the scrape and thud of the runners, he heard the boom of a big gun from the harbour, and the answering thump of an explosion in the hills.

The driver took a route which followed the contour, keeping up the hill, above the town centre. The harbour was out of Joseph's sight, down to his left, but now and then, through gaps in the houses, he could see the warships in the bay, and once, as he was looking, flame spat from one of the *Emperor of India*'s ten-inch guns, followed a second later by the boom of yet another discharge.

'What's wrong with the lady?' the driver called over his shoulder.

'I wish I knew. She had *tif*, and it's some sort of reaction after that.'

The cabby whistled. '*Tif*! She's lucky to be alive. That's what's killed most of these poor wretches.' He jerked his whip at two bodies lying against the wall of a house.

'I know. She didn't get it too badly. She'd been inoculated, and that's what saved her.'

Joseph looked at his watch. Seven minutes past one. They had been driving for twelve minutes. 'How much further?'

'We're nearly there. That's Sergeievskaya, beginning over there. What number did you say?'

'Forty-one.' Quarter of an hour to return to the villa. Back there by half-past one at the earliest. That left half an hour spare.

The street was one of sedate villas set back in their own gardens, less grand than the one Joseph had appropriated, but comfortable and well-built – certainly the kind of area to which a well-to-do widow might retire. The odd numbers were on their right, descending in twos: fifty-one, forty-nine, forty-seven . . .'

'This is it!' He jumped out. 'Please wait.' A low wooden gate stood half-open, with a nearly-pointed cypress just inside it. He dodged between gate and tree, slipped on the ice, recovered himself, ran to the front door, rang the bell. No answer. After a few moments he rang again. Still nothing. He moved quickly across to the window of the front room and peered in: typical heavy furniture, a samovar on a wooden sideboard, icons in the far corner.

Boom! went the big gun in the bay, ticking off another minute. He stood paralysed by indecision. Was it possible that Aunt Olga had taken Katya in and hidden her? Were both women skulking somewhere upstairs? Should he break in and find out? No – he couldn't believe that Katya wanted to escape him.

He looked round wildly. Across the garden, in the window of the house next door, he spotted a pale figure hovering: a woman, watching him. Perhaps she had seen something. At any rate she would know if Aunt Olga was in residence.

He vaulted the fence between the gardens and ran to the door of number thirty-nine. Again, there was a barely tolerable delay after he had rung the bell. At last he heard the key turn. The door opened a few inches. In the gap appeared a little old lady, white from head to foot: white shawl over her head, white face, white hair, white whiskers, white cape, gloves, dress, shoes. She regarded him cautiously and said in a crochety croak, '*Da?*'

'*Prostite,*' he began. 'I'm looking for somebody. Perhaps you can help.' Seeing her grimace with alarm or incomprehension, he forced himself to talk slowly. 'Your neighbour . . . Mrs Smirnova . . . Olga Leonidovna . . .'

The ghost face looked blank. Then she said, 'Smirnova? In Number forty-one? *Nyet.*'

'What d'you mean? Doesn't she live here any more?'

'She never has. I've never heard of anybody with that name – and I've been here thirty years. The family is called Tsypkin. And now there is only Mikhail Mikhailovitch left.'

Joseph felt despair closing in. Had he got the number wrong? No – he was certain Katya had said forty-one. After all, it was his own age. His worst fears were confirmed: she was disorientated and deluded. Aunt Olga – even if she existed – did not live in Novorossisk at all. His mind flew outwards in ever-widening circles of apprehensive speculation, until he realised that the ghost-like lady was speaking again.

'It's funny,' she said. 'You're the second person today.'

'What? Someone else came looking? Not a young woman with fair hair?'

'Yes.'

'In a grey fur hat and *burka*?'

'Yes.'

'Oh my God! What time was that?'

'About eleven. In the middle of the morning.'

'Did you speak to her?'

'No. I just saw her from the window.'

'What did she do?'

'She rang the bell and waited, and then went away.'

'How long did she wait?'

'Ten minutes, perhaps.'

'Oh!' Joseph put his hands to his face.

'Young man, I see you need help.' The croaky voice had become much kinder. 'Is there anything I can do?'

'Thank you. You're very kind. If you see her come back, please tell her to return to the villa *immediately*.'

'To the villa?'

'Just that. She'll understand.'

'Back!' he told the driver. 'Go like the devil.'

The sleigh rocketed over the ice. He forced himself to think calmly. She might, by a miracle, have gone home to the villa already. She might be wandering the town. She might be on her way back to number forty-one. Whatever she was doing, his own time was running out. Already it was 1.45. He would just have to grab the horses and go. The old lady was right: he did need assistance. The only thing to do was to take the driver into his confidence.

'Nikifor,' he called against the wind. 'I'm in a jam. Can you do something for me?'

'What is it?'

'I have to put two horses on board a ship . . .' Joseph launched into a staccato explanation of his plight. He had to stop frequently as jolts knocked the breath out of him. 'If they aren't on the jetty by three, we're finished. Got to get there by then. It's our only chance.'

'What d'you want *me* to do?'

'Find my wife. She's tall, with fair hair, grey fur hat and cloak. Her face is still brownish from the *tif*. When you've dropped me, go back to Sergeievskaya. If she's not there, wait quarter of an hour. If she comes, drive her straight to Quay No 4. The ship's called the *Cuxhaven*. I'll be there to help you get her aboard. If she doesn't come, drive back this way, to the villa, for a last look. If that fails, cruise though the middle of the town and try to pick her out.'

'Easier said than done.'

'I know. Take these. Don't drop them.' Over his shoulder, one at a time, Joseph handed the driver two gold roubles which he had extracted from his belt. 'They're worth 30,000 each. If you get her to the pier, I'll give you two more.'

Nikifor whistled, held each coin up between thumb and forefinger and bit it before sliding it into a pocket. In a few more minutes they slewed to a halt outside the villa's gates. Joseph looked closely at the chain: it was cocked up in a kink, exactly as he had left it. She had not returned.

'Away you go,' he told the cabby. 'And good luck.'

Once more he saddled the horses. There was nothing he could do about cleaning up the garden room: he had neither the implements nor the time. He took a last look round the kitchen and found that Katya had left her small bag of possessions behind. He picked it up and lashed it to the back of Min's saddle. Somehow he must leave a message, in case she returned. Having no pencil or paper, he resorted to soot and the wall of the garden room: blacking his fingers on the fire-basket of the range, he smeared out the legend: SS CUXHAVEN QUAY 4 3PM J. Then he swung up on to Boy.

It was a dreadful journey. The sporadic sniper fire seemed to have increased. Single shots cracked out at random. Every time they approached a corpse, Boy shied and skittered on the ice, dragging Min after him. At every detonation from the harbour he shuddered and tried to turn back. The *whoosh* of shells passing overhead made him jump. Twice he stopped altogether and refused to move on until Joseph gave him a clout on the backside. 'Get on, you stupid bastard!' he shouted. 'If you break your bloody leg now, you'll do for us all.'

As he came down towards the coast, he saw a ship sailing away, with black smoke pouring from its funnel. His heart leapt into his mouth. Pray God that the *Cuxhaven* had not left early. Pray God, also, that the military had had the sense to produce a gangway wide enough to accommodate the horses.

His darkest imagination could not prepare him for the scenes that greeted him at the harbour. The swarm of people on the quays had increased unbelievably: the moles, the harbour walls, the foreshore – every level surface was black with them. Like the sky, their mood had darkened since the morning: anxious and sullen then, they were now in a state of savage desperation.

To his unspeakable relief, he saw the *Cuxhaven* still in the same berth. He manoeuvred until he was opposite her gangway. But then he was forced to a halt. Between him and the ship lay a solid morass of refugees, jammed shoulder to shoulder, chest to back. As he hesitated, a man's scream rose out of the general hubbub, and he saw a figure slump forward, then collapse out of sight. Moments later a woman immediately beyond the stricken man also fell: two with the same bullet. Joseph looked round. The snipers could be in any of a hundred windows commanding the shore. His back felt horribly naked.

There was nothing for it but to plough into the human sea. He set Boy at the backs of the nearest people, shouting out at the top of his voice, 'MAKE WAY!' The first man to be jostled turned, uttering foul oaths. Boy half-reared and struck out with his front feet. The man was knocked down. Cries of rage erupted. Joseph pulled out his Luger and levelled it at the faces right below him. 'Stand back,' he shouted, 'or I shoot!' He was less afraid for himself than for the horses. Anybody could whip out a knife and slit their bellies without him even seeing.

He made about five yards' progress, then became irretrievably stuck. He could neither advance nor retire. Jibes, insults and threats poured up at him. 'Fuck off, grandad!' shouted a young woman. 'Why should you get there if we can't? Leave the bloody horses and take your chance like everyone else.'

Suddenly, from the left, came a diversion. With a vicious, heavy hammer, a machine-gun opened up at point-blank range from the stern of the next ship along the quay. Over the heads of the crowd Joseph saw a whole swathe of people fall – ten, twenty, cut down like corn. Fear cowed the crowd for a moment. He kicked Boy forward again, made another few yards. Then he felt a twitch behind him and turned to see hands removing Katya's little case. Incensed, he fired the Luger into the air, close over the head of the thief, but the man ducked and disappeared among a dozen others. The shot produced an effect exactly opposite to the one he wanted. It seemed to provoke people into action. More hands reached up. He saw the horses' rolled-up blankets disappear, and was powerless to prevent them going. A moment later Min's saddle went. If someone managed to unbuckle his own girth, he would be done for. He transferred the revolver to his left hand and laid about him with his whip.

Suddenly Boy, goaded beyond endurance, bared his teeth and with a terrifying squeal laid hold of the nearest object in front of him. By chance it was the shoulder of a woman, who suddenly found herself picked up and whirled about like a doll. She too screamed violently. People on either side of her were knocked senseless by the impact of her body being flung against their heads. The sudden demonstration of the stallion's power was so frightening that for a moment it eased the pressure. Packed as they were, the nearest people recoiled in terror, or were physically hammered out of reach.

The next thing he knew, he was surrounded by a posse of British soldiers with bayonets fixed below the muzzles of their rifles. Wielding the butts like clubs, and jabbing ruthlessly with the pointed blades, they forced a way through the multitude. Thank God – somebody had been watching for him. On the dockside there was indeed a wider gangway, equipped with cross-bars of wood so that the horses' feet should not slip as they went up. In a moment he and the stallions were at the end of it; then they were on board. He slid off Boy, on to the deck. He found himself being led between winches and air-vents on the after-deck to a central area behind the main funnel where wooden screens had been erected to form the walls of a makeshift stable. As he reached it, he began to sway on his feet, and stood for a moment with his eyes shut, forehead resting against Boy's neck.

'No roof, I'm afraid,' someone said in his ear. 'But we'll sling a tarpaulin over the top for you as soon as we're at sea.'

'Don't worry,' he said. 'This is wonderful.' He was in such a daze that he had not taken in the face of anyone on board. Now, as he looked up, he saw that three young soldiers were standing there and gazing at him with what could only be a form of hero worship.

'Excuse me, sir,' said one of them deferentially. 'Which one's Minoru?'

'This one. And this is Aboyeur. Can you keep an eye on them for a moment?'

'That's what we're here for, sir.'

He was about to ask the time when the single, tearing blast on the ship's horn made them all start. '*Bozhe moi!*' he cried. 'Are we going

276

already?' As if in answer, the deck gave a heavy shudder as, deep down, the screws bit into the water.

He ran the few yards back to the rail. They were still alongside. How could he hold the ship? Only an order from the general could delay it. He spotted an officer: not the young lieutenant who had greeted him in the morning, but another. He rushed to him and cried, 'Where's the general?'

'Who?'

'General Bridges. I must see him.'

'He's gone on board the *Emperor of India.*'

'Who's in charge of this ship, then?'

The siren boomed again. The ship was moving. Water appeared between her side and the dock. Frantically Joseph scanned the mass of hostile faces on the shore. Right in front of him he saw an officer in Cossack uniform draw his pistol, place the muzzle against his temple and pull the trigger. The tall, grey-coated body crumpled and fell into the sea.

Joseph gauged his chances of jumping back to land. The gap was already too wide: five yards, ten. The ship was gathering speed and drawing away. And then – great God! – *he saw her.* There she was. Katya. Right on the edge of the dock. He saw her pale, brownish face, her grey hat, her ash-blonde hair. Behind her stood Nikifor. Somehow he had found her and brought her to the quay.

'Rusalka!' screamed Joseph. 'Rusalka *moya!*'

She heard him. For evermore he would swear that she heard his voice. He saw her head turn as she scanned the ship's packed decks. He saw her mouth open. But at that instant the siren blasted off again.

Whether or not it was the shock of the loud noise so close, whether she was hit by a sniper's bullet, or whether she was simply pushed, he never knew. The next instant she pitched forward and toppled twenty feet into black water.

He saw her plunge under, come up, and float face down. 'Swim!' he roared. 'For God's sake, swim!' He must have tried to jump, because he felt hands grab him and hold him back. But she did not swim at all. Her round fur hat drifted away. For a few seconds her hair spread out round her head as though in a halo. Then her feet went down, her sodden cloak came up and over, enfolding her like the petals of a tulip, and she disappeared beneath the surface of the icy sea.

Acknowledgements

I AM much indebted to all the people who helped me gather information, and I am particularly grateful to the following:

J. A. Allen, Colonel Richard Bromley-Gardner, Susan Carroll (of the Thoroughbred Breeders' Association), Bernard Clements (no relation of my hero), Dr Alice Ellis (Curator of the National Horse-racing Museum), Jonathan Grimwade (Assistant Manager of the National Stud), Susan Rashe (of Lordship Stud), Peter Willett, the staff of the Public Library in Newmarket.

In Moscow, Masha Shustov trawled tirelessly through the records on my behalf. K. P. Bokharov, the only Russian member of the Thoroughbred Breeders' Association, provided useful leads. Trevor and Penny Fishlock offered hospitality both generous and timely.

In England, Tamara Talbot-Rice put her incomparable memory at my disposal, and Leonid and Kira Finkelstein fielded linguistic inquiries with inexhaustible patience.

DUFF HART-DAVIS
December 1990